Praise for *Tell Me No Lies*

"A complex mystery featuring an unconventional sleuth working in an era of unfettered greed."   —*Kirkus Reviews*

"A richly described historical setting provides the backdrop for the tale, in which Phil—a young widow who is a smart, egalitarian woman of the world, welcome at the homes of the elite—uses her social advantages to good advantage. Phil is reminiscent of Anne Perry's Charlotte Pitt and L. A. Chandlar's Lane Sanders."   —*Booklist*

Praise for *Ask Me No Questions*

"Told with wit and humor . . . A spirited and spunky addition to the ranks of aristocratic women sleuths of the early twentieth century."   —Rhys Bowen, *New York Times* bestselling author

"Classy, clever, and fun, this is a propitious start for dashing Lady Phil."   —*Publishers Weekly*

"Ballroom dances, horse racing at Belmont . . . The cast of characters—from good guys to bad—are unique. I can't wait to see what Lady Phil does next!"   —*Suspense Magazine*

"Should prove to be a well-received, long-lived, beloved, and frisky romantic mystery series."   —*Mystery Scene*

"Sparkles from start to finish!"   —Tessa Arlen, author of the Lady Montfort Mystery series

FORGE BOOKS BY SHELLEY NOBLE

SHELLEY NOBLE

Tell Me No Lies

A Tom Doherty Associates Book · New York

This is a work of fiction. All of the characters, organizations, and events portrayed
in this novel are either products of the author's imagination
or are used fictitiously.

A Forge Book
Published by Tom Doherty Associates
120 Broadway
New York, NY 10271

www.tor-forge.com

Forge® is a registered trademark of Macmillan Publishing Group, LLC.

The Library of Congress has cataloged the hardcover edition as follows:

Noble, Shelley, author.
    Tell me no lies / Shelley Noble.—First edition.
        p. cm.
    "A Tom Doherty Associates book."
    ISBN 978-0-7653-9874-1 (hardcover)
    ISBN 978-0-7653-9873-4 (ebook)
    1. Aristocracy (Social class)—England—Fiction. 2. Widows—
Fiction. 3. Murder—Investigation—New York (State)—New York—
Fiction. 4. Businessmen—Crimes against—Fiction. I. Title.
    PS3614.O253 T45 2019
    813'.6—dc23

                                                    2019287272

ISBN 978-0-7653-9875-8 (trade paperback)

Our books may be purchased in bulk for promotional, educational, or business
use. Please contact your local bookseller or the Macmillan Corporate and
Premium Sales Department at 1-800-221-7945, extension 5442,
or by email at MacmillanSpecialMarkets@macmillan.com.

First Edition: November 2019
First Trade Paperback Edition: September 2020

Printed in the United States of America

0 9 8 7 6 5 4 3 2 1

To Gail,
who knows a thing or two

ACKNOWLEDGMENTS

It takes a village to create and develop an idea into a finished book. Many thanks to my agent, Kevan Lyon; editor, Kristin Sevick; and my entire Forge team.

Tell Me No Lies

1

Philomena Amesbury, Dowager Countess of Dunbridge, slowly opened her eyes and peered around the darkened room. She let out a sigh of relief, a ritual she'd gone through every morning since the death of her erstwhile husband, the Earl of Dunbridge, rest his decadent, malicious, morally corrupt soul.

She closed her eyes, smiled complacently as she drifted back to sleep. Not a penniless young widow, disgraced and abandoned by her family and headed for a crumbling dowager house in the wilds of Kent, but at the Plaza Hotel in a delightfully comfortable four-poster bed in her own luxurious apartments overlooking Central Park. And paid for, not by her current lover—alas, she had none at the moment—but by an anonymous official—organization?—who hoped to call on her expertise during the year.

That expertise, she assumed, was murder. Investigating it, not committing it.

Ah. Manhattan. A new life. New adventures. Enchanting men. And the sweet scent of gardenias. *Gardenias?* She turned to her side beneath the soft sateen sheet. The scent was stronger. She stretched out her hand; her fingers came in contact not with a dashing bedmate, but with a stem . . . of a gardenia.

She sat up. It was November. There were no gardenias in any garden at this time of the year. There was also an envelope.

Neither the flower nor the envelope had been there when she'd arrived home well past dawn.

The envelope was sealed. She didn't bother to call Lily to fetch her letter opener, but ripped it open and drew out a single sheet of folded paper. No salutation, no signature. Only one enigmatic sentence.

Rise and shine, Countess, you're about to have a visitor.

A thrill raced through her. There was only one man who called her countess. And she had no idea who he was. She had dubbed him Mr. X, as elusive and mysterious as any dime novel hero—or villain—could possibly be.

But a visitor? Surely not. . . . She groped for the buzzer.

"Madam."

Phil let out a screech and turned to her other side to see her maid, Lily, standing by her bed. "How did you do that?"

"What is that, madam?"

"Arrive before I called for you."

"I came to tell you that you have a visitor."

"It seems I've already had one."

Lily's dark eyes flashed and her hand reached automatically for the dagger she kept strapped to her ankle—a habit that Phil had no intention of trying to break. The girl's gaze flitted to the empty place beside her.

"Alas, not that kind of visitor, as you can see. So you can put that stiletto away."

Lily snorted in a very unsubservient way and leaned over to slide the knife back into its sheath. She stood and fluffed her skirt. "There's a visitor in the parlor, madam. Mr. Pr-r-r-eswick," she said, rolling her r's in the way she did when she was agitated, "sent me to ask you if you are receiving visitors."

You're about to have a visitor. How did her elusive correspondent know unless he'd sent him. Or was he the visitor?

Phil thrust the gardenia at Lily. "Did you leave this here?"

"No, madam."

"Preswick?"

Lily shook her head.

Of course not; her butler would be loath to enter her bedroom at any time but especially if his mistress was sleeping. So the only way . . .

Phil pushed the covers aside and hurried over to the window, threw open the drapes, and looked out the window and to the busy street below.

Her rooms were five floors above the ground. No one, not even the mysterious Mr. X, could have managed such a feat.

"Madam. My lady, come away from the window, you're practically naked."

Phil looked down at her nightgown, the long skirt hanging in tiny tucks from a lace-yoked bodice. It was in impeccable taste.

She turned back to the room where Lily awaited with her brocade dressing gown. "You must hurry."

Who could possibly be calling at this ungodly hour? And why?

"Send Preswick in."

Lily bobbed a knife-sharp curtsey and hurried across the room.

She opened the door and stood back as Preswick stepped in. He was dressed in his immaculate black suit and white gloves, the extra pair he always kept at the ready—for spillages and such, he said, but Phil knew it was also because gloves didn't leave fingerprints—tucked neatly out of sight.

The Amesbury butler was rather long in the tooth, old-fashioned in his notions, but unfailingly loyal. And though he disapproved of her "penchant for recklessness," as he termed it, he'd insisted on leaving his approaching retirement and pension to travel to the wilds of America with his wayward mistress. It was during her visit with her friend Beverly Reynolds, and the subsequent murder of Bev's husband, that he had reluctantly introduced Phil to his secret passion, detective novels.

"My lady." Preswick bowed and looked discreetly away. "Mr. Luther Pratt is here to see you. He apologizes for the early hour but says it's quite urgent. 'Dire,' I believe was the word he used."

Oh dear. What on earth could her host from last night's ball want with her this morning? She was almost certain she hadn't participated in any egregious indiscretions nor led any gentleman on. At present she was only interested in one—or possibly two—gentlemen. She was very discreet when she cared to be.

What could the man want? She'd only met his wife, Gwendolyn, at the Colony Club luncheon last week. She was a delightful though rather frail woman with a quick wit and a gracious demeanor.

Someone had mentioned that Gwen's husband was being considered for a position at some new banking commission that President Roosevelt had promised to form, and a lively discussion about the recent banking crisis—which some were calling the Panic of 1907—ensued.

The women at the Colony Club were quite up to date on political affairs.

Which somehow led to Phil's unexpected and somewhat notorious involvement with a police investigation on her arrival in the city.

The women at the Colony Club were not above relishing a bit of social scandal.

A day later an invitation had arrived for the Pratts' daughter's debutante ball.

And now the mysterious note on her pillow, followed by an extraordinary morning visit by her host. Something was afoot, as Mr. Preswick's favorite detective, Mr. Sherlock Holmes, would say.

"Good heavens, why didn't you say?" Phil said. "Tell him I'll be with him directly."

"Begging your pardon, my lady, but I don't think that nightdress will suffice."

"Lily, my dressing gown."

Preswick discreetly withdrew from the room.

While Lily straightened the collar of the dressing gown and fastened the satin frogs that closed down the front, Phil tried to catch a glimpse of herself in the mirror. Not terrible for someone who had enjoyed copious amounts of excellent champagne and only two hours' sleep. And if she looked a little pale the colors of the dressing gown brought out the brilliance of her dark mahogany hair.

Lily pushed her toward the dressing table, where she quickly twisted Phil's thick long braid into a coil at the nape of her neck and just as quickly fastened it by the expedient method of jabbing several hairpins into her scalp. "It will hold if you don't move your head too quickly."

"Not a problem, my dear, but we will need coffee in the parlor, immediately."

Phil spent the two minutes it took to traverse the hallway from her bedroom to her parlor to drag herself from stupor to acuity and to wonder what on earth Mr. Luther Pratt could possibly want.

And why she had been warned of his arrival.

Preswick opened the parlor door and discreetly withdrew.

Phil stood on the threshold taking a moment to delight in the wonderful freedom of living on one's own, surrounded by beautiful furnishings and all the modern conveniences. Not to mention the freedom of greeting visitors in one's dressing gown.

Luther Pratt stood facing the window, feet apart, hands clasped behind him. He was a robust man, not exactly tall, but seemingly so because of the erect way in which he carried himself.

"Mr. Pratt." Phil came toward him, extending her hand. What *was* the etiquette when one was called on before breakfast?

Mr. Pratt turned, the morning sun creating a nimbus of gray curls around his rather large head as he met her halfway across the room. He was freshly shaven, dressed for the office.

And he most certainly was not the mysterious Mr. X.

"My dear sir, please be seated. Preswick is bringing coffee, then you must tell me what brings you here at such an hour."

He sat on the edge of one of the tapestry upholstered club chairs. "I must apologize . . ."

She sat on the scrolled sofa facing him.

He was still apologizing without ever getting to the point of his visit when Preswick brought in the coffee tray a minute later.

He refused coffee however.

"I've come because my wife, Gwen, Gwendolyn—it was her idea that I should come."

"Yes," Phil prompted, hoping this wasn't a plea for an introduction letter to the king or some other such encroachment. Really, she barely knew these people.

"She says you were such a support to Beverly Reynolds during the tragedy of her husband's"—he bit his lip as if constructing the next word out of the flesh—"um, death and her subsequent crisis."

Phil straightened slightly, ears and mind attuned to the words between the lines. "And are you experiencing such a crisis?" What could have possibly happened during the last two hours?

He leaned forward in his chair. "Yes. There has been a terrible accident. Surely an accident. Only . . ." He rolled his head on his neck, very slightly, his eyes making an arc in the air. "But perhaps not."

"Not an accident?"

"No."

"My goodness. Is there a body involved?" Phil asked, willing him to look at her.

"Yes."

"And has it been moved?"

"What?" His eyes bugged unnaturally. "No. Only . . . I left orders to keep the room closed off to everyone until I spoke with you."

Phil smiled slightly. Her path lay clearly before her.

"Gwen said it was you who saved Beverly Reynolds's reputation, not that Gwen or anyone in my household would hurt the dear boy. But she thought you could be a support to the women, in fact she insisted I come and plead with you to come to our aid. Or do I presume too much?"

"The dear boy?"

"Oh. Didn't I say? It's Perry Fauks. The heir to the Fauks fortune. I believed you danced with him last night."

Perry Fauks. She *had* danced with him. A lovely young man, in looks and manners. Obviously the darling of the young unmarried women who were celebrating Agnes Pratt's debut last night. And the hope of quite a few parents, including, if Phil was not mistaken, the Pratts themselves.

Fauks Copper, Coal and Steel. One of the larger trusts that had so far survived the recent financial crisis. He would be quite a catch. Or would have been.

"Perry Fauks is dead," Phil repeated, just to be sure.

Luther Pratt swallowed convulsively and nodded. "Yes. Can you come?"

To console his wife and daughter? Or was there something larger here? Of course there was; that's why she'd been warned about his visit from the illusive Mr. X.

Could she come? He couldn't keep her away. "Of course I will. But I must get dressed. I want you to return home, make sure that Mr. Fauks isn't disturbed in any way. Keep everyone—absolutely everyone—out of the room where he was killed."

"But—"

"Tell Mrs. Pratt that I will pay a morning call to discuss . . . the color of draperies she's planning to order for the parlor."

"The draperies? But she just—"

"The subject of draperies gives me an excuse to be in the house. Dressmaking would merely give the police an excuse to put both myself and your lovely wife into the carriage and out of their way."

"The police? Must it be the police? I don't know if you are aware. Perry Fauks, though a young man, is the heir apparent of a major industrial trust. He's only a junior partner as of the moment because of his age. Was. Was a junior partner—" Mr. Pratt jumped up, strode to the window. Turned back to Phil. "If word were to get out—"

He collapsed into the nearest chair. "You know of the recent financial crisis?"

Really, men could be so obtuse. How could she not know. A run on the banks because the trust companies didn't keep enough money on hand to pay out when necessary. Add some bad investing and a dip in the stock market . . . Fortunately her allowance—that she had one was thanks to the foresight of her maternal grandmother—was wired monthly from the Bank of England. It wasn't enough to live "in style" as they said, but with the necessities paid for by her unknown benefactor, she'd remained unscathed . . . so far.

"Yes, narrowly averted, I believe, by Mr. Morgan."

He laughed stridently. "By demanding, blackmailing, or strong-arming the banks to put up money to cover the losses whether they had the funds or not. Things are very volatile. Something must be done to keep this from happening again.

"If there is any chance of this being more than a foolish accident, I don't know what it might do in financial circles."

Or to your nomination to the banking commission, Phil thought.

"Did Mr. Fauks have any enemies that you are aware of?"

"Enemies? Why would a boy of that age have any enemies?" He ran his hand over his hair, sending gray curls springing through his fingers. "But of course because of the business, he had serious competitors. Man is a greedy beast, Lady Dunbridge, envious, and sometimes ruthless, but not among our friends. And none who would maliciously cut off a young man's future."

Phil smiled. Surely the man wasn't that naïve. Or did he protest too much?

"But I digress," he said, recovering himself. "You must come,

Lady Dunbridge. Not just for our sakes but . . . but you just must."

"And I will," Phil assured him. "Now please return home; stay there until I arrive and do exactly as I've told you." She held up a preemptory hand. "It's distasteful and disrespectful, but necessary. If it was an accident, there will be no harm done. But if it wasn't, much harm will be done if he is moved."

Mr. Pratt had an odd expression on his face as if he couldn't believe what he was hearing.

"Lady Dunbridge, really, this is most unusual. My wife merely wished to have some female understanding."

"And she will certainly get it," Phil assured him. Just not from her necessarily. And besides, Gwen Pratt didn't seem the type to need cosseting. Unless she missed her guess, Gwen Pratt was one of the reasons for her husband's success. The lady knew her way around a financial discussion. Phil had learned that much about her at luncheon.

"Very well."

"Fauks was a guest in your house, is that correct?"

"Yes, but I don't see what—"

"Please keep the maids from cleaning any room that he might have used last night. And try to keep the situation as much of a secret as possible."

His mouth opened, closed again. Not exactly what he'd bargained for when he came asking her to bring her smelling salts to shore up the females in his house. Which she would also do. Appearances could sometimes be everything and Lily and she had prepared a valise for just such a circumstance.

The social events of the summer had been amusing, but she had to admit she'd been waiting for something to happen that would make her blood race. And since Mr. X had failed to make an appearance himself. Well . . .

She was feeling the thrill of the chase at last.

"One last thing. I believe you have other guests staying in the house."

"Yes, my wife's sister and husband and their two daughters are visiting from Virginia. And my old friend and Agnes's godfather, Godfrey Bennington."

A full house, it would seem. Phil took his elbow and nudged him toward the door. "We'll discuss this later. Go now. Tell Gwen that I will be happy to visit her, shall we say in an hour? Until then, stay calm."

"And the police will have to be called?"

Really, she was a visiting countess, why was he asking her, he must already know the answer.

"Of course they must be called. But not until your wife and daughter are suitably recovered from their inevitable shock." And not until Phil had time for a good look around.

2

Lily was waiting for her, a cup of coffee in her hand, when Phil burst into her boudoir pulling pins from her hair.

"I think the . . ." Phil noticed the brown, side-pleated visiting dress that was already hanging on the door of the chifforobe. "That one," she added superfluously.

"I thought you might be in a hurry," Lily said. "The brown is classic, discreet but chic, well-fitted but not constricting, and appropriate for several occasions."

"Whether it be luncheon or running for your life through the streets of Manhattan," Phil added and cut her a grin. "Yes, excellent." She sat down at her dressing table, and picked up a piece of buttered toast from the tray there.

Lily stepped behind her and began unbraiding her hair. "Though perhaps if you are to meet the police and want to appear *formidable* you might prefer the eggplant and maroon . . ."

Phil grimaced at her maid in the mirror. "I thought we agreed to throw that one out."

"Oh no, my lady. It holds too important a place in your introduction to American crime to be cast off."

"Don't remind me."

"Do you think you will see the detective sergeant today?"

"As much as I would like to renew his acquaintance, I rather hope this won't turn out to be a matter for the New York City Police Department."

"But you think it will."

"All too possible. And if I'm not mistaken, so does Mr. Luther

Pratt. Which reminds me. Pack your 'valise dramatique' with extra hankies. There seems to be a surfeit of women in the Pratt household."

"I am to go?"

"Why yes. You may be needed."

Lily's dark eyes flared. Phil was never sure what that quick light in her maid's eyes meant. Fear, surprise, or anticipation. There was so much she didn't know about Lily. Except so far she'd been utterly loyal.

Phil drank coffee and ate her toast while Lily coiffed her hair. She donned the brown visiting dress and didn't argue when Lily insisted on pinning her new velvet cloche at such an extreme angle that the attached spray of pheasant feathers nearly covered one side of her face.

Preswick saw them downstairs all the way to the hotel lobby, where he reluctantly turned them over to the doorman, who ushered them into the first waiting red taxicab. Phil gave the driver the address, he touched his cap, and they were off to the Pratt mansion farther north on Fifth Avenue.

It was a brisk day; the last of the leaves on the trees in the park still held their color. Lily sat stiffly upright beside her, her simple winter coat covering her spotless, crisply starched maid's uniform.

"Now Lily. This may be nothing more than a terrible accident, but I must warn you. The gentleman who died was young and very handsome. It won't be pleasant."

"Yes, my lady," Lily said, showing her understanding of the gravity of the occasion. She never called Phil "my lady" except in company or when things were extremely serious.

Not a typical mistress-servant relationship, for which Phil was forever grateful. She'd had enough of those to last a lifetime.

Lily was no ordinary servant. She wasn't ordinary in any sense of the word. Phil had decided the moment she'd seen the girl, valiantly fending off the clutches of three customs men to keep from being thrown off the SS *Oceanic*, that she had to do something to save her.

And save her she did. Recruited her as her lady's maid, since her own maid had taken one look at the ship and fled. Phil had finagled her a carte de visite and paid her passage to New York; Preswick had done the rest. And though she still refused to tell them her real name—Phil called her Lily because of her stunningly pale complexion—or where she had come from, or why, she had transformed into a more than passable lady's maid, and more to Phil's taste than any of the prim, nosy, and ready-to-gossip maids Phil had had in the past.

And proven herself more than capable in a scrape.

And so had Phil's butler.

They were quite a team, if she did say so herself.

Several minutes later, the cab pulled to a stop in front of the Pratt residence. The evening before the mansion had been shimmering with light. Torches placed on marble plinths had lit the way up the stone steps to heavy walnut doors. In the light of day, it was a heavy stone building with crenellated frieze columns that rose at least five stories in the air.

Phil and Lily climbed down from the cab and stopped on the sidewalk to collect themselves.

"It looks like La Santé." Lily sucked in her breath, making her lips disappear.

Phil didn't even blink, though she did tuck the morsel away. So Lily had been to Paris; hopefully not to La Santé.

"A prison, hmm. Last night I thought it looked rather lovely, but today it reminds me of one of those large banking establishments down on Centre Street." *Though apropos perhaps,* Phil thought.

"They are the same, are they not? They keep some people in and others out."

"How true," Phil said. "I think we'll converse in Italian today. Most of them will be able to catch at least a few words. I imagine

Mrs. Pratt and possibly her children are fairly fluent. They will all be able to understand but assume you won't be able to understand what they might say in English in your presence."

"*Sì, signora.*"

"But say as little as possible."

Lily's eyes widened.

Phil smiled. "I'm not certain how practiced I am. Something else to add to our study list. Shall we ring the bell?"

They were greeted, not by a butler, but by Mr. Pratt himself. "Pardon the informality, Lady Dunbridge, but I thought the less intercourse with the servants the better. Ah," he said, frowning slightly. "I see you have brought your maid."

"Yes, she goes everywhere with me. Very useful in a crisis and the beauty of it is her English is somewhat limited." She felt Lily stiffen slightly beside her. She didn't like to be belittled even for a good cause. Phil turned to beam down on her and saw her looking demurely and utterly stupid at the brilliantly polished marble floor. Phil could have kissed her.

"Come into the parlor and I'll see if Gwen—"

"Mr. Pratt. This may seem an odd request, but I'd like to see the body first. I'm not ghoulish, nor am I oversensitive. Besides, Lily is heavily armed with smelling salts and other restoratives. But the first thing I learned with my poor friend Bev's situation is to learn everything you can—at once."

She gave him a meaningful look, which she rather thought he missed completely.

The door to their right opened and a man dressed in business attire stepped out. He was tall, with black hair slicked back from a center part. Phil noticed because his head was bent in a preoccupied study.

Luther Pratt startled convulsively.

The man stopped. "Ah, sir. I didn't expect to see you home today and I offered to pick up Mrs. Pratt's powders at the pharmacist this morning. Elva didn't have time to fetch them yesterday with all the preparations." His features lifted from preoccupied to concerned. He looked inquisitively toward Phil, and Phil saw that he was much younger than she'd thought and not at all unhandsome.

"Thank you, Vincent. Very kind of you. And I did mean to be off earlier, but Mrs. Pratt asked me to wait for Lady Dunbridge. If I might introduce my secretary, Vincent Wynn-Taylor."

Phil smiled, nodded. And wished him at Jericho.

"Ah yes," Wynn-Taylor said, while he no doubt desperately searched for the reason she was here and why he had forgotten to put her visit in the day's schedule.

He bowed. Though Phil thought she detected a slight disdain for the whole "peerage malarkey" as one of the shipping magnates had so eloquently put it at the party last night before he passed out headfirst into the deviled eggs.

"How do you do," she returned with her most countess-like condescension. "Dear Gwen mentioned she was thinking about new draperies for the parlor and you know how women are. I promised to come around first thing to discuss some ideas." She gave him a bright smile. One somewhere between one she would give to an eager schoolboy and one reserved for a potential pickpocket she'd just passed on the street. One could never be sure.

"My wife is in the conservatory. I'll just . . . Please tell her Lady Dunbridge will be in shortly," Mr. Pratt said, finally remembering his part in the agenda. "Then I'll join you in the office."

"Very well, sir." Wynn-Taylor nodded to the countess and strode down the hall and entered a room at the far end.

Suddenly galvanized into action, Pratt ushered Phil down the same hallway, Lily following in their wake.

He didn't stop at the elegant curving staircase that led up to the ballroom and living quarters, but steered Phil down the corridor, past several other doors until they were in the back regions of the house.

Then he stopped. "Are you quite sure you are willing to do this, Lady Dunbridge? It's not for a lady."

"Quite sure."

Before Phil could answer, the door behind Luther's head opened and Gwendolyn Pratt slipped out, bringing a distinct medicinal odor with her. Phil just caught a glimpse of Vincent Wynn-Taylor handing a maid a package before Gwen closed the door behind her.

"Oh Lady Dunbridge, I thought it might be you. Thank you for coming."

Phil was a bit shocked at her appearance. Last night the lady of the mansion had been resplendent in a golden charmeuse gown with beaded ocher flounces and a train of glittering wheat-colored organza. She was still impeccably dressed, in a day dress of figured linen, but she was pale and somewhat frail looking.

"I was just bringing Lady Dunbridge to, uh . . . you?"

"All in good time, my dear. But first she must see the body." She sucked in a painful breath. Her husband strode to her side. "Really, my dear. Do not distress yourself. I'll take care of everything."

Gwen waved him away. Turned to Phil. "It's my asthma. A lung disorder. Merely an annoyance. I'll have Brinlow ring for tea or . . . Lady Dunbridge, have you breakfasted?"

She turned to her husband. "You'll do everything exactly as she says, Luther. You must." Gwen turned troubled eyes to Phil, and Phil noticed the deep violet color that contrasted so wonderfully with her blondish-red hair. She was not a beautiful woman, but she knew how to carry herself, and she was intelligent. "We're depending on you."

"Mrs. Pratt," Phil said, trying to rein in Gwen's overly simplistic expectations. She wasn't certain when her friendship with Beverly Reynolds while Bev was under the investigation for the murder of her husband had grown into Phil being the kingpin that had saved the day, and Bev's bacon. It was a role she didn't mind playing and it was partially true, she had to admit. But was it a fluke or did she actually have a talent for this investigation business? And could she really promise Gwendolyn Pratt a speedy and favorable outcome?

"I will do my best."

"Thank you," said Mrs. Pratt.

"In that case, we must be better friends than we already are. To give me reason to be hanging on your elbow when the police arrive. If you could call me Philomena?"

"Certainly," Mrs. Pratt said, finally getting her breath under control. "And you must call me Gwen." She smiled wanly at her husband. "And don't whatever you do, Luther, look shocked at anything we say, and give us all away."

Mr. Pratt's eyebrows rose in astonishment. "I hope that it won't come to that."

"Promise me."

"Very well, but you must wait for us here."

"Yes, Luther." She turned to Philomena. "We will take your advice, if you can help us. I fear this may be more than a tragic accident."

"Hush now, Gwen. You've been reading too many of those gothic ghost tales."

"But you will see us through?"

"I will endeavor to see that suspicion ultimately falls on the culprit and not on the innocent. To the best of my poor ability," Phil added, and hoped to heaven it wasn't this nice asthmatic woman and her stiff but loving husband.

Mr. Pratt opened the conservatory door and Phil caught a glimpse of large potted palms and rattan furniture across a terrazzo-tiled floor, and Gwen Pratt slipped inside.

"I suppose you'd better call me Luther," he said. "Though don't ask me to call you by your Christian name. I'd make a hash of it. This way." They walked all the way to the back of the house, where he stopped in front of a heavy door covered in green baize.

"I'm as progressive as the next man, but have you ever been in the basement of a house?"

"Basement?"

"Yes, that's where he was found. Didn't I say?"

"No, you didn't." And that opened up a vast new arena of possibilities. None with which she was overly familiar. And she doubted if Lily would know much more. After all, she'd only been a lady's maid for a few months, and never in a full household.

Well, Phil had no doubt they would both do their best. She would have to leave it to Lily to obtain what information she could "downstairs."

"I have been known to visit cook on occasion."

"I didn't mean to offend," he said nervously.

"Not at all. Most countesses would never dream of trespassing to the lower realms." She smiled. "They wouldn't be welcome. But as you've probably heard, I'm not your ordinary countess."

He tightened his lips and opened the heavy baize door. The stairway down to the kitchens, storage, and staff areas was fairly wide and well lit, unlike at Dunbridge Castle, where the poor maids had been known to scrape their elbows on the stone walls as they carried trays up to their personages.

It was like walking into a different world. The smell of steam hovered in the air. The clanging of pots and pans, the scraping of chairs, the scuffling of feet as delivery men carried heavy crates of food, echoed from down a warren of corridors.

They turned to the left, and Phil noticed that Lily had moved closer to her.

Halfway down the corridor Mr. Pratt stopped. Looked around, then took out a key. Phil wondered if he was aware of the heads clustered together behind a partially opened door. Three of them at least, and she had no doubt there were others.

She had to work quickly.

They stepped into a large bright room, belowground but with high windows that could be opened to air. Large machines lined the far side of the room, giving it a futuristic quality. Stacks of towels lined up along the long wooden folding table. A line of cord was drawn across the room from which long drapes of lace were drying in the air. Of course, they were in the laundry room, and those odd-looking contraptions must be the new washing machines. The gaps in her education were sometimes staggering.

She turned to Luther Pratt for elucidation.

"We have twelve bedrooms and during a full house as we are close to having now, and with the servants' quarters, the laundry I'm told sometimes gets backed up by twenty hours or so.

"Which it seems happened yesterday with the extra guests and festivities, you know."

Phil nodded. "How long had Mr. Fauks been staying here as your guest?" she asked as she took in her surroundings, thinking what an absurd place for a rich young industrialist to meet his death.

What on earth had he been doing down in this part of the house?

Seducing a housemaid came to mind. Phil couldn't think of a less romantic trysting place. And felt a quiet anger and pity for the poor girls who would spend their entire days washing, drying, and ironing, just to be manhandled by a stranger and be expected to carry on like nothing had happened and hope against hope they didn't become with child.

Any one of them might be the prey of a dashing young man, though Mr. Fauks hadn't struck her as the type to maul a scullery maid. Of course, impressions could be deceiving.

"He came in from Pittsburgh several days ago and was to stay with us for several days to attend Agnes's debutante ball, enjoy the social events, and check in with his business interests. Oh, this is just terrible. What will I tell his father?"

Phil gave him an encouraging smile. This was no time for her host to unravel. They must work quickly, then try to contact the one man on the police force she knew they could almost trust. And pray that he got here before someone with fewer scruples.

It hadn't taken her long to understand that corruption still ran deep within the police force despite President Roosevelt's reforms when he'd been commissioner there.

And if Perry Fauks was killed in the laundry room, then a laundress or other belowstairs servant would be a handy suspect, and would relieve them of having to investigate more prominent suspects and risk censure or even worse by the people who still ran the city.

That would be the easiest outcome and least damaging to the family, especially considering Mr. Pratt's standing in the community. But if Luther Pratt had thought he could sweep this matter under the carpet, why had he called on her? What kind of man was her host?

"This way." Pratt held back a panel of lace and gestured for her to pass through.

They walked between several rows of ironing boards and past a large canvas cart half-filled with white linens. Phil glanced in but saw nothing out of the ordinary.

Pratt stopped suddenly at a pile of white linens spread on the stone floor, then he reached down.

And Phil got a terrible premonition.

He took a handful of material and whisked it away with the bravura of a magician. Not to reveal a rabbit, but Perry Fauks, heir and shining star of the steel and manufacturing future, the darling of hopeful mothers across the country, the object of more than one girl's attentions at the party the night before, lying on his back on a pile of dirty tablecloths. He was dressed in evening wear, his necktie still impeccably tied, as if he had suddenly decided to take a nap.

Or had he been purposely laid out in this dignified pose?

"Did anyone move him?"

"No. Well, not until we . . . we had to . . . He was stuck in the chute."

It was hard to look away, he seemed so peaceful and still handsome even now. But Phil forced herself to look up at the stone wall and square opening in the wall above the body and the tail of sheets and linens that tumbled from the corner like a river of white.

Not a trysting place. A laundry chute.

"You don't mean he . . ." *Really it was too gruesome.*

"The maids were screaming and carrying on so that we could hear them each time a door opened. I was coming down to see what the commotion was when I ran into Brinlow, who was coming to summon me.

"The laundry was stuck and they'd been trying to dislodge a comforter that seemed to be obstructing the way. It took three of them, but when they finally managed to free it, his . . . his feet were sticking out. He was still wearing his evening pumps. They hadn't fallen off as you would expect." Mr. Pratt swayed slightly.

Phil motioned to Lily, who efficiently reached into her emergency reticule and handed Phil a vial of sal volatile.

She quickly passed it under Mr. Pratt's nose and returned it to Lily in a sleight of hand so fast that Pratt, as soon as his eyes stopped swimming from the inhale, looked around in confusion.

But he was calm again.

"So they pulled him out . . ." she coaxed.

"No. Godfrey and I came down. We thought he might still be alive, so we pulled him out and put him here as you see. But it was too late. I sent the maids away with orders not to speak about it to one another or anyone, for all the good that will do.

"It makes no sense. Why would anyone put themselves down a laundry chute?"

"As a prank or on a dare?" Phil ventured.

"Not Perry. No matter how drunk he might be."

"Was he drunk last night?"

"What? Oh, I imagine. The champagne was flowing freely. But Perry was not a child, he was twenty-eight, soon to be one of the most important men in the industrial manufacturing world. He was a very serious young man."

He hadn't struck Phil as irresponsible either, especially not while attending an evening among the cream of the financial

East Coast. Last night might have been focused on the lovely Agnes, but no successful hostess ignored a chance to further her family's position in society and, Phil suspected in Gwen Pratt's case, business.

"But I suppose he must have; you know how young men can be."

Indeed she did. "So where were his friends?"

Mr. Pratt's head snapped toward her. "What? What friends?"

"Whether it was a dare or prank, both are dependent on another party. Whoever the other party was must have run down here to see if he really did it? Or to collect the bet or whatever. And if they did, why didn't they sound the alarm when he didn't appear?"

"Perhaps they thought he had changed his mind."

"Perhaps, but unlikely. My dear sir, if you do that kind of thing, at least one person must witness him going in."

Pratt rubbed his forehead between his fingers and thumb.

Phil gave him a direct look. "What more aren't you telling me?"

Pratt looked down at the lifeless form at his feet. Shook his head.

"There must be something or you wouldn't have come to me."

"I was going to call the police, but fortunately Gwendolyn was coming down the stairs to breakfast. I confided what had happened. She immediately said I should call on you. That all the women of her acquaintance know you were the one who saved Bev Reynolds's reputation."

He was worried about his wife's reputation? Or perhaps his daughter's. Death in one's house is a terrible thing, but shouldn't set off this tizzy of anxiousness. There was more to this story than he'd told Phil. But she was intrigued.

Phil looked quickly around, knowing Lily would be taking note of everything she did. They'd been studying manuals on detection all summer when they could get a moment away from the festivities of Newport, Saratoga, and Hot Springs society.

She tugged her gloves tighter for more dexterity, something

Preswick had taught her, pulled her skirts aside, and knelt down beside the body, ignoring Pratt's sharp intake of breath as she reached toward Fauks's lapel.

She felt a bit squeamish herself as memories of her arrival in Manhattan flashed before her. Reggie Reynolds, dead, her reaching across the body—

Phil shook off the residual horror and studied the body.

His blond hair was still pomaded in place except for a lacquered tress that fell across his forehead in one piece. His skin was pale, almost white, and she didn't need to touch him to know that he would be quite cold.

Phil lifted the edge of his tailcoat with one finger. No sign of injury that she could see. But if not on a dare, then why jump down the laundry chute at all?

Chased by an irate husband perhaps? He was impeccably dressed, properly buttoned and tucked in, not as if he'd dressed in haste.

She saw no sign of a wound or bruising. Not a broken fingernail on his well-manicured hands that would have suggested signs of a struggle to save himself, to slow down the descent, or even a struggle to prevent himself from being pushed inside. Perry must have been unconscious, or perhaps already dead, when he went down the chute.

A sudden shadow fell over the body. Phil stood, just as Lily reached for her ankle.

"Lily, no," Phil ordered as she confronted the newcomer.

"Godfrey," Luther exclaimed, his voice an octave higher than usual.

"You suspect foul play, Lady Dunbridge," said Godfrey Bennington. He didn't look pleased.

"I'm afraid that it is a possibility."

"Gwen said you were down here," Godfrey said without taking his eyes from Phil. He was a tall, large-boned man with a barrel chest and a mane of flowing white hair. Taller in the morning light, it seemed to Phil, than he'd been last night when she had waltzed with him. He'd been an excellent waltzer, surprising since he looked like just the sort to tread on one's toes, but he glided her around the floor with ease and in time to the music without once faltering in polite conversation.

Today, dressed in a well-fitting sack suit of fine wool, he was merely formidable. Perhaps she should have worn the hated eggplant dress after all.

"Well, yes. Gwen wished for Lady Dunbridge to . . . sustain her if . . . when . . . Lady Dunbridge, you remember Godfrey Bennington, my dear friend and Agnes's godfather."

Godfrey bowed slightly; didn't smile.

"Yes, indeed," Phil said. "I would say it was delightful to see you again, except for the . . ." She glanced down at Perry Fauks's body. "The situation."

"I'm not certain if you understand the delicate nature of the 'situation' currently and the last thing we need is . . ."

"Scandal," Phil finished for him.

"Yes, but something more important," Luther said. "These are troubled times, and the death of the Fauks's heir, even because of a stupid prank, might lead to another financial panic."

"True," Phil said, looking from one man to the other. "But we're not talking about a prank gone awry. I'm afraid we're talking about murder."

3

Luther Pratt cast a frantic look toward Bennington.

Not surprise but a momentary panic that had nothing to do with the financial crisis. Just what was going on here?

"Quite," Bennington said. He moved past her and knelt by the body. And before Phil could protest, he turned Fauks over. It was done smoothly and efficiently and Phil couldn't help but think it was something he'd done before. Not just today but many times.

He motioned her closer.

He didn't have to point it out, the tiny hole in the left side of the jacket's back. She could smell the tangy unpleasant odor of blood and other things she'd rather not name.

No accident had made that tiny tear or drawn the blood that seeped around the edges, almost the same color as the dark fabric. It had been an intentional attack. Not by a pistol; there were only torn fibers, not singed ones around the opening as there would have been if a bullet passed through the coat, no residue. But a blade of some sort. Narrow. Thin.

She felt Lily kneel down beside her. She was breathing slowly, shallowly. "Stiletto," she whispered.

Phil nodded and stood. "I think, Mr. Pratt, it is time that we called the police."

Pratt looked at Godfrey. "Must we?"

Godfrey just looked down at the body, his eyes narrowed. Phil wasn't sure he even heard the question.

"You must," Phil said. "You'll never be able to completely hush this up. The staff has seen and probably gossiped among themselves. You can't keep it from your family. They'll wonder where he is and when it comes out that he's dead, wonder why no one told them. It's better just to get it done before it grows past the ability for us to handle."

Godfrey looked up at that.

"Godfrey," Pratt implored.

"I'm afraid, dear friend, Lady Dunbridge is correct. He can't just disappear. He will be traced to this house."

Phil suppressed a shiver. Was he in the habit of making people disappear?

"But this needs to be handled with the utmost delicacy."

"I know just the man," Phil said.

Again Pratt and Godfrey exchanged looks. Phil was beginning to wonder what their relationship was, beyond friends.

"Very well," Mr. Pratt said. "If you can vouch for his discretion."

"I can vouch for his honesty and integrity. And tenacity," she added. "He will investigate until he finds the perpetrator of this crime." She stopped to give them both a good hard look. "But he will not be bribed or thwarted and he will arrest whomever it is, regardless of whoever they are."

Mr. Pratt nodded. "It must have been a burglar he interrupted. It does happen. These people case houses where the residents are out of town or busy with entertainment and the servants are all engaged elsewhere. Perry might have interrupted one and was killed."

"Is anything missing?" Phil asked.

"What? I have no idea."

"I think it's time to inform your honest policeman," Godfrey said. "Who is the man?"

"You must call the nineteenth precinct and request to speak to Detective Sergeant John Atkins. Speak only to him and ask him to come here. Do not overly explain. Just say that there has been a bit of trouble and . . . Well, I'm sure you know what to say.

"If he is not there, have them send someone to find him. Throw your weight around if you must, but delicately. He does not like to be coerced. You may tell him, I precede him. That should precipitate prompt action. In the meantime you must lock the laundry room, and . . . secure the areas around the entrances to the chutes on each floor."

"Impossible," Luther said.

"Well, you must figure out a way, and keep the regular staff off the upper floors until this can be dealt with. And if you could just have your cook see that my maid gets a cup of tea in the kitchen."

He started. "Yes, of course." He strode over to the door, stepped out into the hall.

"Mrs. Cochran!" he bellowed.

The cook appeared seconds later, wiping her hands on her apron and looking harried. "Yes, Mr. Pratt."

"Please take Lady Dunbridge's maid to the kitchen and take care of her. Give her tea or something."

"Yes, Mr. Pratt." She looked around until her eyes lit on Lily. Her eyes widened.

"She's very sweet," Phil assured her. "Her English is not so good."

"Ah." Mrs. Cochran smiled at the maid. "You come along, dearie. Mrs. Cochran will look after you," she said in a loud voice as if volume would make up for Lily's lack of understanding.

Lily didn't even hesitate but went with her.

Phil turned to the two men.

"Just do as I say and all will be well. Now I must join dear Gwen in the conservatory. Shall we go, gentlemen? I have draperies to discuss." Phil swept by the two men, but she waited for them at the door. She had no intention of letting these two have their way with the murder scene more than they already had.

"I'll see you up," Luther said and started toward her.

"As you wish, Lady Dunbridge," said Godfrey, smiling at her in what Phil thought was amusement and perhaps a tad of admiration. Though whether for her skill, her bravura, or her just plain cheek, she wasn't certain.

"I believe Gwen is still in the conservatory," Pratt said. "It's good for her lungs. That and the inhalant that she must use several times a day."

They climbed the back stairs to the first floor, where Pratt opened the door. "My dear?"

The first thing Phil noticed was the smell. A sharp acrid odor that had earlier clung to Gwen Pratt's clothes.

Pratt went inside but Phil stood just inside the door, staring through the hazy atmosphere to where Gwendolyn Pratt, a green and yellow dressing robe covering her clothes, held the glass mask of a nebulizer to her nose. On a nearby table a kerosene-burning vaporizer released clouds of acrid smoke around her head.

Gwen saw Phil and pulled the glass mask from her face. "Lady Dunbridge. Philomena."

"Please," Phil said. "Don't get up on my account."

"It's this horrible asthma. I don't usually use both the nebulizer and the incense, but with the party and the stress of poor Perry's death, I thought the double application couldn't hurt.

"Elva?" She waved at a maid, a plump young woman with fair hair and complexion, who quickly removed the offending dish of incense and hurried away.

Gwen slipped out of her dressing robe and turned to her husband. "Thank you, Luther. I know you have a million things to do today. Lady Dunbridge—Philomena—and I will fend for ourselves."

A tactful dismissal, Phil thought.

"Yes, yes, I do. I'll be here at home in my study if you should need me."

"Thank you, my dear. Now, Philomena, let us go into the parlor. I've ordered cook to serve us coffee and some cakes."

She led Phil into the parlor. She seemed totally recovered from her attack. She stood erect and chatted as well as any hostess would with a morning caller. Only the slightest telltale medicinal odor gave any indication she was unwell.

"Now, what do you think?" she asked as soon as they had sat down in the window alcove where, Phil did not fail to notice, Mrs. Pratt could watch the street.

"I've asked your husband to call the police."

"I thought that might have been what happened. Then it wasn't an accident by misadventure."

"No."

Mrs. Pratt's hand rose to her chest, fingered a medallion that hung around her neck. "But how could this happen, in our own house, under our very noses? A housebreaker? While we were fully staffed and bursting with guests?"

Phil saw no need to try to assuage the woman's quandary. She let her work through to the inevitable conclusion. "Not the servants, surely. Ours are carefully vetted. Not one of my staying guests, nor my family.

"I can't believe this has happened. And poor Agnes. We'd hoped . . ."

"Has she been told?"

Mrs. Pratt shook her head. "She was still sleeping and I've ordered her breakfast sent to her room with a note that I wish her to rest upstairs this morning so she won't look peaked for the coming activities. It's her first season, and to have something like this happen, I'm not sure how to react."

Neither did Phil. Murder was something entirely beyond the pages of Mrs. Kingsland's etiquette book.

"Oh dear." Gwen's breathing suddenly became labored. Her hand came to her chest and she sucked in a jagged breath.

"Shall I ring for your maid?"

"No, no. I'll be fine. When . . . I get . . . excited . . . or up-set . . . poor Elva is already very upset by all of this. Her solicitations and fidgeting just make it worse."

"Then I'll send for Lily. She doesn't speak much English and she's extremely shy," she added, if carrying a knife at your ankle would be considered shy. "But she's extremely efficient."

"Thank you," Gwen said and took a final long breath. "But I'm better now."

The door opened and the butler ushered in two footmen with trays of coffee and finger sandwiches both savory and sweet and placed them on a mahogany side table covered in a Battenberg runner.

Mr. Pratt followed on their heels. As soon as they were gone, he turned to Phil. "I was able to speak with the detective sergeant. He is on his way."

"And Mr. Bennington?"

"He's in my study. He has business of his own that must be conducted today, so I've moved Vincent into the library. I told him what happened. He's very upset. He and Perry were once good friends."

"Once?" Phil asked.

"Oh, when the boys were in school. They both went to Harvard with my son, Morris, whom you met last night. And a couple of others who attended the party."

"They're no longer friends?"

"Of course they are, but having moved on in life, their interests have diverged."

That was a nice way of putting it, Phil thought. Morris, the son of an important banker and possible government commission appointee; Perry, the heir to a fortune. She didn't know about their other friends, but if Vincent was a mere secretary to his friend's father, he hadn't made very good use of his Harvard education. Though perhaps Mr. Pratt was preening him for a future in government.

"Now if you ladies will excuse me, I have the unenviable duty of informing Perry's parents of his demise. And then I must inform Isaac Sheffield. It will be such a blow to the company " He shook his head. "That it should happen in our home." He wandered off.

"Poor man," Gwen said, handing Phil a cup of coffee. "He takes his duties seriously, all his duties." She offered Phil the platter of cakes then took her own cup and looked toward the window. "I suppose we should at least say something about the drapes."

When the detective sergeant arrived, he found two ladies of fashion, heads together over a lifted piece of Brunschwig damask.

Mr. Pratt cleared his throat to get the ladies' attention. Not that they needed it. Phil and Gwendolyn Pratt had been watching from the window as John Atkins arrived. Saw him look up at the address and quickly lowered their heads over their ersatz reason for being there.

"My goodness, he's not what I expected," said Gwen.

"No," agreed Phil. One didn't expect the hero of a dime novel Western to arrive at your door on Fifth Avenue wearing an immaculate Chesterfield overcoat and suede fedora.

"The first time I met him I thought he was a vagrant. He was doing something they call 'undercover' work and was quite disreputable looking."

"Hard to imagine," Gwen said with appreciation.

Indeed it was.

So when Mr. Pratt did his throat clearing and ushered the detective into the room, they were quite ready to meet him.

"My dear, this is Detective Sergeant John Atkins. He's here about poor Perry's accident."

Mrs. Pratt immediately dropped her side of the drapery and hurried forward, stretching out her hand to the policeman's.

Americans never ceased to amaze Phil. In England, Atkins would have used the tradesman's entrance and wouldn't be greeted with anything but disdain. But here was Gwendolyn Pratt, welcoming him and drawing him farther into the room.

Atkins took Gwen's hand but his eyes only briefly left Phil's. She smiled slightly. He was surprised and not pleased.

She'd had the advantage of knowledge of his arrival; still, in the brief moment when Phil finally looked up from her piece of fabric, she was struck speechless. He'd shed his overcoat and was wearing a sack suit of thinly striped gray wool. If she'd met him in public she would have thought him a gentleman.

Well, he was, but by manners, not of class.

"You are acquainted with Lady Dunbridge, I believe." Luther Pratt's words fell into what Phil hoped wasn't a cavernous silence. Heavens, the man was handsome. If only he wasn't such a Puritan.

"Of course," Phil said, coming forward, also extending her hand.

Atkins nodded formally. "Lady Dunbridge."

He touched and dropped her hand. Well, what had she expected. Certainly not *How delightful to see you again*.

He turned to Mrs. Pratt. "I'll try to disrupt your household as little as possible. Mr. Pratt, perhaps if we could . . ." He let the sentence trail off but gestured to the door and the two men left the room.

Phil stared after them in consternation. She hadn't been expecting a warm welcome. And she hadn't really expected him to embrace the idea of her being involved in his case. But surely he must know her being here was not coincidence.

People died at parties all the time. But they weren't deliberately stabbed then shoved down a laundry chute. And the Countess of Dunbridge had never just happened to arrive for a social call in time to view the body the next morning.

She took one look at the closed door and nodded to Gwen. "Excuse me, I'll be back forthwith." She opened the door only to find another suited gentleman. At first she thought it was one of the young men from the party last night, then realized he was standing guard at the door. Well, the department had gone all out this morning. Not a uniform in sight. The detective sergeant got kudos for discretion.

"Sorry, ma'am. I was told to have everyone stay put, I mean where they were."

"Facilities," she said with a giggle.

"Oh, yes, of course." He blushed and waved his hand in a vague direction and let her run up the stairs. As soon as she was on the next floor she ran down the hall to the back servants' staircase and ran down again.

She was quite out of breath when she reached the kitchen level. And slightly disoriented. The kitchen was straight ahead, to her left what looked like a pantry and a panel of buzzers. She turned in the opposite direction, saw two maids hurrying toward her carrying a big tub between them. They saw her and froze. Then curtseyed out of sheer surprise, knocking into each other and sloshing water on the floor.

"Which way is the laundry room?"

They stared openmouthed at her, then one of them quirked her head to the left and Phil sped past them.

The door was closed.

In for a penny. She turned the doorknob; it jiggled but didn't move. He'd locked himself inside. She stood with her hands on her hips and wondered if she could finagle a key from cook's hands. There was a better way that she had been practicing, though she might not be quite up to snuff.

She felt in her coiffure until she found a suitable hairpin. Twisted it according to Lily's instructions—clever maid that she was—then knelt by the keyhole and slid the hairpin into the opening.

As she moved the pin inside the lock, the most amazing thing happened. The doorknob began to turn of its own accord.

Speechless, Phil watched the door crack open and a small hand beckon her in. She didn't hesitate, but held her skirts to her side and squeezed through the opening. She was immediately

grabbed by the wrist and pulled down to the ground, until she
squatted eye level with her ingenious lady's maid.

How? she mouthed.

Lily wagged her finger and crept over to the nearest laundry
cart. Lady Dunbridge duckwalked behind her, thinking what
her mother would do if she could see her now. Fortunately Lady
Hathaway couldn't abide sea travel. Phil was quite safe from her
strictures here.

She and Lily peered over the edge of the cart and could just
see John Atkins moving behind a curtain of lace, silhouetted by
the light of the window like a tableau vivant at the theatre.

Lily motioned her to follow and disappeared around the side
of the laundry cart. But when Phil reached the opening between
the carts, she was stopped by a pair of brown leather dress shoes.
And the woolen-clad legs that were wearing them.

Her head lifted. He seemed extraordinarily tall even for
him.

She smiled up at him and offered her hand, which he ignored.
She stood on her own power and managed to recapture a bit of
her normal aplomb.

"Detective Sergeant."

His expression didn't change. "How did you get in here?"

"Through the door, of course."

"I locked it." His eyes narrowed. "Please tell me you haven't
read any treatises on lock picking during your social whirlwind
this summer."

How did he know about her summer? Was he just surmising
or was he keeping tabs on her? Not for her charming self, she
was sure.

She shrugged innocently and tried not to look where Lily was
crouched behind the laundry cart.

He pointed to the door. "Out."

"Detective Sergeant Atkins. One doesn't order a countess
out." Phil swept past him and stopped at the body. Perry Fauks
was lying on his stomach where they had left him.

"I suppose you have already drawn your own conclusions about the incident."

"Well, yes. Of a sort. He must have been stabbed with some sort of narrow knife. A stiletto perhaps." *But not Lily's,* Phil added to herself. For once they couldn't be suspected of wrongdoing. *Just nosiness.*

"At first I thought he'd had a tragic accident trying to escape from an angry husband."

"In the laundry room?"

"No, before he . . . You do know how he was found?"

"Mr. Pratt said the maids found him early this morning."

"And told you they laid him out, then while I was here, turned him over to show me the wound? It's the only way I knew he'd been stabbed. It wasn't obvious the way he was laid out. Until then I'd only noticed he hadn't struggled on his way down, because I would never have interfered in a crime scene."

One eyebrow raised, then lowered to a frown. "His way down? His way down where?"

"Detective Sergeant. What did Mr. Pratt tell you?"

"He just said he'd been found by the maids, then left me here while he telephoned the next of kin."

Phil sighed. "Perhaps he wanted you to form your own conclusions."

"Or save his own skin," Atkins said.

"I suspect he was more worried about money and another Wall Street panic than being accused of murder."

"Their priorities," Atkins said, and the edge in his voice was unmistakable. "Better to hide and dissimulate than go for the truth."

"We are but mortals, Detective Sergeant."

"Sometimes I wonder," he said under his breath. "So how was he discovered?"

She knew it chafed him to have to ask. And he could have waited and demanded the truth from Pratt or Bennington. Did that mean he was relenting just a little toward her?

"Perry Fauks was found in the laundry chute. They had to pull him out and when they realized he was quite dead, they laid him out and put a sheet over him. Hopefully that's all they did. But they are certainly circumspect."

"They?"

"Mr. Pratt and his friend Mr. Bennington."

"Godfrey Bennington?"

"Yes, do you know him?"

"Of him."

"May I ask why? I just met him last night at the Pratts' ball. He seems very self-assured. Is he someone important? I don't remember coming across his name before. And you don't exactly ask someone his business in the middle of a Viennese waltz. He isn't a criminal, is he?"

"Depends on your philosophy. He has ties to the War Department."

4

"That's the same as the War Office in England?" Phil said the obvious just to give her mind a minute to absorb the information about Godfrey Bennington.

Godfrey had ties to the War Department. *He made money from war.* Phil had never been political minded, but she wasn't unfamiliar with men who were, and who weren't squeamish about profiting from the spoils of fighting, and it had always seemed particularly distasteful.

"I've done all I can here without the coroner. I'll accompany you upstairs, where you will stay while I begin the search of the house."

"I only saw the one man upstairs. Where are the others?"

"There are no others. I was denied a team. Now I know why."

"Secrecy. Reputation. National security?"

"Perhaps." He dipped his head, signaling her to go. They both knew it was about more than discretion. If things turned sour for the participants, pointed to the wrong person as suspect, they might insist on it not coming out at all. They might even try to discredit Atkins.

Lady Dunbridge was not about to let that happen.

"What about the man who was posted on the door of the parlor?"

"He's on loan from central. One man, who has the superintendent's ear. And the super has his eyes and ears in return."

"You can't trust him."

"Not at all."

"You can trust me."

"Can I?"

"Yes. Besides, what choice do you have? You can't possibly do this by yourself and you don't dare alert anyone on the force about what has happened here. The country has just narrowly avoided a disastrous financial crisis. Can you imagine if this were to get out so close on the heels of that event?"

"All too well, Lady Dunbridge." His eyes narrowed. "Just why are you here?"

She hardly knew what she was doing here. Only that they—whoever "they" were—expected her to do something. *But the War Department.* She had to confess she felt slightly out of her depth. But that had never stopped her before, and she had no intention of giving up now.

"I was helping my dear friend Gwen decide on the best pattern to use for her new parlor drapes. That's what we were doing when you arrived."

"I didn't see any pattern books."

"We were merely in the theoretical stage—what colors best accent the wardrobe of the lady of the house, what fabric wears well and what would clash with the furnishings. You know the kind of thing."

"Can't say that I do. I'll have to take your word for it. I had no idea you had expertise in the decorative arts."

"I have expertise in many things."

"I have no doubt of that, Lady Dunbridge. And I don't believe for a minute you are here to discuss drapes. I don't know how you managed to insinuate yourself into the situation, but you need to bow out."

"I was invited and I'm staying to help my friends. I can help you. I've told Luther to keep the servants away."

"I'll see to them."

"They won't allow you to question all the family members. There are young ladies in the house."

"I'll ask Mrs. Pratt to accompany them."

"She's sickly and not up to the task."

His jaw tightened at each answer. If he didn't give in soon, she might be inclined to worry about the longevity of his teeth.

"You'll have to have someone to watch your back."

"I realize that, Lady Dunbridge."

"And help you search for the missing stiletto."

"How did you . . . I suppose you've been reading Gross's *Criminal Investigation* again."

"He is the expert in the field of—"

"I know who he is and I'm certain he would say that you have no business interfering in police business. Now let's go." He took her by the elbow, but stopped by the laundry cart. "You too, Lily."

Slowly Lily rose to her full almost five feet. Lifted her nose in the air. And stalked past him to the door.

"How did you know she was there?" Phil demanded as he steered her out of the room.

"I'm the detective." He locked the door behind them.

Luther Pratt was just coming out of his office when they reached the ground floor. "Ah, Lady Dunbridge, you too? Come into the study."

He ushered them into a dark-paneled room of wall-to-wall bookshelves, filled with books old and new.

"Well?" Luther Pratt gestured to chairs as an afterthought. Phil started to sit, but realized Atkins had not moved. She kept her feet. She had no intention of having two bellicose men towering over her and not listening to a word she might say.

"There is really no reason for us to bother Lady Dunbridge with the details of this event," Atkins said at his suavest and most insulting.

She glared at him, but it was Pratt who after a quick panicked expression pulled himself together and said, "It was Lady Dunbridge who insisted that I call for you personally."

The detective sergeant's focus shifted to Phil with a light raise of one eyebrow. "Was it?" he asked drily.

"Yes, for your expertise." Phil smiled. "And your discretion."

"And I must insist she stay."

"Mr. Pratt, the fewer people involved in this investigation the better. There is no reason Lady Dunbridge need be involved at all."

"She's a big support to my wife, who is very upset over this. It was her heart's desire that our daughter, Agnes, and poor Perry would . . . she is distraught, not to mention Agnes. I don't know how she will take this."

"I will have to speak with both of them."

"What? Not possible. They know nothing of what happened. None of us do. It must have been some kind of prank gone wrong."

Phil shot Atkins an I-told-you-so look.

"Mr. Pratt. The deceased, Perry Fauks, was stabbed to death. There will be an investigation. With or without your cooperation."

He was bluffing—he was one "snitch" away from being pulled from the case. And that snitch was probably standing outside with his ear to the door.

"So it's best that you advise your family to cooperate," he continued.

Pratt darted a look at Phil.

She smiled reassuringly. "And they will be glad to, Detective Sergeant. Not to worry, Luther." She used his Christian name as emphasis. It worked—at least with Pratt.

"I'll see that they are not harassed." She snapped a smile at Atkins.

The slightest tightening of his nostrils. The detective sergeant was not in the mood to be trifled with today. She didn't blame him. Someone had cut off a young man in the prime of life.

"You said he was a guest in the house. I'll need to see his room."

Pratt nodded.

"And anywhere else he might have gone late last night. When was the last anyone saw of him?"

"I-I don't know. I suppose it was Isaac Sheffield. When he left he said he'd had—" Pratt clamped down on the last word.

"He'd had what?" Atkins asked.

"Nothing, nothing, just had a few words."

The detective's jaw tightened. "What kind of words?"

"I don't know. Something about the business. Perry was being groomed to take over soon. Isaac is his New York manager, an old family friend. They occasionally butted heads. But nothing that would . . . no, not possible."

"Is Isaac Sheffield also staying with you?"

"No. Isaac lives with his wife on Park Avenue. Very well-respected businessman."

"I'd like you to gather whoever is in the house this morning. In the parlor, perhaps? I'll need to ascertain Fauks's movements of last night."

"Is this really necessary? I'm not sure the girls are even awake. I believe Godfrey is in the dining room with my son, Morris. And as for the Jeffreys, I believe they were going out for a drive through Central Park this morning. They're fresh-air enthusiasts."

Atkins had taken out his pencil and was busily writing names down in his notebook, but finally looked up. "How many are there?"

"That's all at the moment."

"And the Jeffreys are . . . ?"

"My sister-in-law and her husband."

"When are they expected to return?"

"I don't know. My wife may, but please don't bother her. Her health is fragile and this has already been a strain."

"I will see whoever is here directly, and the others when they return. At the moment, I'd like to talk to Mr. Fauks's valet."

"Yes, of course." Pratt pressed the call buzzer and as if that wasn't enough, stepped into the hallway. "Brinlow!" he bellowed, before coming back to his desk.

The butler appeared a minute later, out of breath and still adjusting his jacket.

"Sir."

"Sorry if I've interrupted your lunch. Ask Mr. Kelly to come to the library. Detective Sergeant Atkins would like to speak with him."

"I'm afraid, sir, that's impossible."

"Mr. Kelly isn't at lunch?"

"He's gone, sir."

"Gone? You mean out?"

"Gone for good. I went up to find out if he knew about his employer. How could he not? But he wasn't there. His room has been cleared out. And no one has seen him this morning. It's like he was never here at all."

"There's your killer, Detective Sergeant," Pratt said. "Why didn't we think of that? You won't need to disturb my household after all."

"On the contrary," Atkins said. "He may be the killer, but we will need evidence to convict him once he's found. And that evidence lies within this house among the residents. In the meantime, I'd like to inspect the valet's room."

Pratt turned to Brinlow, who had made himself invisible during the exchange. He nodded and Atkins followed him to the door.

He turned at the threshold. "Good day, Lady Dunbridge."

Well, that was rather obvious, Phil thought. And totally ineffective. She had no intention of leaving him to pursue this by himself.

"I'll be ruined," Pratt said, sinking into his desk chair.

"Perhaps he'll find some clue that will lead to the man's arrest," Phil said.

"You heard him. He wants to speak to everyone in the house."

"It's how they learn the facts, as you must understand."

"Why? Perry's valet killed him. God knows he'll never work again." He grabbed his forehead between his fingers. "What am I saying? He'll go to jail—or worse." He straightened suddenly. "I beg your pardon, Lady Dunbridge. I was just thinking out loud."

"I assure you, Mr. Pratt, it's nothing I haven't heard or seen before." Though she had to admit, seeing that handsome young man lying dead among the laundry had given her pause.

"I suppose I must warn the family. Godfrey might be able—"

Phil cut him off. "If you want this solved quickly, you and Mr. Bennington must let the detective sergeant do his job. Once the news is out, the press will have a field day for as long as the investigation lasts. The more you cooperate, the quicker it will be. And I, of course, wouldn't think of leaving Gwen at such a trying time."

Detective Sergeant Atkins returned several minutes later. He shot Phil a look that spoke volumes, starting with *why are you still here*, and ending with—if he hadn't been a gentleman—*get the hell out.*

Fortunately he was, at all times, well mannered.

"I'm afraid, Mr. Pratt, it will be necessary to search the premises as well as the laundry chute."

"What?"

Atkins's eyes narrowed to mere slits. "Mr. Pratt. You told me no one touched the body."

"Not once we got him out. We laid him there and covered him up. No one has touched him since. Except for Godfrey Bennington. He turned him over to show Lady Dunbridge the . . ." He couldn't finish the sentence.

"Did anyone remove anything from the scene or the body?"

"No."

"Then I will need to send someone down the chute to look for any possible evidence."

"What evidence?"

The murder weapon for one. Could it be stuck in the chute? Was it hidden somewhere among the sheets? Phil hadn't had time to search.

Or had someone removed it after the body was discovered? With her new insight into Godfrey Bennington, she didn't think he would have any compunction about tampering with the scene.

And what about Luther Pratt? Was he complicit in an attempt to cover up the real reason for Perry Fauks's murder?

"In that case," Phil said, "you'll need someone small enough to fit in the laundry chute and still be able to look around for clues. Perry wasn't a large man and he got stuck."

"How did you know that?" Atkins asked.

"He was wedged in the chute. They had to forcibly pull him out," Phil said complacently.

Pratt rubbed his chin. "I don't have anyone on my staff small and agile enough to do that. Perhaps I could ask the chimney sweep."

Phil pursed her lips. "Small to be sure, but perhaps not as needle-witted nor as honest as necessary. But," she added before Atkins could stop her, "I know just who will have such a person, and who will be completely discreet."

And he would also keep her abreast of what was found.

Both men looked at her. Pratt with curiosity, Atkins with resignation.

"I'm afraid no one is completely discreet," Pratt said tentatively.

"Discreet—and loyal," Phil smiled.

"You have such a person?"

"I believe I do," Phil said.

Atkins glowered at her. "You can't possibly mean Lily."

"Good heavens, no. She's much too delicate for such an endeavor."

Atkins made a noise that from a less cultured man would have been a snort.

"Really, Detective Sergeant," Phil said. "You don't need a policeman, or a chimney sweep, or even a lady's maid. You need a jockey."

5

"A jockey?" Luther exclaimed.

"A jockey." Phil knew Atkins wouldn't like her idea, so she plowed on before he could explode. "I'm sure Bobby Mullins would be only too happy to loan us one from the stable."

"Mullins? That—" Atkins caught himself before he expounded on his views of Bobby Mullins, ex–prize fighter, confidant of thugs and thieves, denizen of Manhattan's seamier society.

Bobby had turned over a new leaf since then, but not before running the gamut of unsavory professions until finally ending up as the loyal right-hand man of Reggie Reynolds, notorious gambler, womanizer, racehorse owner—and husband of Phil's best friend.

After Reggie's murder, Bobby had switched his loyalties to Bev and, because of Phil's involvement in solving Reggie's murder, Phil.

"He's the manager of Holly Farm stables. I'm sure he would lend me—us—one of his men."

"I have no doubt," Atkins said, through clenched teeth. But he knew she was right. The police were constantly battling a war on two fronts. One to catch criminals, and two, dealing with the powers that be when the investigation skirted too close to the upper crust of society.

She could see the detective sergeant's mind at work. She didn't envy him. As one of the holdovers from the department's brief experiment with honesty and efficiency, he was respected by few and despised by many who augmented their own salaries with graft, bribes, and extortions. Being a cultured man—Phil hadn't so far learned just how that had come about—he was naturally sent to deal with the upper echelons of society when it was impossible to merely look the other way.

It constantly put him in an untenable position, alert to deceit from his own people, and out-and-out hostility from most of the people he was sent to investigate.

He could use her help, though he would never admit it.

"Bobby can expedite the investigation."

"I think it's a capital idea," Mr. Pratt said. "If you really trust this Mullins character."

"With my life," Phil said somewhat hyperbolically. Bobby's loyalties were few, but unwavering. She hoped it was never put to the test, but she expected Bobby would do his part to save her if it ever came to that.

"But I can't have rough characters coming in and out of my house. I have women and young girls in residence."

"I will ring them and ask them to come, shall we say tomorrow morning? I'll tell them to arrive at the servants' entrance and carry a crate so it will look as if they're tradesmen. Bobby has experience in the theatre."

Atkins cut off a snort.

Well, Bobby did have experience, if you counted consorting with the ladies of the chorus.

Atkins didn't make a move to stop her. And why was that? Usually he would have thrown her out by now.

"I'll be glad to call out to the farm and arrange it with Bobby. And of course I'll be here to make sure all goes well."

"Not necessary," said Atkins.

"*Au contraire.* You intimidate him, and put him on his guard. But I—"

"And your inimitable charms?"

"Thank you, can get him to do what we need."

"Very well," Pratt said.

Atkins nodded his acceptance, possibly his defeat? He would thank her someday. Hopefully when they found an indisputable clue in the laundry chute on the morrow.

A muscle in Atkins's jaw worked as he turned back to Pratt. "I must ask you to seal every opening to the chute as well as the entire laundry room until a search can be accomplished."

"But what about the laundry? And what do I tell the servants?"

"That the sanitary department will be here tomorrow for its yearly inspection," Phil suggested without missing a beat.

The two men stared at her.

"Every laundry chute should be habitually disinfected." *Especially after a dead body had passed through it.* "Now, if you gentlemen will excuse me, I think I should check on dear Gwen and then make arrangements for tomorrow."

She swept past the two men, past Brinlow who stood just outside the door, and met Gwen in the foyer as she was about to go upstairs. She stopped on the first step and looked over the banister at Phil.

"Any news?" Gwen asked.

"Yes. It looks like Mr. Fauks's valet is missing. Suspicion has fallen on him."

Gwen slumped and caught the rail. "Oh, thank goodness."

"You should rest," Phil said, coming around the newel to lend her support.

"I will, but first . . . someone must tell Agnes what has happened." Tears welled in her eyes. "All her hopes dashed. It's almost too much to bear."

"Let me help you upstairs," Phil said and took her elbow.

"I don't know how to thank you, Lady Dunbridge—Philomena. You're so calm. So collected. I envy you your aplomb." They reached the second floor; halfway down the hall, Gwen stopped by a door. They could hear giggles coming from inside the room. It must be Agnes's room.

"I'll leave you to your daughter," Phil said.

"Oh no, please, if you don't mind."

Phil really had intended to search Perry's room while Atkins was otherwise occupied, but it would have to wait. She was here to give support after all.

They found not one but three young girls sitting on a bed covered by a thick eider down quilt. Heads together, they whispered and laughed as they sipped chocolate and munched on muffins. When Phil and Gwen entered, they all jumped, nearly upsetting the breakfast tray.

"Oh, Mama. You scared us to pieces."

Gwen forced a smile. "Sorry, my dear. Are you exchanging secrets about the young men at the ball last night?"

Agnes blushed. She was a pretty girl, not like her mother and not really like her father either. Blond curls had escaped her nightcap and curled beguilingly around her cheeks. Her eyes were bright blue and large; she reminded Phil of one of those girls pictured on soap advertisements.

"Agnes, your manners."

Agnes scooted off the bed, setting off a swell of ruffles and lace of her dressing gown.

"Oh, I beg your pardon, Lady Dunbridge, I didn't see you standing there. How nice of you to come?" The sentence ended in a question. Why on earth should a dowager countess she'd only briefly met last night be visiting in her boudoir?

The other girls also stood. Curtseyed.

"And this is Maud and Effie, my sister's children," Gwen said. "You met them last night, Lady Dunbridge."

"Should we go, ma'am?" asked the one on the left.

Gwen shook her head. "No, Effie. I'm afraid I have bad news. You might as well all hear it at once. There's been a terrible accident."

"Papa!" Agnes cried.

"No, child, your papa is fine. It's Perry Fauks."

"Perry? What kind of accident?"

The twins, Effie and Maud, whom Phil hadn't bothered to differentiate at the ball last night, inched closer to each other.

"What kind of accident, Mama?"

"It seems he fell down the laundry chute."

"Stupid man. Isn't he too old to play at that? How badly is he hurt? Serves him right."

Effie and Maud nodded their heads in agreement.

"I'm afraid . . ." Gwen cleared her throat. "He's dead, my dear. A terrible thing."

Agnes frowned. "He can't be."

Effie—or maybe it was Maud—gasped and covered her face.

The other sister—Maud or Effie—cried, "Oh no," and threw her arms around the other sister and they clung to each other so closely that their masses of black curls and similar expressions evoked images of the two-headed lady Phil and Lily and Preswick had seen at Coney Island at the beginning of the summer.

"I am so very sorry," Gwen said and tried to hug her daughter, but Agnes pulled away and sank back against the bed. "He's dead?"

"Yes, my dear, I'm afraid so."

"Poor Perry."

Phil turned to the twins. "Perhaps you should go wait for your mother to return."

One of them nodded convulsively, and Phil noticed she had a tiny mole on her neck. "Come, Maud."

Phil took a quick look at Maud's neck as she passed by. No mole. Good, now she would be able to identify them if need be.

Maud hesitated, before Effie took her elbow and pulled her across the room. "She'll be glad he's dead," Maud said as the door closed behind them.

Well, well, Phil thought. She looked quickly at Agnes. The girl hadn't shed a tear. Shock could do that. Grief would come soon enough.

Gwen began helping Agnes back into bed, so Phil took the opportunity for a quick look around. The room was done up in flounces, swags, and ruffles in various shades of pink and green.

Curlicues and furbelows adorned the drapes and chairs and dressing table.

She wandered over to the table. A pair of gloves that hadn't been taken away by the maid. Odd, that they had been forgotten. Phil picked them up, turned them over. Found nothing. She didn't really think this child had stabbed Perry and shoved him down the laundry chute.

But one never knew.

Agnes's dance card was open on the tabletop and a pink rosebud was wilting on the top.

Memorabilia, cards, and favors from various trips were strewn across the surface. Nothing to aid Phil in finding Perry's killer.

After another quick look around, she quietly left the room and stood just outside the door considering what to do next. With the men downstairs and Atkins searching the valet's quarters, this would have been a perfect time to visit Perry Fauks's room, if she only knew which one it was. Unfortunately she didn't know the layout of the house. She was obviously in the family's wing. The guest bedrooms could either also be on this floor or the floor above.

She was contemplating the efficacy of just opening doors and taking the chance of surprising someone at their toilette when a door at the end of the hall opened and Effie—or was it Maud—slipped out, closing it quietly behind her. Then she sped down the hall away from Phil and disappeared around the corner.

Phil naturally followed. She slowed at the back of the house, then peered around the corner. Maud looked back so quickly that Phil barely had time to hop back into the corridor. When she peeked out again, she caught sight of the train of Maud's dress going into a room. Not a room. Up the servants' stairs.

What was the girl up to?

Fortunately, Effie, or Maud—Phil needed to get a closer look to be sure which one it was—was in too much of a hurry to notice the square of light that appeared on the stairs when Phil opened the door. She shut it quickly, dimming the light to the square windows on each landing.

The girl paused on the landing above, then went through the door to the third floor. Phil stopped when she got to the landing, then stuck her head out the door. The girl had disappeared.

Phil walked slowly along the hallway trying to hear any sound that might be coming from the bedrooms on this floor, but the guests were either out or still sleeping.

Well, Phil could wait. And hope to heaven Detective Sergeant Atkins didn't find her skulking along the corridor before she found out what Effie or Maud was up to. She'd just stepped forward when a door opened, and Maud—or Effie—ran headlong into her.

"I beg your—" The girl broke off. "What are *you* doing up here?"

A quick look revealed the lack of a mole on her neck. *Maud.* "Following you, my dear. You seemed distressed. I wanted to make sure you were all right."

"I'm fine." Maud shoved one hand behind her back, but not before Phil saw the sheet of folded paper.

"Love letter?" Phil guessed.

"It's mine."

"But this isn't your room."

Maud shook her head. "It's just a silly note I wrote. I wanted it back. Now that he's . . . he's . . . dead."

She burst into tears. Phil quickly slipped a supporting arm around her and relieved the note from her hands.

"The police will probably want to see this."

"No. They can't. Please give it back. It doesn't mean anything. It was just a joke. Agnes will never forgive me. Mother will kill me. Please."

"If that's so, then perhaps all will be well."

"I didn't kill him."

Phil blinked. "What makes you think someone killed him?"

"I-I just do."

"You must have a reason to think that."

Maud shook her head, setting off an agitation of curls.

"Come now." Phil made a slight motion with the hand that held Maud's note. Just enough to get the girl's attention.

"I don't. Please let me go."

Phil supposed it hadn't occurred to the girl she could merely walk away.

"Is that Perry's room? Is this where you retrieved your note?"

Maud's eyes bugged. Answer enough. Now how had she known which was Perry's room, unless she had been there before?

"Why don't you go back to your room. I'll take this for safe-keeping. If the police need to see it, I'll hand it over to Detective Sergeant Atkins. He's very discreet. If you're innocent, you have nothing to worry about."

"Innocent?" Slowly she dropped her hand. "Take it. I don't want it. I'm sure you'll have a good laugh at me when you read it."

"I doubt it. You're not the first girl to do something silly. Now run along and try to forget that anything just happened." Phil waited until the girl slumped away, then looking quickly each way, she slipped into the room.

The guest room was like many she'd seen, lifted straight from an English country house or French château and deposited in a smaller space in a New York mansion. A large four-poster bed of dark mahogany commanded the room. It was prepared for the night with one corner turned down, but unused. No one, including Perry, had been in Perry's bed before he was killed.

She quickly searched the carpets for scuff marks, even drops of blood, though she didn't expect to find much. Fauks's shirt and jacket had soaked up most of it. And though it was hard to tell against the black wool, it was even harder to see among the deep jewel tones of the oriental carpet that covered the floor. And as far as scuff marks—there were none.

She moved on to a carved dresser and wardrobe, both in the Hepplewhite style. She was tempted to look inside, but she knew

John Atkins would be walking through the door any minute with the same purpose in mind. The same purpose, but perhaps not for the same reasons.

Phil wasn't even certain why she felt she needed to stay a step ahead of the intrepid detective. He was thorough, intelligent, and honest, as far as she knew. But if her elusive benefactor had known of the murder early enough to warn her of Luther Pratt's visit, there was something more here than a spontaneous crime of passion or accidental manslaughter.

She opened the top drawer of the dresser. It was a shambles, with linens, socks, and pajamas rudely pushed into heaps. The detective sergeant would be furious. Especially if he thought Phil had made such a mess.

And of course she wouldn't, but she couldn't very well tell him Maud had torn through them looking for her letter. Not yet.

She dismissed the thought. One day even the straitlaced detective would accept that there are some things women might just do better than men.

She moved quickly to the writing desk. The surface was clean, she took a little peek in the drawer beneath. The typical guest amenities. Clean sheet of stationery, pens, envelopes. She shut the drawer.

But the wastepaper basket. There was a temptation too strong to resist.

And it appeared to be a treasure trove. Quite a few torn strips of paper. The same stationery she'd seen in the drawer. Her pulse quickened. Had Perry been having trouble writing a letter? Phil wondered. Or breaking off his flirtation, surely not an affaire, with Maud?

She leaned over and stirred the papers with one finger, trying to see some indication of their contents without actually touching them. Most had been torn into strips, and she finally had to lift one out to see what it contained. Love letters and, if she wasn't mistaken, all in Maud's hand. So more than one little note, and he'd torn all but one. At the very bottom, one sheet was merely crumpled.

She deliberated for two seconds. After all, it was already crumpled, what did it matter if she opened it and then crumpled it again.

She scooped it up, opened it, and smoothed it against the desktop. It was an article about balloons cut from a newspaper. She leaned over to read the crinkled print.

An announcement of the testing of air balloons by the War Department the following week on Long Island.

War Department. Godfrey. *Balloons?*

Interesting. That he had this article might mean no more than Perry was boning up his conversational skills for social chats with Godfrey. As heir to Fauks Copper, Coal and Steel, he might have many things in common with the older man.

And the fact that he crumpled it up and threw it away might only mean he was finished with it.

Phil, however, wasn't. She re-crumpled it and dropped it back into the wastepaper basket. She'd leave the paper but she would ask Preswick to do some research on war balloons as soon as she returned home.

But Maud's letters were different. Obviously they hadn't meant as much to Perry as they had to Maud. And the fact that she knew which room was his didn't bode well for the girl.

A girl in her position could lose every chance of a future in society if she had strayed too far.

Phil wouldn't be responsible for wrecking the girl's future if she could help it. She'd take the letters for safekeeping until the time they were needed, and if they weren't? Well, no need for the world to ever find out about them.

When she was sure she'd collected every scrap, she shoved them all in the pocket of her morning dress and hurried back downstairs—down the front stairs this time—and returned to the drawing room to find not Gwen, but Luther and Godfrey and another younger man, who seemed vaguely familiar.

"How is Agnes taking it?" Luther asked, coming to meet her.

"Gwen is with her. She's holding up the best she can." Phil hoped that was true.

"You remember my son, Morris."

Morris was sprawled in a club chair. His hair, which tended to curl like his father's, was neatly pomaded in a center part. His demeanor left much to be desired.

Spoiled. Bored. Going to seed already. Phil knew the ilk.

"For God's sake, Morris," Luther Pratt said between tight lips.

Morris unfolded from the chair, languidly bowed over Phil's hand, and gingerly eased himself back down.

"I do beg your pardon, Lady Dunbridge, but I'm sure you can understand. Have a bit of a head this morning. My sister's debut, a cornucopia of my father's excellent champagne, several cigars, and a walk along the river with some fellow revelers have made me an anathema to good company."

He smiled and relapsed into a silent heap in the chair.

Luther Pratt shot him an acid look. "Please be seated, Lady Dunbridge. Detective Sergeant Atkins is telephoning to alert the police to be on the lookout for the valet, Mr. Kelly. And also to summon the coroner and the mortuary van. Are you sure this man can be discreet?"

"Ha," said Morris. "When have you ever known a copper to be discreet? He'll cost us a fortune."

"Don't be vulgar," Luther snapped.

Morris shrugged.

"I assure you, you needn't worry about that," Phil said, bristling at the assumption that Atkins could be bribed.

"I beg your pardon."

She nodded slightly. Perhaps he was just a concerned son, worried that his father's reputation and good name, not to mention his rise among the political elite, might be irrevocably damaged by the death of Perry Fauks.

"It is very kind of you to support Gwen during this difficult time," Godfrey Bennington said into the silence that had fallen over the group.

"Not at all. So many people, Gwen particularly, have shown me kindness since I've arrived, I'm delighted to be able to return the favor."

She didn't miss the quick sparkle in his eye. Had he guessed that it was more than her compassion that had brought her here? He suddenly became much more interesting.

He wasn't ruffled at all at Fauks's death. Not like Luther Pratt. But then Godfrey wasn't about to become the head of a powerful banking committee.

He was, however, attached to the War Department. Could such a situation be disastrous to him, also? He didn't seem at all concerned.

She realized he was watching her, a smile hovering on his lips. Was he just being friendly? Waiting for her to put the pieces together? What was his place in all of this?

Phil sighed. Really, this detective business was getting no easier. She had become suspicious of everyone.

The door opened and another young man strolled in.

"Hey ho, Morris. Brinlow wasn't about, so I saw myself in." He stopped mid-step. "Sorry, sir. I didn't expect you to be home. My apologies. I came to pick up Morris and the girls for a day on the lam. Where *are* the girls? Aren't they ready?"

He looked from Mr. Pratt to Morris. Frowned. He was obviously no stranger. Middle height, an athletic build, and dressed in motoring weeds. Phil could see the slight indentions from where he'd been wearing driving goggles.

"Anything wrong?"

"Perry's dead," Morris said in a laconic voice.

"Drank too much last night, did he? Well, we'll go without him. Serves him right for hogging all the girls on the dance floor."

"No, Harry. I mean dead. Deceased. No longer living."

Harry's eyes widened and he turned back to Mr. Pratt for

verification. "Can't be. He was in prime twig. Don't tell me he fell down the steps or something."

"He was killed, Harry. By his valet as far as we know. The man has disappeared."

Harry sat down in the nearest chair. "So much for Perry's great business coup. Murdered?"

"It appears so," Morris said. "Glad you held on to your money?"

Harry let out his breath. "I'll say. But poor Agnes. How's she taking it?"

"She's distraught, as you can imagine," Mr. Pratt said, breaking into the two men's conversation. "The police are here and we're all still trying to make sense of what happened."

"Perhaps I should . . . go?"

"Good idea," Morris said and stood with more energy than he as yet had displayed. "I'll go with you. I can't stand much more of this sitting around."

"Morris," his father said, "I really think—"

"If that policeman wants to question me, tell him to come round tomorrow. I've had enough. Ta." He bowed to Phil and he steered Harry out the door.

"Pardon our poor manners, Lady Dunbridge," Godfrey said. "That was Harry Cleeves. His father is head of one of the city's major investment companies. Barely escaped collapse. One of the lucky ones. Harry is one of the new set, not much on manners, but heavy on enthusiasm."

"Please, don't be troubled by it. But tell me, what were they talking about, Perry's big coup?"

"Oh, just talk. Those young men are always scheming some way to get rich without working. I just don't understand the younger generation, so much energy just to fritter it away."

"Detective Sergeant Atkins may be interested in learning more about Perry's latest scheme."

"I don't see how it could possibly be of interest to him," Luther said. "Just something to confuse the investigation."

"Which I'm sorry to say," Godfrey added, "will not last much longer."

Phil's eyebrows went up.

"I'm afraid I was forced to go over the detective sergeant's head. In my defense, no good can come from him digging into very volatile matters. He'll be allowed to search the chute tomorrow, and do a cursory questioning of the staff, while the police pursue this valet. But after that, as far as we and his superiors are concerned, his involvement of the Pratt family will be at an end."

"You're ending the investigation?" Phil blurted. "But why?"

"My dear Lady Dunbridge, I too have my superiors."

6

Well, she hadn't expected that. Now she must readjust her opinion of Godfrey Bennington. Not only was he a good family friend, a doting godfather, he was well connected, powerful, and, she imagined, ruthless.

She didn't envy Atkins, though she suspected he was used to these strong-arm tactics. He always seemed to be assigned to the more delicate investigations, whether because he was more cultured than most policemen or whether they were trying to make things so difficult he finally quit, Phil could only guess.

The mantel clock struck the hour. It was later than she thought and time to take her leave. She didn't expect to see Atkins again today. Once he'd finished questioning the servants, he would be hustled out the back door and sent on his way.

Besides, she was getting hungry. She'd only had a slice of toast for breakfast, and the sandwiches the Pratts' cook had sent up had sat uneaten and were finally taken away.

"Perhaps I could call Mr. Mullins and arrange for tomorrow's search," she said to Luther, "and then I'll collect my maid and be on my way."

"Of course." He escorted her back to the study. "I'll tell Brinlow to send your maid up and leave you to your privacy." He bowed slightly and closed the door.

She placed the call to Holly Farm. When at last Bobby Mullins answered, she told him about the plan for needing someone small enough and willing to climb down a laundry chute.

Bobby laughed. "Well, that wouldn't be me, would it, your

ladyness?" Once a welterweight boxer, Bobby had put on a few stone over the years; "stocky" would be a polite term for what Bobby was these days. "But I got a bunch of little guys willing to make an extra buck, I mean—"

"Excellent, of course he will be reimbursed," she said before Bobby could start haggling and give himself a cut. "But I must warn you, this is a police matter."

"Gorn, not again."

"I'm afraid so. A young man died at a residence last night. A very important residence. Discretion is required."

"I don't know how you get into these things. I'll bring Rico. I'll wear my bluest suit and see that he does the same. Rico is okay with you, your ladyness? His English is pretty so-so. And he knows how to keep his mouth shut." *And he was sweet on Phil's maid, Lily.*

She gave him the address and Luther Pratt's name.

There was silence on the end. Then a whooshing sound as if Bobby was blowing out air. "I'll say this for you, your countess-ness. You sure do run in some pretty high-up circles. Don't tell me he's dead. I don't think the banks could take it. He and his kind nearly queered the whole stock market. Lucky they didn't all lose their shirts."

Interesting that Bobby should know of Luther Pratt's financial dealings. Of course, before he'd cleaned up his act to run the stables, Bobby had had his hand in a lot of money deals—some legal, some anything but.

But things had changed. Phil knew she could count on him and the other men at the farm.

"Detective Sergeant Atkins will be here to give Rico instructions. Shall we say eight o'clock?" She thought Bobby groaned but whether at the mention of the detective or the early hour, she could only guess.

"We'll be there."

"And Bobby, no offense, but could you come to the servants' entrance?"

"No offense taken. We'll bring some tools, so nobody won't know we're not tradesmen."

"Excellent. I knew I could count on you. Until tomorrow."

"Aw revoir," Bobby said. He was laughing when she ended the call.

Godfrey stopped her by the open door of the taxi as she was leaving. "I've decided to take the whole family out to Foggy Acres, my estate on Long island, as soon as Detective Atkins has finished with his search. Keep them removed from the situation until the valet can be apprehended and the talk dies down.

"I hope I can count you as one of my guests. I'm sure Gwen would love the company."

"But what about Agnes?" Phil asked, frantically putting together the ramifications of the entire list of suspects leaving town. "It is the beginning of the season. Must she withdraw from society due to Perry's demise?"

"No. Nothing was settled between them, thank God. Though there was speculation. Which is another reason to get her away. A few days to let the gossip die down and she'll be welcomed back into society without a thought.

"And while we're away I'll keep the young people entertained. I can scrounge up a few couples for dancing. There is still plenty of game for the gentlemen. Quite a few of my neighbors live there year-round. And there are plenty of others who would love to take the drive out to be able to claim themselves as Foggy Acres guests."

"I see. In that case, Mr. Bennington, I would love to come."

"Godfrey, please. I believe under these circumstances, formality becomes rather ridiculous."

"I agree."

"I will have my Daimler call for you."

"Godfrey. I'd love to come, but I'll be driving my own auto."

"I see. And how many staff will be accompanying you? I have plenty of room."

"Just my maid, and perhaps my butler, an old family retainer. I think he might enjoy a few days in the country. I'm afraid he's a little out of sorts in America." She mentally apologized to Preswick, who was having a second youth since landing in New York harbor. Phil even suspected he was "stepping out," as they say, with a certain cook he'd met recently.

She and Lily climbed into the taxi. Phil was tempted to tell the driver to let them off at Central Park. She liked to stroll every day.

But it was gaining evening and there was much to be done if she was to solve a murder and outfit herself for a country house party. Hopefully it wouldn't be as boring as English parties, where the gentlemen spent their days "bagging birds" and the women sat around with one amusing non-athletic gentleman to entertain them.

Phil generally joined the shoot, though she'd never enjoyed killing birds. She rather liked them, especially their feathers, which adorned many of her hats, she was embarrassed to say, but one had to get one's feathers somewhere.

"Well?" Lily asked.

"Later." Phil nodded, indicating the driver. You never knew who might be willing to sell secrets to the newspapers; she'd learned that at an early age and to her immense chagrin. And even though the rattle of the engine made conversation nearly impossible, she didn't dare take a chance of the driver overhearing.

So they sat in silence while they drove back to the Plaza.

The taxi let them off at the main entrance on Fifty-Ninth Street.

While Phil fumbled in her purse, Lily reached into her own pocket and paid the fare.

"Clever girl," Phil said. "Always prepared." A quality she

needed to cultivate in herself, and immediately. Because between the murder, the War Department, and her secret employer, she was bound to have a full dance card.

Before they entered the lobby, Phil made a quick detour to the corner newsboy hawking the afternoon edition of the *Evening Post* and bought a copy. Surely it was too early for word to have gotten out to reporters. But they were indefatigable news-hounds and it was best to stay abreast of the news.

She folded the newspaper and tucked it under her arm. Turned to avoid a passing shoeshine boy and stopped. Turned back around, but the "boy" who was actually a rather tall man disappeared around the corner of the hotel.

She inhaled, but it was gone, that exotic pipe tobacco that her mysterious note-leaving friend preferred. She was tempted to run after him, but that would be unseemly and besides, she knew he would be gone. Since their first meeting, he'd appeared several times in different disguises and disappeared without her ever managing to catch him.

"What is it, madam?"

"Lily, did you smell that?"

Lily wrinkled her nose. "Just fumes and horse droppings."

"Hmm." Phil took a last look down the street and decided she must have imagined that telltale scent.

"Good afternoon, Lady Dunbridge." The doorman tipped his hat and opened the door for them.

"Good afternoon, Douglas. Did you recognize that shoeshine boy who just passed?"

"Boy?" Douglas crinkled his brow.

"An adult shoeshine person, rather."

"No, can't say that I did. Though there're plenty of 'em hanging around. Did he bother you?"

"No, I was just curious."

"Yes, madam."

Phil went inside and headed straight for the row of four bronze elevators that took guests all the way up to the nineteenth floor. Her favorite elevator operator, Egbert, was waiting at the first lift and she and Lily stepped inside.

"Lovely day, Lady Dunbridge."

"Yes indeed, Egbert." His voice was a lyrical tenor and his greetings always reminded Phil of a song.

He shut the grate and they ascended to the fifth floor.

She let Lily and herself into her apartments. It was a wonderful sense of freedom, this coming and going at will. Preswick, of course, frowned upon the custom of letting oneself into one's own apartments, but he'd finally stopped grumbling aloud.

He of course appeared before they had both stepped over the threshold.

"High tea, immediately," Phil declared.

"Yes, my lady."

"For three. I refuse to have my tea while the two of you stand over me like starving refugees. We'll all have tea. In the study room where I can spread out my newspaper and you can both take notes on what we found out today. We've a lot to do if we're going to the country at week's end."

"The country?" Preswick said.

"Yes, and you will accompany us, Preswick. It's to be a country weekend in a place called Foggy Acres or some other Dickensian-sounding name." Phil laughed. "These Americans. I'll explain all if I may only have my tea."

Preswick bowed and hurried to call the waiter who would order tea to be sent up by dumbwaiter from the subbasement kitchen. And which would arrive hotter and fresher than most food served in the great homes across England and probably America.

"Now, Lily, get me out of this hat and we'll reconvene to compare notes."

By the time her hat was returned to its hatbox, Phil had changed into an at-home gown of mauve chiffon, and had transferred the torn strips of paper from her pocket to a small silk reticule. She carried the bag, her newspaper, and the note down to the smaller sitting room, where a lavish tea was spread out on their study table.

She sat down, dumped her paper and bag on the table, and piled her plate high with liver paste, watercress, and cucumber and cheese sandwiches, while Preswick poured tea.

"I must say, this delivery system is excellent," Phil said, taking a sip of tea. "Delicious."

"Humph," Preswick said. He'd been trying to get the kitchen to make English scones. The French chef was not amused until he found out that Lady Dunbridge had a favorite recipe. Which, of course, she didn't. It never occurred to her to bring recipes to America—if she'd had any, which she didn't. Nonetheless, Monsieur Lapparraque humored Preswick and turned out a reasonably edible scone.

As soon as Preswick deigned to sit, Lily sat down and reached for a sandwich. While they ate, Phil apprised Preswick of the murder of Perry Fauks. "Lily and I got a firsthand look, though I imagine Detective Sergeant Atkins was more thorough."

"We would have found more but he made us leave," Lily added. "But I saw when the black van came."

"The coroner?"

"Yes. Three men, two carrying a cot. The detective sergeant took them into the laundry room, but he locked the door behind them. I tried to listen but they were talking low. Then they came out again and cook told me I was to stay in the kitchen and not wander around the halls. She called me a heathen." Lily's face hardened. "But I just smiled and pr-r-r-retended not to understand her-r-r."

"Very good," Phil said. "She's an uneducated woman and is to be ignored."

Preswick poured Lily more tea.

"So tell me what else you found out downstairs today."

"Pfft, those ser-r-r-vants. They were told not to talk, and that's all they did all morning long."

"So your presence didn't curb their tongues?"

"I just sat and looked stupid, and didn't react to anything they said and they yammered on for hours. Yammer, yammer, yammer."

Preswick cleared his throat. "That is not the proper word for a lady's maid, Lily."

"But I like it. Yammer-r-r-r." She grinned at him. "But I won't use it."

"I told her to only speak in Italian today."

"Ah," said Preswick, putting his cup down.

Phil pushed the tiered plate of sandwiches toward him. He hesitated and then chose one of cheese and cucumber.

"I wish I'd had my notepad," Lily said. "But I think I remember most things. Mostly they were just hysterical and saying they were afraid to stay."

"So no question about it being an accident?"

Lily shook her head. "The laundress saw the blood. It was on one of the sheets. But it was put in the fire."

Of course it was, Phil thought. What else had they "tidied up" before she arrived?

And where was the weapon? Had they tidied that up, too? Phil mumbled an expletive under her breath. She was certain that both she and Detective Sergeant Atkins hoped it was stuck in the laundry chute somewhere. And not on its way to the garbage dump.

"What else did you learn, Lily?"

"Three of the laundry maids. They went down to sort the day's laundry and he was stuck in among the sheets. They screamed and carried on until the laundress came over then sent for Mr. Pratt. The men had to pull him out. That's when they saw the blood. The laundress wanted to bleach it, but Mr. Pratt said to burn it."

So Luther had given the order. Fastidiousness or stealth? "Go on."

"Mr. Pratt and that other one with the lion's hair laid him out and tried to see if he was still breathing, but he wasn't. Then they sent the girls away and told them not to talk, and cook took them to the kitchen for tea."

"And were there conjectures about how the man died?"

"Just silly talk. Rr-r-r-robbers or madmen. *Stupido.*"

"Yes, I'm afraid it might be a little closer to home." Phil took a minute to describe to Preswick going to Agnes's room, following Maud to Perry Fauks's room.

"Maud Jeffrey. I don't think you saw her today, Lily. She's one of Agnes's cousins. A twin. You both will see them when we all go to Long Island."

"You think this cousin killed him and stuffed him down the laundry chute?" Lily asked.

"Not unless she had help," Phil said. "She's quite petite."

"Small individuals are known to have unnatural strength when under duress," said Preswick. "One of the girls from the village lifted a wagon off her father when it collapsed on him while he was trying to tighten the wheel."

"No!" Lily said, her eyes wide. "Is that true?"

"Do you question my veracity?" Preswick asked indignantly.

"No, Mr. Preswick," Lily said contritely. "But is it true?"

He raised an imperious eyebrow.

Lily grinned back.

"But I did find this." Phil wiped her fingers on her napkin and opened the silk bag she'd brought to the table. She turned it over and shook it until the table was covered by strips of torn paper, as well as Maud's confiscated note.

She lifted the note and unfolded it.

"What does it say, madam?"

"It's a love note. And rather silly schoolgirl stuff. But Maud sneaked away to retrieve it from Mr. Fauks's room."

She read it aloud. A short, pitiful exclamation of affection and a plea not to marry her cousin Agnes. "Well, the girl was certainly carrying a torch for Mr. Fauks, but there's nothing here that sounds desperate enough that would cause a young girl to kill her lover.

"Though I suppose we should read the rest." Phil looked at the strips of paper in front of them. "Do we have glue and paper? Perhaps we can reconstruct these."

While Preswick went to fetch the supplies, Phil and Lily started arranging the strips. It took under an hour to put them all back together. Most were silly, like the one Phil had confiscated. Two were pleas to meet Maud at night. There were no dates, but they did raise the possibility that Maud had met him the night of the party and might have been the last person to see him alive.

Or possibly the first to see him dead.

"I suppose I must hand them over to Detective Sergeant Atkins. I hate to do it, they're such humiliating evidence of a schoolgirl crush. Except, maybe not so innocent."

Phil sighed. She herself wasn't so old—at twenty-six she was in her prime, perhaps a little jaded; she *had* seen much of the world—that she couldn't sympathize with those pangs of love. She'd definitely have to turn them over to Atkins. And ask him to be gentle with the girl's heart.

She pushed the notes to the side of the table and reached for another sandwich. "Let's see, what else," she said as she munched on the liver paste sandwich. "I suppose I shouldn't share this since it's pure speculation, but the Pratts' daughter, Agnes, was about to be engaged to Mr. Fauks, or so they expected. But when Maud of the love letters left the room, I overheard her say, 'She'll be glad he's dead.' I believe she was referring to Agnes.

"I've asked Bobby Mullins to bring a jockey to climb down the chute tomorrow morning to look for clues. He may bring Rico."

Lily's nose went up. "Oh, that one."

"Yes, that one."

"Is it dangerous?" asked Lily, melting a little.

"No. I'm sure the detective sergeant will contrive some sort of harness to keep him safe while he's looking for clues."

"What kind of clues will he be looking for in a laundry chute?" Preswick asked.

"The missing weapon for one. It appears to be a stab wound from a very narrow knife. If it isn't in the chute, they will have to search farther afield."

"Any suspects thus far?"

"The valet disappeared. The police are looking for him. But there is a whole house of people, including the Pratts' son, Morris, a rather smug, unlikable young man.

"There was also a Mr. Isaac Sheffield at the ball last night. The victim was to inherit his family's Copper, Coal and Steel trust, which is now being run by Mr. Sheffield, until Perry was deemed mature enough to take over. Which will never happen now. But it could be a motive.

"Mr. Sheffield lives in the city with his wife. Preswick, if you could ask around, peruse some newspapers, see where he stands in this financial crisis business. Godfrey Bennington, he of the lion hair, is somehow connected to the War Department. Luther Pratt is a very influential banker, managed to survive the Panic, and is expected to be appointed to a big government committee to prevent such things in the future.

"Everything could unravel for him if this isn't solved efficiently."

"Yes, my lady."

"And what if it brings scandal to his house?" Lily asked.

"Then it will. But it is the price one pays. Tomorrow I will return, ostensibly to help Mrs. Pratt with her new parlor drapes. Preswick, call to a fabric house and have them send over some appropriate samples, in blues and ochers, drapery colors, you know better than I.

"Oh, and what do you know about balloons?"

"Balloons, my lady? I imagine they sell them in the park."

"No, the kind that carry people and instruments. There is a test of such balloons scheduled for next weekend. I saw an article crumpled up in Perry Fauks's wastepaper basket. And I've just been invited to a house party by a man who works for the War Department and whose estate is located near to where the government is testing balloons while we're in residence. It seems too coincidental not to do a little research."

"Very well, my lady. I can take the trolley down to the library tomorrow."

"Thank you. And now that my hunger is somewhat assuaged . . ." Phil stood up and a piece of paper fell from her skirt.

"Now what's this?" She leaned over and picked it up. "Odd. There were no missing pieces from the notes. It must have been in the wastepaper basket along with the others." She peered at it. Rectangular and torn at either end. Initials and numbers and Greek to her.

"If I might, my lady."

Phil handed the paper to Preswick.

"Do you know what it is?"

"Yes, my lady. It's a ticker tape."

"Which is?"

"It sends the most recent movements of the stock market over the wire. The initials stand for the name of this particular company. The numbers represent the fluctuation in stock prices since the last reporting."

"Can you tell what the company is?"

"No, but I can stop by the exchange tomorrow and find out, though . . ."

"Though what?"

"I doubt if this company will even exist tomorrow. From the numbers displayed, the company's losses are most likely unrecoverable."

7

Phil arrived at the Pratt mansion a few minutes before eight the next morning.

"Good morning, my lady," Brinlow said as he took her coat and hat. "The workmen have arrived and are on the fourth floor with Mr. Atkins. Mrs. Pratt isn't down as yet, but if you would like to wait in the parlor, I will inform Mr. Pratt that you have arrived."

"Thank you, Brinlow, but that won't be necessary. I'll go directly to the fourth floor."

"Would you care to take the elevator, my lady?"

"Yes, indeed I would, Brinlow."

He bowed, handed her coat off to a waiting footman, and took her to a door inlaid with mother-of-pearl and exotic woods near the back of the foyer. It opened to reveal a cage that could accommodate several people.

Excellent, Phil thought. Now she wouldn't have to sprint up four flights of stairs and arrive disheveled and out of breath to face the detective sergeant. He was bound to be in an unconciliatory mood.

"After you, my lady."

Phil stepped inside. It was rather a rickety ride up, in comparison to the smooth-running elevators at the Plaza, but still eons away from the cold hard steps of Dunbridge Castle. The longer she was in America, the more she loved it.

Brinlow opened the doors onto the fourth floor and a hallway saturated with sunlight from a back window. She could hear the sounds of activity and after thanking Brinlow, she hurried toward it.

The first person she saw was Bobby Mullins, his bright orange-red hair, as always, defying the generous amount of pomade he used to keep it tamed. His black bowler was sitting out of the way on the floor. He was wearing his best plaid suit, brushed and looking slightly looser than it had been the first time she'd met him.

Bobby must be getting exercise running the stable and training facilities at Holly Farm.

He and another man, who Phil took as a tradesman, were arguing about the best way to send Rico down the chute.

Rico himself was standing back looking skeptical. He was a small man, even for a jockey, with almost black hair framing his face. He saw her and nodded, but his face fell when, she imagined, he saw that she had not brought Lily.

She had left Lily home for just that reason. Rico needed his wits about him today and Lily would be a distraction.

Besides, she had more important things for Lily to do today.

She found Atkins farther along the hallway leaning into what must be the opening of the laundry chute on this floor.

"Good morning, Detective Sergeant."

He started and knocked his head on the top portion of the chute before easing out and standing upright.

Phil winced, not only for his head, but for the cut on his cheek and the blue bruise along his jaw.

"A barroom brawl, Detective Sergeant?" she asked.

There was the slightest tightening of his nostrils. Not in the mood to be trifled with today.

"Surely Perry Fauks's death didn't lead you to the rough side of town."

"I was on another case. We've been known to work more than one at a time."

Things must not have gone well. "Dare I ask, did the bad guys win?"

"Depends on which bad guys to whom you refer."

"We're ready, sir." The man who Phil had taken for a trades-man was rolling a winch down the beautiful antique runner.

"Hold it there, Higgins, until I finish here."

"Is this where you think Fauks went in?" Phil asked as the detective sergeant bent down to peruse the floor around the chute.

He cast her an irritated look over his shoulder.

"I take that to mean there isn't evidence either way. Shall I help you look?" She put her actions to the suggestion and be-gan searching the carpet for anything that might give them an idea of where to start looking.

Atkins straightened up. "All right, Higgins. Bring it over. And be careful of the carpet."

Higgins pushed the winch up to the chute opening. He was followed by Bobby, chewing on an unlit cigar, and Rico dressed like he was about to go down to the coal mines. His torso was concealed in a leather harness, and he wore a metal cap with a light attached to the front and a strap under his chin. He looked terribly uncomfortable.

Phil gave him an encouraging smile.

"Ready, Rico?" Atkins asked.

Rico made one sharp nod.

Atkins clipped him to the rope by a metal hook and lifted him into the opening.

"Go slowly like you were instructed. Take all the time you need. If you find anything, deposit it with the officer waiting at the next opening then keep going. I'll meet you at the end."

"Yes, sir," echoed up from the chute.

Atkins motioned for the machinist to begin uncoiling the rope. "Slowly," he ordered. "You okay in there?"

"Yes, sir," echoed back from the chute.

Atkins backed away. "Bobby, you're in charge of making sure everything goes all right here, I'm going to the third floor."

He strode off down the hall.

Phil followed him so closely that when he stopped at the next landing, she nearly fell over him.

"Go downstairs."

"Then bring in more men to help you."

His look said it all.

"Oh my. Now what are they afraid of?"

"I don't know what you're talking about."

"Whoever is tying your hands on this case." *And who is tying theirs?* she wondered. How powerful was Godfrey Bennington?

"Lady Dunbridge. I know you probably mean well, though actually I'm not at all certain. But I've been given three days to solve this case before the family leaves for a country house party."

He started walking down the hall.

"Then you should take advantage of an extra pair of eyes and hands."

"Go. Away."

They arrived at the third-floor laundry chute. This floor also had a guard on the opening.

"No signs of a struggle, sir."

Phil looked around. The carpet on this floor was more plush than the one on the fourth floor. But the officer was correct, there were no scuff marks or splashes of blood anywhere. She'd walked down this same hall following Maud the day before, and she hadn't seen any then either.

Fauks must have been murdered somewhere else and his body carried to the chute. They would have to search all the rooms. It would take more time, time the detective sergeant didn't have.

They waited by the chute opening and moments later, a pair of shoes, then legs, then torso passed by the opening. Then Rico's face.

A bang echoed from inside the chute; Rico rebounded and came to a stop. "Nothing yet."

Atkins nodded. "Keep going."

Two bangs and Rico's face disappeared from view. The bangs must be Rico signaling them to stop and start.

Phil followed Atkins to the second floor. Here Rico tossed out a scrap of paper and a pair of lace-trimmed undergarments.

Phil tried not to laugh at the look on Atkins's face, but she couldn't help herself.

He, however, was not amused. He handed the underwear to the guard, and after a cursory look at the paper slid it into his pocket.

"Carry on."

Rico knocked on the metal and disappeared again.

Atkins turned to the guard. "Have you searched the surroundings?"

"Yes, sir. Nothing."

He walked away.

Phil ran after him. "Do you think he was dead before he got to the laundry room?"

He ignored her. She followed him down the stairs to the next opening.

"There didn't seem to be bruising on his face or hands. If he were conscious wouldn't he have tried to stop himself?"

Not getting an answer, she continued. "Is it true that bruising doesn't occur after death?"

He shot her a look. "Sometimes it's hard for me to remember that you are a countess."

"Is that a good thing?" she asked, slightly thrown off her game.

"No."

"Are you saying I'm comporting myself in a manner in which a member of the peerage should not?" she said at her haughtiest.

"I wouldn't dare."

"Detective Sergeant, a man has died. You are under certain constraints. I am not. I can help you."

"Why? And don't tell me because you want to help your good friends the Pratts."

What could she say? *I think I'm supposed to look into these things because there was an anonymous note on my pillow saying to expect a visitor.* It sounded like something right out of a gothic novel. He wouldn't believe her.

A pity, because with a little cooperation, they might come to an acceptable outcome a lot sooner.

"Well?" he prodded.

"I do want to help the Pratts through this ordeal. And you have to admit, I have access to places and people that you don't."

She placed a hand on his sleeve. "I don't pretend to know about investigations. But a young man has been cruelly murdered. A young woman is distraught. The financial world is teetering on the edge of another disaster. Let me help."

Rico's head appeared in the opening of the chute, he shook his head.

Atkins sighed. Rico knocked on the chute and was lowered out of sight.

Phil and Atkins watched him go, both falling silent. Maybe she should proceed on her own. She turned away.

And saw a glint in the crease between the wall and the carpet edge. Probably a sequin or diamanté from a ball gown. Still, she knelt to pick it up.

It wasn't a sequin, but something much more valuable.

"What is it?" Atkins asked, coming to stand over her. She stood and found herself very close to the man. He stepped back.

She turned it over in her palm to reveal a yellow-orange gem, cut with many facets. She tilted her hand so the light caught it from another angle and it turned a fiery red.

"If I'm not mistaken this is an Imperial topaz."

"From a gown?" He bent his head to look closer. Phil could feel his breath on her hand. It was quite a scintillating feeling.

"Not a gown. This is a very fine stone. And very valuable. At one time it was only allowed to be worn by the Tsar."

Their eyes met over the topaz.

"From a necklace? An earring?"

"More likely a tiara." She turned it over with the tip of her finger. "See? It's cut flat in back as if it was attached to a flat surface. A brooch or possibly a ring in a prong setting . . . but what a waste of a brilliant stone."

He raised one eyebrow. "Are you feeling tempted?"

She laughed. "Absolutely. But I'll surrender it, peacefully. Hold out your hand."

He did and she dropped the stone into it.

"Do not lose it."

"No." He took a small envelope out of his pocket and slid the jewel into it, then returned it to an inside pocket.

"If it came from a piece of jewelry, a lady's maid would be remiss not to have noticed. Shall I ask Mrs. Pratt to inquire? Or perhaps, she'll be visited by someone who has discovered it missing."

"No. Leave this to me."

"I hope you're not feeling tempted yourself."

The look he gave her was more than her quip should have evinced. "Oh really, Detective Sergeant, tit for tat. It was just a little joke." She smiled. "One must learn to laugh at oneself, don't you agree?"

"Perhaps, but not in this case."

She glanced at his chest where the gem lay inside his breast pocket. "Do you think it has anything to do with Perry Fauks's murder?"

Phil, Atkins, and Bobby were waiting like a welcoming committee when Rico's feet appeared in the opening of the basement laundry chute. And Phil felt a sudden chill imagining what the laundry girls must have felt when they'd pulled out the linens to reveal Perry Fauks's dancing shoes.

Atkins helped Rico out. As soon as he was standing up he held out empty hands. "Nada."

Bobby set about releasing Rico from the harness, then yanked on the rope, which immediately began to recede back into the chute.

Rico's clothes were covered with lint, and he sneezed violently several times as Bobby began brushing it off while he checked arms, legs, and hands. After all, Rico was one of Holly Farm's up-and-coming jockeys.

"I am fine," Rico said. "The rope held me safe."

Atkins was staring into the laundry chute as if willing it to reveal the secrets of Perry Fauks's demise. Then he turned to the others.

"Well, thank you, Rico. See my sergeant by the stairs. He will have a little something for your work."

"Oh no, mister. We do it for the lady." He smiled shyly at Phil.

"We'll be sure to see the sergeant before we go," Bobby said, pushing Rico toward the door.

"I suppose," Phil said, "this means we must search farther afield."

"We," Atkins said, stressing the word, "will do no such thing. You will go back upstairs to your drapery or whatever other excuse you've come up with for being here, and leave the investigation to the professionals."

"Very well." She lifted her chin and left him. It wasn't until she got to the door that he said, "But thank you."

"Not at all," she said, and feeling perhaps unwarrantedly satisfied, she went upstairs to discuss new drapes.

She never made it to the morning room. She was still standing in the hallway, considering whether to try to do some investigating on her own or begin the questioning, when she felt Atkins come up behind her. Was he following to make sure she was gone?

Really, the man was infuriating. She could stamp her foot, but his opinion of her un-countess-like demeanor had rankled. So she merely nodded politely.

He ignored her and joined an officer who was now guarding the parlor door. "Is everyone in the parlor?"

"Yes, sir, as you requested."

Phil hurried over. Brinlow opened the door to the parlor and before Atkins could muscle her out, Phil slipped inside.

Not the most graceful entrance she had ever made. But needs must . . .

They were all there, almost exactly where she'd left them the day before. Godfrey and Luther standing by the fireplace, only today they both held brandy snifters. Morris sitting somewhat straighter in the club chair, though an empty glass rested on the armchair beside him. Gwen was sitting upright on the settee, next to Agnes, whose hands she held in hers. The Jeffrey family was absent.

Agnes's cheeks were flushed. She had dressed in a somber dark green dress, high necked and not at all what a young girl making her debut should be wearing. She glanced up at Phil with frightened eyes.

"It will be quite all right, my dear," Phil said sympathetically as she came over to say hello to Gwen, who was dressed in a dark purple moiré silk—a color Phil was coming to hate, and which only served to make Gwen look sickly pale.

Atkins had stopped just inside the door and stood surveying the occupants. "Where are the Jeffreys?"

"Out for their morning ride. Taking advantage of our proximity to Central Park. And really, Detective Sergeant Atkins, there's no need to bother them," Luther said. "The girls know nothing. Ruth sent both of them to bed right after dinner, long before the party wound down. And Ruth and Thomas followed shortly afterward. They keep a different schedule even when in New York. Early to bed, early to rise."

"Nonetheless, I'd like to speak with them."

Pratt nodded curtly. "I'll tell Brinlow to send them in when they return." He rang for the butler.

Atkins looked around, zeroed in on Morris. "Then perhaps, Mr. Morris Pratt would like to start?"

"Me?" Morris said. "I don't know anything. Of course, there's a lot I don't remem—" He broke off, suddenly straightening. "As you wish, Detective." He followed Atkins out of the room.

It was an interminable wait until Morris returned, looking if possible even more surly than before he left.

"He wants to speak with Agnes," he said.

Agnes nearly catapulted from her seat. "Me? Mama, must I?"

Gwen looked at Phil.

"There's no reason to be frightened, my dear. Detective Sergeant Atkins must ask everyone questions so that he can construct a timetable of where Mr. Fauks was and when. Just answer to the best of your ability and tell the truth."

"But my head is all ajumble," Agnes whined. "I don't know what happened. I was having so much fun; it's my first season."

"You must do your duty," Phil said, cringing at her own words. Duty should be a choice, not an infliction. But not, alas, when murder was involved.

Gwen pushed herself from the settee and took her daughter's arm. "Yes, my dear, you must pull yourself together. I'm sure the detective sergeant will let me stay with you."

Phil wasn't sure of that at all.

"Absolutely not, Gwen." Luther strode over to his wife and daughter. "I won't have you wrecking your health for this ridiculous impertinence. I'll go."

"No, Papa," Agnes cried.

"I'm going out for a while," Morris said as they passed him. "This is just getting too tedious to bear."

"You'll do no such thing," Gwen told him. "Your sister is very upset and she needs her family around her."

Morris sighed. "If you say so." He smiled at his sister but there was no sympathy in it. No love lost between him and Agnes? Of course, siblings did have their difficult moments. Phil shuddered at the memory of a few of hers. The last being over her decision to forsake her rightful place as Dowager Countess of Dunbridge and take off for America. She'd yet to receive a letter from any of them.

"I'll be in the billiard room, if you need me." Morris patted Agnes's shoulder and sauntered off down the hall.

Agnes whirled around. "Uncle Godfrey, must I?"

Godfrey's lips thinned, but he managed a reassuring smile. "Yes, my dear. It will only take a few minutes and then it will be over. Just tell the detective the last time you saw Perry last night and all will be fine."

Agnes shrank back against her mother.

"Lady Dunbridge?" Gwen entreated.

Phil rose to the occasion. After all, that was why she was here. "Why don't we both accompany you to the library."

They guided the trembling girl down the hall and knocked on the closed library door.

8

"Enter."

Phil smiled reassuringly at Agnes and opened the library door.

Atkins was standing by the desk. His eyes narrowed as Phil, Gwen, and Agnes squeezed through the door. It was quite ridiculous, Phil had to admit.

Atkins managed to find a smile, though Phil could tell he was near the end of his tether. She wondered why.

"Perhaps just her mother," Atkins suggested, tacitly acknowledging their reason for accompanying Agnes.

Agnes shot a frightened look to her mother. "No, no, I'd rather Lady Dunbridge. If that's okay, Mama."

For a moment, Gwen looked befuddled. Then she nodded. "Of course, my dear. I understand."

And so did Phil. What secrets did Agnes Pratt have from her parents? Had she been a naughty girl? Or, perish the thought, was she guilty of murder?

Atkins held the door for Gwen to leave and Phil calmly swept Agnes farther into the room. She could feel the girl shaking against her.

He closed the door and motioned for them to sit, not in one of the chairs placed facing the desk, but on a small settee near the bookshelves.

She recognized what Atkins was doing. He'd placed Agnes where she would feel more comfortable and where he could watch her physical reaction to his questions without having half of her hidden by the desk.

She had just read about this technique in Mr. Gross's *Criminal Investigation* that she'd bought at the beginning of the summer. Actually, she'd learned a similar technique at the feet of some of the most powerful ladies in London society, but applying that knowledge to solving a murder had only gone so far.

Study had been called for. And for the last five months she and Lily and Preswick had been learning the finer points of investigation.

Agnes sat on the very edge of the seat. So close that one twitch might plummet her to the floor. Phil gave her hand a reassuring squeeze.

Agnes looked back at her with her big doe eyes. Phil couldn't remember having seen such a sweet, helpless expression. She certainly couldn't remember a day when she'd been that innocent, or even that innocent appearing. She wondered what John Atkins was thinking.

He pulled a chair close to the settee, smiled slightly, and sat down.

All of Phil's instincts rose to the alert.

"Now, Miss Pratt," he said, not unkindly. "I know this is a very upsetting time for you, but I need your help."

Ha, thought Phil. And she settled back to watch him at work.

"What time did you last see Mr. Fauks?"

Agnes glanced at Phil, then said, "I don't know. It was at the ball. But . . ." She bit her lip; in a less innocent girl, it would have been a nibble. "After midnight and . . . yes, I saw him again after supper, so maybe two o'clock?"

"And where was that?"

"Where?"

Atkins smiled slightly. "Yes, was it in the ballroom? Supper room? Upstairs?" He threw the last one out in a voice as bland as whey.

"The ballroom, I guess. No, I saw him in the foyer after that."

Atkins waited, attentively, for her to continue.

Once again she cast a glance at Phil. *Oh dear, there was something she didn't want to tell the detective sergeant.* Phil could guess.

Agnes squeezed Phil's hand.

"What did you talk about? And Miss Pratt. Please know that your answers are confidential unless they are needed as testimony in a court of law."

Agnes burst into tears. "I didn't do it. He wanted me to, but I didn't want to."

Atkins cut a look to Phil. She took the hint and put her arm around Agnes. "Now, now. What did Perry want you to do?"

Agnes shook her head, as tears sprang to her eyes. "To . . . to go upstairs," she mumbled into Phil's shoulder. "With him."

Phil exchanged a look with Atkins. Champagne and dancing and desire. Stupid man. You didn't take a girl at her debut ball.

"And you told him no?"

Agnes nodded. "Of course. Can I go now?"

Tears were streaming down her face. Atkins reached in his pocket for a handkerchief. Phil incongruously wondered how many handkerchiefs he lost in this way and how many he could afford on a policeman's salary.

Atkins stood and walked to the window, giving Agnes a minute to collect herself.

Phil took advantage. "There, there," she said. "It's all right. These things happen."

"He said everybody did it, and I was being a silly schoolgirl. But Mama says, a girl shouldn't let men take advantage."

"And she is correct," Phil said. *A woman should always be the one who decides whether she's taken advantage of—or vice versa.*

Atkins turned from the window. His face was free of emotion, but he'd turned a shade paler. She remembered that from before; most people turned red when they were angry, but John Atkins went white. Phil was struck by a pang of sympathy for the man; he must hear terrible things, much worse than this, day after day.

He sat down, leaned forward, resting his elbows on his knees. A nonaggressive pose. "After you saw him in the foyer, where did you go?"

"I don't really remember. He was mad at me."

"Do you know what he did?"

Agnes shook her head. "I didn't see him again. I know Morris said he and some of the fellows were going out, you know, 'slumming,' he called it. Whenever Perry was in town, Morris would invite him to go out with him and his friends."

"And were these friends at your party?"

"Some of them. Harry Cleeves, and Newty—Newton—Eccles. Maybe a couple of others. I can't remember. Vincent used to go with them, but not anymore since he came to work as Father's secretary."

Probably concerned about his reputation, thought Phil. And his future if Luther Pratt became a member of the banking commission.

Atkins had been busily writing in his black notebook; now he stood.

"That will be all for now, Miss Pratt. Though I hope you'll be willing to talk to me again if I have more questions?"

Agnes sniffed and let Phil dry her eyes with the now soggy handkerchief.

"Now see, that wasn't so bad, was it?"

Agnes shook her head. "Don't tell what I said."

The same thing Maud had said. Phil most likely would have to show him the notes, but not with Agnes in the room. There was no reason to add insult to injury, if there was any evidence that Perry Fauks was carrying on with his intended's cousin.

At one time Phil might have found this kind of intrigue amusing, but not so today. She must be getting old, because Agnes's unhappiness was all too depressing.

"Miss Pratt, you never have to allow anyone to make you do things against your will. Understand me?"

"But . . ."

"No buts. . . . It isn't right that any man should force himself on you. Now thank you for your time." A tic of his head and Phil pulled Agnes off the settee and headed her toward the door.

She'd been momentarily distracted by Atkins's assurances. She'd seen a little window into the things he cared about. She couldn't say she was surprised, but she was glad to see it.

But before they reached the door, it opened and a man stepped inside. Phil recognized him as Pratt's secretary, Vincent Wynn-Taylor.

Wynn-Taylor pulled up short. "I beg your pardon. I didn't realize. I was just coming for the daily account book."

"Vincent?"

"Aggie?" Vincent stretched out his hands and took an involuntary step toward her before re-collecting himself. "Agnes, what is happening here?"

"The police wanted to know about Perry."

"Does your—" Wynn-Taylor got no further.

"Mr. Wynn-Taylor. Please take what you need. This room is being used for the investigation and is off-limits until further notice."

"Yes, of course. I apologize. I had no idea."

Vincent crossed to the desk, took out keys and unlocked a drawer from which he retrieved a large black ledger. Then with one more quick look toward Agnes, he left the room.

Phil stood back to admire the detective sergeant's rapid change from compassion to authority. He did them both so well.

He also had seen what she had seen. Wynn-Taylor's reaction at seeing Agnes being questioned by the police had been more than mere surprise. Or the concern of an employee. Did his interest lie in that direction the same as Perry's? He didn't stand much of a chance if monetary considerations carried the day.

Except the heir to Fauks Copper, Coal and Steel was conveniently dead.

"Thank you, Miss Pratt. You've been most helpful." Atkins

opened the door to find both Pratts waiting anxiously outside. Gwen saw her daughter's face and rushed to her. "My poor dear."

"Look here, Atkins," Luther snapped.

"It's okay, Papa. I just got scared. I didn't know what to expect. Mr. Atkins was very nice." The doe eyes turned on the detective sergeant, beseeching.

"She was very brave and I appreciate her clearheadedness."

Phil's eyes widened, not doe-like, but in surprise. This wasn't the by-the-book, come-hell-or-damsel-in-distress attitude she'd seen in their previous investigation. Now what had made him act so out of character? Or perhaps the question should be, What was he up to?

As she stepped past him, Atkins said, "Lady Dunbridge, a moment if you please."

"But of course."

He closed the door on the others' astonished faces and turned to face her.

"Rather tarnishes the golden boy's reputation," she said. "Not to mention opens up another line of inquiry." One that she really should make him aware of. Agnes wasn't the only girl involved with Perry. Agnes might not have wanted him, but Maud clearly did.

She opened her mouth but before she could confess about the letters, his eyes narrowed. "I hope you don't intend to . . . ?"

"Poke my nose into your investigation?"

"I was searching for a more polite way to say it."

"Always the gentleman." *Unfortunately,* she thought.

"If you think you can set yourself up as a self-appointed protector of the rich, forget it. You were a help I'll admit in the reckoning of Reggie Reynolds's murder, but that doesn't make you an expert. And I find your presence—"

"Delightful? Invigorating? Come now, Detective Sergeant, I can't help it if murders occur among my friends. You do have an awful lot of murders in this city, do you not?"

"I don't for a moment believe this was another coincidence. A more suspicious man than I might suspect you of more than curiosity."

"Oh, come now. Two murders do not a—what do they call it?—an accessory? make?"

He closed his eyes for a moment. Counting to ten? Then gestured to the settee.

"So what have you found out that I haven't?" he said, sounding resigned.

"Nothing yet." At least nothing she was willing to share just yet.

"But you will. I suppose you know that Godfrey Bennington has already been on the telephone to have the investigation shut down."

"He did mention it."

"Damn." He flinched. "I beg your pardon."

"Not at all. But who exactly is the man? I know you said he was connected to the War Department, and he's friends with the Pratts and Agnes's godfather, but does he really wield as much power as that?"

One eyebrow dipped. "Really? Godfrey Bennington has his fingers in every pot. Local as well as national. So if you're planning to involve yourself in this case, and I'm sure you are or you wouldn't be here today—"

"I explained why I was here."

"Drapes. Yes, and do you really expect me to believe that?"

"No. But since I plan to be around at least until your investigation ends, I'd best have a good reason to be here."

"Why? What interests you here? It has to be more than idle curiosity."

That was a good question. She wished she knew the answer. "They're my friends, Detective Sergeant." She sighed. "What comes after detective sergeant?"

"What?"

"'Detective sergeant' is such a mouthful. Now something like

'inspector' rolls off the tongue. Inspector." She drew out the syl-
lables. "See?"

She swore she could hear him grinding his teeth. "Will there
be anything else? No? Then I'll bid you good day." She rose.

He managed to get to the door before her. He did move
quickly when he needed to.

"Oh, and I would not discount the two Jeffrey girls if I were
you. Maud and Effie." There, that should suffice for the time being; nudge him toward Maud and let her have the opportunity
to tell him about the love notes herself. If she didn't, then Phil
would be forced to encourage her to do so. But she absolutely
refused to betray another woman's possible peccadilloes unless
absolutely necessary to the investigation. "I just thought I would
mention it. I'm certain you would have questioned them eventually."

"Have no worries about that, Lady Dunbridge. I may be plod-
ding, but I'm thorough."

I bet you are, Phil thought. Too bad he was also so thoroughly
a gentleman.

Brinlow was waiting to show Phil up to Gwen's private sitting
room. She followed him dutifully down the hall, past Agnes's
bedroom, past the laundry chute opening and the place where
they had found the Imperial topaz.

Her excitement of the find had ebbed somewhat. It might belong to anyone who had wandered upstairs to the ladies with-
drawing rooms, which she had reason to know were in the far
corridor, and had decided to take a look-see in the upper rooms.
It might not be missed until the next ball, at which time the
lady's maid in charge of such things would be given the sack for
not noticing sooner.

Brinlow stopped at the next door and knocked before announcing Phil. Gwen's sitting room was a cheerful, delicate
space, furnished with a feminine touch. A Sheridan writing desk

stood at a bow window overlooking a tiny garden. Gwen was stretched out on a chaise longue, but she sat up when Phil entered the room.

"I sent Agnes to her room. Poor child. I think I must have the girls take her out shopping or something. I can't expect her to sit pining for a man who hadn't even declared for her, when she's on the brink of the season. Can I?"

"No. I think you should carry on. Discreetly, of course, as you would for any friend who had passed."

"That's what Godfrey says, but it seems . . . I don't know. I suppose when they find this valet, things will be set to rights."

"Most likely," Phil agreed.

"Did they find anything in the laundry chute? I've been so beside myself I forgot to ask."

Phil was dying to say, *Yes, do you know anyone who owns an Imperial topaz?* But she kept mum as directed. She would show Atkins that she could be trusted—within limits, of course. He needed her. He knew he did; she could go places and question people that he as a policeman, no matter how cultured he might appear, would not have access to.

She'd proven that during what she liked to think of as "our last case." She really didn't understand why he was so loath to accept her help. It was common knowledge that the police used paid informants. At least in the lower classes, so why not in her class?

After all, wasn't that exactly what she was? After a fashion. Actually, her duties weren't quite clear, if they were indeed duties. But why else pay for her keep in expensive apartments like one would a mistress without expecting something in return.

"These arrived a little while ago," Gwen said, rising to walk to the far side of the room where a tower of fabric books was stacked on a small oval table.

"My heavens," Phil said. "We have our work cut out for us."

"I may be enticed to redo the draperies after all. I didn't think Luther would like to have the parlor cluttered with them, so I had them brought here. Besides, we'll be quite undisturbed here, and I have news."

"Do tell."

"I don't know if Luther told you, but he called Isaac Sheffield's office yesterday to inform him of Perry's death. Isaac wasn't there. Evidently he had gone out of town early yesterday morning. No one seemed to know why or exactly where. It must be something to do with this banking situation. It has made the whole business world a tinderbox."

"So he doesn't know about Mr. Fauks?"

Gwen slowly shook her head. "Not at the time, but I do know that after you left, Detective Atkins visited his home to ask his whereabouts. Evidently Isaac's wife, Loretta, refused to let him in."

"So Sheffield hasn't been located?"

"I don't know. Luther tries to scuttle me out of hearing distance every time they discuss something." Gwen breathed a little laugh. "These men, I don't know why they persevere in this notion that we need to be protected from the difficulties of life."

Phil murmured something. She'd stopped depending on men to protect her the day she was force-marched down the aisle toward the Earl of Dunbridge.

"Anyway, I took the liberty of telephoning her earlier today. Just to see how she was. She didn't come to the ball. She doesn't get out much. Well, actually, she hasn't been the same since her daughter died. They only had the one child. A daughter. Rachel. She and her infant son died of the influenza, oh, about two years ago. They were staying with Loretta and Isaac at the time.

"Loretta has never really recovered. A shame. She used to be quite fun. Perry often stayed with them in the past. She's bound to be affected by his death. And if Isaac isn't there to support her . . ."

"Do you think she knows where he is?" Phil asked.

"Surely he would tell his wife that he was going out of town."

Phil wasn't so sure about that. If he'd been at the ball late and left early the next morning. It could be coincidence, but it did have all the trappings of a man on the run.

"With her husband away, perhaps she would enjoy a morning call?" Phil suggested.

Gwen's eyebrows rose. "That's just what I told her. Shall we say ten o'clock tomorrow? I'll have the carriage brought around."

Phil was not really interested in attending the Follies that night. She and Bev had seen Mr. Ziegfeld's extravaganza twice last summer at the rooftop of the New York Theatre. Entertaining, amusing, slightly risqué, perhaps it was just what she needed after two days of murder investigation.

And where better to hear the current *on-dit* than at intermission in the most popular revue of the season. Had news of Perry Fauks's death made it to the grapevine? Were opinions being touted, gossip being spread?

Tonight would be the show's last performance. There was bound to be a crush.

And the Countess of Dunbridge was taking her scintillating self to the theatre to find out what the town was talking about.

"Hmm," she said as she looked at Lily's confection of a coiffure in her dressing mirror.

"What is it, madam? Is something amiss?"

"Not at all, Lily. Just thinking about the investigation."

"Well, you should think about your toilette or you'll be late."

"You are right, of course. There's just something that bothers me."

"What is that?"

"I don't know."

"Huh. Mr. Preswick and I will confer while you're gone."

"Good idea. Maybe you will come up with a solution."

Lily affixed a narrow tiara of emeralds at the crown of her head.

Phil perused their sparkle in the mirror. "I wonder if Detective

Sergeant Atkins asked if someone was missing a valuable topaz from some piece of jewelry. It's almost as if they expect the valet to be arrested."

And that thought was given more credence when she arrived at the Grand Opera House on Twenty-Third Street and joined her friends, Olivia and Frank Quincy, in their box.

Hellos were said and small talk ensued. A few words from Frank about the near miss of the financial crisis which was quickly hushed by Olivia with "you promised no talk of business tonight."

Ah, but murder was a different thing.

"My goodness, would you look at that," Olivia Quincy said from behind her opera glasses, which were trained on a box across the theatre where a party was just entering.

Phil didn't need her glasses to recognize the lion's mane of white hair. Godfrey Bennington had come to enjoy the Follies. Now she raised her glasses. Maud and Effie were there, their black curls arranged in similar swirls and twists.

The couple with them must be Ruth and Thomas Jeffrey, whom she had yet to meet. Ruth was a duller version of her sister. Thomas was tall, with brown hair and a thick mustache, and appeared to be scanning the audience. Looking for someone in particular?

Godfrey nodded to someone in another box. Saw Phil and nodded to her.

Phil nodded back. They all seemed quite normal. No one turned en masse to look. A buzz didn't go through the audience. It seemed Perry's death was not the subject of widespread gossip yet.

So intent was Phil in her study of the family that she almost didn't notice the man who sat alone several boxes away, his own opera glasses turned toward Godfrey's box. Phil raised her opera glasses and he came into view.

She caught her breath. How ridiculous to be staring at another pair of opera glasses, staring back at you.

She lowered hers, just as the lights dimmed and the orchestra burst into music. The people across the theatre were lost in shadows and she knew when the lights rose on intermission, the box the man had occupied would be empty.

But she couldn't very well excuse herself from her hosts at the beginning of the show to rush around to the other side to catch him. So for the third time, she sat through the songs and the girls in their short dresses and big hats, the feathers and silly plot of John Smith and Pocahontas. She would have to bide her time. Until the intermission.

When the lights rose again, Phil's eyes were already trained on the watcher's box. As Phil suspected, the box was empty. She scanned over to Godfrey's box. The first thing she noticed was that Thomas wasn't there and Ruth looked displeased.

Godfrey bent over her and said a few words, then he too left the box.

It was only a few minutes before he entered the Quincys' box.

It was a formal call, no talk of murder. Phil introduced him to the Quincys, they spoke for a couple of minutes, and he departed as the lights for the second act went down.

It seemed interminable, before the curtain closed and the cast began their numerous curtain calls. Phil had to fall back on the time-old excuse of a headache to part from her friends as soon as they were out of the theatre.

"We totally understand," Olivia said. "We've all been burning the candle at both ends and the season has barely started. But you, Phil, have put us all to shame. You could have blown me over when Godfrey Bennington appeared in our box this evening."

"Oh really," her husband complained.

"Well, he wasn't coming to see me, I can assure you."

"Good to know," said her husband. "Let me put you in a taxi, Phil, and pay Livy no mind. With all the hoopla over this banking thing, even I'm feeling a bit off my game."

"But you're okay," Phil said, suddenly realizing the repercussions were not over yet. In fact, they might just be beginning.

"Oh, I'll see it through. Not to worry about me. But some. Whew, it's been a brutal fall, I can tell you. Ah, here's a taxi."

As Phil stepped off the curb, someone brushed against her. She turned to look but saw nothing unusual, just the normal bustle of people leaving the theatre.

But as the taxi pulled away, she noticed that her purse was open. Hoping she hadn't been the victim of a pickpocket, she quickly looked inside.

Nothing was missing, but something had been added. A torn corner from the evening's program. Two names were handwritten in a script she recognized. *Morse* and *Heinze*. *Tell Atkins*.

She turned and looked out the window at the crowded sidewalk. *Where are you? And why won't you show yourself?*

9

When Phil let herself into her apartments, Lily and Preswick were waiting at the study table, books and papers open and ready. Both were a little blurry-eyed and she made a note to give them some time off tomorrow.

Phil quickly exchanged her theatre gown for one of her silk kimonos. *Wonderful things, kimonos.* And joined them.

"I took the liberty of picking up the evening papers, my lady." Preswick handed her several folded sheets. "Would you care for a cocktail or a cognac?"

"A cognac would be divine," Phil said and opened the *Times*.

"'An Accident with Deadly Consequences. Perry Fauks, son,' etc., 'and heir apparent of Fauks Copper, Coal and Steel, passed away Tuesday evening during a ball to celebrate,' etc., etc." She ran her finger down the article. "No mention of how, though I suspect it won't be long until that news is leaked to the press. Let's see. 'Mr. Isaac Sheffield, New York manager of the company, was not available for comment.' Some mention of the ball and who attended." Phil dropped it to the floor. "Well, that didn't take long." She picked up *The Sun*.

"Oh dear. 'Prank Takes a Tragic Turn. Heir to Fauks Copper, Coal and Steel died Thursday night from a fall that occurred during the debut ball of Miss Agnes Pratt.' Interesting. But it pretty much has the same information as the *Times*. Well done, Detective Sergeant. Though I suspect much of the restraint came from Godfrey Bennington. Now, if we can depend on the family to be as discreet."

She dropped the papers to the floor. "Now let us see how we can contribute to this investigation."

The three of them opened their notebooks, a system they had been perfecting in the months since their first case.

"So we know that he was killed with a narrow sharp blade, as Lily says, something like a stiletto, or some other narrow fine blade. Most likely killed or at least unconscious before he was shoved down the laundry chute." Phil shook her head. It was such an ignominious way to die. "He was dead when he was found. No active bleeding." She took a sip of cognac. "Lily?"

"The girls when they were talking said they had been pushed out of the room as soon as the men came."

"So they didn't do any cleaning up?"

Lily shook her head. "Only the sheet they burned."

"So there is still no murder weapon that we know of. The only things found in the chute were . . ." She glanced at Preswick. "A scrap of paper, a pair of lady's drawers, and quite a bit of lint."

They all took a moment to write their notes.

"I saw no scuffs on the carpets near the chute, nor in Perry Fauks's room. Which means . . ."

"He was carried to the chute," Lily said.

Preswick cleared his throat but didn't reprimand her for speaking out of turn. Progress to be sure. "Or he was accosted in the hallway in front of the opening, stabbed, and pushed inside," he added.

Phil looked at her notes. Many possibilities, not one clear explanation.

"I did find an Imperial topaz on the carpet nearby the opening on the second floor. It's a valuable stone. If someone has lost it, surely they would have noticed by now and called on Mrs. Pratt to apprise her of the loss."

"Do you think it is a clue?" Preswick asked.

"I have no reason to think so, but it's not to be discounted. There were close to two hundred people at the ball that night, but most of them would have no reason to be in that section of the second floor."

"Atkins didn't ask the family about the gem, at least when I was around. I wonder why."

"Perhaps he didn't want to tip his hand," Preswick said.

Phil and Lily both looked at him in surprise.

"I believe that is the expression."

"To be sure," Phil agreed, studying her notes. "And then there are Maud Jeffrey's love notes to Perry. And Agnes, who according to everyone but Agnes expected a marriage proposal from Perry. But Atkins questioned her today. She asked me to accompany her."

"Very clever, my lady."

"It wasn't my cleverness. She didn't want her parents to hear what she had to say, but she needed support to say it. She intimated that he was insisting on more than she wanted to give, if you understand me."

Both Preswick and Lily nodded seriously.

"Let's see, what else? Oh yes, while we were in the study, Vincent the secretary came in for some papers. And there's something between those two. Not necessarily love, but definitely attraction.

"Isaac Sheffield has for all intents and purposes disappeared. His office say he's out of town on business but won't say where. Gwen Pratt and I are calling on his wife tomorrow.

"Everyone caught up? Good. Did I miss anything?"

"The ticker tape, my lady."

"Yes, Preswick. Were you able to ascertain anything about it?"

"It is the stock market initials for Fauks Copper, Coal and Steel. Its stock has dropped eighty-seven percent in the last few weeks. The bulk of it in the last few days."

"That's bad," Phil said.

"Devastating, my lady."

"But that wouldn't be Perry's fault. Sheffield's? Perhaps Perry found out and confronted Sheffield. They fought and . . . Well,

I'll tell the detective sergeant about it and see if he thinks it's important.

"And now for the pièce de résistance." Phil reached into her kimono and pulled out the scrap from the Follies program. "Someone—and I believe it might have been our old friend, the master of disguise—bumped into me in the street outside the theatre tonight. I found this in my bag when I got in the taxi."

"'Morse and Heinze,'" Preswick read aloud, then looked at Phil.

"I have no idea what it means. But it must be important. To-morrow, Preswick, ask if anyone among your town acquaintances can decipher it."

"What shall I do?" asked Lily

"Pack for the country."

Much to Phil's surprise, Loretta Sheffield was "at home" when Phil and Gwen arrived at her doorstep the next morning.

"Dear Etta," Gwen said, stepping forward to take their hostess's hands in hers. "I'm so sorry that you missed Agnes's ball, but Agnes loves the brooch you sent. She asked me to tell you that it was one of her favorite presents."

Loretta smiled wanly. "So kind."

"I've brought my friend, Lady Dunbridge. I knew you'd want to make her acquaintance."

"I'm honored, Lady Dunbridge. Won't you both be seated?"

She gestured to a sitting area on the far side of the parlor, where a dark Victorian sofa and two uncomfortable-looking parlor chairs were placed before a many-paned window that seemed to prevent any direct sunlight from creeping into the room.

The atmosphere was oppressive, dark and out of date as if time had stopped inside this room, perhaps in the entire house, and certainly within their hostess, who had probably been quite handsome as a young woman, but now wore the dour expression of someone who had borne many burdens and not borne them well.

She was petite, excruciatingly thin, with dark hair streaked with gray.

They all sat down and Loretta Sheffield rang for tea. Phil settled in for what might be a long and arduous visit before they got to the actual point of why they'd come.

But Loretta fooled her. "Gwen, how on earth did this happen?"

Gwen blinked in surprise. Then collected herself quickly. "Isaac told you then. I wasn't sure . . ."

"Isaac? No. His office called looking for him. That nice Mr. Stokes broke the news. Luther had called him to inform Isaac, but Isaac had gone 'out of town.'"

Phil perked up at the slightly acidic tone of Loretta's statement. She recognized a euphemism when she heard it. Now what exactly did Loretta mean and was she going to enlighten them?

"And then some odious policeman came here yesterday. I suppose to inform Isaac of the news. I didn't see him, but my butler said he had the actual effrontery to appear at the front door."

And since he'd been denied, it fell to Phil to find out what she could.

"Did your husband learn of the terrible . . . event . . . before he left for his business trip?" Phil asked innocently.

"I have absolutely no idea." Loretta waved to the maid to bring in the tea tray.

When she'd gone, Gwen said, "It must have been a sudden trip. Have you spoken to him?"

Loretta looked up briefly, but went back to pouring. "No. Milk? Sugar, Lady Dunbridge?"

"As is, thank you." Phil took her cup, watched as Loretta went through the pouring ritual twice more, and thought she might scream with impatience.

"You must be sorely affected by poor Perry's death," Gwen said, taking another tack.

"Yes, very," Loretta said.

Phil was surprised to see her smile slightly.

"He was like a puppy when he was younger, full of enthusiasm and grand ideas, always getting into mischief. Some of it harmless, some less so. I blame his family for not giving him more responsibility. He was very bright, full of schemes, but they would never listen to him."

And to Phil's utter astonishment, she began to cry.

Gwen switched seats to sit beside her on the settee. "Oh my dear, I had no idea you were that close."

Loretta pulled a handkerchief from her sleeve, dabbed at her eyes. "We weren't really. He used to stay with us when he was in town. Before . . ."

Gwen frowned. "Before he began paying attention to Agnes?"

"Oh no, Gwen. Nothing like that. He just got impatient and was always at loggerheads with Isaac. Perry urged Isaac to give him more power, but Isaac refused. Isaac's hands were tied—it was stipulated by the trust that Perry wouldn't be able to assume his rightful place in the company until he turned thirty. I sometimes heard them arguing and would quail, waiting for it to end."

And Isaac Sheffield was at the ball; Luther had heard him arguing with Perry during the evening. And now Sheffield was conveniently away on a surprise business trip—or something else.

On the lam came to mind. Really, these Americans had such interesting expressions.

"But we mustn't bore Lady Dunbridge with our worries," she added and offered Phil a plate of dry-looking sandwiches.

Phil smiled, but shook her head. "Oh, I assure you, I'm not bored. I briefly met the young man at the ball."

"Cut off like that," Loretta finished. "I just don't understand. Mr. Stokes said it was some kind of accident, but I was so shocked that I didn't really follow what he was saying, something about him falling down a laundry chute. But that's not possible."

Gwen glanced at Phil, asking for guidance on how much to say.

Loretta sighed. "It seems so senseless."

If Phil was going to mention that it was murder, now was the time. She might not have a better one. "We're afraid that he didn't actually fall. He was most likely dead before he entered the chute."

Loretta stared at her. Her mouth slackening as the news seeped into her mind. "Dead already? How could that be?"

Neither Phil nor Gwen enlightened her.

"Someone pushed him into the chute? Deliberately?"

"The police are afraid that might be the case."

"Good heavens." Loretta reached for her cup, put it down. "And Isaac—"

"Must have been told about it and gone immediately to Pittsburgh to inform the family and deal with whatever business matters—" Gwen said.

She was interrupted by a very unladylike snort from Loretta. "Business matters. He hasn't gone on a business trip. Or to pay his condolences to the family. At least he didn't pack a valise. I had his servant check. I doubt if he's even heard the news."

"But his office said . . ." Gwen began.

"What they often say when he takes a personal day."

"What on earth do you mean?" Gwen asked.

Phil held her peace. Loretta might clam up at any time once she remembered there was a virtual stranger listening to her story.

"Oh, Gwen. It's no secret. He has a mistress. He spends quite a bit of time there."

"Oh my dear, I had no idea. But please, don't feel bad. It seems to be epidemic these days. Perfect respectability on the outside."

"And rotten to the core inside," Loretta said with so much vehemence that Phil flinched.

"Do I shock you, Lady Dunbridge? I doubt it. You are a woman of the world, or so they say. I hope you won't hold it against me that I'm in this situation or that my husband is unfaithful."

"Not at all," Phil said. "I completely understand and sympathize." She did indeed; the earl had had his share of illicit affaires, some truly illicit in the legal sense. She'd had a few of her own. Perhaps more than a few, but none that hurt anyone besides herself and her own reputation.

Though after meeting Loretta, Phil could understand why a man might seek some levity in his life. But surely he could have been more discreet and prevented humiliating his wife.

And if he was with his mistress, he might be unaware of events. Or he might know more than he wished to tell. But how to wheedle the mistress's name out of Loretta, if she even knew it.

"Men," Phil said.

"Oh, do not excuse them," Loretta said with more energy than she had yet shown, color lighting her face briefly, a smoldering fire in her gray eyes. "Most people would say that my grief had driven him away, but it was just the opposite. He didn't have the fortitude to face life with his own guilt."

"Loretta," Gwen said sympathetically.

"That's what it is, Gwen. He killed our daughter."

"Loretta, no. The influenza killed Rachel and the baby."

"He refused to call the doctor."

"No. Why would he do that?" Gwen blurted out, on the verge of tears herself. "Oh, I do beg your pardon."

Loretta shook her head. "He was angry at her. So he let my daughter and grandson die. I hope he burns in hell." She broke down, and clung to Gwen. Phil watched the two women rocking together, both freely crying, and wondered how soon she could suggest they leave.

It would only be a matter of minutes before Loretta Sheffield realized that she had said too much and would begin to resent them for it. And Phil couldn't for the life of her see how a daughter dead from influenza could possibly have anything to do with the murder of Perry Fauks.

A few minutes later, Loretta showed them to the door, once again the drained, pale woman she'd been when they arrived.

Phil took her hand and held it long enough for Loretta to know that her grief was understood and safe with them.

"Call on me whenever you like," Gwen told her. "We've been too much without seeing you."

"Thank you."

Phil and Gwen started down the steps to Gwen's carriage, waiting at the curb.

"Mrs. Kidmore-Young," Loretta said.

Gwen stopped and turned, looking up at their hostess from the sidewalk.

"I beg your pardon?"

"Tell the police that they'll most likely find him at Mrs. Kidmore-Young's."

"I-I will," Gwen said. "And remember. Anytime I'll be happy to see you."

Loretta shut the door and Phil and Gwen climbed into the carriage.

"Who is Mrs. Kidmore-Young?"

"Loretta must be mistaken. Mrs. Kidmore-Young is a widow and inimitably respectable. A paragon."

"Alas," Phil replied. "Still waters run deep, as they say."

"Not with Ida Kidmore-Young. She was married to one of the most noted pastors in the city."

"A preacher's wife?" Phil leaned back against the carriage seat. "Will wonders never cease?"

"But surely she's mistaken," Gwen said. "She seems to be tormented in her mind.

"She used to be a lovely woman, quite popular and outgoing. I never could understand what she saw in Isaac. A parsimonious man—I don't mean she ever went without, but with his affections. To my mind he never gave her the attention she deserved. And whatever affection had lasted between them over the years was snuffed out with the death of her daughter and grandchild."

"It is a sad story," Phil said, "but influenza can be deadly. Why should Isaac Sheffield carry such guilt? They might have died even if their doctor had come."

Gwen pursed her lips. Looked out at the passing scenery. "Well. This was merely a passing rumor. And we never believed any of it, but . . . Oh, I suppose it doesn't matter now."

"I can be totally discreet," Phil assured her. "You'd be surprised at the things I've learned about the elite Manhattan society." The tell-all diary locked in her safe attested to it. And her discretion was unquestioned because she hadn't used any of it . . . yet.

Gwen sighed, looked out the glass of the carriage window. "At the time, there was talk that perhaps the baby wasn't the husband's. And that's what Isaac and Rachel had argued about and it had made him late for his train. He was going out of town. He asked Perry to call, but by the time Perry had fetched the doctor it was too late for both mother and child."

"Perry was there?"

"I had completely forgotten this until Loretta mentioned it, but some vicious tongues questioned whether the baby was Perry's. You know how people are."

Phil did indeed. She'd been the brunt of her share of vicious gossip, some false and some a little too close to the truth for comfort.

"Loretta has always blamed Isaac for the lapse."

"So he turned his affections elsewhere?" Phil said. "I fear someone must pay a visit to Mrs. Kidmore-Young."

"Oh no, Lady Dunbridge . . . Philomena."

"Your name won't enter into it. I'm not sure how to go about it. I can see that it will be a delicate matter."

"Loretta must be mistaken."

"I hope you're right. But there seems to be only one way to find out where he might be."

Phil spent the carriage ride back to the Pratt mansion piecing together things she had learned from Mrs. Sheffield and wondering the best way to tell John Atkins about what she'd just learned.

He needed to know the information about Sheffield's possible mistress. A respected preacher's widow. No one would be pleased if that tidbit got out. And there could be terrible backlash on John Atkins, not to mention herself, if it did. Society didn't like to see a paragon brought down. Well, most of the time, they didn't. She'd have to be terribly discreet.

By the time the carriage drew up to the mansion, she was in deep thought and so evidently was Gwen Pratt, since they both were startled when the door opened and the coachman let down the steps.

Gwen stopped her on the sidewalk. "Must you involve Mrs. Kidmore-Young?"

"I'm afraid I must. But I'll be very careful with what I learn. Do you know Mrs. Kidmore-Young's address?"

Gwen looked down, kneaded her hands. And finally told her the address.

They went into the house, co-conspirators. Luther and Detective Sergeant Atkins were both in the parlor.

How fortuitous, thought Phil, grimly. She would have appreciated a few minutes to consolidate her information and make a few educated inferences before turning over what information she had to him.

"Ah, there you are, my dear." Luther strode across the room to greet them at the door. "How was your visit?"

"It was lovely, my dear. Now if you and the detective sergeant don't mind, I really must go see about Agnes." She turned to Phil, shouldering out the two men. "Will you forgive me, La— Philomena?"

"But of course. And I must be going, too."

"Don't forget—"

"To telephone you tomorrow about the drapes. I won't forget."

Gwen hurried from the room, and Phil turned to the men just in time to catch John Atkins's sardonic expression.

"Perhaps I can offer you a ride back to your hotel, Lady Dunbridge."

She narrowed her eyes at him. "Why, thank you, Detective Sergeant, as long as you don't expect me to ride sidesaddle on your motor bicycle. I'm not really dressed for such an adventure."

He smiled. Well, if she stretched her imagination she might call it a smile.

"Actually I have a driver waiting outside."

"In that case, I gladly accept."

Phil was somewhat surprised to see a French Panhard et Levassor awaiting at the curb. It hadn't been there when they'd arrived a few minutes ago. Unless it had been waiting down the street.

The driver opened the door and Atkins handed her in.

"I hope your reputation doesn't suffer from being seen driving without a suitable chaperone. Shall I let you off a block from your hotel? We wouldn't want the doormen to talk."

"Oh, don't be ridiculous. And sarcasm doesn't become you."

He laughed and the auto rumbled down the street.

"I didn't realize the department also employed the use of automobiles."

"Actually we have four, but this happens to be the commissioner's, loaned for this particular occasion."

"So the Pratts wouldn't be embarrassed by a departmental horse or motorbike parked at their door?"

"Quite," he said.

"Mr. Pratt must be very important to warrant such attention."

"He is."

"More important than Godfrey Bennington?"

"In certain circles."

The cab turned down Fifth Avenue, the air crisp, a wet chill suffusing the air. "Do you think it will snow?" she asked.

"What? No. Too early."

They fell into silence. She knew Atkins was a decent conversationalist, so why this silence.

Phil took a breath. She knew by now he wouldn't volunteer any information if she didn't have something to trade. She wondered if there was a police term for "tit for tat."

Phil turned toward him and leaned in closer so as not to be overheard. "Do you want to know what I found out?"

He glanced toward the driver. "I knew it. What have you been up to?"

"Gwen and I made a morning call to Loretta Sheffield."

"So I heard."

"Is that why you're so cranky?"

"I'm not cranky."

"Well, I am. It was a trying morning and I'm ready for my lunch."

He had leaned in closer to her but now he moved away. "If you're angling for an invitation, I'm afraid that won't be possible."

"Afraid for *your* reputation, Detective Sergeant?"

This time his smile was genuine—and quite devastating. It didn't last.

"Are you going to tell me what you found out?"

"Well . . ." She didn't know quite where to start. "We paid the morning call on Loretta Sheffield. As it turns out, she didn't know where her husband was."

"He's away on business."

"So his office says. Mrs. Sheffield told us that he didn't come home, didn't pack his valise. She thinks he's with his mistress."

She waited for his reaction, which though he tried to control, was all too obvious.

"Don't feel bad. As much as you hate to admit it, sometimes it's necessary to depend on a woman for results."

"And did she name this mistress?"

"She did."

He turned toward her. Their knees touched and he quickly eased away. "Who is it?"

"Well, that may be a problem."

10

"Lady Dunbridge, are you going to tell me the name of this mistress before we reach your hotel? Or do you expect me to guess?"

"I'll tell you when we get to the lady's house."

"Oh no, I think I can handle this without you."

"Evidently she's a very prominent member of society."

He expelled a deep sigh and dropped his head back on the seat. "Are you trying to tell me I should not pursue this?"

"Probably not if you care for your job. Not that I think that will stop you. I don't know the lady in question. But she's the widow of a very prominent clergyman."

"Oh God."

She suppressed a laugh. "You do seem to pull these sticky assignments."

"On purpose. I'm one of the few detectives who can hold my own in a drawing room, and they hope I'll screw up so they'll have a reason to fire me."

She stopped laughing. "That must be stressful."

"All in a day's work."

"Well, Gwen was reluctant to get involved. It is rather a difficult position. I would go myself but I don't know the lady."

"Thank you, but I believe I can handle this one."

"You mean you want me to wait on the sidewalk to help you up after the butler throws you out?"

"I mean I'm dropping you by your hotel and will visit the lady myself."

"She won't let you in, any more than Mrs. Sheffield would. And she has so much more to consider, though being a widow, she should feel free to act as she likes. But of course, there is that terrible man and his Society."

"Anthony Comstock and the Society for the Suppression of Vice?"

"Yes, that's the one. I can't imagine that you actually put up with his outrageous strictures. Sick individual. Bev told me he once visited a whorehouse over fifteen times, just to make sure there was illicit behavior going on. Idiot."

Atkins snorted. "I beg your pardon, but you do have a way of surprising me."

"Why, Detective Sergeant, what a lovely compliment. I suggest you have the driver take us to the corner of Thirty-Seventh and Park and wait for our return."

"Just give me her name and address."

"I'm afraid her name and address have slipped my mind. You'll have to ask Mrs. Sheffield if she can remember."

"One day you're going to push me too far."

Phil doubted it. John Atkins was as strong and honest a man as she had ever met. And one who as yet had never let his composure slip.

He gave the driver the new directions and a few minutes later they were standing on the corner of Thirty-Seventh and Park.

"You needn't wait," he told the driver; the driver nodded and drove away.

"I suppose you have your reasons for sending the auto away?"

"Yes," he said. "Now, which way do we go?"

"I believe it's this way." Phil began to walk east. It was a lovely street lined with stately townhouses. Trees, now nearly leafless, were planted at equal intervals in square plots filled with ivy. They passed several brownstones until they came to a lovely Beaux Arts row house, its light limestone façade banded by rows of sculpted waves separating each of the three stories. On the ground floor, tall French windows opened to a small cast-iron balcony.

"I must say religion seems to be flourishing in Manhattan."

"What do you mean?" he asked, eyeing her suspiciously.

"This is the home of Mrs. Ida Kidmore-Young."

Atkins groaned.

"Is she terribly respectable?"

"Terribly. Her husband was one of the most respected deans of one of the largest churches on the east side."

"Oh dear," Phil said. A movement in an upstairs window caught her eye. She looked up to see the faces of several young girls pressed to the panes looking down. Phil smiled and they quickly disappeared from view.

"Either His Reverend Kidmore-Young was very virile or we may not be visiting Sheffield's mistress, but his abbess."

Atkins cut off an expletive in the nick of time. "Perhaps I should speak with her alone." Atkins reached into his breast pocket.

"Stop it. If you're just going to storm in and arrest them all, we'll never learn anything. Perhaps *you* should wait outside."

Atkins knocked on the door, and it was immediately opened by a large, dark-skinned butler, who managed to dwarf the impressive figure of the detective sergeant.

Phil stepped in front of Atkins before he could reveal his identity. "I'm Lady Dunbridge and this is—"

"Oh, I know who he is."

"We've come to call on Mrs. Kidmore-Young," Phil continued. "We seem to have lost one of her husband's parishioners."

The butler grinned. "I'll see if Madam is receiving." He shut the door in their faces.

"Well, I must say, I've never been left waiting on a stoop before."

"Welcome to New York, Lady Dunbridge." Atkins was trying not to smile or laugh. Phil was certain he was glad to see her comeuppance. Never mind, she would make a convert of him in the end. *Convert?* Too much religion for one afternoon.

The door opened again.

"This way, my lady," the butler said not without a tinge of amusement. He frowned at the detective sergeant but allowed him to pass.

He led them through a high entryway, into a parlor overly stuffed in the manner of the late Victorian style. Phil shuddered at the excess.

"Madam will be with you shortly." The butler left them to the dim light of the room.

Atkins went to peruse the portrait over the unlit fireplace. A man in the robes and red sash of ecclesiastical hierarchy.

"The good reverend?" Phil surmised.

The door opened and a tall woman entered. She was dressed in a tweed morning dress, buttoned at the throat, but whose tailoring suggested an hourglass figure. Her hair was pulled back at the nape of her neck. Her face was pale, made even paler by the brilliant blue of her eyes, which Phil was convinced held a sparkle of amusement.

"Lady Dunbridge, you must forgive Daniel, he thought you were . . . well, let's just say some of my callers use all sorts of nom de theatre.

"And you are Detective Sergeant Atkins. Won't you both be seated?" She gestured to a curved plush sofa, then sat across from them in a high-backed chair. "Detective Sergeant, I've heard you are a fair man."

"I try to be."

"I understand that you are here in search of a missing person. I'm afraid I'll be of little help to you. I am a lonely widow and don't get out much in the world." She addressed this little speech to the detective sergeant but she shot a curious glance toward Phil.

Phil took the cue. "Mrs. Kidmore-Young, please. We mean you no trouble. But an accident has occurred and we have been unable to reach Mr. Isaac Sheffield. It's important that he contact us as soon as possible."

The slightest look of alarm crossed her face.

Atkins cleared his throat. "He has not appeared at his place of business in two days and his wife has not seen him."

"Ah, did Loretta send you here?"

"She gave me your name," Phil admitted.

"Foolish woman. Is the earl still alive, Lady Dunbridge? You must forgive me, I don't follow the English peerage too closely."

It was said without irony, just a statement of fact, but it did take Phil aback.

"No, he died nearly two years ago. I'm a dowager and living in New York now."

"It was not a happy marriage?"

Phil forced herself not to look at the detective sergeant. She was surprised to become the subject of the interrogation. She laughed, slightly forced, but not bad under the circumstance. "I'm afraid the whole world knows that it was not."

"Those marriages seldom are. Isaac Sheffield's marriage is not a happy one."

"So he came here?"

"Yes, not to see me in the way poor Loretta suspects. Not entirely."

"Not to meet you but meet his mistress?"

She nodded slightly

"*Une maison de rendez-vous?*"

"As you say." She looked at Atkins. "I do nothing wrong here, merely provide a salon for gentlemen and ladies to dine and converse and snatch a few hours away from their sometimes mundane, sometimes hellacious, lives. If they do more, it is none of my business."

"Pardon me for saying so, but you run a whorehouse."

"You're mistaken, Detective Atkins. I hire people to cook, clean, and wait at table. They are safe in my employ from unwanted advances, even from wanted advances."

"And what about the young girls we saw upstairs? I imagine some of them are underage."

"I imagine most of them are. They live here. I house, clothe, and educate them. I do not use them. Though perhaps you cannot understand that."

"Explain it to me then."

Phil sat back to watch this battle of the wills.

"My husband was a proud man, a just man, a godly man, though perhaps a bit didactic. He served God all his life and all he got was a heart attack and an early grave. And when it came to the support of his wife and children, the Church conveniently developed a case of amnesia.

"Fortunately, I'm from a wealthy family. Wives of established clergymen generally are. It never occurred to them that I would need his pension. But I did. My children did. I put a word in an ear or two but they laughed me off, and said Herbert wished to have his pension returned to the Church for good deeds.

"Fortunately the house was mine. And I've been able to keep it by my own ingenuity for the sake of myself and my girls. I've hurt no one in the process and have managed to provide for a few.

"Yes, Detective Sergeant, *my* girls—three of my own, and at the moment four others. There have sometimes been more and sometimes fewer, but I give them a chance for a life outside drudgery or worse, and I've done it without defiling them, in the way you are forgiven for assuming they might be. Can you say that for your righteously indignant purveyors of morality?"

Atkins looked her straight in the eye. "Unfortunately not usually."

"At least you are honest. My husband was the head of his congregation, but I also felt a calling, if not from God, at least from Justice, herself."

"And have you been successful?" Phil asked, genuinely interested in the answer.

"There have been a few who didn't stay. But all in all I won't be afraid to meet my maker when the time comes."

"And was Mr. Sheffield and his companion here night before last or anytime since then?"

"No, Detective Atkins. He wasn't."

"Are you sure?"

"But of course. My dinners are very exclusive, very private, and never at the same time."

"And very expensive?"

The little nod of the head. "As you say."

"And before that, when was the last time you saw him?"

She stretched her hand over to a round carved table and picked up an old-fashioned bell. Rang it. The door opened immediately and the butler entered.

"Daniel, ask Cylla to bring the guest book."

Daniel flashed the detective a quick look, but bowed and backed out of the room.

A few minutes later, a girl entered carrying a mahogany leather-bound ledger. She had long brown ringlets pulled back by a simple blue ribbon. A calico dress, stylish but not ornate. A child still.

"Thank you, Cylla."

The girl curtseyed and turned to leave, and Phil saw that a scar cut the length of one side of her face.

Phil heard Atkins's slight intake of breath. For herself, Phil's breathing had stopped altogether. Such a lovely face marred so hideously. And yet the girl didn't seem self-conscious at all.

When the door closed behind her, Ida opened the book. Ran her finger down the page, turned to the next page, and stopped. She looked up. "Cylla came to me four years ago. She was ten; three of the older girls had gone to the market and they saved her from a ruthless pimp. They managed to get her away, but she nearly bled to death before they got her here.

"They were afraid to ask for help along the way." She leaned forward suddenly. "Do you know what it is to fear like that, Detective Atkins? Or you, Lady Dunbridge? I don't and I never want any girl to have to fear like that again.

"I provide a place of solace for a few girls and a few wealthy, unhappy gentlemen. There is no commerce between them. Arrest me if you must. But I will tell you this, you will be doing justice a disservice."

"I have no intention of interfering, if indeed there is nothing illegal going on in this house."

Mrs. Kidmore-Young laughed sharply. "And will you be the judge?"

"I am merely the instrument of the law. And I hope I uphold those laws with a sense of compassion."

"I hope you do, too, Detective Sergeant." She looked back at the ledger. "He was here last Thursday. I have not seen nor talked to him since." She riffled ahead in the ledger, flipped back. "And he has scheduled a dinner for the first Thursday of next month. A holiday dinner. Now, if you have no further questions . . ."

"And will you divulge the name of the woman he meets?"

She lifted her chin. "I'm afraid I can't tell you."

"Or won't?"

"Can't. I told you I was discreet. I don't know which ladies they bring. As long as they *are* ladies, I don't care."

She stood, signaling that the interview was over. "When I see Isaac, I will tell him you wish to speak with him, but when he returns I'm sure his place of business will inform him."

"Mrs. Young. A man is dead; no one, not Mr. Sheffield's wife or his business seem to know where he is. Or if something has happened to prevent him from returning."

Ida pressed her hand to her chest. "Dead? Who?"

Atkins's jaw tightened. He wasn't going to tell her. Phil didn't see why not. It would be in every newspaper by tonight. She was surprised is wasn't already.

"His associate Perry Fauks," Phil said into the silence.

If Mrs. Young's face could grow paler, it did in that moment. She reached for the bell. Daniel appeared so quickly that he must have been waiting just outside the door.

"Daniel will show you out."

They had no choice but to go.

They went down the steps and Phil couldn't resist looking up at the second-floor windows. One of the girls was back. And waved shyly. Phil thought she recognized Cylla, before Atkins took her arm and led her down the sidewalk.

"*Maison de rendez-vous?*" He stared at her. "How do you know these things?"

Phil laughed. "I'm a woman of the world. But I dare say you'd be amazed at what many of your sequestered wives and mothers actually know."

"I don't have a wife and my mother is dead."

"Oh, I am sorry . . . about your mother. There's still help for the other."

"Why, Lady Dunbridge, are you proposing?"

"Ha. Not if you're talking about marriage; that is one thing I will never do again. And alas, you are too respectable to do anything else. But if I wanted a husband, you are exactly what I'd choose: upright, honest, moral . . ."

"And terribly dull . . ."

"Not necessarily . . . ?"

She caught the glint in his eye.

"But I'm not looking for a husband." She glanced up at him through her lashes. "So where do we go from here?"

"I'm going back to the station. I suggest you get ready for whatever ball, soirée, or entertainment you have planned for this evening."

Not exactly what she had in mind, but . . . "Are you going to arrest her?"

"Do you see any reason why I should?"

"No, but your mere presence could destroy her reputation without her doing any wrong."

"Then I suggest you invite yourself to tea and find out who his mistress is."

Phil stopped in the middle of the sidewalk. "Good heavens. Are you asking me to investigate?"

"I wouldn't presume." They started walking again.

"She won't give the name of his mistress away, even to me," Phil said. "Her survival depends on her discretion. Something women understand all too well."

"Including you?"

"My passions have led me into some dangerous waters."

He quirked one side of his mouth. "Our passions generally do."

They'd come to the end of the block and Atkins stopped her. "I believe there is a taxi stand on Thirty-Ninth Street."

"Why *did* you send the driver away?" she asked.

He inhaled and his nostrils flared, as she had noticed he did when exasperation was about to get the better of him.

"Never mind then."

"I was loaned the car for the visit to the Pratts so as not to cause alarm arriving in a police wagon."

"But not for cavorting with countesses?"

"Something like that. Though I'm hoping the driver didn't recognize you. I think he's more of a *Racing Daily* man than *Society News*. But also I have some other business I want to discuss."

"Without it getting back to your superiors?"

"I am not an underhanded man."

"I'm perfectly aware of that, Detective Sergeant. What would you like to discuss?"

They began walking along Park Avenue.

"I've talked to the servants and as expected got nothing. None of them were upstairs after the last time Perry was seen alive."

"Not even the personal servants?"

"They say not." He held up his hand. "Of course, the few ones that admitted waiting on their employers say they saw nothing."

"And the murder weapon?"

"We've searched the laundry room and Mr. Fauks's room. And the servants' quarters. It's procedure."

"Naturally," she said. "Anyone with a brain would not have hidden it in those places. And there are plenty of knives around:

the kitchen, the scullery, the butler's pantry . . . But surely not one that thin and narrow."

"A few. A boning knife is thin, but too flexible to cut through fabric and . . ." He trailed off.

Phil made a mental note to add the study of knife types to her growing lexicon of investigatory learning. As a member of British peerage she was only required to know how and when to use the many implements in a formal place setting. Never anything that belonged in the kitchen. But perhaps Preswick . . .

"I'm sorry, Detective Sergeant. You were saying?"

"I said that Mr. Pratt has balked at giving me free rein, and my superiors backed him up. Because of the recent financial panic and the standing of Luther Pratt in the banking community, they would like to gloss over the matter as quickly as possible. So much so that they're perfectly willing to pass it off as a burglary."

"Is anything missing?"

"Not that anyone has said or noticed."

"And the topaz? It's quite valuable and if it fell from a larger set, a parure for example. A set of—"

"I know what a parure is."

"I beg your pardon. One never knows."

"That a policeman might know these things?"

"A gentleman," she corrected. "Gentlemen seldom pay attention to ladies' accessories."

He barked out a laugh. "You can thank my Investigative Techniques professor."

"Professor? I thought policemen learned on the job and worked their way through the ranks."

"Generally they do."

They'd come to the corner and Atkins held her elbow until a wagon passed, then ushered her across the brick paving stones of the street. It was obvious he wasn't going to say more about himself and she was running out of time—she could see the line of taxis at the end of the next block.

"I'm certain that Luther Pratt wants to find the truth," she said.

"Most people do. As long as it doesn't affect themselves or their families and doesn't create a scandal."

"You think it's one of the family."

"I don't surmise. I follow the evidence."

She took his point. He was the professional and she was not.

"And they've been given permission to all quit the city for a house party this coming weekend. A house party," he repeated in disgust. "Out of my jurisdiction and out of my hands unless they all deign to return."

"That didn't stop you before."

"The Tenderloin is not the Gold Coast of Long Island."

"No," she agreed. "You need someone undercover."

"What?"

"Remember the first day I met you?"

"Yes. Over Reggie Reynolds's body."

"I thought you were a bum. But you told me you were investigating something 'undercover.'"

His eyes narrowed. "I'm afraid my superiors will not allow access to Mr. Bennington's home in that capacity. Besides, the family already knows who I am."

"True," she said. "But I'm going as myself. A perfect under the cover." She smiled triumphantly.

"A perfect 'cover.' But no."

"You just said it would be perfect."

"But not for you."

"Are you saying the police will prevent me from attending the house party?"

"You know that's not what I'm saying. We don't use civilians in that way. That is not how the police department works. At least not in New York City."

"Of course it is. And you're not even subtle about it. You often depend on a—I believe the word is 'snitch,' is it not? I will be your snitch." She had one-upped him there. She knew he wouldn't condone her actions, but he couldn't really prevent her. But would he take whatever information she gathered, knowing it wasn't gathered by the police proper? Time would tell. She had no intention of letting this opportunity to help go by.

They reached the taxi stand without speaking further. Took the ride uptown to the Plaza in silence. When the taxi stopped he handed her out.

"Will you come in for tea? The tearoom at the Plaza is delightful and neither of us has had lunch."

He breathed out a laugh. "Some other time perhaps. I have to fill out my report."

"And you'll keep me abreast of any progress in the investigation?"

"Something tells me, it will be the other way around."

"Perhaps." She smiled, nodded slightly. "Good day, Detective Sergeant."

She started to get out, remembered the scrap of paper in her bag she'd been slipped at the theatre. "I almost forgot. Do you know anything about something or someone called Morse and Heinze?"

"Not offhand, why?"

"Someone suggested I mention them to you."

"Who?"

"I don't know his name." She smiled brightly. "A 'snitch,' I imagine. Adieu, Detective Sergeant."

She hurried across the sidewalk toward the hotel entrance and saw the shoeshine man from the day before standing near the front doors.

Ridiculous, surely she wasn't being watched. There was only one way to find out. She glanced quickly around to make sure the detective's taxi had pulled away, then headed straight toward him, but as Douglas opened the door for her, he slipped inside using the far door.

She hurried after him; surely one of the bellmen would stop him. Street vendors were not allowed inside the Plaza. But when she reached the lobby she saw him disappear around the corner of the main lobby.

Egbert tipped his cap to her, expecting her to take the lift, but she hurried after the elusive man. But when she reached that section of the corridor, he was nowhere to be seen. She looked around, caught the slight whiff of tobacco that proved he had been there. She moved more slowly down the corridor past the gentlemen's bar and looked inside.

No shoeshine man, but plenty of cigar smoke.

He must be heading toward the Fifty-Eighth Street exit. She walked more quickly, looked into the restaurant. No sign of the man. When she reached the entrance to the tearoom, she hesitated. She wasn't going to find him, she was hungry, and the glass dome of the tearoom cast a welcoming spray of color over the tables and chairs and potted palms.

She was about to give up the chase for a table in the tearoom, when a small woman, wearing a dark dress and a wide-brimmed hat, heavily veiled, exited.

Surely not. Not even Mr. X could create such a transformation as that. And not that quickly. Could he?

The woman tucked her head, and fairly ran down the corridor. Several men who had been lounging in the hallway stood up and hurried after her.

Hunger forgotten, Phil went in pursuit. She overtook the woman as she reached the gentlemen's bar. Grabbed her by the elbow and spun her around.

"Just what are you up to now?" she demanded. And stared down at a face she knew very well.

"Good heavens. Daisy?"

Daisy Greville, Countess of Warwick, the most beautiful woman in England, and budding socialist, stared back at her. "Phil? Phil Amesbury?"

"What are you doing here?" they asked simultaneously.

"I'm trying to elude those vultures," Daisy said. "News-papermen. They hound me everywhere. Do you know of a back entrance?"

"I know of something better. This way." Phil took hold of Daisy's elbow and they raced across the marble floor to where Egbert waited by the open elevator door.

11

"Quick, Egbert, we're being pursued." Phil pushed Daisy inside.

He grabbed the accordion frame and pulled it closed just as several hands reached for the gate.

The elevator ascended smoothly, leaving the scrambling journalists behind, and didn't stop until it reached the fifth floor. "I'll just wait here until you're safely inside."

"Thank you." Phil hurried Daisy down the hall to her apartments. She'd already fished out her key, not wanting to take the chance of being overtaken by an overzealous newspaperman who had taken the stairs.

She pushed Daisy inside right into Lily holding a feather duster.

"We're being pursued," Phil explained, then saw Lily drop the duster and pull up her skirts, giving them a glimpse of the wicked knife she kept strapped to her leg.

"Good heavens!" exclaimed Daisy at the same time Phil cried, "Not that kind of pursued."

Lily dropped her skirt and curtseyed. "Sorry, my lady," but eyed Daisy suspiciously.

Daisy eyed her back but with curiosity. Lily helped Phil out of her coat, then hesitated before turning to Daisy.

For a moment the two women, countess and maid, stared at each other. Then Lily reached out to undo the buttons of the countess's coat.

Phil looked on proudly, silly though it was. It was the first time Lily had dealt with another English peer and she was doing admirably.

Lily curtseyed and carried the coats away.

Phil turned to Daisy. Beneath the rather drab overcoat, she was wearing a dark green double-breasted suit of Cheviot wool. More in keeping with her new persona as spokeswoman for the underclasses than the notorious socialite she'd been until recently.

"I want to hear everything," Phil said. "But have you had your lunch or tea? I haven't, and I'm absolutely famished."

"No," Daisy said, still looking astonished. "I was to meet a business associate for lunch in the tearoom downstairs. But he failed to come. And when I tried to leave, I realized a mob was waiting outside for me."

"Lily, please have Preswick ring down for a gigantic tea, and bring some ice to the parlor *tout de suite*."

Lily curtseyed and hurried off down the hall.

"Now let's make ourselves comfortable." Phil led the way into the parlor, unpinning her hat as she went. She tossed it onto an occasional chair by the door, which, since no one ever sat in it, had become her catchall.

"Tea will be here shortly, but really after the morning I've had, a martini would be in order. Or do you prefer sherry?"

"A martini sounds divine." Daisy dropped onto the couch and proceeded to lift her veil away from her face, spent several seconds pulling pins out of her hat, and tossed it onto the cushion beside her.

Preswick appeared with the ice bucket and Phil followed him to the drinks buffet.

"Thank you, Preswick." He bowed to Phil, bowed to the Countess of Warwick as if she were a regular visitor, and left the room, swiping up Phil's hat as he passed by.

"Is that the Amesbury butler?" Daisy asked.

"Yes. He was about to retire when I boldly and against everyone's advice crossed the pond to a new life. He decided I couldn't go alone, so he came with me."

"And your maid? Don't tell me *she* is from the Amesbury staff."

"No. I picked her up as she was being arrested for trying to stow away on the ship. Since my own maid had refused to leave the country, I snatched her from the jaws of fate and Preswick did the rest."

"Good heavens, you put me to shame."

"No, my dear, you actually care about the hundreds of poor waifs you clothe, house, and train; this was purely self-interest."

"That does help explain her unusual accoutrement. Does she always carry a weapon?"

"Yes." A habit Phil had no intention of putting an end to. And one she had been considering adopting for herself.

"I won't ask why. Where on earth does she come from?"

"I haven't the slightest. Nor her real name, her age, or anything else about her. I tried at first, but she became so reticent that I soon gave up. I call her Lily; have you ever seen a more beautiful complexion?"

"She is striking. As long as she doesn't slit your throat while you sleep."

"Not Lily. I trust her with my life."

"That sounds ominous. What have you been up to?"

"I'll tell you," Phil said, handing the countess a glass and taking hers to sit in the slipper chair across from her. "But first tell me what has brought you to New York."

Daisy took a sip of the martini and sighed. "Oh, this is good. First of all, I'm here as 'Mrs. Greville,' not the Countess of Warwick, for all the good that did. They were waiting for me at the dock. I had to sneak out from the captain's cabin while he diverted the newshounds, the dear man."

Daisy's expression became animated as she told Phil of her escape from the ship to the Webster Hotel on West Forty-Fifth Street.

She was twenty years older than Phil and Phil had to admit still the most beautiful woman in England. Petite and fine-figured. Her hair more simply dressed than in her younger days, which Phil thought was a purely political move on Daisy's part. She was still a brilliant blonde, though she did look tired. Perhaps the ocean voyage had taken its toll.

"When did you arrive? What have you been doing? I haven't heard a word about you being in town."

"A few days ago. It took two whole days to recover. And the several times when I did try to leave the hotel, I was hounded to death by those journalists; they're like jackals."

"So you live here, Phil?" Daisy asked, slipping into their old casual ways. Though not friends exactly, they had often attended the same balls, soirées, and house parties, especially those of the prince regent, with whom Daisy had carried on a long-term affaire.

"Yes. The hotel just opened a month ago. I have a butler and a lady's maid and *c'est tout*. All our meals are delivered by elec-tric dumbwaiter or there is a Residents Only dining room down-stairs. They do everything here. I don't care if I ever see another drafty castle as long as I live."

"Lucky you. I can't afford mine and yet I'm stuck with it."

"Well, I was forced from mine, by Amesbury's heir."

"So I heard. No one likes him. Very stuffy fellow."

"And how is Brookie?"

"Oh, he's the best of husbands, he's never in England and is busy when he is. He's always tolerated my affaires, as I have his, and now he puts up with my flights of do-goodery as he calls them, even puts up with other people's opinions of me. They all think I've lost my mind."

Phil had been one of them. Daisy had gone from outrageous

to political, taking up the socialist cause and opening schools for poor children and work cooperatives for tradeswomen. Good things to be sure, but it wasn't until Phil had fallen into her new—dare she say "line of work"—that she began to understand the satisfaction of having a mission.

"But how came you here?" Daisy asked. "I heard you were staying with Bev Reynolds."

"I intended to, but Reggie had the poor taste to get himself murdered, a nasty affair. Bev left for the continent, so I moved here."

"Very posh. And who is the gentleman?" There was a glint in Daisy's eye from the old days.

"Gentleman? Oh. All this?" Phil shrugged.

"It's outfitted in some lovely furniture. That Louis Quinze chaise, the writing table. It's Directoire, no? It's all so lovely and tasteful."

"It is," Phil agreed.

"Come now, Phil. Fess up. Dunbridge's estate didn't pay for it. I have it on authority that we're both as broke as the proverbial church mice.

"Though I realize it's none of my business and I know there are some who are still to this day reluctant to confide in me. Babbling Brooke." She laughed. "I haven't used that name since Greville became the earl. And yet it persists. How ridiculous. I know how to hold my tongue when it suits me."

Phil laughed and took their glasses to be refilled. "I'm certain of that," Phil said, though she didn't plan to say too much. Daisy was perfectly right. She could hold her tongue until it benefited her not to.

When Phil returned with the new drinks, she sat next to Daisy on the couch. "I'll tell you, though it really must go no further."

Daisy leaned forward. "My lips are sealed."

"The fact is . . . I have absolutely no idea who is paying for the apartment."

Daisy's eyes glinted with speculation. "Phil, don't be coy."

"I'm not. I assure you."

"No gentleman? Surely someone has caught your eye."

Phil nodded, a gentleman *had* caught her eye. Two actually. But one was a Puritan. And the other. The other was too elusive for even her machinations.

"When Bev left town I was sent a letter offering me this apartment."

"And you really have no idea?"

"Well, it could possibly be Daniel Sloane, Bev's father. In appreciation of me, um, sticking by Bev in her hour of need. They closed up her brownstone and left me a bit stranded."

"Oh?"

"And as you pointed out, I'm quite broke."

Daisy looked shocked then broke out with a peal of laughter. "My God, but you're refreshing. Why did you ever leave London?"

"I didn't have much of a choice."

"Oh yes, the earl's early demise, and there *was* your last rather brazen affaire de coeur with Claude DeLouche." Daisy laughed.

"My father was not amused. Then the newspaper articles—"

Daisy squealed with delight. "I almost forgot that. You were involved in that murder investigation. That must have been the last straw—" Her eyes popped. "Are you still? Wasn't Reggie Reynolds killed while you were here?"

"The day I arrived," Phil said.

"Oh Phil, the investigation? You didn't . . . did you?"

Phil shrugged. "I helped in my own little way."

"Oh, do tell."

She gave Daisy the official story with a few juicy details added to make it seem reasonable. She couldn't tell what really happened. Her life and the lives of others still depended on it.

"But tell me about you, what brings you to New York? And incognito."

"Business, my dear friend."

Phil raised her eyebrows.

"I kid you not. Brookie had several mines and ranches over here, though God knows we haven't made a penny from them. I was hoping to sell them and reinvest the money.

"I got wind of a chance to take advantage of the banking and stock exchange situation here, so I jumped on the next ship over. That's who I was supposed to be meeting downstairs.

"I hoped to sell him the mines and reinvest that money plus a little I've set by to get in on a major steel venture. I had an appointment to meet him at the tearoom at three o'clock. But he didn't show. I can't imagine what happened."

"Steel?" A frisson of unease sped up Phil's spine. Fauks Copper, Coal and Steel. Coincidence? "His name wouldn't happen to be Isaac Sheffield, would it?"

Daisy shook her head. "No. This gentleman is the head of a large family trust. He's planning to use his business and other smaller trusts to compete within the growing steel market. It could be very lucrative, and I could finally do some of the projects that I've been wanting to do."

"His name?"

"Oh, didn't I say? A Mr. Perry Fauks."

At that moment, the doorbell rang, and a minute after that, the floor waiter rolled a food trolley into the parlor, followed closely by Preswick.

"Where would you like this, Lady Dunbridge?"

"Over by the window, please. Is that good with you, Daisy? The view is delightful."

Daisy smiled, distracted.

The waiter lifted the covers of platters of salads and cold meats and cheese.

"Shall I serve, my lady?"

"No, thank you, Preswick, we'll fend for ourselves."

Daisy waited until both men were gone, then leaned over the

table. "What's the matter, Phil? Why do you look so odd? Do you know Mr. Fauks?"

"Not really," Phil said, choosing her words carefully and thinking, *the plot thickens*. "Actually I danced with him at a ball just the other evening. You came all the way to New York from London to discuss selling your mines to him?"

"Well, not just that, but as I said, he had a venture I wanted to invest in. You know the king has always been helpful in guiding my investments."

"Well, I heard about this on my own. Lord Fitzgerald had just returned from a meeting with him, and was quite excited. He gave me the tip, all on the Q.T., you understand."

Phil breathed out slowly. Daisy was in for a rude awakening.

"I can't imagine why he was absent today. I know he was planning to return to Pittsburgh, is it? In a few days. That's why I took the fast ship here. We telegraphed several times. I'm sure the meeting was for today. I would have telephoned his office downstairs, but for those odious men. Do you have a telephone here?"

"Yes, but I wouldn't call his office," Phil began, setting down the canapé she had just picked up. "I'm afraid Mr. Fauks won't be able to meet you."

"What? Don't tell me I'm too late."

"In a manner of speaking. Mr. Fauks is dead."

"Dead? He can't be. Lord Fitzgerald said he was quite young."

"He was murdered. And Daisy, this is just between you and me, though I expect you'll be able to read about it in the papers tomorrow or the next day."

"Murdered? He can't be. I came all this way."

"It's true. I saw him myself. He was stabbed to death."

Daisy's eyes widened. "Good heavens. Don't tell me you're involved in another investigation."

"Just an innocent bystander," Phil lied. "He was staying with, uh, friends of mine. I just happened to be calling the morning after the daughter's debut ball to offer my congratulations and to tell them how much I enjoyed the evening. And he had just been discovered."

"In the house?"

Phil nodded. "We believe he was killed during or shortly after the ball."

Daisy knit her brows. "What a terrible way to make one's come-out."

"Yes," Phil said. "It's the daughter of one of the big banking families in town. I believe there were expectations in that direction."

"Oh dear. Now the poor child is without a prospect." Daisy sighed. "And unfortunately so am I."

"It can't be as bad as that."

"It is." Daisy leaned back in her chair, her plate of food forgotten. "I've made this trip for naught. And am thoroughly undone."

Phil understood Daisy's desperation. Keeping an estate was difficult at the best of times. Living a lavish life and keeping up estates were nigh impossible. And philanthropy was generally the first to go.

"Oh, I know that sounds selfish, but I had set my hopes on this scheme. Not just for me. I had plans for the money. Real plans, not just for my frivolous life. Actually, I no longer go out in society very often."

"So I've heard. They say you've taken up the socialist cause."

"I have. I've wasted so much of my life, going blissfully from one entertainment to another, causing trouble and relishing in the scandal. But there are so many people who have nothing. Nothing, Phil. I just couldn't ignore it any longer. People on our own estates who are close to starving just because of one dry season.

"Brookie is always off on his soldiering, and the estate manager doesn't care as long as his books are correct. And suddenly I just woke up.

"You probably think I'm crazy. But one day you'll get sick of it all, Phil, long for something more, want to leave your mark on the world, leave it a better place. I don't mean handing toothbrushes to soldiers going off to war, or knitting socks for African children who have no shoes. But teaching people the skills that can lead to a better life—something that we've always enjoyed by chance of birth. I just want to do something useful."

"You have, Daisy."

And Phil, though she couldn't explain it to Daisy, felt the same way. She was doing something useful. Not to mention she was having more, not exactly fun, but more stimulation than any of her life in England had given her.

Daisy sniffed and reached for a sandwich. "Society laughs at me behind my back.

"It wouldn't be so bad if the socialists accepted me. They don't even laugh at me; they despise me, because I haven't given every-thing I own away, but they don't even want what I have. They just don't want me to have it."

"Surely they understand that most of everything you have is owned by Brookie."

"Including my children."

Even though they aren't all his, Phil thought. "Well, if you gave it away you couldn't do all the things you do for anyone else."

"True. It's a paradox, isn't it?"

"Well, all may not be lost. Isaac Sheffield actually runs the company. Perry would not have taken over until his thirtieth birthday." Phil wondered who would take over now, or if this had secured Isaac Sheffield's place in the company. But in that case, this was the least appropriate time to disappear.

"I'll go to visit Mr. Sheffield at his company tomorrow." The glint was back in Daisy's eye. "Did you say banking family?"

"Yes. The Luther Pratts. If you tell me what you know about Mr. Fauks's scheme, I may just introduce you."

When Daisy left a half hour later, Phil knew more about stock trading than she'd ever thought she would need to know. She'd finally had to stop Daisy long enough to get paper and pen and write everything down.

She still didn't understand the half of it, but she had no doubt that she could find out.

"Madam," Lily said, coming up behind her as Phil looked out the window to the street below. A horse-drawn carriage turned into the park. People hurried along the sidewalk, the wind whipping at their coats and hats. The little newsboy stood at the stone entrance, hawking his papers, wearing a jacket too little and too thin for this weather.

Winter was upon them. Soon the holidays would be here. It would be a cozy holiday with only her and her two servants. Their first in their new home. They would get a tree and buy presents.

She might even send gifts to her family. *If* she bought them gifts. She hadn't heard anything from any of them, which she supposed was a good thing. Still, talking to Daisy made her a tiny bit wistful . . . until she remembered why she left.

No, she had too much important work to do before she thought of Christmas.

"Madam?"

Phil came back to the present. "Yes, Lily?"

"Are you going out tonight?"

"Not tonight. It's a good thing it's the beginning of the season and I have a few free evenings still. I'd forgotten how exhausting investigation can be. I think I'll have a nice long soak and a quiet evening at home. Then we'll exchange notes tomorrow over breakfast. I'm sure there's something I'm missing. I have a feeling this is going to take all our wits."

"Very well. Shall I draw your bath?"

"Yes please, then you and Preswick can have the evening off. Maybe there is something playing down at the Nickelodeon that you would both like to see."

Phil meant to take her notebook to bed and organize all the things she'd learned in the past two days, but between Daisy, the martinis, and the bath, she found that her eyes insisted on closing. She yawned, stretched, tried to remember what she'd been thinking, something about trust companies. That was it . . . what was the difference . . . between . . .

The next thing Phil remembered was opening her eyes to darkness. Lily must have returned and turned out the lights. She must have been tired, for she hadn't even heard them return home.

She nestled down in the soft comforter. But something wasn't right.

"Lily?"

"Sorry to disappoint you, Countess, but not Lily. She and Preswick are safely in their beds."

She stilled.

"Don't scream," he said.

She had been about to do just that. But it had been purely reflex. She wasn't afraid. There was no mistaking her visitor now.

"How did you get in?" She looked automatically to the window, where a sliver of moon cast the only light into the room. The window was closed.

"Really, Countess, do you really expect me to scale the Plaza façade to reach you? It's five flights straight up." His voice was smooth, not too deep, but rich, an American accent. Tonight anyway. He did several accents very well. Well enough to fool her. "I wouldn't want to attract a crowd."

"Come closer so I can see you."

She felt him move, but he skirted the window, staying to the corners of the room where the moonlight didn't penetrate.

She reached for the lamp, but a hand appeared out of the darkness to clamp over her wrist, halting her progress.

"Why don't you want me to see you?"

He didn't answer.

Emboldened, she said, "Are you still dressed as a shoeshine boy?" She couldn't help but gloat a little. She'd spotted him; it was only natural that he should visit her tonight.

"Tsk, tsk, Countess. You should know better. I wasn't the shoeshine boy."

"But he—ugh, you gave him a cigarette and he smoked it."

He chuckled in the darkness.

It sent a tingle through her limbs.

"I was one of the journalists bear-baiting your friend, the other countess."

"Daisy? She's not under suspicion, is she?"

"Everyone is under suspicion. You might get her an invitation to the shoot this weekend."

"You know about the shoot? Do you know where Isaac Sheffield is?"

"I'm hoping you'll find out."

"Will you be there?"

"Perhaps. And now alas, I must leave you. But soon. I'll—" He didn't finish his sentence, but moved in quickly enough to kiss her, full on the lips.

The man could kiss, and while she was still recovering, he disappeared into the dark.

Phil couldn't very well follow him out the window, if that was the way he'd come. It was a favorite method of his. She didn't even bother to run to the door, chase him down the hall. Tomorrow, she would ask Egbert or the other elevator operators if they'd seen her visitor. Of course they would say no.

And then she realized something else. He'd smelled like soap. He'd made sure she followed the pipe scent on the newspaper boy and he'd outwitted her.

So he had changed the rules. No matter. She could keep up . . . somehow. And why was he playing with her? She thought she was supposed to be helping him.

Unless they weren't really working for the same side.

12

Morning came all too soon. Phil waved away Lily's suggestion of breakfast in bed, and got up.

Lily proceeded to brush Phil's hair until it shone with red highlights. She obviously had been reading the latest fashion magazines, because when she was finished, waves rode upward from Phil's temples to be pulled into a loose coil at the back of her head.

Phil decided on one of the new walking dresses she'd ordered from Paris for the fall. A smoky gray messaline silk with a Gibson collar, a tucked net yoke with gilt buttons down the front.

Phil lifted her arms. The sleeves were fitted and tucked but gave her ample range of movement. She turned in a circle; the skirt was full, but unlined. It might be a bit drafty in cold weather but it wouldn't slow her down.

She smiled, remembering a day when that thought would have held a very different connotation than it did today. And yet hope sprang eternal. There was no man in her bed as yet, but that could change . . . and very soon.

"Very nice. I think I'll be able to make it through without changing until tea time. Really, how did I change clothes five or six times a day in England. What a hideous waste of time."

She strode down the hall to the small butler's pantry that served as office and makeshift kitchen when needed. Breakfast had arrived via those remarkable dumbwaiters, and she sat down at the table, which was already set up with pens and papers and a copy of the morning newspapers.

Preswick served, then cracked the top off her soft-boiled egg. He would have stood at her shoulder until she finished but she waved him to one of the other chairs. "Sit, both of you. I suppose you've breakfasted already. But do pour coffee for yourselves."

"We're quite sated," Preswick said for both of them. "Lily, you may be seated."

Lily pulled out a chair, sat down, and waited for Preswick to position himself in the chair opposite, before she reached for a tablet and pen.

Phil took a moment to sip coffee, a morning habit she'd picked up from Bev Reynolds and immediately adopted into her own household, such that it was.

She reached for a piece of toast and dunked it in the egg, took a bite. "Let's see what the papers have to say." She opened the first of two newspapers that were folded on the table at her elbow.

"'Valet Wanted for Questioning in Fauks Heir Death.'" Phil put the paper down. "I suppose this was inevitable, though I wonder if the information is being fed purposely to the journalists. So far they are several days behind where the actual investigation is.

"Will they question Isaac Sheffield's whereabouts tomorrow?" Phil put down the paper. "I think I'll pay another visit to Mrs. Kidmore-Young." Seeing the blank faces of her servants, she realized she hadn't apprised them of her visit to the clergyman's widow with the detective sergeant yesterday.

"She's the widow of a distinguished clergyman who runs a house of assignation, though our lips are sealed. Sheffield seems to be a personal friend of hers. She was not forthcoming yesterday. Perhaps without the strong arm of the law sitting across from her she'll be more cooperative.

"Now there are a few things I need the two of you to do today.

"The Countess of Warwick came to New York to do business with Mr. Fauks. They were to meet yesterday in the tearoom, which would be a logical place to meet. However, obviously he didn't come. She didn't know about Mr. Sheffield at all. She planned to sell Fauks her copper mine and invest in some scheme of his. Harry Cleeves, who was a friend of Perry's, also mentioned Perry's 'scheme.' It might be purely coincidental, but between the banking panic and the stock market volatility, I don't think we should leave any possibility unconsidered.

"Preswick, see if you can discreetly ask around and find out what the scheme was. And how Isaac Sheffield is involved. And if this Heinze and Morse have anything to do with it."

"Yes, my lady. If you will not need my services here this afternoon," said Preswick, in his most butler-like voice, "I may be able to find out some information down in the business district."

"Excellent." What he meant was he'd make the rounds of the pubs listening to the gossip of the clerks who were taking their lunch.

There were definitely advantages to having a butler who was versed in the stories of Sir Arthur Conan Doyle's famous detective, who as it happened was a master of disguise like her Mr. X. Really she had a good mind to give it a try sometime.

"What shall I do?" Lily asked.

"You will stay here and prepare my wardrobe for a weekend in the country. Several walking skirts, the gold silk chiffon for evening, and the rose, and call round to Eglantine's. Tell Madam I'll need a sporting outfit appropriate for a weekend shoot. Though I have no intention of shooting grouse or anything else."

Lily's face fell.

"I'm sorry, my dear, but we must be prepared. We'll be taking the Packard, so have our touring coats cleaned and pressed."

"What ar-r-re you going to do . . . my lady?" Lily asked. She was not happy to be left with the domestic arrangements. Phil didn't blame her, but someone had to do it, and that was her job.

On the other hand . . . "Though perhaps you should come with me to Mrs. Young's house. She has several girls whom she saved 'from the streets,' if you know what I mean."

"Of course I do," Lily said, her eyes downcast.

"Perhaps we could finagle a way for you to get to know some of them while I'm visiting. I'll tell Mrs. Young that I saved you from a similar fate—"

"But you didn't. I wasn't—"

"Of course you weren't. You were valiantly fighting off a passel of burly customs officials. And you were winning, too."

Lily's eyes flashed and she grinned. "I was, wasn't I?"

"Which is nothing a young woman should brag about," Preswick reminded her, though there was a tiny bit of respect and affection beneath his words.

What an interesting situation her household was, Phil thought. And she wouldn't have it any other way.

"But I must have Mrs. Kidmore-Young believe that I've brought you for a lesson in humility."

Lily's face became so abject that Phil did laugh out loud. "But subtly, Lily."

"But of course, my-y-y lady." Lily hopped up from her chair. "And while you are finishing your breakfast, I will call Madam Eglantine to order your shooting dress." She bobbed a curtsey and fairly skipped out of the room. *Maybe her maid was even younger than she thought.*

Phil exchanged a look with Preswick, who was trying very hard to hold his countenance. But she was happy to see that life in America was affecting even her loyal, stodgy, die-for-her butler. She thought he was actually beginning to enjoy this new life.

There was one thing she hadn't mentioned to either of them. And she probably should. That was her visit from her mysterious . . . *patron?* She didn't think so. Having a patron would be too much like being a kept woman, which she had been occasionally, and didn't like overmuch.

Colleague? They didn't exactly share information. And being colleagues was a little too businesslike.

Rival detective? Now there was something to get her blood racing. And the trio, no, the triumvirate of Mr. X, Detective

Sergeant Atkins, and her—though she was the only one who knew it—would be unstoppable.

She popped the last bite of toast into her mouth. She would tell them tonight. Before she might be visited by him again. She really wouldn't want Lily to slit his throat or even for Preswick to engage him in fisticuffs, if they came upon him without warning.

An hour later, after a brief difference of opinion about which hat the countess should wear, Preswick, dressed not in his butler uniform, but in a tweed cutaway suit, his bowler hat tucked under his arm, saw the two of them downstairs to the taxi stand. Lily won out and Phil agreed to the new small platter hat, festooned with satin rosettes and embellished on each side with brown and black natural bird wings. And for the first time in her life, Phil thought about where those ornamental wings had come from.

"Are you sure you won't take a taxi?" Phil asked Preswick.

"Thank you, my lady, but I prefer the autobus. Pick up the tenor of the times, so to speak."

Listening for what people were talking about. He'd have his ear out for how much of a stir the death of Perry Fauks was making on the populace.

He waved them off, and Phil immediately turned to Lily, who looked very sweet in her fall coat and her simplest fall hat, black felt adorned with braid and a simple silk flower at the side. They'd bought it for just such an occasion.

"You look charming," Phil said encouragingly. The coat had been more expensive than the modiste had thought proper for a maid, but she was a lady's maid to a countess. It was befitting that she should dress a little better. Besides, she'd been delighted. How could Phil say no.

They arrived at the Thirty-Seventh Street brownstone within a few minutes. "Ready?"

"Yes, my lady," Lily said primly.

"Then into the fray, my dear."

They stepped out of the taxi. Preswick had very astutely given Lily the fare. Really, Phil made a mental note to herself to start carrying more ready money, especially coins for fares and ices and such, in her purse.

They ascended the steps and were greeted by the same butler.

"Good morning, Daniel. I've come to see Mrs. Kidmore-Young." She smiled disarmingly. "I do hope she's receiving this morning. I've brought my maid."

He looked down from his towering height. Lily briefly cast shy eyes up at him before quickly lowering them.

He stood back and let them into the foyer. "You may wait here while I see if she is at home."

"That won't be necessary, Daniel," Mrs. Kidmore-Young said from the staircase. "You may take their coats." She tipped her head toward Phil. "If the countess is making a long visit."

Phil hoped she was indeed. Lily unbuttoned her coat in a fashion befitting her position. After a quick look about, Lily handed Phil's coat to the butler, letting him know with a look that she noticed there wasn't a footman.

Lily was always astounding Phil, not just with her ability to absorb the vast amounts of information handed down by Preswick about servant rules, but her agility in reacting to every situation. Something Phil herself knew you learned out of necessity.

But where had Lily learned hers?

Mrs. Young saw them into a second parlor, a sunny room at the back of the house where a fireplace was banked low and was surrounded by several comfortable-looking chairs. A newspaper lay on a side table next to one of them.

With walls painted in a light yellow, it seemed less ponderous than the visitors' parlor.

"And this young woman is . . ." Mrs. Young began.

"My maid. It's an interesting story actually."

Mrs. Young gestured to the chairs in front of the fireplace. Lily stood where she was.

"Sit down, child. There are some magazines on that table over there that might interest you."

Lily quickly looked around and sat down at a round table covered with books and magazines.

"This is our personal parlor, for me and my girls, all my girls."

She and Phil sat down. Mrs. Young rested her elbow on the chair arm. "Now tell me, Lady Dunbridge, to what do I owe the honor of a second visit?"

"Several reasons actually," Phil said, reassessing the woman. She was all business this morning with very little of the warmth Phil had seen when she was talking about "her girls" the day before.

"First of all, I wanted Lily to see other girls who were able through help to see a better life."

"And is not Lily appreciative of her place in your household?"

Phil immediately felt contrite. And that wasn't good. She could bluff her way through this, but she suddenly didn't want to. But she did need information that might be had from Mrs. Young. And she realized that she wanted Lily to meet other girls her age. Maybe what she really wanted was to find out more about Lily.

"Of course she is." Phil leaned forward. "I don't believe she was raised to be a maid. Actually, I just found her." She told Mrs. Kidmore-Young of finding Lily on the docks. "We don't live an orthodox life here, as I'm sure you can understand. And I thought it would be nice for Lily to have some contact, no, friendships with people more her own age."

"And how old is she?"

"I have no idea. Nor do I know her real name nor where she comes from."

"Can she talk?"

"Of course she can talk." And was happy to do it. "She just

won't talk about herself, and I have stopped asking. We rub along quite well."

"It seems to me she holds the ace in the deck of your relationship."

Phil thought about it. "Is that an ecclesiastical metaphor?"

For the first time Mrs. Young's face lit with amusement. "Oh Lord, Henry would roll in his grave. And I say let him."

She rang the same type of dinner bell as she'd used before and it occurred to Phil that the house had not been modernized. Another example of either her husband's sole attention to God or to her own indifference.

Daniel entered the room.

"Ask Penny to come down, please."

He left and Mrs. Young turned to Phil. "As you can see we also do not have an orthodox household. Penny is my oldest daughter. I'll ask her to introduce Lily to the others, if you think she will go with her. But, Lady Dunbridge, I will not have her questioning them about what goes on in this house. They won't tell her. The underside of our way of life is that it must be kept secret. All our lives depend on it."

"I understand and so does Lily."

Mrs. Young raised her eyebrows. "Are you sure?"

"Most definitely. Our way of life also depends on secrecy."

"You intrigue me. And I'm not quite sure why you were here in the company of the police yesterday. It could be very bad for your reputation."

"True, but I've found myself embroiled in unusual circumstances since the day I arrived in your city."

"Yes, the Reynolds affair, so I've heard."

"Well, I seem to be in a similar situation with the death of Perry Fauks. Mr. Pratt thinks I can be helpful as a support to his wife."

"I dare say Gwendolyn Pratt is not so helpless as she appears."

"To tell you the truth I agree with you," Phil said.

The door to the parlor opened and a young woman stepped into the room. She looked just as her mother must have looked at her age. And Phil adjusted her impression of Mrs. Young as being older; if this was her eldest, she couldn't be more than forty.

"May I introduce my daughter Penelope. Penny, this is the Countess of Dunbridge. And this is Lily, who would like to meet your sisters."

The girl curtseyed and took Lily away.

As soon as they were gone, Mrs. Young said, "Now, for the real reason you are here. I will not divulge the lady's name."

"I really don't care about who she is, unless she was with Sheffield after the Pratts' ball."

The two women eyed each other speculatively.

"Mrs. Kidmore-Young, I understand your need for privacy, so I will tell you something in the strictest confidence. Mr. Fauks was murdered." She took a moment for her statement to sink in. "That is one of the reasons the police wish to find Mr. Sheffield."

"He wouldn't murder Perry Fauks, if that's what you're thinking."

"Perhaps that's a judgment you can make. I unfortunately don't know the man. And if you do know his whereabouts, it would behoove you to tell me."

"Why?" she said shortly. "So they can have a convenient arrest?"

"I assure you, Detective Sergeant Atkins is not that kind of man."

"So I've heard. But he's not calling the shots, as they say, is he?"

Mrs. Kidmore-Young had her there. There were powerful men impeding his search for the truth. But it was a way of life for him.

"He will do his best to find the guilty party."

Mrs. Kidmore-Young sighed heavily. "Good men," she said. "Sometimes I wonder if it's worth it."

Phil stared at her, stunned.

"I see that I've shocked you. Nothing against your Mr. Atkins. I assume they've contacted the Fauks family. I would think that Isaac would be in Pittsburgh to break the news in person."

"He may well be, but no one, including his business and his family, knows that for certain. He's not in contact with them. If he's somewhere else, whether guilty or innocent, he needs to communicate with Detective Sergeant Atkins. It's only a matter of time—my guess is by tomorrow—before the headlines will announce that he's missing and his fate will be in the hands of the masses. So if you know where he is . . ."

"I do not."

"Or why he would run?"

"You don't know that he's run anywhere."

"No, but we need to find him. What if he, also, has met with foul play?"

"No." Mrs. Young clutched her hands together. A very pious gesture for a not-so-pious woman. She genuinely cared for Mr. Sheffield. Though from everything Phil had heard about him for the last two days, she didn't see why.

A hard businessman, parsimonious and cold, if his wife was to be believed. An unhappy person, oppressed by guilt, who turned to other women for understanding, not at all a stellar recommendation. But a typical one.

"Mrs. Sheffield said it was his guilt not hers that had caused the cleft between them. What is he guilty of? And would he kill because of it?"

"What?"

"You must confide in me. I'm trying to solve the murder, and Mr. Sheffield's disappearance makes him appear guilty. Are you shielding him because your affection for him makes you unable to judge?"

Mrs. Kidmore-Young laughed mirthlessly. "No. He, like all men, has his faults, but I don't think he would kill."

But anyone might if the circumstances were hellacious enough, thought Phil. "The business under his management is on the brink of failing. His wife blamed him for the deaths of their daughter and grandchild. Gwen Pratt said there were rumors at the time that Perry Fauks was the real father of Rachel's baby."

Mrs. Kidmore-Young was at war with herself. Phil could tell that. She liked the woman, but she had to push her into telling whatever secrets she knew. "What does he feel guilty about? Does it have anything to do with Perry Fauks?"

"I would never speak against my friend."

"Very altruistic," Phil said. "But what about justice? You've taken in these girls; what if something happened to them?"

"Perry Fauks was no innocent."

At last they were coming to the point. Phil waited. It wouldn't pay to push Mrs. Young too quickly. And she'd rather have her as friend than foe.

Mrs. Young had lowered her head as if she were praying, and perhaps having been a clergyman's wife, she was. Asking for guidance perhaps? Phil was certain she knew something. So she waited quietly for Mrs. Young to come to her decision.

Finally she lifted her head. Looked Phil straight in the eye. But instead of an explanation, she asked Phil a question.

"Do you have children, Lady Dunbridge?"

Taken aback, Phil shook her head. "I—"

"No need to explain. Better to not bring children into a love-less marriage. I mean no offense."

"None taken," Phil said. "I was sold on what people used to call the 'marriage mart.' And though the phrase has gone out of style, the custom hasn't."

"A barbaric custom." Mrs. Young took a deep breath. "Where to start. The Sheffields had one child, a daughter, Rachel. They doted on her. She made a very advantageous match, happily with a man whom she loved, and who loved her.

"They lived in South America because of his job with the government, but they visited New York several times a year. During those years Perry had come of age and was being groomed to take over the family business. But he was a wild boy as so many young men are these days, so the family would send him to New York each year for a few months to learn the business and some discipline.

"Since Isaac managed the trust, it fell to him to introduce Perry to the workings of things and prepare him to take over when he turned thirty. And to curtail his intemperate ways.

"Much of his time in New York, he stayed with the Sheffields, sometimes at the same time as Rachel and her husband . . ." Mrs. Young paused as if feeling a twinge of pain. "Sometimes Rachel came alone as she often did during the season, when it was summer in Buenos Aires and the heat became oppressive."

Oh dear, thought Phil. She was pretty sure she knew where this was going.

"One day, Rachel wrote to say she was in the family way and she and her husband had decided to send her home for the duration of her confinement." Mrs. Young smiled sadly. "You can imagine Isaac and Loretta were over the moon.

"The baby was born and all was well. At first." She tilted her head back, closed her eyes, beseeching heaven? Or blaming it? "Then the talk began as it always does. Idle hands and malicious minds.

"And someone finally made the observation that Rachel had been in New York without her husband at the same time Perry Fauks was staying with the family. Exactly at the right time to have fathered the baby.

"It was utter rubbish, or at least should have been. But as you know, once a false idea takes hold it's very hard to eradicate."

It was a story Phil had heard many times before. "And was it a false idea?"

"I don't know. Perry never confessed. I'm not sure they ever confronted him.

"The baby flourished, but Rachel didn't. It had been a difficult birth as births so often are. Then the influenza struck."

"And did they blame Perry for Rachel's death?"

"Loretta blamed Isaac."

"For introducing Fauks to the household?"

"No. Because he left town on business when Rachel was ill. He promised Loretta to call for a specialist before he left, but he was in a hurry to catch his train and left it to Perry to call. Perry should have called, said he called, but if he actually did call, it was too late."

"But they might have died anyway."

"Of course. But Loretta accused Perry of delaying on purpose."

"So he wouldn't have to clean up the mess," Phil said. "And she blamed her husband for not doing it himself."

"Not in words, but Isaac knows she blames him, and God help him, he blames himself."

And if they both blamed Perry for besmirching their daughter and then being responsible for her early death and the death of their grandchild . . . They had the best of motives for wanting Perry dead.

Revenge.

And now Perry Fauks was dead and Isaac Sheffield was missing.

13

Daniel rang for a taxi and within a few minutes, Phil and Lily were traveling uptown.

"They liked me," Lily said.

"Well, of course they did."

"But they are smart ones."

"The girls?"

Lily nodded.

"So is Mrs. Kidmore-Young. Did you find out anything useful?"

Lily looked away. "I . . ."

Sensing perhaps Lily had been having fun instead of investigating, Phil said, "I didn't get much either. Did you at least have a little fun?"

Lily nodded. "They were playing a game and they let me join in. A guessing game."

Phil felt a frisson of wariness. Perhaps Lily really was younger than she'd thought and perhaps Mrs. Young's girls were a little more cunning?

"Mostly they talked about getting married."

"Oh?" asked Phil. "Are any of them thinking about marriage?"

"Seems all the time. I asked if any young men came courting." Lily paused to roll her eyes. "They all got real quiet. They've been told to keep mum, I'm sure. And I didn't want to push them."

"And you did just right," Phil told her. "They understand the importance of security."

Lily nodded. "As do I."

Neither of them said more, but Phil couldn't help but wonder if that was Lily's way of saying that Phil could count on her loyalty, or that she had reason to stay mum about herself and her past. Fascinating and a little daunting.

"I did say, sad like, that we didn't get many visitors here. Well, we don't . . . usually. And I asked them if they had parties and callers. And Penny, the one who came downstairs for me, said they didn't either, and it could be very dreary.

"Then one of the other girls said, 'We don't but—' And Penny told her to mind her manners and she shut up."

Lily sighed. "Then we went back to playing that game."

"Did you enjoy the game?"

Lily smiled. "I won."

"Good for you. Now I'm going to drop you off at the hotel to finish packing our things and to see if Mr. Preswick has returned. I'm going to visit the Pratts. If I'm to finagle Lady Warwick an invitation, it would be more polite to do it in person."

The taxi stopped at the entrance of the Plaza to let Lily off. Phil gave the driver the Pratts' address and they drove away, Phil looking from side to side for anyone who might be watching their departure. Everything looked absolutely normal.

But not so at the Pratt mansion.

She rang the bell; it took a long minute before the door opened and Brinlow, looking a bit harried, said, "Good day, Lady Dunbridge." He bowed, stepped back to let her enter. "The mistress is . . . If you'll just come this way."

"Is that you, Luther?" Gwen Pratt appeared at the top of the stairway. "Oh, Lady Dunbridge. Philomena." She made a little nervous hand gesture, picked up her skirt, and hurried down to meet Phil.

"Thank goodness, you're not Luther. Though I suppose he

will have to be told, if we can't find it before he comes home. How could I have done such a thing?

"I've misplaced my letter opener," she explained. "Please forgive me if I sound like a witless ninny, but it's very valuable. And priceless to me. Luther gave it to me as a wedding present, oh, twenty-five years ago."

"Not at all. Why don't I help you look?"

Gwen shot her a smile that was so grateful and unguarded that Phil thought she could really learn to like Gwen once they'd gotten a chance to know each other in normal times.

"Come upstairs to my sitting room."

Gwen's maid was looking under the cushions of a cretonne love seat, but she quickly straightened up and bobbed a curtsey. "Shall I leave you, madam?"

"No, no, Elva. Keep looking. I just can't imagine where I left it."

The maid went back to searching.

Gwen crossed over to the writing table and pulled open the drawer. "I always keep it in this drawer. But I've searched it three times already and it refuses to appear." She shut the drawer again and threw up her hands. "I'm very careful normally not to leave it lying about. Not only is it very sharp if someone were to come upon it unawares, but its handle is encrusted in precious gems."

That information gave Phil pause. A sharp blade, a gem found on the carpet where Perry Fauks might have been pushed down the laundry chute. The laundry chute just two or three doors down the hall from the sitting room.

A sudden frisson of anticipation sharpened Phil's attention, but she held her tongue. Better not to raise the alarm. The missing letter opener might have nothing to do with Perry's death. Then again . . .

"Perhaps if you describe it to me," Phil said.

Gwen turned from the desk, sent a harried look around the room. "Luther found it on a trip to Austria." She took a breath. "It originally belonged to the Tsar . . . of Russia. Not the most comfortable letter opener, the blade is too long, too sharp, and the handle is rather heavy, gold and inlaid with gems but as a token of . . ." She sighed, took a breath that ended in the slightest wheeze.

Elva stepped toward her mistress.

Gwen waved her away.

"Jewels, like rubies and sapphires and the like?" Phil asked.

"Yes, do you think it really was a theft that Perry interrupted?"

Phil chose her next words carefully. "Possibly. It could be worth a lot of money if it belonged to the Tsar."

"Yes, yes, it did," Gwen said. "It's studded with three Imperial topaz. Luther told me this type of stone was only allowed to be worn by the Tsar and Tsarina." She smiled reminiscently. "'Fit for a queen,' he said."

Across the room, Elva knocked over a vase of cut mums.

"Sorry, madam," she said as she hurriedly stuffed the flowers back in the vase and began sopping up the water with her apron.

"No matter, Elva. Have Barbara come finish drying the table; you run along and get a dry apron. And when you've done that, please go to the conservatory and set up my nebulizer. I don't have time for the incense this morning."

Elva lingered.

"Go on now, it was just an accident. We're all a little not ourselves these days."

Though Phil thought Elva was more so than the others. Was it the idea of a murderer on the loose, possibly among the household? Or was it that Elva understood something her mistress didn't? If the opener was not just missing, but stolen, the first place they would look for it would be among the servants.

And Elva was the most likely candidate since she was Gwen's lady's maid and had access to her belongings. And if it turned out to be the murder weapon . . .

The coincidence was too much to ignore.

"I don't know what's gotten into her," Gwen was saying. "She's usually completely efficient. We'll all be glad to get away to Long Island."

"Perhaps you took it into another room," Phil suggested, cutting into the momentary silence. "When was the last time you remember using it?"

"Let me see. Vincent sees to most of the mail down in the study. He usually brings my personal mail here for me to read, but with all the invitations and responses coming in, I might have taken it downstairs to the library."

"Perhaps we should ask him, on the outside chance"—a slang phrase Phil had picked up at the racetrack—"that you left the opener there."

Gwen's breath became more labored with each step down the stairs.

"Would you rather rest? I can ask him if you don't think it presumptuous of me." Besides, she'd like to get a closer look at Mr. Wynn-Taylor. He was one of the members of the household with whom she'd had little commerce.

She left Gwen to Elva's ministrations and went to interview the secretary.

Vincent Wynn-Taylor was sitting at the large kneehole desk, in Luther's study, his dark head bent over an open accounts book. He looked up as Phil came into the room.

It was the first time that Phil was able to get a good look at him. The few times she had seen him, he was in a hurry, bent over his work, or that one brief interchange of looks with Agnes.

He was a striking young man, dark eyes beneath straight eyebrows, raised now in surprise, a rather large beaked nose that was more distinguished than caricature, and thin lips. Friends with Morris and Perry in their school days, and now working for Morris's father.

He started to stand, but Phil waved him back down. "Don't get up. Mrs. Pratt has lost her letter opener. She thought she might have brought it in here."

"I haven't seen it," he said.

A little sharply, Phil thought. Perhaps he didn't like to be interrupted while he worked. Especially with something as insignificant as a missing letter opener.

He did make a cursory glance around the desktop, rolled his chair back and pulled out the top drawer. "No, not here. Perhaps one of the maids misplaced it."

Phil took a quick look around. "Thank you. I'm sure it will turn up."

"Of course. If I do see it, I'll let Mrs. Pratt know immediately."

Phil poked her head in to report to Gwen and found her sitting in a rattan chair, the nebulizer's glass cup covering her nose and mouth.

Gwen removed the cup long enough to smile her thanks, but quickly returned it to her nose and mouth and inhaled deeply. It took a few seconds before her breathing became regular again. She attempted to take the mask away, but Elva held it to her nose.

"Another few minutes, ma'am."

Gwen cast a helpless look toward Phil.

"Take your time. I'll just go wait in the parlor."

Luther, Godfrey, and Morris were all in the parlor, the two older men standing before the fireplace, drinks in hand, and Morris, as usual, sprawled in the armchair, a drink at his elbow.

Luther and Godfrey turned from the hearth as she entered. Morris uncurled from his chair, albeit slowly, as Luther strode toward her.

"Brinlow said you had arrived. Please come in."

"I just came to see how Gwen was feeling and I didn't realize it was so late," Phil said and sat down on the sofa.

"Where is Gwen?"

"She's in the conservatory. She was having a little difficulty breathing. Nothing serious, but using the nebulizer."

"Brinlow didn't tell me."

"I dare say he wasn't aware. We've been upstairs."

"I see. If you'll . . . Godfrey, perhaps you could pour Lady Dunbridge a sherry—or tea, would you prefer tea? If you'll just excuse me."

Phil watched him hurry from the room. How would it be, she wondered briefly, to have a husband who actually cared about you? Well, she would never find out. One husband was more than enough for her.

"Please, Lady Dunbridge, have a seat. You'll have to forgive Luther. I'm afraid very much against custom, he's still smitten with his wife. Will you have sherry? Or will you join us in a whiskey and soda or do you prefer gin?"

"Gin, please." She couldn't abide sherry, it reminded her of tedious afternoons at Dunbridge Castle.

Morris rolled his eyes and reached for a magazine from a stack on the table next to his elbow.

Godfrey handed her a glass and sat on the sofa beside her. She didn't want to talk in front of Morris, but the obnoxious young man refused to excuse himself. So she turned her shoulder to him.

Oh well, it wouldn't be a secret for long anyway.

"I must tell you, Mr. Bennington."

"Please call me Godfrey. I think we've all come way past the pleasantries."

"Only if you call me Philomena."

A groan came from the lump on the chair. "Does that go for me too, Lady D?"

"No, it does not," Godfrey snapped. "If we're keeping you from something . . ."

"Not at all." Morris took a sip of his drink and turned the page.

"I think," Phil said under her breath, "I should tell you. Gwen's letter opener is missing. I think we should contact the police."

"Over a . . ." He lowered his voice. "Over a missing letter opener?"

"A very expensive letter opener, and a very sharp one." She decided not to tell him about the topaz until she'd talked with the detective sergeant.

Godfrey's expression didn't change and his eyes didn't leave hers. He was probably a good card player, she thought, and a very manipulative businessman.

"Really, Lady Dun—Philomena, do you think that is necessary? It could be anywhere. Stuck in between the pages of a magazine, dropped behind a piece of furniture, fallen into a wastepaper basket. One of the girls might have borrowed it and forgotten to return it. The three of them have been getting so many invitations, it's not an easy task to keep up with."

"Yeah," Morris added laconically. "Agnes is always borrowing things and not putting them back. You should ask her."

So he was listening. Not as bored and uninterested as he appeared—or wanted to appear.

Godfrey made no attempt to appear uninterested. "Or do you mean—"

She tilted her head. First to remind him of Morris sitting across the room from them, and to let him know he was on the right track.

At that moment, the door opened and Luther stepped in. "She's feeling much better and said if you would excuse her, Lady Dunbridge, she'll just take a little rest in preparation for tomorrow's drive."

"Of course," Phil said.

"She told me about the letter opener being missing. I'm sure it will turn up."

"Perhaps," Godfrey said. "But Lady Dunbridge thinks we should inform the police."

"What on earth for? I'll have the servants look while we're at Foggy Acres."

"Perhaps you might ask Detective Sergeant Atkins to oversee that search."

"Why waste the poor man's time?"

Godfrey and Phil both looked at him incredulously. Was he being intentionally obtuse or trying to deflect possible blame? Surely he wasn't trying to protect his wife. Phil didn't believe for a minute that Gwen had murdered Perry Fauks. She certainly wouldn't be able to stuff him down the laundry chute by herself. Which means she would have needed help.

Phil pushed the thought aside and took a sip of her drink.

"Luther," Godfrey said. "Don't be obtuse. Lady Dunbridge, Philomena, thinks it might be the murder weapon."

"Good Lord." Luther sat down in the nearest chair. "It does have a wicked blade, but there must be dozens of such blades in the household."

"The police have already searched the kitchens," Godfrey explained.

Phil looked quickly over to him. How did he know that? She didn't. Probably from the servants. She really needed to get Lily more involved. Perhaps at the country house. Why had she ever thought that having Lily speak only in Italian would be an aid in her investigation? Well, she would have to leave it to Lily to find a way.

Morris dropped his magazine on the table and stood. "Whose side are you on, Lady Dunbridge?"

"Morris," Luther snapped.

"You invited her into this house and now it seems she's poking her nose where it don't belong."

"Do you have something to hide, son?" Luther stood taller and Morris's mouth dropped.

"Are you accusing me of killing Perry?"

"Of course not, but Lady Dunbridge has been kind enough to help us through this ordeal, and I don't need this attitude from you."

"I apologize, Father, and to you, Lady Dunbridge. I'll just take myself off now. See what's happening at the club. I won't be in for dinner."

"But you will be in for the trip to Foggy Acres."

Morris bowed sharply and strode out of the room.

"I apologize for my son, Lady Dunbridge. I'd like to say he's having growing pains, but he's a grown man. One without much ambition, I'm afraid."

"Everyone reacts differently to stress, Mr. Pratt. Those of us who can stay rational, must."

"Yes."

"Now I really must be going. I have a million things to do. I'll just have Brinlow telephone for a taxi." Phil rose.

Godfrey did, too. "Luther, why don't you see to Gwen, I'll see Lady Dunbridge out. No need for a taxi. My automobile is outside. I'll have my driver take you home."

The three of them walked into the foyer just as Gwen came out of the conservatory. She hurried toward Phil. "I just wanted to thank you for—"

The words were interrupted by a loud expletive, followed by Effie and Maud, already dressed in their fall coats, fleeing down the stairs.

Standing on the landing, Thomas Jeffrey shook his fist at them. "This is the last straw. I will not—will not—pay for any more of these shopping sprees. Do you understand? It ends now."

A crash from down the hall as if someone had dropped glass. The girls didn't stop but ran to the front door. Fortunately Brinlow was there to open it for them.

Thomas looked down, realized he had an audience. "Oh, I beg your pardon."

"Really, Thomas," Luther began. "Brawling on the stairway like a common—"

"I'm terribly sorry. Unforgivable. Girls. They're enough to try a man's soul." He tried for a laugh. Failed miserably. "So sorry." He backed away.

"I must apologize for Mr. Jeffrey's outburst," Luther said.

"An inexcusable breach of etiquette," Godfrey added.

Gwen took Luther's arm.

Phil hardly heard them. Beyond them, standing in the open doorway of the conservatory, was Elva, shards of glass strewn on the floor around her. She didn't move but stared out at them, her face etched with shock, perhaps fear.

"What is wrong with that girl?" Luther snapped, his nerves obviously stretched.

Down the hall Elva crouched down and began to gather the glass in her apron.

"Well, no harm done," Godfrey said. "And he's right about those girls. They're spoiled rotten. And don't scold, Gwen. You know they are. But we mustn't keep Lady Dunbridge standing in the hall. Brinlow."

Godfrey took Phil's coat from the butler and helped her on with it himself, then he walked her out to the auto, an impressive black Daimler.

"Families are complicated beasts," he said. "Though I don't suppose I need to tell you that."

"No indeed," Phil said. "I have one myself."

He smiled.

He stopped her on the sidewalk. "These are trying times, and we all want what's best, but you must pardon me if I'm a bit selfish. This is my goddaughter's first season. I wouldn't have it spoiled for anything."

Even murder? Phil wondered.

"I won't ask the police not to investigate, though I admit I may have the ear of the top echelons for the department and the city. I'm also an honest and just man, but I walk a thin line, Lady Dunbridge."

"Oh?"

"Between trying to do what is right, and trying to do what is best for the common good."

"Are they not the same?"

"Unfortunately not always. I will do what I can and what I feel is appropriate. I will telephone Detective Sergeant Atkins and apprise him of the situation, and ask him to oversee the search while we are gone. It's against my first inclination but I'll do it, under the auspices of an inventory to see what the thief and murderer might have stolen."

She nodded. She also would be talking to Atkins before she left and she thought Godfrey Bennington knew it.

"That being said, do you really think the murderer might be a member of the family?"

"I hope not," Phil said, stressing the word. "But from what I've learned so far, I'm not convinced that it was a simple case of interrupted burglary. But that is for the police to discover." She looked up. "Do *you* suspect someone?"

"None whatsoever."

She didn't believe him, so she made a stab.

"I don't suppose you have any idea where Mr. Sheffield is?" Phil asked.

"Not at all. I just hope when he does turn up, he'll be in a condition to tell us where he's been." He opened the automobile door for her. "Now on a lighter note. We will have the pleasure of your company at Foggy Acres this weekend."

"Ah, that was another reason I dropped in today."

"Don't disappoint me, please."

"I'm afraid I'm in a bit of a quandary at the moment. A friend of mine just arrived in the city from London and I promised to show her around this weekend."

"Well, bring her, too. The more, the merrier."

"That is very generous of you. I'm not sure she is prepared for a country weekend. She came for business."

"That's fine. We're less formal than you would expect. I'll put her on the guest list. What is her name? We have a man on duty at the front gates."

"It's the Countess of Warwick."

"Daisy? Daisy Greville is in town? How did I miss that?"

"You've had other things on your mind," Phil said, surprised at his sudden enthusiasm.

"Yes. Well, she must come, too. We're old friends. Her husband, Brookie, and I go way back."

Did they indeed?

And just how big was Godfrey's place in all of this? Doting godfather and loyal friend, extraordinarily rich and by his own admission very powerful, connected to the War Department, and now a good friend of Daisy and her husband.

It was time to find out the exact nature of his business. And before she left town tomorrow. Perhaps Daisy could enlighten her.

"There won't be too many women?" she said. A situation that could kill a house party faster than smoking chimneys and mice in the woodwork—or even a murder investigation.

"With Perry's demise and Isaac not attending, we're already short a man. Not to worry, I'll have Luther bring Vincent along. And I do have a few friends in the area."

I just bet you do, Phil thought.

"Where is she staying?"

"The Webster, I believe."

"Then I'll call her immediately. I hope she isn't too busy with one of her cockamamie socialist events." He shook his head. "Socialists."

"I'm sure she would love to attend," Phil said.

"Then if you would be so kind as to call her and add your pleas to mine . . . If she says yes, *you'll* have no excuse not to come." He kissed her hand. Probably to distract her from the fact that he seemed more enthusiastic about Daisy's possible attendance than Phil's.

"Two countesses at one weekend party. My neighbors will be green. I'll dine on the coup for the rest of the season."

Phil laughed. "My guess is your neighbors are already green and you have more invitations than you could possibly accept. But I will do my best not to disappoint you."

"Good. Good. I plan to go out in advance, but the family will be glad to count you both among their party. They have quite a caravan of cars and carriages."

"Thank you, but I have a few things that need to be done before I quit town. I'll drive myself and Daisy out."

"I'll send over directions to your hotel. And have a carrier pick up your luggage and Daisy's."

"Thank you." Phil climbed inside and he shut the door.

"*À demain*, Philomena." He stood watching as she drove away.

Well, well, well, Phil thought as she returned to the Plaza. The coincidences were beginning to add up. Running into Daisy in the lobby of her own hotel. Daisy here to meet with Perry Fauks. Mr. X breaking into her room to tell her to invite Daisy to the country party. And now the host insisting they both come.

But could any of this shed light on the murder of Perry Fauks?

14

Traffic was always heavy this time of afternoon and Phil had plenty of time trying to piece together what she'd learned today. She ended up with more questions than answers, the foremost being why Godfrey and Mr. X were so insistent that Daisy attend the weekend in Long Island.

Did they both know something she didn't know? Something to do with either Daisy's socialism, which Phil had no intention of getting involved in, or her businesses, which Phil knew nothing about except that Daisy had planned to sell her mine to Perry Fauks.

And what about Vincent Wynn-Taylor? He seemed a hardworking, serious young man. Once friends with Morris Pratt and Perry, but no longer of their set. Phil wondered if he felt resentful that he had to work in a subservient position while the others seemed to have it all.

Morris Pratt was just the opposite, if appearance served, lethargic, jaded, arrogant, and rude. There was a scapegrace if ever Phil had known one, and she had—quite a few. But she could see no apparent reason for either of them to kill Perry.

When the auto finally came to a stop in front of the Plaza, Phil thanked the driver and took a minute to admire the vista of the park across the street—while her eyes scanned the sidewalk and street to see if there were any lurking shoeshine boys, journalists, or any other disguises that might be amusing to Mr. X. He obviously enjoyed his work, though why he would be keeping watch on the hotel, she couldn't begin to guess. But if he was, there were a few questions she wanted to ask him.

She didn't see anyone who might be he, but as she turned toward the entrance of the hotel, she did notice that the young newsboy, standing on his usual corner, was paying her an inordinate amount of attention. Perhaps he was daydreaming and his focus had landed unintentionally on Phil, but Mr. X—really, she had to find a better name for him—had used a boy to deliver a message before.

She waited for several automobiles and carriages to pass, then crossed the street to the park.

"Paper, miss?" The boy held out a folded copy of the afternoon edition of the *Times*.

"Are you being paid to watch me?" she asked, taking the paper. If he took off, then she'd have her answer. But the little urchin dragged his cap off his shaggy unwashed hair and grinned.

"This is my corner, but yes, ma'am. He said you needed somebody to watch your back. You being new here and all alone in the world." He poked his chest with his thumb. "That's me."

"Well, I certainly feel better knowing that," Phil said and handed him a penny. "And how do you report back to him?"

"Oh, I tell Clancy and he telephones out to the farm."

The farm? "What farm?"

"Gorn, Holly Farm where they train the horses. Mr. Mullins says if I do good, he might give me a job out there." He ended the statement with a shiver. Which might be from enthusiasm, but more probably because a gust of chill wind had just cut through the street, and his threadbare jacket was anything but warm.

This was probably just the kind of boy Daisy Greville wanted to help with all her socialist ideals.

Phil fished in her pocket and came out with a dime.

"Who is Clancy?"

"Just a guy where I stay," he said, greedily eyeing the dime.

"And where is that?"

"Oh, down in the Tenderloin."

All the way across town and the bastion of their nemesis and the most dishonest policeman in town, Charles Becker, whom Bev Reynolds had nicknamed the Fireplug.

Treacherous environs and a long trek for a small boy. A trolley ride at least. Phil hoped that Bobby was paying him directly and that neither Clancy nor Becker was taking a cut.

"I can't say no more. Mr. Mullins says you're messing with people who are dangerous."

"Why didn't Mr. Mullins come tell me this himself?"

"He's got a big race out at Aqueduct today so he's kinda tied up."

"When will he be available? I'll telephone out to the farm."

"He don't want ya to call 'cause o' ears, ya know?"

It took Phil a moment to understand. "Ears? If he's afraid someone will listen in, the hotel is very discreet."

The boy gave her a universally understood look of disbelief. "I don't know about no fine hotel. But I do know about ears."

Phil imagined he did.

"They do it all the time, them girls what put you through, from the switchboard thingy. They all listen in on conversations. Everybody knows it ain't safe to say stuff over those machines. They'd sell anything for the right price." He glanced greedily at the dime Phil still held. "You just count on me. I'm true blue."

True blue with a cocky attitude. A perfect Artful Dodger in the making. No, not Dickens, but her own Fifty-Ninth Street Irregular. "Excellent. I'll depend on you. Will Mr. Mullins be back at the stables tomorrow morning?"

"'Spect so. He likes to get the horses back to the farm as soon as they're rested. That way nobody can do any funny business on 'em."

Phil nodded. "Please let him know that I'm driving out to Long Island this weekend, and I'll stop by the stables on my way."

"Yes, ma'am."

She handed him the dime; he dropped it in his cap and shoved the cap over his head.

"What's your name?"

The boy frowned. "Just a friend."

Phil smiled. Another cautious one. "Well, Just a Friend, thank you very much."

"Yes, ma'am."

A man had stopped to buy a paper and the boy turned from Phil to make the transaction. Phil could hear his high, thin voice hawking his papers as she crossed the street to the Plaza.

Several men were standing outside the hotel, possibly waiting for friends, or the next taxi, though there was a line of four or five of them waiting for fares. None of them acknowledged her as she passed. She didn't smell the telltale tobacco that said one of them knew her much better than the others. So she went inside.

Lily was waiting for her in the lobby of the hotel.

"My goodness, where are you going?" Phil asked.

"I was—" Lily stopped to bob a quick curtsey. "I was watching from the window and saw you cross the street."

Phil nodded her understanding. She handed Lily the newspaper. "Let us go upstairs."

But before they could step into the elevator, the concierge came striding over. He was a dapper, middle-age gentleman with graying hair combed back from a high forehead.

"Good afternoon, Lady Dunbridge. These came for you." He held several letters, which he handed over to her.

"Ah, Mr. Nolan. You didn't have to do that. Preswick would have fetched them."

"It is my pleasure. You have several invitations and a letter from Europe."

She took the envelopes from him, glanced at the one on top. "Thank you. It's from Mrs. Reynolds." Something she was certain he already knew from the return address.

"I hope she's enjoying her trip?"

"It's very restorative, I'm sure," she said with a smile, her new irregular's warning about "ears" freshly imprinted on her mind. Not only ears, but eyes. "Good day, Mr. Nolan."

He nodded crisply and waited for her and Lily to enter the elevator.

As soon as they were upstairs, Phil dropped the invitations on the entryway table, handed Lily her gloves and coat, and took Bev's letter to her writing desk. She reached for her letter opener. Paused, thinking that of course she knew exactly where it was. It never left her desk. Right side. Tip pointed to the wall.

So where was Gwen Pratt's? A very valuable instrument with special meaning. Not something one would likely misplace.

She opened the letter and read.

Lily came back into the parlor.

"What did that boy want?"

"Why Lily, were you spying on me?"

"No, but it isn't safe."

"Oh pish, it's broad daylight on Fifty-Ninth Street." As if that were a reasonable answer. "But of course you're very right. Things happen to people in all different venues. It was one of Bobby Mullins's 'informants,' I believe is the word. Bobby is worried about us.

"It seems we are dealing with some dangerous men. But not in the normal sense, I don't think. I can't imagine Godfrey Bennington—" She stopped. Actually, she could. As jovial and well mannered as he was, part of her could imagine him taking matters, literally, into his own hands. And doing it ruthlessly.

And if he thought Fauks might be responsible for Rachel Sheffield's pregnancy and not trying to save her and the baby's life, he might not want Fauks courting his godchild.

Though it would be easy enough to warn him off.

And the Pratts. If the scandal had held water, surely they wouldn't have even invited Fauks into their home.

And where was Isaac Sheffield?

"Madam." Lily's voice prompted her back to the here and now.

"Sorry, just thinking. Is Preswick back yet?"

"No, madam, though I should think he would have returned in time for your tea."

Phil glanced at the mantel clock. "A little past. I think I might contrive to make myself a cocktail."

"Still, he should be here," Lily said, glancing out the wide window.

Could it be that her prickly lady's maid was worried about her mentor? He was very strict with her, and though she chafed at his strictures, it had yielded amazing results. Though Phil had to admit Lily wasn't just a diamond in the rough as they had imagined. Phil guessed that their Lily had at one time seen better days than the ones she was living when they saved her from arrest that day on the Southampton docks.

"Well, let's hope he's been able to learn something for his trouble." She crossed to the drinks cabinet. "Ring down for your tea. And have them send up plenty of sandwiches. I'm quite ravenous."

Phil made herself a martini and sat down with the afternoon paper. "'Search Continues for Suspect in Fauks Heir's Murder.'" She read the article, then tossed the paper aside.

Phil was on her second drink when she heard the front door open. Lily hurrying down the hall from her room. Mumbled voices.

A minute later Lily came into the parlor, scowling. "He says he'll just tidy up and will be with you shortly." She sniffed. "He smells like beer."

Phil tried not to smile. If Preswick didn't watch out, Lily would be ruling them all. "He was probably doing undercover work."

"Humph," Lily said. "I'll ring for more hot tea."

Preswick, Lily, and the new tea arrived in the parlor at the same time.

"Ah," Phil said. "Do help yourself. Preswick, sit down and tell us, did you have a productive day?"

"Thank you, my lady. I had a late luncheon, but I will avail myself of a hot cuppa."

Preswick poured himself tea, and went to sit at the luncheon table by the turret window. He reached into his jacket and pulled out his notebook and pencil, and placed them on the table.

Phil retrieved her own notebook from the desk and joined him, followed by Lily, who took her notebook from her apron pocket.

Phil smiled with satisfaction, the epitome of a cozy little family with a murder to solve.

"Now what did you learn?"

"Quite a bit, though it was necessary to engage in a small bit of prevarication," he confessed.

"And a lot of spirits," mumbled Lily under her breath.

This gained her a sharp look from Preswick.

"Needs must when the devil drives," Phil reminded her. "Now tell us everything." Phil poised her pen above the fresh page of her notebook.

Preswick took a sip of tea and sat up straighter. "I took the trolley over to Lexington, where I caught the underground down to Wall Street.

"Once I was there, I spent some time at various news and coffee stands, ostensibly to buy a newspaper for the financial news, but really trying to catch a bit of conversation or a headline that would aid our investigation. The atmosphere was nothing short of frenetic, much talk of short sells, and sell-offs, and cash availability. The volatility of the stock market, a concern about the strain on the monetary system caused by the runs on banks, the constriction of available cash and the ability to pay out loans."

He turned to Lily. "Not enough cash to make loans or trade stocks," he explained.

Lily nodded but without much enthusiasm. Phil sympathized.

She'd really rather be chasing criminals than trying to understand the nuances of investing.

"But at last it paid off. Two gentlemen at one stand were discussing whether one of them should sell off stock. The other advised him to sell as quickly as he could. I caught the name Fauks. So when they'd bought their papers, I followed them."

Lily's interest perked up, and so did Phil's.

"They walked quickly, standing close, and it was hard to hear what they were saying, but the sidewalk was crowded with pedestrians so I was able to wedge myself closer until I was standing right behind them."

Phil smiled, imagining Preswick tailing the unsuspecting businessmen. He was obviously very pleased with himself.

"The first gentleman became very agitated. And the second one said in a very exasperated way . . ." He paused to look at his notes and read, "'Where have you been? Sheffield can't be found. Fauks's stock is plummeting. There's speculation that he saw the writing on the wall and absconded. I wouldn't want to be in his shoes.'

"Then a fire truck passed by and I missed the next part of the conversation, but by then people had collected at the curb waiting to cross, and so I was able to stick close by.

"When they reached their place of business, they had to pause to open the door against the crowd." He consulted his notes. "The second man said, 'Use your head, man. It was copper that started this run on the banks. J.P. bailed out Tennessee Coal, but don't expect him to help anyone else. Get your money out before it's too late.'"

"Were they talking about Fauks Copper, Coal and Steel?" Phil asked.

"I couldn't say for certain—they never mentioned it again after that first time, and then the one went inside and the other hurried down the street."

"Who is J.P.?" Lily asked, looking from one to the other.

"J.P. Morgan," Preswick said. "He is an extremely rich banker, and a steel magnate, who forced banks and trusts to put up money to cover the run on the banks last month. He put in his own money and bailed out the brokers who had invested in Tennessee Coal, Iron and Railroad, who had pledged their stocks for loans to stave off the bank run, but then couldn't pay."

Preswick looked at Phil and Lily's blank faces. "It's very difficult to understand," he assured them. "I was having trouble myself."

Phil doubted that. Her staid butler was continually surprising her.

"Then I remembered Mr. Tuttle—you remember Mrs. Reynolds's butler—had some funds in stocks and I thought he might be able to help.

"I went into one of the exchanges and telephoned him. He's keeping house for Mrs. Reynolds's father while they're in Europe.

"He suggested luncheon at a pub where the brokers go. I met him there and we spent several hours listening and trying to interpret what was going on.

"At one point we fell into conversation with a mature gentleman, not so excitable as most of the others. I told him I had just retired and was thinking about investing in Fauks Copper, Coal and Steel.

"He warned me against it. He said the banks might be saved for the time being, but with Morgan saving the Tennessee coal company, all the smaller companies will either sell or fail."

"I see," said Phil. "And if Mr. Morgan buys up everyone else or lets them fail . . ."

"He'll own all the steel," Lily said, frowning.

"He'll have a monopoly on the major building material of the century," said Phil. "But isn't there a law against monopolies?"

"Yes, but he did just save the banking system," Preswick pointed out.

"Favoritism," Phil said.

"I believe that is the word, my lady."

Is that why Perry was killed? What Bobby was worried about? *Heavens,* was this why she'd been sent to investigate this case?

"I think," Phil said, "we should study up on the financial situation."

"Fortunately, I returned with several good articles on the subject."

"Excellent. This all begins to make sense. Well, some of it begins to make sense."

"Were you able to learn more from Mrs. Kidmore-Young?" Preswick asked.

"Yes. But it's all very hush-hush, as it should be. No reason to speak ill of the dead. Unless absolutely necessary."

She told them about going to the Pratts' and the missing letter opener. "The jewel I found in the hallway could have very easily come from the handle."

"You think that poor lady with her bad breathing murdered him?" Lily asked incredulously.

"Not at the moment. But I do think I should inform Detective Sergeant Atkins. First I must telephone Daisy Greville and convince her to attend this house party with us. And then I think I must meet with Atkins this evening."

"Shall I ring the police station for you?" Preswick asked.

"No, thank you, Preswick. I'll telephone myself to see if he can join me—for tea." Seeing their faces she added, "I don't want to discuss the business over the telephone."

"Why?" Lily asked.

"Ears," Phil said. "I learned a little about the telephone company this afternoon from a wise young newspaper boy who, if you see him skulking about, is one of us."

She rang up Daisy.

It took some cajoling.

She had come on serious business, not to gad about with the elite. She had nothing to wear to a weekend party.

"You came all the way to America without the proper wardrobe?"

Daisy confessed that she did have a couple of evening gowns. But nothing for a country weekend.

"Eglantine's can outfit you acceptably in a trice. Use my name." She gave Daisy the telephone number.

She'd granted her maid a few days off to visit relatives.

"No matter, Lily can see to us both. No more arguing. Members of the banking interests will be there, Daisy. Very rich men, bankers and financiers. There will be scads of opportunity to make deals. It would be a shame to have come all this way and not be able to invest."

"Who is giving this party?" Daisy asked.

"Didn't he telephone the hotel? Godfrey Bennington."

"Godfrey? No, he didn't, but . . . of course I'll come."

"Have your luggage sent downstairs tomorrow night and a truck will pick it up the next morning. I'll pick you up at ten sharp Thursday morning. And don't think about changing your mind." Phil rang off and called the nineteenth precinct station. Luck was with her and Atkins came on the line.

"I have something to discuss with you."

"Yes?"

"It's rather sensitive. Shall we meet in the park? Our bench?"

She heard a sound that was either a cough or a choke.

"Say in an hour?" It would take her that long to freshen up and take a circuitous route in case she was being followed.

15

Thirty minutes later, Philomena Amesbury, Countess of Dunbridge, stepped off the elevator into the Plaza lobby. She wasn't
dressed for an evening's soirée or drinks party but in a walking
skirt and jacket of navy blue twill. A woolen cape hung about
her shoulders and the wide-brimmed felt hat trimmed with
ruched silk ribbon was perched securely on her head.

She made no secret of leaving the hotel, but stepped into a
taxi and told the driver to drive slowly around the block.

She turned just enough to see that one of the "journalists"
had jumped into the cab behind her.

"Slowly if you please."

"Lady."

The other taxi stayed behind them as her driver turned the
corner and drove down Fifth Avenue. When they reached Fifty-
Seventh Street, she said, "You may let me out here."

He tossed her a look that said he didn't appreciate being taken
out of line for such a short drive, but he pulled to the curb; she
paid and got out. The second taxi stopped several yards away.
From the corner of her eye she saw the man climb out. She also
saw a small newspaper boy running down the sidewalk in pursuit.

She didn't wait, but made her way down the street, slowly as
if window-shopping. She knew exactly where she was going and
if all went well, she would still be in plenty of time to meet the
detective sergeant—and without her "tail."

She was fairly certain Mr. X wouldn't be so unimaginative,

so this was either a journalist or someone who had gotten wind of her involvement and wanted to find out what she knew or put a stop to her interference. Either way, she had no intention of letting him succeed or follow her to the park.

She stopped at the show window of a small store on the south side of Fifty-Seventh. When she was certain the man had seen her, she stepped inside the shop. She didn't think he would follow her inside Martinson's Ladies Foundations.

A bell jingled over her head as she entered the store.

The clerk, a robust woman of middle age, came to greet her. "We'll be closing shortly if Madam would like something specific."

"Yes," Phil said breathlessly. "I do believe I'm being followed. A cutpurse or something. Do you have a back door?"

The woman looked alarmed. "I'll telephone the police."

"No, that isn't necessary. My husband told me not to come out this late, but I didn't listen."

The woman pursed her lips. "I 'spect he knew best, now didn't he?"

Phil nodded contritely. Looked around. He'd taken up a position outside the door and was pretending to look in the window.

"Nasty-looking character," the clerk said. "This way. It lets out onto the alley and there's a cut-through two doors down. It's not a fitting place for a lady, but . . ."

"Thank you very much. You don't know how much you've helped me."

They hurried through the back of the store and the woman unlocked a heavy wooden door. Phil stepped out into a garbage-filled alleyway. Fortunately the chill of autumn prevented it from assaulting her nose. She sped along the brick pavement, her hand to her hat until she reached the passage the woman had told her about. One quick look showed that it was empty. She could see traffic on the street through the opening ahead.

She hurried toward it, slowed down before she reached the

sidewalk, then peered around the corner of the building. The man was still there looking in the window. Holding her hat to her head, she stepped out onto the sidewalk and moved toward him, as any other pedestrian might.

But as she reached him, she pulled her hand from her hat and along with it, six inches of strong steel hatpin.

She stopped behind him, and stuck it into his neck, not far, just enough to get his attention.

"Move, and it will be the last thing you do."

He stilled.

Well, that was successful. "Who are you?" Not Mr. X. Even in his most outrageous disguise, he'd never smelled of cheap liquor and body sweat.

He said nothing. She pressed the tip a little deeper into his neck.

"I'm just a mere businessman looking in a shop window."

"You followed me from the Plaza Hotel. I want to know why."

"What are you talking about?"

She gave him a little jab.

"Okay, okay. I'm a journalist!"

"For which paper?"

"With . . . with—" He moved so fast, she was afraid for a moment that she'd actually stabbed him, then his hand gripped her wrist and twisted it. She managed not to drop the pin, but she was certainly at a disadvantage. She stomped in the vicinity of his foot. Missed, tried again.

This time she made contact and he cursed at her.

A shrill whistle sounded close by. Not a police whistle, but a human whistle. The little human who had made it was running across the street.

From several directions, more boys ran toward her.

"Stay out of what don't concern you. Or you'll be sorry."

"Who sent you?" She twisted away, but he'd seen them coming and he took off down the street, several of the larger boys going after him. The others crowded around her.

"Are you all right, lady?" Just a Friend asked.

"I am now, thanks to you and your . . . men. You saved my bacon." The corner clock began to strike the hour. "Now I must hurry if I'm not to be late."

She crossed the street and they fell in beside and behind her. Seems she was to have an escort to the park.

She welcomed the company.

John Atkins was waiting for her just inside the stone wall of the park entrance.

"Copper," one of the boys warned, and they all spread like leaves in the wind.

Atkins was not amused.

"A strange group of companions," he said, offering his arm as any other gentleman would walking in the park with a lady.

"Bobby Mullins has decided I need someone to watch my back."

"And do you?"

"It seems so." She told him about the man and the threat. "What does that sound like to you?"

He was silent for a few seconds. When he did speak, he said, "Lady Dunbridge, why is it that you manage to insinuate yourself into the stickiest of investigations?"

"Detective Sergeant, I can hardly be blamed for stepping off the ship into Bev's husband being murdered. It was pure coincidence."

"No, but you certainly took up the reins, so to speak."

She smiled. Reggie had been an avid gambler and racehorse owner. "If you must know, I was afraid of whom you might arrest."

"And this time? Was it pure coincidence?"

"I'm friends with the Pratts, and Gwen asked me to give her

my support. It was the least I could do. And you know how women are."

He raised an eyebrow at that. "How are women?"

"They talk among themselves, and it seems that I'm known as the great comforter."

He barked out a laugh and led her to a bench by the small pond where they'd met before to discuss another case.

"Is it too cold to sit? We can keep walking."

"No, this is lovely and quite frankly my knees are still a little shaky from my encounter."

"He didn't hurt you."

"Not really. I had this." She pulled her hatpin out of her hat where she'd returned it.

He leaned away. "Don't wave that thing around. You're lucky you didn't kill the poor sod."

"He would have deserved it. He threatened me."

"Tell me exactly what he said."

She told him. "It sounds like someone doesn't want me looking into Perry Fauks's murder."

"That someone would include me."

"But you wouldn't send a thug to threaten me."

"No, because I doubt it would do any good. And I'm afraid of hatpins." He smiled and she forgot what they were talking about. He really should do that more often.

"So who do you think would?"

"I can think of several people. And I suggest you stay away from them."

"Like the Fireplug?"

"Who?"

"Bev's nickname for your nemesis Sergeant Becker."

"An apt description. He doesn't usually get involved in banking matters, but there are other people who do. And they have no compunction about ridding themselves, and the world, of annoyances."

She swallowed. "Duly warned. Do you think Perry was murdered because of the banking panic or the stock market plunge?"

"It's hard to say. This seems to be another case where they want answers but tie my hands."

"It must be very frustrating."

"It is." He looked at her curiously.

"Well, maybe I can help."

He shook his head.

"Just listen. We're all on our way to Godfrey Bennington's estate in Long Island for the weekend. If it's one of the family or close friends, they'll all be there."

"Be careful and stay out of it."

"Of course, but listen. And I want you to know that I deliberated before deciding to tell you."

He turned toward her and rested his arm along the back of the bench, which made their positions a little more intimate, but also, she realized, gave him a view of the path and anyone who might be lurking nearby.

"Remember the jewel I found on the floor outside the laundry chute?"

"You said it was part of someone's jewelry."

"I said it could have been. But today I arrived at the Pratts' house to find Gwen desperately searching for her letter opener."

"And this letter opener was studded with fine jewels?"

"Evidently. We searched everywhere she could think of that she might have left it. To no avail."

"Steel blade?"

"She didn't say. But as I was holding my prisoner at bay with my hatpin a few minutes ago, I had to admit that the letter opener might have been the murder weapon. I haven't seen it, but most of that ilk would leave a rent in fabric about the same size as the one in Perry's jacket."

"You may be right."

"Which doesn't mean Gwen killed him and stuffed him down the laundry chute."

"You have such a way with words."

She smiled. "It was a gift from her husband, whom she actually loves, and almost priceless. The Imperial topaz alone is worth thousands. A thief might have found out about it and thought with everyone busy at the ball, it would be easy to put inside a jacket and escape unnoticed."

"There was no sign of a break-in. Are you suggesting it was one of the guests?"

She sighed. "I suppose. Preswick told me today that men are beginning to panic over losing money in this latest stock market drop. Englishmen are renowned for blowing their brains out over loss of a fortune. Maybe someone was desperate."

"Possible. Or angry. Or jealous. But as I said, there's not much I can do, except declare this a robbery gone wrong. They'd love me to find some poor slob to arrest."

"Like the valet?"

"Unfortunately."

"You don't believe he did it."

He was silent.

"Why is that? Have you . . . You have. You've found him."

"Hiding out in Pittsburgh. They sent him back this morning. But I didn't tell you that."

She was flattered. He actually had confided in her.

"You don't think he did it?"

He shrugged, looked out over the water. "He says he didn't do it, but ran because he knew the police would frame him."

"And are they?"

"They've already charged him."

"So you're no longer investigating?"

"Not officially."

"You don't think he did it?"

"He can't prove that he didn't do it."

"Did they find the murder weapon?"

"I'm not at liberty to discuss the case," but he shook his head.

Things were looking bleak for the valet. "What about jewels? Maybe he took them out of the handle to sell."

"Stay away from this."

"Why? I'm trying not to irritate you."

"It's not that." He half smiled. "Well, you do, but mainly it's dangerous. I don't want you to get hurt. And there is nothing I can do to protect you."

"You're just going to let them sweep this under the carpet?"

He didn't answer and he didn't look at her.

"You can't just give up."

"I'll keep looking for evidence, but without access to the Pratts . . ."

"But I still have access."

"No."

"Is that it? You're just giving up? I guess your heart just isn't in it."

"My heart? My integrity, my honor, my reason for being a policeman is at stake." He stopped, looked away.

Phil touched his sleeve. "I told the Pratts that you would search for the truth no matter where it landed."

"I won't be responsible when you go too far and get hurt or worse. Go to Long Island. Dance all night and shoot pigeons all day, but please don't do anything to put yourself in harm's way . . ."

His words gave her a rosy feeling for two seconds until he continued with "or screw up my investigation."

"I won't, but I can't ignore it either."

He had nothing to say to that. He knew she was right. And he knew that she wouldn't stop. But she wished for a moment that she could explain.

They left a few minutes after that.

He stood on the park side of the street while she crossed and went into the hotel. A perfect gentleman, he didn't want to wreck her reputation of being seen with a policeman in case someone recognized him. Which the boys certainly had.

She turned when she got inside the door and looked back. He was still standing there. He touched the brim of his hat and walked off down the street.

16

"'Suspect in Steel Magnate's Murder Apprehended.'"

Phil dropped the morning *Times* on the breakfast table the next morning. "Perry has certainly come up in the world since his death. From heir to magnate. They found the valet back in Pittsburgh."

"Always it is the servant," Lily groused.

"For once," Phil said, "you and the detective sergeant are of like mind."

"He doesn't think the valet did it?"

"His mind isn't made up and neither is mine. What would cause a servant to kill his master in the middle of a ball? An argument over the amount of starch in his collars? The theft of a letter opener, even a jeweled one, even after being used as a murder weapon, might be a motive, but would hardly be of such intense emotions in so many circles."

"Are we going to prove him innocent?" Lily asked.

"If he is innocent, then we certainly will."

Preswick poured her another cup of coffee.

"What say you, Preswick?"

"Would you care for anything else, my lady?"

Phil smiled up at him. "Not a thing in the world, my dear Preswick."

Phil arrived at the Pratt household just as the door opened and Thomas Jeffrey strode out, valise and briefcase in hand. With only a dip of his stiff-brimmed hat, he jogged down the last few steps and strode off down the sidewalk.

Brinlow showed her into the ladies parlor where Gwen was seated with Ruth Jeffrey, who sat with a canvas of needlepoint across her lap; skeins of yarn nestled in the curve of the sofa. Phil noticed immediately that she'd been crying.

"Am I interrupting?" Phil asked superfluously. Obviously she was. "I saw Mr. Jeffrey leaving as I came in."

"Called back to Washington," Ruth said, showing a tight smile and dabbing at her eyes with a delicate handkerchief. "They have no regard for his time. Or his family. But I don't mean to complain."

Gwen smiled sympathetically, but she seemed distracted.

"That is a shame," Phil said. "Will he miss the house party?"

"He promises to meet us there at least in time for the shoot. But who knows? He's at their beck and call, night and day. Sometimes I wonder if they can sign their own names without his help."

"Well, he must have a very important position to be so needed."

"He does. He's advisor to Mr. Cortelyou," Ruth said proudly. "Secretary of the Treasury. But it can be tedious when your husband is always running off to do business, not to mention the expense of living in Washington." She sighed and twisted a piece of yarn around her finger as if she'd forgotten she had an audience.

Gwen gave her a look that would have quieted a more observant person.

"Don't think we're ungrateful to Luther for opening doors for us, but I can't tell you what I spend in entertaining alone. And with the girls about to debut . . ."

"Well, then don't, my dear Ruth. I'm sure Lady Dunbridge doesn't care to hear about your domestic arrangements."

Ruth flushed. "I beg your pardon, Lady Dunbridge. I'm not

fit company today. If you'll excuse me." She stuffed her needle-
work into the tapestry bag and hurried from the room.

Gwen sighed. "You must forgive my sister, Philomena. May I
still call you Philomena now that this nasty business seems to
be at an end? I hope we can become friends."

"I consider you a friend already, Gwen."

"My sister is much tried, but she does her best."

"I'm sure she does. And she's lucky to have such a magnani-
mous brother-in-law. He recommended her husband for the
job?"

Gwen tightened her lips. "Between you and me, something
he's rued ever since. Actually it was Godfrey who found him a
place in the War Department's requisitions office. It's an important enough job, he does liaise with the Treasury people, but an
advisor he's not. I tell you this so you will not be mistaken by
his sometimes overinflated sense of himself."

So Thomas wasn't living up to Luther's expectations. A common enough state in families where one member is more successful than another. But Secretary of the Treasury, War
Department, financial crisis. She was beginning to feel just a
little at sea. How did all this impact on the investigation of Perry
Fauks's murder?

"If Thomas would only be content in being an underling. But
he sees himself as more. And always asking Luther to put his
name forward for some position or other. He's barely able to hold
his own as it is.

"My sister, on the other hand, is quite capable. She should
be the one advising the secretary. Unfortunately she's relegated
to planning social activities without enjoying the resources that
most people in her position enjoy. A man needs to be rich to
last in politics, or they pay the price—one way or another. Poor
Ruth. But to each his own."

She shook herself. "Well, he's promised to be back by Saturday's shoot. And all will be well on that front."

"Yes, of course." Phil was wondering how to get the conversation back on the topic of Washington politics, when the door opened and Godfrey Bennington strode in.

"Ah, Lady Dunbridge. Delighted to see you." He cut a look toward Gwen. "I ran into Ruth on the stairs."

"Not to worry," Gwen said. "I'll see her out of the doldrums before we arrive."

"I know you will. You are a brick." He turned to Phil. "And we'll see you and Daisy Greville tomorrow?"

Phil tilted her head. "But of course."

"Well, then, I'm off to oversee the preparations for the weekend. And now that the suspect is apprehended we might actually have a delightful few days." He bowed. "Until tomorrow, ladies."

When he was gone, Phil stood. "I think you also have family matters to see to. And I have packing to do. If all is well, I'll return home to do so."

Brinlow telephoned for a taxi and Gwen escorted Phil into the foyer.

"Oh, I meant to ask, how is Agnes holding up?"

"Quite remarkable, I must say, but she takes after me. Strong New England women." Gwen laughed deprecatingly. "You wouldn't know it to look at me."

Phil demurred. She didn't think Gwen, except for some occasional shortness of breath, was weak at all.

"She even seems excited about the weekend."

Morris's voice rose suddenly from the back hall.

"My goodness, such a bustle this morning," Gwen said.

"Sorry, Vince. I'm driving out with Harry and Newty; we'd give you a ride but there's no room."

A muted voice which must belong to Vincent Wynn-Taylor. "Don't worry, I know my place, Morris." The sound of footsteps receding down the hallway.

"Those boys. That whole crowd has always been competitive," Gwen said. "But I do feel for Vincent. He's the only one who won't inherit a fortune."

And therefore no longer a peer, nor acceptable as a suitor for Agnes.

A few minutes later, Phil climbed into the taxicab. She knew immediately it had been a mistake. As soon as the taxi turned onto Fifth Avenue, they were met by loud auto horns, bells, shouts, and neighing horses. Phil sat forward and looked past the driver into a sea of automobiles, trucks, and carriages. All brought to a standstill.

Behind them traffic had stopped, wedging them tightly between two vehicles. There was no room to budge. Phil was contemplating the efficacy of abandoning the taxi and walking home through the park, when she saw a familiar figure weaving through the vehicles toward the park. Tall, barrel-chested, wearing a brown, stylish overcoat and a felt homburg and carrying a walking cane. At first she thought he might be coming to rescue her. But he didn't slow down as he passed behind her taxi and strode up the sidewalk toward the Metropolitan Museum.

So much for leaving for the country. Perhaps he had decided to wait for traffic to clear. *And visit the museum while he waited?*

Perhaps Phil would do the same. A visit to the museum would be just as good for thinking. And if they happened to be going in the same direction . . .

"I think," she said, reaching into her purse, "that you should try to maneuver yourself out of this traffic." She handed him what she owed with extra for his time. "I believe I'll walk through the park."

She didn't wait for his response, which was bound to be acrimonious, but got out of the taxi. Waving fumes and grime from her nose, she darted between the vehicles, her eyes trained on that dapper homburg.

She wasn't completely taken by surprise when instead of going up the steps to the museum, he took the path that led into the park.

She waited at the entrance until she saw which path he took, then followed slowly behind. The park was in full glory of fall colors. Some of the trees had already shed their foliage and the ground was dotted in browns, golds, and oranges.

Godfrey wasn't strolling, not like a man marking time. He seemed to know exactly where he was going and was in a hurry to get there. But where? Ahead of them, the white Egyptian stele, known as the obelisk, rose above the trees. Beyond it, a row of trees grew around the banks of the reservoir.

Phil spent most of her walks in the south end of the park, but she had seen the obelisk on many occasions during her visits to the museum. She couldn't imagine why Godfrey was in such a hurry, unless perhaps he was meeting someone?

Her interest piqued, Phil studied the several paths and the surrounding trees. And saw two men walking briskly in the opposite direction. Neither of them looked familiar, not even in disguise, so she turned her attention back to Godfrey.

He didn't stop at the obelisk, merely slowed down and looked around him. Phil smoothly turned to look at a bush and when she surreptitiously looked back at him, he had moved on.

Damn the man. She hurried after him and reached the obelisk just in time to see him stepping into the trees by the water. She sincerely hoped she wasn't about to discover him relieving himself in the lake. That would be embarrassing to both of them.

She stepped behind the obelisk, peered out in time to see another man slip out of the underbrush.

A clandestine meeting. The temptation was just too strong to ignore.

Phil stepped off the path, and keeping out of sight of the two men as they talked, she managed to work her way through the bushes close enough to see the back of Godfrey's hat.

She could only catch a glimpse of the other man, who was shorter and slight, and wearing a black suit and no overcoat.

At first she thought he might be a bum, looking for a hand-out, until Godfrey grasped his shoulder. For a brief moment she got a look at the man's face. Dark eyes, thin cheeks, hatless, with thin pomaded hair, a little mustache. No one she'd seen before.

Surely it had to be something untoward. Or was she making too much of a coincidence? Then Godfrey reached inside his breast pocket, handed something to the man, who clapped his arm and hurried away.

Godfrey turned to retrace his steps and Phil ducked behind the tree.

What a dilemma. Godfrey was going back to the street. The man was moving quickly, passing behind the museum in a most furtive way. A quick decision needed to be made. She followed the furtive man. It had a nice ring to it, The Furtive Man.

He continued along the path behind the museum, which, as far as Phil knew, went farther into the interior of the park. Not somewhere she wanted to go unaccompanied.

She was already getting a prickly feeling up the back of her neck. She glanced behind her. No one was there. She passed beneath a bough of trees; the furtive man looked around as if he knew he was being followed, then plunged off the path and into the shrubbery.

She was certainly not going to follow him into the woods or the water. She turned to go. A man was standing on the steps at the back of the museum. Dressed in a gray tailored overcoat and felt trilby, a trim beard of indeterminate brown, he was the epitome of fashion. And she knew who he was. It was the ironic slant of his hat that gave him away.

He tilted his head in her direction, then turned and disappeared into the colonnaded entrance.

It was a challenge that she couldn't resist. She hurried after him, but of course there was no dapper gentleman waiting for her inside the gallery. Fortunately it was a free day so she wasn't held up waiting in line for a ticket.

She walked through the domed gallery, looking in archways, keeping alert for a familiar posture, a sudden movement. In one room, two ladies were bent over a display case of figurines. In another a young man sat on a bench studiously contemplating a painting.

She moved on. Stopped. Came back, the student was gone.

She moved on to the next gallery just in time to see the tail of an overcoat round the corner of the gallery door.

The chase was on and Phil felt a thrill she seldom felt these days. She hurried after him, but not too fast. She'd never catch him, not in a straightforward way. He was much too good for that. But she might trip him up yet. With the success of her encounter with the journalist outside the foundations shop, she felt confident she could find him before he disappeared again.

She stood in the hall considering her options. He'd been moving toward the Fifth Avenue exit and would most likely pass through the Greek sculptures to get there, but first he would have to pass several exhibits that, if she recalled correctly, were quite crowded with artifacts.

The rooms became more populated as she neared the exit. She walked slowly but purposefully toward the gallery to her right. Just in case he was waiting, teasing her with a glimpse. For a second all she saw was oriental tapestries. Then he stepped out of a group at the far end and strolled toward the door.

She quickened her step toward the retreating figure but as soon as he disappeared into the next room, she hurried back into the main hallway and raced toward the Greek gallery.

A quick look around told her that she'd beaten him there. He'd have to pass through in order to get to the exit. She slipped behind a life-sized marble depiction of two wrestlers. One had fallen to the ground, his arm lifted in defense. His body gave her camouflage and an extraordinary view of his . . . *Good heavens.*

She pulled her eyes from that delectable detail and peered through the legs of the standing wrestler.

Mr. X did not make an appearance. The two ladies from the gallery she'd passed walked in, arms linked and taking their time. Phil crouched down until they passed on, then she peered out from behind the statue and scanned the gallery.

Nothing. She was about to admit defeat when she felt a breeze behind her. She stood, turned around, right into his arms.

"Really, my dear, you're absolutely inspired this afternoon."

"You," she said, backing away and almost sitting on the wrestlers' plinth.

He shook his head. "Did you really think it would work twice?"

"Twice? What are you talking about?" She was asking questions, but she was really studying his face. Looking for any distinguishing characteristics that she might recognize when they met again. But it was impossible to tell what was really him and what was artful deceit.

"Your encounter with the sordid character at the ladies foundations store. You were clever, but you made an amateur's mistake."

"And what, pray tell, was that? I caught him off guard."

"You did. But you need to learn to never wield a deadly weapon if you're not willing to use it."

"I would have poked him."

"Ah, but would you have killed him?"

Phil swallowed. Surely she would never have to kill a foe or anyone else for that matter. She steeled her nerve.

"I was afraid it might be you," she said by way of explanation.

"Really, Countess. I'm hurt that you think I would be so clumsy."

"If you were there, why didn't you come to my rescue?"

"I didn't want to be *de trop*. Besides, you seemed to be well guarded."

"*My irregulars.* Do you know who the villain was?"

"I know who he worked for."

She wanted to know who, but what she asked was, "Worked? He no longer works for this employer?"

"Unfortunately his employer, as you call him, found it necessary to have him, um, dispatched."

Phil shuddered in spite of herself. "Not you?"

He laughed quietly. "Not in this instance. But don't think I'm incapable of certain, shall we say, unsavory necessities."

"So who *did* he work for and why was he following me?"

"To the first, you're better off not knowing. And for the second, we're not sure."

"We?"

"I'm not sure. But I would guess a mere intimidation technique. The poor fool couldn't see his way past—and no offense meant here—a woman and a bunch of children."

"Are you warning me off?"

"God no. I love watching you work. Your method is nothing if not creative, and charming. But following this particular lead would be as fruitful as playing at thimblerig. I need you elsewhere."

"Why are you interested in Perry Fauks's murder?"

"I'm not really except that it brings us together. Other than that, it merely coincides with other interests."

This was the longest she'd been face-to-face with him in the light and she was quickly memorizing everything she could. As if she would easily forget any of their encounters. He was taller than she by a good six inches; she forced herself not to look at his feet in an effort to see if he was wearing lifts in his shoes. She searched for telltale signs of spirit glue along the brownish-red mustaches and muttonchops, a style that had been out of style for years. She vaguely remembered her grandfather wearing them when she was still a child.

He stood smiling back at her, amused, knowing exactly what she was doing. Why was he being so reckless? Or was it arrogance, believing that she would never be able to identify him. He was infuriating.

And then another thought occurred to her.

"You aren't even following me, are you?"

An elderly couple passed by and cast disapproving looks at them. Well, perhaps they *were* standing a bit too close for museum etiquette. He took her arm and steered her to another statue, this one a nude young woman holding a water ewer over her head.

More to his liking no doubt.

"Actually no, but we do seem to be running in the same circles."

She laughed. "I feel like I'm running in circles."

He smiled. He had the most engaging smile, though she was under no false illusions that he would not be ruthless if need be. It made her blood rush. An altogether unsettling feeling.

"What am I supposed to be doing?" she demanded.

"Enjoying Manhattan with all its wonders."

She started to press him, but held back. What if they weren't working for the same people? What if she wasn't even really working for anybody? She'd never been given direct orders or any clue as to who was paying for her apartment at the Plaza.

Not him. That would be too demoralizing. Hardly better than being a lover's kept woman—without even the pleasure of the lover.

"Actually, I'm rather interested in the Countess of Warwick."

Phil was nonplussed. And heartbroken. Well, maybe not her heart, but . . .

He flicked her cheek. "Don't be jealous."

"I wouldn't bother," Phil said at her haughtiest. "She has a good twenty years on me."

He laughed and was immediately hushed by a group who had just entered.

"Make sure she gets to the house party."

"Will you be there?"

"Perhaps. Now really I must run." He kissed her hand. "And you must be more careful. That was a beginner's mistake. Take a taxi home. Adieu."

He walked out of the gallery as if he had no place better to go, and she let him. She was ready for her tea, or better still, a martini.

When Phil finally reached the Plaza, she bought a copy of the evening edition of the *Post*, "hot off the presses" from a grinning Just a Friend—making a mental note to have Preswick purchase him a warmer coat—and took the paper upstairs to read.

The news was not good. The suspect may have been apprehended, but the afternoon editions had moved on. "Stocks Continue to Plummet, the Latest Victim, Fauks Copper, Coal and Steel."

Another headline a little lower down. "Head of Fauks Copper, Coal and Steel Missing." Followed by this question. "Is he another victim of a killing spree, or was he an accessory to the deed? Was this a plot to corner the market?"

And beneath that a grainy photo with the caption, "Isaac Sheffield Missing." A grainy image of a thin-cheeked man, with dark pomaded hair and mustache. The same man Phil had seen with Godfrey Bennington not an hour before.

17

The Packard was brought round at nine-thirty sharp the next morning. Its yellow surface gleamed as bright as the sun on a clear crisp day. Not a blemish marred the polished windscreen. That would soon be remedied when they reached the open road.

Better the screen than her person, thought Phil.

She sighed with satisfaction. There was something empowering being behind the wheel of an automobile. And though in town she'd been relying on taxis rather than the Packard mostly, she was glad to be behind the wheel today.

So much better than a carriage or the railway. And quicker. The Packard could reach speeds of fifty miles an hour on the open road, as she had reason to know. And even though she'd traveled at nearly twice that in France in the Darracq of a certain captivating race car driver, she had no need or desire to try to emulate him in any way.

Besides, it was impossible to appreciate the scenery at that speed.

Today, with the top pulled up, plus the lap blankets folded on the backseat and the thermoses of coffee the hotel had packed for the drive, they should be quite cozy.

The truck had picked up her trunks and her servants' valises, but there were still lunch baskets, makeup cases, and other packages to be packed. When at last they were all strapped to the back of the Packard, Lily adjusted the scarf around Phil's hat, Preswick tucked his bowler under the seat, and they all climbed in and drove to the Webster Hotel on West Forty-Fifth Street.

Daisy was waiting in the lobby. She was dressed in a day dress of navy foulard, figured in white and trimmed in Valenciennes lace. One of the narrow-brimmed hats advertised for the coming season topped her hair and a beige woolen coat with fur collar was folded over her arm.

So much for her not having a thing to wear.

"I'll have Preswick take care of this," Phil said and she slid the coat from Daisy's arm. "We have a bit of a trip. I have to make a quick stop at the Reynolds' horse farm. We'll have lunch there. And then on to Foggy Acres. You'll be better off wearing this touring coat."

While the bellhops strapped Daisy's carrying cases onto the back of the Packard with the rest of the personal luggage, Lily and Phil dressed her in one of Phil's driving coats, which almost dragged the ground, but would suffice as long as Daisy didn't have to walk too far.

Lily handed her a pair of goggles and wrapped a wide net shawl around her hat and affixed it with a big bow beneath her chin.

She balked, however, when she realized Phil would be driving.

"You don't drive?" Phil asked. "Well, we'll have to remedy that while you're here."

"Thank you, no." Daisy pressed her lips together, dimpling her cheeks, and let Preswick help her into the passenger seat.

They took the bridge across the East River with Daisy clutching the seat with both hands. Soon enough they'd left the bustle of the city behind and were tooling down the country road to Holly Farm.

They sped along fields now fallow, the harvest long since past, leaving brown stubble where a few months before lush green grasses had grown. Cows and sheep still foraged, but it wouldn't be long before snow covered the landscape.

Phil could feel the cold on her cheeks and hoped Daisy wasn't too uncomfortable. She'd finally relaxed but still sat tall, looking every inch a countess, as the wind buffeted the tails of the scarf about her face.

Phil couldn't imagine her among the socialists, picketing and striking, and giving speeches from the back of a farm truck.

But Phil admired her dedication and determination to make the world a better place. Phil was helping in her own little way, but she had to admit she'd much rather chase criminals than stand in a picket line.

In their own way, they were both fighting for justice and a better life for all. She and Daisy might someday be the heroines of their own dime novel. Phil chuckled and shifted the Packard into a higher gear. It shot off down the road.

Holly Farm looked much different than it had when she'd visited last summer. Besides the shorn grasses and the leafless trees, the private road that led to the house and stables had been paved. She stopped the Packard at the white-framed farmhouse and was happy to see the ducks who made their home by the little pond at the front of the house running to greet them. Lily always packed breadcrumbs to feed them. They hadn't forgotten.

Though weren't they supposed to fly south for the winter? She'd have to ask.

"It's charming," Daisy said. "Does someone live here?"

"Bev and—" Phil stopped; there was no "Bev and" with Reggie dead.

"Bev uses it when she comes out to check on the training sessions," Phil said. "It's primitive but adequate. Why don't you go inside with Lily and Preswick. I just need to have a word at the stables. Lily, see to her ladyship, please."

Lily, who had just taken the picnic basket from Preswick, handed it back to him, and curtseyed.

"Yes, my lady." Then shot an anguished look to Preswick.

"I'll bring the Countess's cases up."

Daisy broke into a peal of laughter. "Is there anything more absurd than two countesses and one set of servants?" She turned a saucy look toward Phil and the twenty years between them melted away. "Though I suppose we should call *you* dowager?"

"Not if you value your life," Phil quipped back.

"Oh Lord, how I've missed having fun." Daisy turned toward the house and practically tripped away, Lily running quickly after her to open the door.

Phil pulled off her scarf, and strode up the drive to the red painted barn and training areas, where two blanketed horses were being walked in the paddock.

As she neared the barn she caught sight of an air balloon drifting above them and she paused to watch it soar and dip on the wind.

"Lady Dunbridge!"

Bobby Mullins came out of the stable, his hand raised in greeting, his unruly hair flashing red and orange in the sun. He was dressed in one of his favorite plaid suits.

"I was just checking on our new mares," he said, coming up to shake her hand. "Glad you could make it. I got news."

"You brought up more colts from Virginia?"

"No, we'll do that in the spring. Bought these two at the track. Had 'em checked over after the races. They both lost and that was the end for their owner. A deal too good to pass up."

He tilted his head, which she took to mean he wanted to talk to her out of hearing distance.

He opened a door on the side of the stable barn and led her down a hall to a small office. It smelled like stale cigar smoke, and Phil steeled herself to a few minutes in the unwholesome air.

He pulled a stack of racing forms off the extra chair, flourished a handkerchief that she hoped was clean, and slapped it at the chair's seat.

"Have a seat, your . . ."

Phil waited for him to find an appropriate ending. He never

seemed to remember the protocol and frankly she enjoyed his creativity.

"Your . . . ness."

As if the abbreviation would suffice.

It did.

"Yes?" she encouraged.

"I hear you're going up to Foggy Acres for the weekend."

"I am," Phil said, wondering how he knew that. Then again, Bobby had his own network of informants.

"There are gonna be some big cheeses—I mean some high-stakes folks there. Some of them what might be responsible for what happened to Abe Sorkin."

"Abe Sorkin? Gambling?"

"Stock market." Bobby lifted a cold cigar butt out of the ash-tray on his desk and stuck it in his mouth.

Phil braced herself for the choking smoke, but he didn't light it, just sat chewing the end for a ruminative minute. Then he took it out of his mouth and pointed it at her.

"Until yesterday Abe was the owner of those two fine mares you just saw. They showed real good but didn't win. He sold 'em to me right there at the track. I thought it was just him being pissed off and all, begging your pardon, but he was depending on those nags to save him from bankruptcy.

"They both lost and so did he. His whole fortune—pfft." His fingers splayed in the air. He stuck the cigar back in his mouth and clamped his teeth around it. "Gone. Every last dime. Lost his shirt on account of dumping everything in a short-sell scheme."

"Ah," Phil said. "Not to worry. I have no intention of invest-ing in the market at this time. But I appreciate your concern."

"Ain't your concern I'm worried about. It's your neck. Last night, ole Abe blew his brains out."

"But what does that have to do with me?"

"One of them fine folks up at Foggy Acres killed Abe Sorkin as sure as they killed that Fauks fellow."

"They shot Mr. Sorkin?"

"They cheated him."

"But I thought the crash was averted," Phil said.

"For some, but some, like Abe, took a bath. Word on the street is it ain't over yet. More people are going to bite it." He returned the cigar to the ashtray and picked a piece of tobacco off his tongue.

"Now what generally happens is either people start jumping out of windows or other people help them do it so's they won't talk."

"Talk about what?"

"Fixing the market."

"It's illegal to manipulate the stock market."

Bobby snorted. "Miz—Lady Dunbridge, this is New York, nothing is illegal if you don't get caught. But here's where it might interest you. One of Abe's boys told me he went into a scheme to buy up other companies that would give U.S. Steel a run for its money. Stupid if you ask me. Bound to fail. But then old Abe got cold feet, but when he went to get his money out, it wasn't there."

"Because of the run on the banks," Phil said.

"Not the bank. Abe had cashed out at the bank and put it all in Fauks Copper, Coal and Steel."

"And Fauks's stock is nearly worthless," Phil added.

"Not worth a hill of beans. But Abe ain't usually such a fool. When it started to sink, he went directly to the Fauks office and demanded to sell back his stock to them. Turns out they'd never heard of him or his money."

"That doesn't make sense," Phil said, trying to put this together.

"Their records showed that he'd never invested in Fauks Copper, Coal and Steel." Bobby leaned back in his chair and slapped his knee. "If that ain't a scam, I've never seen one."

"Has he no recourse?"

"Hell, Lady D, he already took it. Went home and killed himself. If Fauks or somebody was cheating people, fleecing them, some people at that house musta had knowledge of it."

"Do you know who?"

"Nope. Nothing has hit the street yet. Which means someone up top is keeping mum."

Someone at the top? Sheffield? He managed the company. Luther? He was courting Perry to become a member of the family. She suddenly wondered about the state of the Pratts' finances. Or even Godfrey. He'd tried to stop the investigation from the start.

"Just watch your back. The boys and me are here if you need us."

"Thank you, Bobby."

"It's nothing. I was Reggie's right-hand man. Gotta take care of his wife and her friend."

He walked her back to the yard.

"Damn those people." He pointed up to where a balloon—the same one or another one—was passing overhead and appeared to be losing altitude.

"They agreed not to fly over the farm. It scares the horses. And if one of these babies gets injured, they're gonna pay. Eddie, Rico!" he called. "Get those horses in the stable!"

The two jockeys ran into the paddock, rounded up the two mares, and pulled them toward the barn.

"I'm gonna have to get tough with them guys."

"Who's doing it?"

"The dang government. Some aero-naw-tical weather-predicting tests. Hell, if you want to know what the weather is, look out the window."

Weather. Fauks had been reading an article about weather balloons.

"Ask me, they're spying on us. Well, maybe not us exactly, though I know some owners who'd give their eyeteeth to snoop around our training techniques. They say they got some new kind of something that makes navigation better. They've been flying back and forth all week."

The jockeys had reached the barn, but one of the mares jerked her head, caught sight of the balloon, and pulled frantically on the rein. Several other stableboys ran out of the barn to help bring her inside.

"See what I mean? They're driving us nuts, and they won't do a thing about it. Back on Monday one of them crash-landed right in the middle of the training track. Tore up the surface. Lucky none of the nags got hurt. They gotta pay for the repairs, but damn it set us back."

"What happened to the balloon?"

"Bashed in all the equipment and a few heads. One of the pilots broke his leg. Nobody died, but if a horse had been on the track there woulda been hell to pay. If you'll pardon the expression."

"I will. That's terrible. When are they finishing the testing?"

"Hell if I know. When they all crash, I guess."

"Shall I try to find someone to intercede?" Phil asked. There should be someone in Phil's little black book of scandal that she could, as Bobby would say, "squeeze" for a favor.

"Shall I ask Godfrey Bennington? I don't know if he can help, but I know he's connected to the War Department. He might know someone."

Bobby slapped his knees and guffawed. "If you ain't something. It's his balloons."

Phil had plenty to think about on the way to Foggy Acres. It was a lovely drive with the last colors of fall holding on among the evergreen trees as they danced in a bright blue sky. It was hard to imagine a place called Foggy Acres while driving beneath the brilliant sun.

The road narrowed, rose and dipped and finally snaked beneath an overgrowth of trees. The temperature dropped considerably. And Phil was more than ready to be sitting before a warm comfortable fire with a glass of brandy in her hand.

The road forked; Phil turned to the left and began looking for the gates to Foggy Acres.

She would have driven right past it if it had been summer with the trees in full growth. As it was, two tall sculpted cedars framed an ornamented wrought-iron gate that rose a good ten feet in the air.

She stopped the auto in front of the closed bars.

The door to a stone guardhouse opened and a small man dressed in a normal sack suit came out. Phil was glad to see that he wasn't costumed in some outrageous livery parroting British servants.

He opened the gates, Phil drove through, and the gates shut behind them. "Just like a gothic horror story," Phil called over her shoulder to Preswick and Lily.

"Let us hope not," Daisy said. "If Godfrey and you have spirited me away from business for a damp weekend in a rustic country house, I may learn to drive myself."

Phil laughed. "It's an adventure." An adventure and the perfect opportunity to get to know the people who were in attendance the night of Fauks's murder.

She accelerated and soon they drove out of the tunnel of trees and into more brilliant sunshine. A formal lawn, still lush with green, stretched out before them and beyond it, a rise of land where Godfrey's mansion rose like a colossus in front of them.

"If ever there was a misnomer," Phil said. "No fog, and hardly rustic."

It was tasteful, large but not overbearing, and not monstrously overbuilt like some of the cottages she'd visited in Newport. An edifice built by someone who didn't wear his wealth on his sleeve. Or perhaps did, but just in an understated way. Someone who had no desire or need to impress. It made him much more interesting than the rank-and-file millionaires all trying to outdo the other.

It was two stories of red brick and limestone with a grand stairway that led to massive carved doors, sheltered by a rounded portico of frieze columns, and topped by a wrought-iron balcony trimmed in gilt. Large windows were aligned in symmetrical rows on both floors, promising a well-lit interior.

They drove around the curve of the drive and came to a stop in front of the main entrance. The doors opened immediately and several servants, all dressed in simple black livery, filed down the steps to open the doors to the auto and take their luggage.

They were followed by Godfrey Bennington.

Phil quickly leaned toward Daisy as they went to greet him. "I forgot to warn you. They think Lily only speaks Italian."

Daisy's eyes widened. "Why on earth?"

"Later," Phil said. Godfrey was upon them.

"Delighted, delighted," he said, and kissed Phil's hand. He turned to Daisy.

"Daisy, my dear. It's been ages," He kissed her on both cheeks, then he embraced her like a long-lost friend.

Hmm, thought Phil.

Godfrey swept them up the steps and into a large marble foyer that took Phil's breath away. Above them a massive crystal chandelier shot prisms of light over a double-curved staircase of dark wood with an ornate wrought-iron handrail. On the landing above them, a smaller chandelier echoed the light down three separate hallways.

Impressive, tasteful, and outrageously expensive. And perhaps just a bit of humor? A suit of medieval armor stood between the two staircases flanked by two tall plinths, each holding models of aeroplanes introduced by the Wright brothers a few years before.

A genial-looking woman, a little past middle age, dressed in a buttoned dress of gabardine, appeared from a doorway to the left.

"Ah," Godfrey said. "I'll leave you ladies in the good hands of my housekeeper, Mrs. Nicholson. She will see that you have everything you need."

"This way, please," Mrs. Nicholson said, and began to climb the stairs.

"Drinks at six," Godfrey called from below them. "I've invited a few people."

Phil raised an eyebrow. She had no doubt that Godfrey would be the consummate host this weekend. And would keep them all busy and their minds away from the murder that had driven them here. She just hoped she would have a few quiet moments to find out why he met with Isaac Sheffield in the park, where Mr. Sheffield was now, and the reason he continued to keep him hidden.

Mrs. Nicholson led them up the stairs and to the left. "This is our west wing; you should be quite comfortable. There are two rooms with adjoining parlor and also rooms for your staff."

She stopped at a door on her right. "Lady Warwick, Mr. Bennington has put you in the Yellow Room." She opened the door and they all stepped inside. The room was wallpapered in a delicate gold. A canopied four-poster bed sat prominently against one wall and French doors opened onto what looked like a balcony.

Daisy laughed delightedly. "Charming."

"I'll send Margaret up to help you get settled."

"Thank you," Daisy said.

"Through here is your shared parlor."

They followed Mrs. Nicholson into a bright sitting room, with a row of French doors that led to a balcony.

"And Lady Dunbridge . . ." the housekeeper paused while she opened a connecting door. "Mr. Bennington has put you in the Lilac Room."

"It's lovely," Phil said. The bed was Louis Quinze style with an elaborate gilt headboard with pale mauve panels draped behind it, against a patterned wallpaper of lilacs and green leaves. She was pleased to see that the room also opened onto a balcony.

She did love a room with a balcony. She would have to warn Lily that the Countess of Warwick, if Phil had read Godfrey's welcome, might be receiving an unannounced nocturnal visitor.

It wouldn't do for Lily to skewer their host thinking he was an intruder.

As for herself . . . who knew who would be among the guests?

18

After Mrs. Nicholson had left, Phil crossed the room, opened the French doors, and stepped onto the balcony, which she realized conveniently ran the length of the back of Godfrey's mansion. Below her was a wide brick patio with two sets of steps that led down to a wide green lawn surrounded by formal gardens planted for fall in asters and mums and colorful ornamental greens.

Beyond the gardens were woods, and in the distance, wide glimpses of sparkling water, which had to be Long Island Sound. Phil couldn't imagine why Godfrey had chosen to call this delightful hideaway Foggy Acres.

The sound of laughter caught her attention and she looked over the balustrade to see a badminton game was in progress on the wide still-green lawn. Effie and Maud Jeffrey were testing their skills against Morris and Harry Cleeves. Agnes and Vincent Wynn-Taylor stood off to the side, waiting their turn.

The girls wore soft woolen jackets but the men had stripped to their shirtsleeves in a show of defiance to the weather, except for Vincent, dressed in a business suit, perhaps in deference to his position as secretary.

Maud or perhaps it was Effie stretched up to return the shuttlecock Harry had just served, but a sudden gust of wind shot it beyond her reach and out of bounds. Vincent jumped agilely and snatched it out of the air.

Agnes clapped and laughed and Harry trotted over to clap him on the back and retrieve the shuttlecock.

They all seemed in high spirits. No one, not even Agnes, seemed to miss the presence of Perry Fauks.

Especially not Agnes, Phil thought. A little too happy for someone whose fiancé had just been murdered, but not entirely a surprise. It had been apparent in her talk with Detective Sergeant Atkins that Agnes had been disgusted by Perry's touch, though duty may have compelled the girl to accept his proposal when he offered. Phil could relate. No wonder Agnes was relieved at his death.

She was smiling and laughing as Vincent came back to stand by her side, closer than they had been standing a minute before.

There was no doubt of the attraction between them. And Phil knew it was not unusual for a girl to fall for a poor young man who couldn't compete with the attractive suitor her ambitious parents had planned for her.

She would have to delve further into that relationship.

Then there was Maud. Agnes may not have wanted the man, but Maud Jeffrey did. And Phil wouldn't make the mistake of dismissing them as mere children.

Phil had been younger than either of them when her parents sold her off to the derelict Lord Dunbridge. There had been more than a few times she'd wished him dead. She hadn't acted on it, of course, but she might have found someone who would, one of her many liaisons, perhaps.

Phil shivered and went back inside. She wouldn't mark Agnes and Maud off her suspect list just yet.

She changed out of her driving clothes and into one of her favorite Poiret tea gowns, an aquamarine and blue flowing silk chiffon, with a passementerie of rose and gold beading around the high waist, and joined Daisy in the private sitting room that separated their bedrooms.

Here, like her own guest boudoir, every detail spoke of attention to what would please a lady, with comfortable chaises and padded chairs and several lovely oil paintings on the wall that Phil was almost certain were originals.

Daisy was draped along a pink velvet chaise with the air of a nymph from an Impressionist painting. "Lord," she said when she caught sight of Phil. "You look divine. Poiret, isn't it? I'm sure he's going to be all the thing in a season or two."

She sighed. "Now that we're here, I wish I had brought a wardrobe more appropriate to the drawing room than the picket line."

Phil perused the tray of sandwiches and fresh fruit before sitting on a matching chaise on the opposite side of the tea table.

It was a perfect arrangement where confidences could be exchanged and gossip could flourish in private. And since Daisy and Phil had more to gossip about than most women, it was a perfect setting for their tête-à-tête.

However, they would have to change for dinner soon so Phil had better get on with her interrogations, starting with the subject of Daisy's relationship with Godfrey. But before she could begin Daisy asked, "Now what's all this about Lily speaking Italian?"

Phil gave her a quick explanation of her not-so-brilliant idea. "I thought it would loosen tongues if they thought she couldn't understand what they were saying."

"Did it?"

"No. Mainly it's just an encumbrance. But no matter. You'll just have to play along. At the moment, I'm more interested in hearing about you and Godfrey."

Phil considered a bowl of fresh strawberries. "He really didn't know you were in town?"

"I didn't tell anyone but my lawyer I was coming. I'm desperate to get things done and in a hurry. I didn't want to have my time eaten up by society."

"And yet here you are."

"Because neither you nor Godfrey would take no for an answer."

Nor would the enigmatic Mr. X. It was so infuriating. Couldn't he at least have given her a hint as to what she was supposed to find out? And she felt a bit of a traitor to Daisy. Unless she was somehow involved in the murder, which seemed preposterous. How could a meeting to sell mines involve her in a murder when she'd just arrived?

"Tell me about the two of you," Phil said.

Daisy smiled reminiscently. "It was a whirlwind affaire de coeur, and many years ago. Really he was quite amazing." She looked at Phil under her lashes and over the tea table. "I expect he still is.

"Brookie and Godfrey were friends. We were young, at least younger. But you know how quickly those kind of things run their course and burn out; thrown together at a party, a flirtation, a dalliance, one thing leads to another. Brookie went off to Africa for several weeks, Godfrey was staying at the Brown Hotel."

She smiled a sad, rueful smile. "I was quite smitten, we couldn't get enough of each other, then he went back to the States. Brookie came home. And life went on. Godfrey got frightfully rich and, well, Brookie, you know how he is with money."

Alas, Phil did.

"Everything Godfrey touched, like Midas, turned to gold. Every scheme poor Brookie tried seem to die on the vine. Take these Mexican mines. We haven't seen a penny, though he did get some good butterflies out of it."

"He still collects butterflies?"

"Yes, a barbaric hobby. Poor beautiful creatures." Daisy shuddered. "But what about you, Phil? No affaires de coeur or any other kind since coming to America?"

"Alas, no. But it's only been six months or so, and I've been busy establishing myself."

"But it must be so expensive."

Phil smiled, not at all disarmed by Daisy's wide-eyed innocent reaction. She was a master at eliciting information. "True, but at least I'm no longer tied to a philandering spendthrift of a husband who never let me have a dime. I make do."

"Well, I do like Brookie, and we rub along well enough by living our separate lives. If women didn't have to cede all their possessions upon marriage . . ." She stopped, pursed her lips, an expression that couldn't contain her mischief. "We wouldn't be able to blame our losses on our husbands."

They both laughed.

"Is it really as bad as that?" Phil asked.

"Worse. I had to close my school for boys; other of my projects are tottering on the brink."

"And selling your mines to Perry Fauks was going to remedy that?"

"It could have. That and reinvesting in his mergers."

And if she had she might be worse than broke today. And if that was true . . . Phil had to remind herself Daisy hadn't arrived until after Perry's death.

"Daisy, when did you arrive in New York?"

"Last Saturday, for all the good it did me."

Saturday. The day of the Pratts' ball. Hours before Perry's murder. Phil shook herself—she no more thought Daisy killed Perry than she had, but could her arrival have set things in motion? She didn't see how.

"I'd also planned to speak with some prominent socialists, one in particular who runs a socialist newspaper in Philadelphia. I've been wanting to start a socialist newspaper if I could just raise the funds. I think I could reach more people that way. Well, it's academic now."

"Daisy, I wouldn't despair. Bobby says that it is a bad time to invest in the stock market."

"Bobby? That odd ex-boxer at the farm?"

"Yes. He tends to have the latest *on-dit* in the criminal and quasi-legal world."

"And Mr. Fauks was doing something illegal? Phil?"

"I have no idea, but evidently there are a lot of shady dealings with stocks and bonds, something I'm not really versed in."

Could it be that? A falling-out among thieves? But who were the thieves? "I just know that some investors have lost everything. Maybe you should consider asking Godfrey for advice."

"I would never sully our friendship by asking for money."

"That's not what I meant. I'm sure he is more able to put you in contact with a better advisor than Perry Fauks. From everything people have said, Fauks was an immature young man being groomed to take over the family business but not allowed much say in the day-to-day operations.

"If they gave him an investment to work on, it would hardly be one to make or lose a great fortune."

"Lord, now what am I to do? I did call the office but no one there seemed to know of any investment that Perry worked on. In fact, they seemed very surprised and said that Perry was not in charge of investments and offered to put me in touch with their manager, Mr. Sheffield."

"Whose whereabouts are unknown," Phil said. Except by Godfrey Bennington. And perhaps even he didn't know where Sheffield was at this moment.

"Do you think he's involved in Mr. Fauks's death?"

"Sheffield? I don't know, but I believe the police want to question him." And Phil certainly did.

Daisy slumped back on the chaise. "He was my last hope. I might as well go home."

"What about the speeches you planned?"

"I was hoping to present some talks to prominent socialist groups, but not one of them wanted to talk to me. It's so lowering—not even the socialists like me."

"Don't despair, Daisy. You'll figure something out. Women always do." *Or perish,* Phil thought but didn't share that with Daisy. "Actually, that's not such a bad idea. Why don't you do a lecture tour in the States?"

"You think people want to hear an English countess talking about socialism?" Daisy asked, brightening.

"No, my dear, I don't. But they'll pay good money to hear the latest society gossip. As Daisy Greville you wouldn't have much clout, but as the Countess of Warwick . . . I bet they'd flock to the lecture halls. You could probably fill Carnegie Hall."

"Take money for gossip? It seems so sordid."

Phil burst out laughing. "Why not? You'll be fulfilling a need; what you do with that money is up to you."

"Hmmm. I'll give it some thought. But enough about my problems. What about you? I want to hear everything you've been up to since you arrived." Daisy poured herself another cup of tea. "Everything."

Phil told her about spending the summer in Newport. "They've transported entire French châteaux, Italian villas, English country seats and plunked them down at the sea shore."

The sailing.

"Floating palaces to rival those of Europe. And the scandal that goes with them."

The parties.

"Mamie Fish is the most eccentric character. She gives outrageous dinner parties at her Newport mansion Crossways. Invites everyone and then insults them all evening. She's one of the most popular hostesses in town.

"Mrs. Alfred Vanderbilt, on the other hand, very high in the instep. She gave an alfresco luncheon at Oakland Farm. Very rustic. By far the most attended of the season.

"It was fun but not exciting. Everyone complained that it was a lackluster season because everyone was feeling the pinch of the stock market crisis. And that was before all this banking nonsense even happened."

Phil rattled on, giving just enough scandalous tidbits to keep Daisy from asking any more questions about the murder investigation.

"Oh, how I envy you your youth and energy," Daisy said, looking over the sandwiches.

Phil laughed. "You're in your prime."

"I have a good twenty years on you, my dear. And recently I've been feeling each of them more than the one before."

Phil could think of nothing to say. She had no intention of being broke and at the mercy of others in twenty years. Which meant she'd better start earning her keep now.

Lily appeared in the doorway. "My—" She stopped mid-curtsey. "*Signora. E ora di vestirsi per cena.*" She finished the curtsey.

Daisy trilled a laugh. "Famous. *Buon pomeriggio,* Lily."

Lily bobbed another curtsey and cut a look toward her mistress.

Phil stood. "Goodness, is it that late? Shall we meet back here and go downstairs together?"

"But of course," Daisy said. "We will be doubly impressive that way. Godfrey has a wonderful sense of humor. He'll love it. I'm so glad you talked me into coming. *Grazie, mia cara amica.*"

So down they went, Countess of Dunbridge and Countess of Warwick, Phil in a gown of iridescent teal with an over jacket of fine soutache embroidery, and Daisy in a crenellated gold crepe, with taffeta florets and wide-ribboned waist. Pausing at the top of the wide stairs until Godfrey, who was welcoming three new arrivals, turned and saw them.

The look on his face, even though Phil knew most of it was meant for Daisy, was very gratifying.

They took their time coming down the stairs, arm in arm, careful not to step on each other's hems, a feat learned from many years of deportment lessons.

"Ah, you both look beautiful beyond compare." Godfrey bowed seriously then turned to his guests.

"May I introduce Ambassador and Mrs. Whitelaw Reid."

"A pleasure." Phil nodded and shook hands.

"I've had the pleasure of meeting the ambassador and his wife," said Daisy. "How do you do?"

The ambassador smiled. His wife did too, a bit tightly, Phil thought.

"And this is my neighbor Maximillian Rosarian."

Maximillian bowed, managing to look attentive and charming at the same time without offending either one of the countesses by not taking either of their hands. "An honor to meet you both. And please, just Max. Imagine burdening an infant with such a cumbersome name."

Perhaps, thought Phil. She smiled and tried to take in every detail of this charming gentleman's presence. He was, as some female novelists might write, devilishly handsome. Dark chestnut hair, lively brown eyes, tall enough to be a good dance partner, and . . . She didn't know him.

No flicker of recognition. A charming twinkle in his eye, but not the twinkle she was looking for. Surely she would be able to recognize her elusive . . . dare she call him colleague—no matter what his disguise. And yet she didn't.

Godfrey was the perfect host, congenial to all, but an entity unto himself. Assured of his position in the world and powerful enough to keep it. Then Phil thought of him in furtive conversation with Isaac Sheffield in the park and wondered just how far that power extended.

He gestured them through an arch into the parlor. As Phil turned to go, she managed to lean close enough to Max to smell the faint residual hint of his pipe tobacco. Not the one Mr. X smoked.

But this could also be a ruse to deceive her as he had done by giving his cigarette to one of the newsies. But why?

Wouldn't it be better to work together sharing information? She didn't even know what information she was after. Was she here merely to support Gwen as she'd said, to make certain that Daisy attended, or to catch a killer or more?

And then it occurred to her that this subterfuge and unwillingness to share might be a part of her training.

But really, how could you enjoy yourself if you were constantly on the lookout for evidence that might or might not be clues, following trails that might lead nowhere.

She had to admit that this was more nerve-racking than dealing with the straightforward John Atkins. It was gratifying to know that even though they locked horns on occasion—actually on *most* occasions—she always knew where he stood. It was secure. *Gratifying,* but not as titillating as always being off balance with her elusive Mr. X.

Gwen glided toward them, looking fully rested and resplendent in a mauve and pearl gown of tiered Belgian lace.

The young people—how that phrase disconcerted her—were gathered near the windows where the reflections of lanterns in the garden created fireflies of color in the night.

It was a huge room with high ceilings and outfitted in English antiques and oriental carpets. Tapestries hung on the walls and life-sized statues were situated among the furnishings like extra guests.

A hand-painted screen covered the large marble fireplace, unneeded because of the central heating system. A momentary chill skittered across Phil's arms as the memory of freezing at dinner in Dunbridge Castle reared its head. She quickly pushed it aside.

Ah, the luxury of modern life. She would never go back.

They were immediately served champagne and Godfrey left them to welcome more guests.

Phil made small talk with Ambassador Reid and his wife, all the while keeping one eye on Maximillian Rosarian. After the briefest of attentions, he had moved to the far side of the room to say hello to Agnes and the others and Phil was reminded of the night she'd first seen the elusive mystery man. He'd kept his distance that night, too.

More guests arrived and more introductions were made. Ruth came downstairs on the arm of her husband, Thomas, back a day early.

"Ruth must be happy to have Mr. Jeffrey back in time for dinner," Phil said to Gwen.

"Actually, Philomena, I don't think I've seen Ruth happy since she married Thomas. Hopefully something good will come of this. She's hoping that Thomas will be appointed as attaché to the ambassador."

"Indeed," Phil said.

Gwen pursed her lips. "Ah, here is Colonel Baiole." Gwen introduced Phil to a spritely-looking older gentleman, with a shock of white hair that refused to be tamed by pomade and a full white mustache that curled at the ends.

He bowed and held out a palsied hand, cool and bony. It reminded Phil of long-ago visits with her grandfather, a dim memory that nonetheless seemed very real. And just a little sad.

Then she looked more closely as he bent over to kiss her fingers. Could he possibly be Mr. X? She couldn't keep calling him Mr. X—Aloysius? Lochinvar? He was a master of disguise. It was possible. Actors changed their looks and personas from one role to the other. Colonel Baiole was just the kind of character he would enjoy.

The conversation was lively and soon the room was filled with the crème de la crème of Long Island society. As quickly as glasses were emptied, a waiter appeared to take them away, and another appeared just as quickly with fresh ones.

Phil soon lost count. She took a new glass from the waiter who had appeared at her elbow. While she sipped, she looked for the whereabouts of Max Rosarian. Of course, she couldn't see him, hidden away, perhaps intentionally, by the other guests. And when they sat down at dinner, she and Daisy were placed on either side of Godfrey, and Gwen, who was acting as hostess, had Max and the ambassador at the opposite end of the table.

The dinner was not only delicious but well orchestrated so that the stock market, the banking crisis, and the murder were meticulously avoided. Gossip abounded but nothing of import as far as Phil could tell.

But after dinner, when Agnes and her cousins and friends had removed to the card room, and the men had joined the ladies in the parlor, they just could not resist speculating about the morrow's shoot.

But it was talk of the balloon ascension that roused Phil's interest. Godfrey was in his element. A side that she hadn't expected.

"You must forgive me," Godfrey said in a quiet moment and finding himself beside Phil. "Air travel is the future. And whoever masters the skies will master the world."

"Goodness," Phil exclaimed. "Do you want to master the world?"

He smiled, an expression rife with more than one meaning. "Perhaps, just my little corner of it."

She nodded.

"Fog's set in," said Luther, looking out the window and drawing everyone's attention to the clouds of lamb's wool settling over the lawn. It was decided that those who were driving should be leaving for home and they all assembled in the foyer to say good night.

"Godfrey, if it doesn't clear off by morning," said Max, "you'd better come up to my place for your birds."

"I thought you were leaving tomorrow for London?" Ambassador Reid said.

"Actually I'm leaving tonight for the city docks, but I'll alert my groundsman to set up for you. I've seen quite a few coveys, but I haven't had time to go out even once and the season is almost done. I'll be glad to thin out the flocks, so help yourself."

"When do you plan to return?" Phil asked.

"Soon, I hope. Unfortunately I'll miss Godfrey's balloon ascension. And hopefully, opening night at the opera."

"Oh, Max," Gwen said.

He laughed. "Philistine that I am. But if all goes well, I'll see you before Christmas."

He turned to Phil. "You've had such a crush around you all evening, Lady Dunbridge, I'm afraid poor man that I am, I couldn't have the pleasure of getting to know you better."

He bowed over Phil's hand. "We will have to wait to further what I hope will be a better acquaintance until I return."

Phil tilted her head slightly in acknowledgment. If this was Mr. X he was laying it on a bit too thick.

Nonetheless, she'd leave a light on in her bedroom tonight. If he really was leaving, there might be important intelligence she needed to know.

"Max!" Thomas Jeffrey was hurrying down the hall from the back of the house. Phil had noticed that he'd not returned with the men after dinner, but had forgotten all about him. He'd been steadily emptying his champagne glass all evening and if Phil had wondered about his absence, which she hadn't, she would have supposed he was passed out on a couch somewhere out of sight.

Max tilted his head. "Yes?"

"Can I catch a ride into town with you?"

"Thomas, no." Ruth rushed up to stand beside him. "The ambassador."

"Business, my dear. So sorry. But I've just been called back to Washington."

Phil saw Godfrey and Luther exchange looks.

"But of course," Max said, frowning a little. "If you're ready to leave now."

"Just let me get my coat."

"Thanks for a delightful evening, Godfrey."

"Glad you could attend. I'll walk you out." The two men left the room.

"Well," said Daisy. "I wonder what that was about."

Thomas ran out from the cloakroom, pushing his arms into his coat sleeves as he hurried toward the front door. As he passed Phil, he reached into his coat pocket and pulled out his gloves, dislodging a piece of paper that drifted to the floor. Phil scooped it up meaning to call after him, then changed her mind.

It had a familiar feel. A quick glance showed her what she already suspected.

Thomas Jeffrey may have been called back to town, but Phil suspected that it wasn't to Washington, and that whatever his business was, it was with the stock market and not the government.

She folded the piece of ticker tape he'd dropped and slipped it into the neckline of her jacket.

Godfrey returned, rubbing his hands. "Who's for a brandy?" He offered his arm to Daisy. The others followed.

So that was that. The guests were gone and she hadn't had a moment with Mr. X. Hadn't even figured out which one he was. Maximillian Rosarian? Could Mr. X be an ordinary citizen like Sir Percy Blakeney from Baroness Orczy's delightful novel? For all she knew he could be Colonel Baiole. More than once during the evening she'd been tempted to snatch the mustache off the illustrious gentleman's upper lip.

Of course she couldn't take the chance.

The girls went up to bed; Morris and his friends went off to the pool room, except for Vincent, who took himself to bed. He wouldn't be joining the men in the morning because he insisted he had work to do.

"Not to worry," Luther assured the others. "It will burn off by the morning, though we may have a few lingering clouds."

"I don't suppose any of you ladies will be joining us?" Godfrey asked.

None of them would, including Phil, who could shoot tolerably well. She didn't enjoy the activity, not so much because of maidenly squeamishness, but because Lord Dunbridge had enjoyed it too well.

"Foggy Acres has lovely grounds. You must take in the ponds in the gardens, and if you're up for an excursion and the weather permits, we'll all go down to the beach for a picnic.

"Feel free to amuse yourself, but I must warn you the fog does roll in during the evenings just as it did tonight. And sometimes during the day when the weather inversion is like it was today.

You don't want to get too far from the house when it does. A veritable pea soup.

"Gwen, please remind the girls not to go past the brick walls into the woods. It's easy to lose your way once the fog sets in. Our groundskeeper lost his young son when he wandered away from his cottage and fell into the lake. Horrible business. I should probably put a fence around it, but it is so lovely I hate to spoil it.

"And there are plenty of other places to explore without having to send out a rescue party to find you."

He smiled genially as to take the edge off his words. But it merely served to make the admonition that much stronger.

Didn't he know that kind of warning just made one want to see things for themselves? It certainly had that effect on Phil. At the back of her mind she wondered if he was worried about their safety or if there was something beyond the wall he didn't want them to see.

It wasn't until much later, after Phil had changed, not into her nightgown, but into an orange and black figured kimono of Chinese silk. After she'd sent Lily to bed with the orders not to disturb her until morning. After she'd turned out the lights and stretched out on her bed to read Sir Edward Henry's *Classification of Fingerprints*. After she'd closed her book and fluffed her pillow and was about to turn off the reading lamp, that she heard the latch click on the French doors.

The door opened slowly, bringing a gust of cold air. A figure dressed completely in black slipped through the narrow opening.

She wasn't afraid. She had Lily's stiletto under her pillow.

She held still, peering into the shadows to catch her first glimpse of him. But he lingered in the dark.

She knew it was him. Her pulse raced a little, but not so much so that she lost her head. She slipped her hand beneath the pillow, slid the stiletto close to the edge, and sat up.

"Don't you ever make a proper entrance?" she asked.

"Only when the lights are on," he said from the dark.

"But the lamp is—"

The lamp went out.

19

Phil didn't move. She felt the bed dip as he sat down. He had crossed the room like a panther—well, at least like a cat. Any self-respecting lover would have at least tripped or banged his shin on the several things she'd spread about as booby traps to catch him off guard.

A finger touched her cheek, traced a line to her mouth, across her bottom lip where it curved and he gently grasped her chin. "I'm a bit jealous."

His voice was barely above a whisper, not low, not light, but rich and smooth and practiced and she wondered if it was really his, or one of the accents he did so well. The other times they'd met alone, he'd spoken in an American accent. She was pretty sure that it was not assumed.

"Why?" she asked, finding her voice.

"I saw you making eyes at Maximillian Rosarian all night."

"That wasn't you?" That explained why Max had seemed so remote. He was actually Maximillian Rosarian. Her eyes were becoming accustomed to the dark and she could make out his silhouette, feel the heat of him, and smell the faint aroma of the recognizable tobacco.

"That oily charmer? Really, my dear." He shifted position, slid his hand beneath her head.

He leaned closer. So close she could feel his breath on the open décolleté of her kimono. She leaned into him, his hand slid behind her—then he moved away.

"Expecting to use this?" he asked.

She saw the glint of the stiletto he held before her eyes.

"I wasn't sure what to expect."

He chuckled quietly.

She didn't see what was so funny. "I thought he was handsome. Were you the colonel?"

"No."

Thank goodness she hadn't tried to rip off the old man's mustache.

He pushed her down to the pillow, stretched out beside her, propping his body upright on his elbow.

"But it's nice to know you were looking for me." His free hand roamed along the edge of her kimono.

If she had been a young innocent, she would have blushed, trembled, demurred. But being a dowager, she let him roam. She had time, and evidently so did he.

"Who were you?"

"You made a very understandable mistake. You were looking for me among the guests, among the dashing young men."

"Uh-huh, or the decrepit old geezers."

"Touché, but wrong again."

"Then who?"

He drew closer and nuzzled her neck. He was clean-shaven, almost as if he already knew she couldn't abide hairy kisses. "Did you enjoy Godfrey's champagne? I made sure your glass was filled all evening."

She pulled away. "You were one of the waitstaff?"

"A man of many talents." He went back to her neck. "I really shouldn't tell you these things, but you're such a quick study, you're almost too good. Too soon."

His hand moved inside her kimono and she had to stifle a sigh. It had been a while since her last lover . . . she batted his hand away and sat up. "What do you mean too soon? Too soon for what?"

"You are dealing with powerful men, my dear. Ruthless businessmen. There was a reason Perry didn't run the trust. He was much too naïve and reckless and arrogant, as young men tend to be."

"Says you from the grand heights of old age?" He couldn't be too old, not with that body, that agility.

"Not too old, as I will soon demonstrate. Fauks's murder is one of many small parts in a bigger mare's nest."

"Are you saying he was murdered because he knew too much?"

"Perhaps, perhaps not; murder except at the lowest level is rarely what it seems."

"And what is the lowest level?"

"Passion," he said, and fit his actions to the word.

Phil awoke to a scratching sound.

"My lady. My lady?"

My lady? Phil sat up. "Lily? What's amiss?"

"Nothing . . . my lady."

More awake now, Phil said, "One moment!" She turned to find an empty bed. But what had she expected? And how would she explain it if he hadn't gone?

"Come."

The door to the dressing room opened a crack. Lily peered into the room, looked around, then stepped all the way inside.

"Is he gone?"

"Who?"

"Him."

How stupid. She had completely forgotten to ask his name. "Yes." Alas. It was a night she wouldn't soon forget and would hopefully soon be repeating. But business before pleasure.

"What time is it?"

"Past ten."

"Dear me. Coffee, please."

Lily curtseyed and went out.

"My lady" *and* a curtsey first thing in the morning? Either Preswick's lessons were finally seeping in or something was afoot.

Phil slid her hand beneath the covers to the empty space beside her. Cold. Gone for a while, before dawn most likely, just like Romeo. She couldn't help but chuckle at that comparison. *More like Oberon than the hapless young Montague.*

Phil stretched, relishing in the memory of a few high points of the night, then sat up abruptly as one particular subject sprang to the front of her mind.

Where was Lily's stiletto?

A frantic search among the bedclothes found it beneath her pillow, just where he'd found it. She leaned over to place it on the bedside table and noticed the small black smear on the pillow.

She ran her finger along the spot. Dye. He dyed his hair and black would be hard to remove. Today she would pay attention to any staff members with dark hair, though in the back of her mind she knew that would be fruitless. He wouldn't be so obvious. He was probably miles away by now.

Phil slid out of bed and picked her kimono from the floor where it had fallen rather early in the night's encounter. She checked the French doors. All were completely closed. A neat lover, she noted. Outside the fog had burned off just as Luther said it would. She wondered if the men would stay out all morning or retreat into the warmth of the house and their brandy and cigars.

Lily returned with coffee and toast.

Phil let out a squeak. "That was fast."

"Mr. Preswick brought up the tray for me."

"Why?"

"He didn't know if you would be requiring one cup or two."

Phil groaned. "I suppose he's still waiting outside?"

"Yes, my lady. He said he would stay to make certain you had no immediate need for his services."

Like engaging her nocturnal visitor in fisticuffs over her honor, such that it was. Or pistols at dawn? "You sound just like him," Phil said, picking up her cup. "I suppose you might as well tell him to come in."

Lily's eyes only rounded a tiny bit, before she curtseyed and hurried to the door.

As Phil waited, she couldn't help but smile with affection for her loyal retainer, even as a shiver of contrition passed through her. She had no illusions as to how much Preswick knew about her life away from the earl. But this was the first time she'd indulged in her "vagaries," as her father called them, under the same roof as her faithful butler. She wasn't at all certain what his reaction would be. Though a good butler would pretend to know nothing. And Preswick was nothing if not the consummate butler.

The door opened and Preswick, looking even more somber and nonjudgmental than usual in an immaculate black suit, compliments of Godfrey's laundress, stepped in. Lily stood behind him, peering around his elbow.

Phil swallowed. "Well, Preswick. Am I to have a scold this morning?"

"I wouldn't presume, my lady."

"But you brought up my coffee yourself."

"I took the liberty of anticipating that it would be welcome."

"And you were correct." She cut to the chase. "How did you know to expect a visit from our elusive Mr. X last night?"

"I deduced that with the party and the extra staff hired for the occasion, it would be a perfect situation for him to insinuate himself into the company."

"And again you were correct." Phil had anticipated—dare she say hoped for—the same.

She put down her cup. "Bennington hired extra staff?"

"Yes, my lady." Preswick refilled her cup and handed it back to her.

"I see. I had expected him to be among the guests, but he

said he was one of the waitstaff. I should have paid more attention but I was too busy suspecting the guests."

"Only natural, my lady, but I did offer my services to Mr. Tillis
to coordinate the downstairs service with the one above. I was
able to observe his instructions to the hired staff, and I must say
they were impeccably trained."

"None of them seemed even slightly out of place?"

"No, my lady. In fact, they worked with almost military pre-
cision. Either Mr. X is a military man himself or he's very good
at what he does."

Indeed he was. She'd had ample opportunity to experience
that the night before.

"If that is all, my lady. I will try to ascertain more about the
temporary staff."

"Excellent. Though I don't think we need worry overmuch
about him making another appearance. At least not in that guise.
And Preswick . . ."

"Yes, my lady."

"He said we were dealing with ruthless men, and that we
should be careful. That goes for you and Lily also."

"Yes, my lady." He strode quietly out the door.

Phil turned to Lily, who was standing well out of the way.
"Were you expecting a row?" Phil asked, more than a little relieved herself to have escaped Preswick's real opinion.

"No, my lady."

"Then stop calling me 'my lady.' There are some things you
must learn to accept about the way we live."

"I like it very much, my—madam."

"Excellent."

"Only Mr. Preswick sometimes worries about—"

"My reputation?"

"Your safety."

"Ah. But there is no need to worry. The three of us will do
famously."

Lily only glanced down to where she had safely restored the stiletto to her ankle strap. "Yes, madam."

"I think I shall wear the russet walking dress this morning," Phil said, reaching for her cup.

"The one with the split skirt? You're going out?"

"One never knows. I may take it into my head to explore the gardens."

"Yes, my lady."

"You don't approve?" Phil asked, but Lily had already quitted the room.

Phil sat down at the dressing table, but her mind was not on her toilette. It was on the last romantic murmurings of her mysterious lover. "Don't go to the shoot tomorrow, though I'm certain you can hold your own against the pigeons."

"I don't really care about the shoot at the moment," she'd murmured back.

"Nor do I. But stay with the women . . . where you can do the most good."

Now she wondered what he'd meant. Because he'd said no more and she wouldn't have remembered if he had.

Where she could do the most good. Not just a ploy to keep her away from the shoot because he thought it was too dangerous for her? He would never insult her by trying to protect her.

He needed her at the country house. And so did Atkins, though neither would ever actually admit it. So she would stay in and find out what she could. Besides, how much information could you overhear with the air constantly reverberating with gunshots?

"What do you find so amusing, if I may ask?" Lily said, hanging up the walking dress.

"You most certainly can. I was just thinking how men expect women to solve their problems without ever really telling us what the problem is."

Lily frowned as she began unbraiding Phil's hair.

"Perhaps because they don't really know what the problem is themselves."

"Now that is a thought worth pondering."

"Yes, madam." Lily coiled Phil's hair to the top of her head, while Phil sipped her coffee. It was hot and strong, just what she needed.

"Did the Jeffrey twins bring their own maid?"

"Yes. Two of them."

That was interesting—each had their own maid as well as Ruth? An expensive practice, and if what Gwen said about living beyond their means was true—and why would Gwen lie about that—certainly that was an expense that could be cut. But so much of success—and failure—was about keeping up appearances.

"Are the maids friendly?"

Lily paused, the hairpin she was holding aimed directly at Phil's scalp. It slid neatly into place.

"You mean did I 'pump' them for information?"

"What an imaginative turn of phrase. I don't suppose you learned it from Preswick."

"No, madam. At the stables."

Phil fought with a smile. "I think it's very colorful, just please don't say it in front of Preswick."

Lily grinned. "Yes, madam."

"But did you? Pump them?"

"Oh yes, though it was a little difficult with me speaking only Italian."

"Oh yes, I keep forgetting."

"Fortunately, I can listen in all languages."

Phil grinned. "Clever girl."

"They are always complaining about the twins. How demanding they are, always competing to look best. They are very spoiled." She took another hairpin. "And Miss Maud is no better than she should be."

"Ah." Phil waited for the hairpin to find its place. "A phrase you picked up from the scullery maids, no doubt. Anything in particular?"

"That's just the problem. She's not particular."

"Oh dear." Phil took a bite of toast and stood while Lily helped her into the walking skirt and matching jacket. She would have worn it to the shoot if she'd been inclined to go. The soutache braid of the jacket lent it a somewhat military air.

"Go downstairs and insinuate yourself to the staff. Then we'll meet after lunch with Preswick and plan a course of action."

With the men gone and Gwen and Ruth breakfasting in their rooms, Phil and Daisy decided to do the same. They met in their connecting sitting room.

"I managed to talk with Godfrey about my investments last night," Daisy said over a plate of ham and eggs.

"And?"

"He was surprised that Mr. Fauks would be interested in buying my mines, since evidently Fauks had no power to buy or to sell anything in the company. And he told me not to sell or invest in anything until I talked to him."

"And are you going to talk to him?"

"I suppose. But he's very much against the socialists. He thinks I'm being irresponsible. Of course he would. He thought I was irresponsible years ago."

And he was probably right, Phil thought. "Well, I'm glad you consulted him." She'd like to talk to Godfrey herself on a totally different subject. But there had never been an opportunity . . . as yet.

As Phil was pouring them a final cup of coffee, a note arrived from Gwen asking them to join her and Ruth in the downstairs morning room.

"Ugh," Daisy said. "That Ruth is a dour one."

"True," Phil said. "It promises to be a long morning."

They found Gwen and Ruth downstairs in the morning room,

bright with many windows and a view of the terrace. A tray of coffee and tea and sweets had been laid out on the sideboard. Gwen was pale and Phil wondered if the wet, cold weather was affecting her breathing.

Ruth barely acknowledged them as she bent over a square of needlepoint.

They sat down; Daisy picked up a magazine. Phil looked out the window where a few wisps of fog clung to the landscape.

"In the old days we'd meet the men to dine alfresco," Daisy said a little wistfully, and Phil wondered if suddenly stepping into her old lifestyle was making her rethink her socialistic views of property.

"We often do so here, too," Gwen said, sitting forward for Elva to plump the pillows behind her. "Some of the ladies even shoot, though it's a bit too much for me."

Elva backed away, stopped to fiddle with the vaporizer that was used to heat Gwen's medicinal incense.

"Oh Elva, would you please stop fussing."

"Sorry, Mrs. Pratt."

Gwen waved her away. "That will be all, thank you. I'll call you if I need you."

"Yes, ma'am." Elva bent at the knee and hurried from the room.

"She's a wonderful maid," Gwen said. "But this situation has made her overly protective and nervy. Jumps at the least provocation. Though who can blame her—all our servants are upset, and I'm sure word has gotten out with Godfrey's.

"Do you think we did right to quit town, Philomena? Godfrey thought it would be best just to remove ourselves until the air cleared, but I feel like I'm shirking my duties. And poor Loretta Sheffield. She has no one. What must she be feeling?"

What indeed, Phil thought. With the newspapers speculating on her husband's death or his calumny. And where was the man? And what did Godfrey know? Had he, unbeknownst to the rest of them, turned Sheffield in to the police? Had he indeed killed

Perry Fauks? It didn't seem to Phil they were any closer to catching the killer than they had been the day after it happened.

"I think I'll take a walk outside," Phil said.

Daisy raised both eyebrows at her.

"I take that to mean that you won't be joining me?"

"Not in this weather. I spend too much time as it is out in the raw air to talk to the masses. Since I'm here, I'm going to snuggle into a cozy chair and read these lovely ladies magazines that have been provided for our entertainment." She frowned. "Monday I'll go back to making the world a better place."

Phil smiled, understanding more than Daisy realized. She deserved to have a day of relaxation. As for Phil, what she needed was exercise and time to think.

"Have fun," Daisy said, turning the page of her magazine. "Don't get lost."

Phil retrieved her hat, coat, and muff from Lily and went out the colonnaded doors to the flagstone terrace she could see from her bedroom. The air was cold and crisp and would be uncomfortable if not for the sun shining palely through a hazy sky.

It was a large terrace, delineated by a low columned parapet, with wide brick walkways leading off to each side. A huge stone double staircase led down either side to a wide lawn, green even now. She went down to the lawn and turned to admire the house.

It was even more magnificent than the front entry. Topiary boxwoods sat like giant wedding cakes across the front; the balcony's wrought-iron rail ran along the second floor above the terrace like a filigree necklace.

She could see the lights from their private rooms and imagined Lily there cleaning up the remnants of her toilette.

The lawn, the gardens, the distant sparkle of the Sound peeking through the woods. It was quite spectacular.

But the predicament that had brought her to Foggy Acres kept her from fully enjoying the view.

John Atkins, who needed to solve Perry's murder, was absent. Mr. X, who didn't seem particularly interested in the murder,

was here. She was almost certain he was working in some clandestine way for some specific reason. But why? And for whom?
The government? A cartel of businessmen? A group of concerned
citizens?

A secret society of criminals?

Perhaps the same entity that put Phil up at one of New York's
most exclusive hotels in order to "call upon her again" and that
was so secret that it precluded her even knowing what she was
investigating?

She walked down a grassy boulevard lined with mature lin-
den trees, saw a path that led through what must be a beautiful
rose garden in the spring. Now, the bushes were cut back, skel-
etal without their glossy leaves. In the center of the garden a
fountain stood dry and naked. As she reached it, the sun slipped
behind the clouds; the air took a sudden chill and for some reason, so did Phil.

Where the water had glistened in the distance before, it was
now hidden by a rolling curtain of what must be fog.

Phil sighed; now she understood why the estate was called
Foggy Acres. Hopefully, this fog would stay in the distance. She
turned down a path through the trees, trying to piece together
the many aspects of Perry Fauks's murder. The many people
whose lives were affected by his death. The people who might
be innocent and those who might be guilty.

She came to a lake, quiet, serene, and incredibly lonely. And
beyond the lake, far into the forest, she could make out the roof
of a house or cottage. A neighbor. Perhaps Maximillian Rosarian.
Or the groundskeeper's cottage.

There was no sun here and it had become quite uncomfortable even in her winter coat. She turned to retrace her steps and
noticed the wisps of white mist that wove among the nearby
trees and began to rise like ghostly fingers from the surface of
the lake. The fog had appeared without warning and was coming in fast, spreading along the ground like living clouds.

This was the lake Godfrey had warned her about.

Even the intrepid Countess of Dunbridge knew when to retreat. To her right she saw the steps that led back to the brick walk of the mansion. But before she could reach them, they disappeared into the mist. Her toe found them before her eyes did and she felt her way upward.

When she reached the top, she was relieved to see daylight ahead; the fog seemed to be chasing her back to the house. She hurried up the path and came face-to-face with Godfrey and Luther returning from the hunt.

"Lady Dunbridge!" Godfrey exclaimed. "What on earth are you doing out here in the elements?"

"Getting a bit of fresh air," she said, pretending to be oblivious to the encroaching fog. "I had no idea I was within range of the shoot."

"No, no. You were perfectly safe. The fog started coming in an hour ago, so we gave the shoot up early, and stopped in at the colonel's for a drink. But please, come with us back to the house. A few more yards and you might have fallen down the stairs. Or worse, into the lake."

Phil automatically turned to look behind her. Saw nothing but fog and a tiny faint glow of light, like a captured firefly facing certain death.

"What is—" she began.

"We should hurry." Godfrey took her arm and hurried them all up the path to the house.

When they reached the house, the men excused themselves to change and Phil went into the parlor to see if Daisy was still about.

Daisy was there, as was Agnes and her cousins, as well as Morris, Harry, Vincent, and Newty Eccles, who had decided not to "tromp around in the fog all morning shooting at shadows."

"Ah, Lady Dunbridge," Harry Cleeves said, half rising from his chair. "You find us in a state of hopeless ennui. But please join us."

Morris rose even less in his chair than usual. However,

Vincent stood and bowed. "I was even given the day off to amuse myself." As if he needed to explain. It was hard to believe that this serious young man had once been crony to the others.

Phil sat down next to Daisy.

Agnes turned from the window where she'd been standing. "The fog is coming in, and now we'll be stuck inside when we could all be at the horse show at Madison Square Garden."

"And see if Roosevelt got his way about women's style of riding," said Effie.

"I hope he does," Harry said.

"How would the great man prefer we ride?" Daisy asked with just a touch of irony.

"Astride of course."

"No more sidesaddles? That would mean a whole new wardrobe." Daisy winked at Phil.

"And I'm missing Maddie Flowers's Italian tea," Agnes said. "She's going to have everything served while the guests are sitting in gondolas. It will be so beautiful."

"Stop complaining," Morris said. "You should be thanking Godfrey for removing you from ruin."

Agnes gasped. "I'm not . . . not ruined. Am I?"

"Not unless you've been a naughty girl," said her brother. He smiled in a snide way that made Phil want to slap him.

"I haven't been."

"Really, Morris," Harry interrupted. "There's no call for teasing Agnes in such a way. It isn't funny. Think of the ladies."

Morris cast a look in Phil and Daisy's direction. "I beg your pardon, my ladies, if I offended you."

"Not at all," Phil said. "Though you might have offended your sister."

He smiled back at her, then bowed to his sister without rising from his chair. "I beg your pardon, Sis. But even you must realize that Godfrey has done us the greatest favor by abducting us away from the scandal. And inviting our friends to help us enjoy our forced exile. What's a few gondolas when your whole future is at stake?"

Agnes's gaze flitted around the room, lingered a little too long on Vincent, who was sitting bolt upright in his chair, one fist clenched by his side.

Perhaps Agnes had had other plans all along, thought Phil.

Morris yawned. "Well, not to worry, Godfrey has promised you a balloon ascension tomorrow."

"Oh yes, the balloon ascension. That will be grand, won't it?" Agnes exclaimed in a burst of enthusiasm. It only lasted a second. "If the weather permits," she said, her bottom lip protruding in a pretty little pout.

Maud sighed. "I want to go home."

"You're not helping," Harry said. He picked up a copy of the *Daily Eagle* he'd evidently been reading. "No good news here. Banks, banks, banks. Ugh. Now Borough Bank has gone under the hatches, given sixteen months for full repayment to depositors. It will be amazing if any of us get out of this unscathed."

"Fat chance," said Newty. "Isn't there any good news?"

"Well, it didn't fail. That's good."

"Yet," Newty said.

"Well, listen to this, President Roosevelt just came up with a plan to . . ." Harry ran his finger down the page. "Here it is. 'Relieve the current situation and guard against future disturbances due to insufficient money to meet the demands of business.'"

"And how is he going to make the trusts do that?" Morris said. "They don't want to keep even five percent cash on hand. He'll never get them to go for it."

"He'll put J.P. on it," Newty said.

"Old man Morgan? He'll own us all before it's over," Morris groused.

"Boring old business," Agnes said petulantly. "Isn't there anything amusing?"

Harry riffled through the pages. "Here's something that

should cheer you up, the latest installment of 'The Avengers' from the *Daily Eagle*."

"'The Avengers,'" Agnes said, clapping her hands. "I love that serial. Read it to us, Harry."

Harry folded the paper over and flopped back in his chair. "Just to catch you illiterates up to this installment . . ." He began to read. "'Morris Barnes, a dissipated rounder' . . . hey, Morris, he must be named after you."

"Very funny."

"'. . . is murdered in his cab in London. His apartment has been ransacked by a young and beautiful woman, who then bumbles into the lower apartment of Herbert Wrayson, a serious newspaper editor.'" Harry lowered the paper. "That has to be you, Vincent. Mr. Serious."

"We could put on a play," suggested Agnes. "Who else is in it?"

"We have plenty of characters." Harry winked at her. "But who would play the beautiful young woman?"

Agnes beamed at him.

He smiled back and continued reading. "But it says here she is apparently of superior rank, but estranged from her father and living with Baroness de Strum. So she must be very upper crust. We just happen to have two delightful members of the peerage among us, but how do we decide between them?"

Daisy laughed. "You're a darling, but I can hardly be considered young. I must bow out of the honor."

"*Au contraire*." Harry grinned at her, absolutely flirtatious. And the serious socialist of yesterday, Daisy, flirted back.

"Or you, Lady Dunbridge? Will you be . . ." He looked down the page. "Now what is her name, this paragon whom Wrayson falls desperately in love with? Ah, the plot thickens. She swears she isn't involved in the murder but knows the reason for it."

Phil willed Daisy not to look at her.

"Do you, Lady Dunbridge? Have all the answers?"

Phil trilled a laugh. "Not one, I'm afraid."

"Desperately in love?" Newty guffawed. "I don't know, Vincent. Are you up to the task of violent passion?"

"Of course he is," Agnes said, and smiled encouragingly at Vincent, who sat unmoving.

"You have a champion," said Harry.

Vincent stood suddenly and went to the window. "I don't think we should be making light of murder considering he was a friend of ours and the murder was committed in our hom— presence."

"Oh, don't be a spoilsport," Newty said. "It's not our fault that Perry and his valet chose to fight out their problems. Terrible manners."

Phil picked up a magazine and pretended to read.

"Do you suppose he caught the valet stealing from him?" Newty persisted.

"Most likely," Morris said.

"I don't want to hear about that horrid old murder," Agnes said. "Keep reading, Harry, do."

"Your wish, etcetera," Harry said. "Let's see. Sidney, Morris's greedy brother, arrives from South Africa in desperate search for funds he believes Morris has hidden. Are you sitting on a fortune we don't know about?"

"That's a laugh. I had to beg cab fare from Vincent the other day." Morris sighed. "He turned me down, the monster."

"I didn't have it," Vincent said, unbending a little.

They all laughed.

"Well, I think you're all being just beastly," said Maud and ran from the room.

"Lord, she's getting tiresome," Harry said. "You'd think *she* was in love with Perry. Oh sorry, Agnes."

Agnes looked contrite, but only for a second. "What happens next?"

"I'll go see to her," Effie said and followed her sister out.

"A couple of drooping violets, those two," Newty said. "Don't know why Bennington invited them."

"They're my cousins," said Agnes.

"Well," Phil said, taking the lull in the story to make her escape. "You'll have to find another heroine. This countess is off for a nap."

It was time she had another little chat with Maud Jeffrey.

20

As soon as Phil was in the hallway she started listening for any clue as to where Maud and Effie had gone. And heard voices coming from a room across the hall. She hurried to the door to listen, expecting to find Maud in tears and Effie consoling her like any good sister would do.

She heard so much more.

"You're ruining the whole weekend."

"So what if I am? I hate Agnes. She could have married Perry, but no, she's out there flirting with Vincent, like Perry wasn't even dead. Vincent! How could she? He's a secretary." A sob. "He's not nearly as handsome as Perry. Why?"

For a few moments all Phil heard was sobbing.

"She always gets what she wants. She's a snake in the grass."

"Gee, Maud, that's just not true."

"It is so. I bet she killed Perry, just so I couldn't have him."

Effie gasped. Phil moved closer.

"That's a horrible thing to say."

"I don't care, she's glad he's dead. I hate her. She's ruined everything. I want to go home."

"You're being a spoiled brat. Why don't you show some concern for someone other than yourself for a change."

"You don't know anything. So just shut up."

"Fine, be that way." Footsteps across the floor.

Phil retreated into the shadows of the staircase.

Running steps. The doorknob rattling and Phil had just

enough time to duck behind the curved staircase as Effie stepped into the foyer.

Maud followed her out. "If you knew what I know . . ."

Effie stopped and turned toward her sister. Phil eased out from her hiding place.

"What do you know?"

"Shh. I can't tell."

"Fine. Then don't. I'm sure I don't care." The swirl of Effie's hem as she turned to leave.

"Where are you going?"

"Back to the others."

"My life is over."

"Oh please. Stop being so dramatic, Perry Fauks didn't even know you existed."

"He did, too. He said he wanted to marry me, not Agnes."

"Don't talk so loud." Effie pulled Maud behind the stairs. Two more steps and one of them would see Phil. She didn't want to interrupt their talk, but she was stuck between them and the wall—the wall and a narrow door.

One of the coat closets, most likely. She turned the handle and squeezed inside, leaving the opening just wide enough to see through.

Effie pulled Maud closer. They were now hidden from anyone coming into the foyer, but they were directly in Phil's line of sight.

Maud's hands covered her face as she sobbed.

Effie grabbed her by the shoulders and shook her. "I hope you didn't give away anything you shouldn't. You'll be ruined for sure."

Phil couldn't hear the answer if there was one.

"He'd never have married you. You're not rich enough." Effie huffed an exasperated breath. "You are so dense. He didn't want to marry you. He just wanted what he could get for free."

"That's not true."

"True. Besides, Mama and Papa would never allow it. I heard them talking. Papa was really angry. He told Mama he'd never let Perry marry either of us, that Perry had a reputation and he couldn't be trusted. And she agreed that it wouldn't do even if he weren't almost engaged to Agnes."

"That's not true. Mama and Papa would jump at the chance of either of us marrying a fortune."

Effie just shook her head.

Maud looked up, stopped crying. "They were arguing? When?"

"Never mind, I shouldn't have told you. Forget what I said."

"When?"

"The night of the party. I had run upstairs for my wrap and they were in the hallway."

Maud's expression changed from self-absorption to fear. "You were upstairs that night? Did you hear anything?"

"I just told you."

"I mean anything else?"

"No. What else would I hear?"

"Nothing . . . nothing." Maud was moving toward hysteria. "You don't think that . . . that Papa killed him?"

"Of course not. How asinine. You really think our father would kill someone to keep them from marrying you? You're the most self-centered person on earth."

"Then why is Perry dead?"

"His valet killed him. Maybe Perry caught him stealing something. Maybe Perry tried to stop him. I don't know. And neither do you, Miss Know-it-all." Effie turned and huffed away in a swirl of taffeta skirt.

Now if Maud would just leave, so would Phil.

What she'd just overheard—Maud's accusations that Agnes had killed Perry, the argument between Thomas and Ruth Effie had overheard, Maud afraid her father might have killed him— sounded like the typical overreaction of two competitive sisters, the hope of one, and the exasperation of the other. Phil remembered a few overwrought fights with her own sisters.

This latest argument at least had served to convince Phil of two things. Maud was playing a dangerous game with her reputation, and Agnes had given up all pretense of grief over Perry's demise.

Lunch was served late to accommodate the dispirited shooters. "Couldn't see the loaders much less any grouse or pigeons," Luther said, but smiled at his wife. "So you're stuck with us for the rest of the afternoon."

Morris, Harry, and Newty had taken a car over to the nearest town looking for fun. Maud claimed a headache and stayed in her room. Vincent sat next to Gwen, upright and concentrating on his food. Agnes and Effie seemed particularly quiet.

It fell to Gwen, who was definitely having trouble breathing, Daisy, and Phil to keep the conversation going. Luther tried to hold up his end, but Godfrey, normally the perfect host, seemed preoccupied. And when a telegram arrived during the fruit course, he excused himself, apologizing, "Alas, business that will not wait." He bowed himself out of the room.

By the time coffee had been served, it was evident that Gwen was in distress.

Luther looked concerned. "My dear, shall I call for Elva to set up the nebulizer?"

Gwen waved him off. "It was just a momentary spasm. I'm much better now. No need to be alarmed. I'll just take some of my lozenges." She turned to Phil and Daisy. "I have these little attacks off and on throughout the day sometimes when the weather is like this."

After lunch, Agnes and Effie cajoled Vincent into a game of cards. To which Luther gave his full approval. "Have some fun, my boy, no work for us today. For myself, I think I'll adjourn to Godfrey's commendable library."

"Where he will nap the afternoon away," said Gwen, with obvious affection.

The women retired to their own rooms. Phil had no intention of napping, but she would use the time to summon her servants to a council of investigation.

But before she reached the top of the stairs she heard the sound of a motorcar, the front door opened, and the three young men came inside.

"Hey ho," Harry exclaimed. "Couldn't find our way to the main road, barely found our way back. Never seen it like this before." They shrugged out of their driving coats and shoved them at the butler, who took them with barely a curl of his lip.

"Where are the girls?"

"I believe Miss Agnes and Miss Effie are in the game room."

"Tillis. We're starving, could you have cook bring us some sandwiches and beer?"

The butler bowed and departed beneath his load of coats.

Phil found Daisy stretched out on the chaise in their sitting room. Phil didn't feel like sitting. She crossed to the French doors and looked out at the fog. "Godfrey looked preoccupied during lunch."

Daisy looked up. "He did. Something to do with those balloons that we saw over at Bev's farm."

"What does he do with balloons exactly?" Phil asked. "Bobby said the government was doing tests, something about collecting data on the weather."

Daisy shrugged. "He's always been an aeronautical buff. Even helped finance some of the test flights of those brothers that built those flying machines."

"The Wright brothers."

"Those are the ones. Now he's pressuring them to create a prototype for the War Department. I think that's why he's so

against me getting involved with socialists. He's such an estab-
lishment man. I don't know why he doesn't understand that
when you make conditions better for workers, you make conditions better for everyone."

"Hmm," Phil answered, only half listening; she'd seen movement on the terrace below. Someone was moving through the fog.

Godfrey had warned everyone about going out in the fog. Who
would do such a thing now? It was impossible to tell who it
was as the figure moved across in and out of the fog. Phil saw a
shoulder, a hat, a raincoat. The figure was moving quickly
toward the brick pathway that Godfrey had used to return her
to the house earlier in the day.

He turned around as if someone had called him, or he was
making sure he wasn't followed, and for a split second, Phil saw
his face.

Godfrey Bennington was taking the same path he'd warned
her about. He disappeared for a moment, then a sickly yellow
light appeared in the mist. He'd brought a torch. The man was
up to something.

And Phil was going to find out what that was.

With Lily and Preswick both downstairs, she didn't dare wait
to have her warm coat brought up. She ran into her dressing
room, pulled on a shawl over her day dress, and ran down the
stairs.

She let herself out the door to the terrace and into blindness.
She stood for a moment on the wet flagstones, trying to orient
herself. She knew she had walked straight out the door, but already her sense of direction faltered. She would have to pay extreme attention to where she was going.

She could only see an occasional shape in front of her. Earlier
that day, in the sunlight, the area had been a confection of lawns,
gardens, and woods. Now it was a menacing, unrecognizable
terrain, straight out of a gothic horror story.

But this was the twentieth century and Phil was no damsel
in distress.

She made a precise right turn, walking as fast as her thin-soled shoes and lack of visibility allowed. The bricks were slippery with condensation, and Phil let out a sigh of relief when her hand touched the thick pillar that denoted an opening to the wide brick walk. She peered ahead but could find no light in the unrelenting gray.

But she was certain he'd come this way. She trailed her fingers along the top of the short balustrade, using it to guide her. And if necessary it would guide her back.

The salty air was acidic in her nose and on her tongue. The balustrade ended. She knew she had come to one of the paths that led to the gardens. Tried to remember how many such openings she had passed that afternoon on her way back from her walk. But she had been paying attention to Godfrey and hadn't used all her faculties to good use. What kind of detective was she?

She stopped, strained to hear any sound in the dense fog. Was that a footfall on the walkway? If he had turned onto the grass, he wouldn't make a sound in this weather. He had warned her to stay away from the lake, had trundled her away when she ran into him this morning.

But was it her safety that really concerned him, or did he have another reason for keeping her away? He was on his way there now, she was certain.

She sidestepped, groping for the other side of the opening. When her hand touched cold stone again, she hurried on.

She came to the next opening in the wall. Was this it? She took a step—into air. Landed with a thud several inches below the walkway. She'd come to the stairs.

She held on to the railing and descended while the fog swirled around her. She was concentrating so intently that she almost missed the little yellow ball of light that bounced in and out of the fog. He must be going around the lake. To the house she'd seen earlier?

And for the first time since deciding to follow him, she

wondered what on earth she would say if she did catch up to him. What if this was just an ordinary visit to a friend? Under the cloak of a heavy fog? If it was innocent, why not have gone there this morning before the fog had settled in?

Foggy Acres indeed. She'd laughed at the name as they'd driven up to the mansion the day before. She was no longer laughing.

She reached flat ground. The earth was spongy. It took a frightening amount of time to feel for the solid stone of the path. She had to pay attention. If she veered from the path she might succumb to the same fate as the groundskeeper's boy.

She shuffled along, staying on the path, as she searched for the little bouncing light, but fog tended to turn light back in on itself, leaving it as an indistinct glow at best and a phantom decoy at worst.

It was moving erratically. Not in a straight line. Phil tried to plot the points of light and not be beguiled into running straight toward the latest appearance. By now she was sure the lake was between them.

Her shawl became heavy and damp around her shoulders. Once she snagged it on a branch or a bramble and spent valuable time pulling it free while trying not to become disoriented or losing sight of her quarry.

What could be so important that Godfrey would go out in this weather? Then she saw it, hovering in the air. A flare of a large rectangular light that swallowed the smaller one whole. And then they both disappeared. It took several seconds for Phil to realize it wasn't magic but the house in the woods. Someone had opened the door to let Godfrey in.

And shut her out.

Something wailed. A night creature, her brain said. Still, she turned and ran—straight into a man, his hand held over his head. Phil raised her arms to ward off the blow, but she was too astonished to run. She sucked in her breath, but nothing happened. Slowly she lowered her arms. Stepped a little closer. Felt

a cold stone foot, an ankle, a calf. She didn't bother to feel farther. She was too weak with relief.

A statue. One of the many that adorned the grounds.

Phil let out her breath.

And was grabbed from behind.

"Don't scream," he whispered.

"What are you doing here?" she whispered back.

Mr. X breathed out a laugh. "I imagine the same thing you
are."

"Whose side are you on?" Ridiculous as the situation seemed,
she really needed to know that he was on the side of justice.

"You have to ask? Can you find your way back to the house?"

She shook her head.

He blew out breath. "Does that mean, no you're lost or—"

"No, I'm not leaving."

A finger appeared two inches from her face.

"Don't tell me what to do."

"Then be quiet."

Voices inside the cottage suddenly grew louder. An argument.

Without speaking, the two of them inched forward. The
Countess of Dunbridge and an unknown accomplice. The light
turned out to be a casement window, and they pressed into it.

They were standing so close that Phil could feel the contours
of his body. No heavy coat to impede his actions—wasn't he cold?
Or could he be the devil incarnate as she sometimes suspected.

Concentrate.

Godfrey was standing at a table. A man was seated with an
empty plate and a bottle of wine in front of him. A stack of papers
and a briefcase lay at his feet.

Dark thinning hair, brilliantined to his skull. Phil had seen
that face just this past morning on the front page of *The New
York Times.* And in the park.

"Isaac Sheffield," she whispered.

Mr. X. nodded.

"Did you know where he was?"

"Shh."

She moved.

He grabbed her arm. "Where are you going?" he said in her ear.

"To find out what this is all about."

Godfrey's head snapped toward the window. Almost as if he'd heard them. Which he couldn't have—they'd been whispering.

He turned toward the door.

Phil stepped back right into her partner in crime.

"Sorry, my dear, you're on your own." He pressed something small and hard and cold into her hand.

She looked down at it. A pistol?

"What?" She looked up just in time to see him disappear into the fog. She heard a crack as if someone had knocked on a door. She just hoped it hadn't been his head on a tree.

The front door opened and Godfrey stepped out.

What was she supposed to do? Shoot him? She didn't even know that the pistol was loaded.

So she did what any self-respecting countess caught eavesdropping would do. She took the offensive.

She marched around to meet Godfrey face-to-face.

"Ah, Lady Dunbridge. Of course. I should have expected this," he said.

Phil swore he was smiling.

Her blood ran cold. Maybe she *was* as silly as any of those poor distressed damsels in novels.

"I suppose you want to know what's going on."

"I would indeed. Beginning with why you are harboring a possible murderer."

"Very well. Come inside."

She managed to slip the pistol into the pocket of her skirt before allowing Godfrey to escort her to the door.

Isaac Sheffield looked haggard and afraid. But he jumped to his feet when Phil and Godfrey entered the room.

Introductions were made. Sheffield shook her hand. It was

totally absurd. If she hadn't just put her pistol away, she would hold him at gunpoint and march him straight to John Atkins.

Unfortunately it was two men against one countess and John Atkins was miles away.

21

"I didn't kill him," Isaac Sheffield said. "I didn't kill him, but I could have. After what he did." He cast a furious look toward Godfrey.

Was this simply a case of revenge for his dead daughter and grandchild? Why wait until the party of his friends, where he was most likely to be caught? It didn't make sense. Unless something had happened that made him finally snap.

Phil felt for him. She had no children of her own, probably wouldn't, she was past twenty-five and a widow. But she could sympathize; just not enough to condone murder.

"You have to give me time."

For what? Phil wondered.

"I remember you from the party, Lady Dunbridge. I don't expect you to understand any of this. You've probably never had to worry about the lives of thousands of people and the fate of a nation."

Was he making some excuse for his actions? "I assure you I have been responsible for hundreds of people who depended on the earl's estates for their livelihood. But I don't see what that has to do with Perry Fauks's murder."

Again he looked at Godfrey. "I don't even understand why she is here." Sheffield rubbed his face with both hands. A man at his wit's end.

"It's rather academic, Isaac."

Phil couldn't agree more. "I think Mr. Sheffield needs to tell his story, whatever it is, to the police."

"I can't. Godfrey, you know that. It will create another panic. One that may destroy more than a few trusts."

Phil looked from Sheffield to Godfrey. Something was going on here that she didn't understand. Something bigger than Perry impregnating his daughter and her subsequent death. More than revenge.

"Mr. Sheffield, you can't stay in hiding. The police are looking for you." Phil paused. He had a wild look about him. He had no intention of talking to the police.

She swallowed. "What exactly is going on here?"

The two men looked at each other as if trying to decide telepathically what to do with her. She took the opportunity to slide her hand into her pocket and grasp the pistol's stock.

Both men turned toward her, but not before the pistol was aimed at a point somewhere between them.

Sheffield reared back in his chair. Godfrey just stared at her, not the pistol. After a moment he shook his head. "I knew you must be more than Gwen's concerned friend. But you didn't come up on any lists. What exactly do you want?"

To stay alive? "I *am* a concerned friend. A man was murdered in Gwen's home. A man who I'm told was expected to marry Agnes. You men will go on about business and whatever else you do. But Gwen is stuck having to face society while she attempts to save her daughter's future. Women must stick together in these times."

Heavens, she'd sounded just as vehement as Daisy when she was spouting her socialist ideas. And for the first time, Phil understood a little of how she must feel.

"Perhaps you were trying to save Agnes from the same fate as Rachel and decided to take the matter into your own hands."

Sheffield's mouth dropped open. "Who told you about Rachel? Not my wife."

"What are you talking about?" Godfrey asked.

"Not your wife, but Mrs. Kidmore-Young."

Godfrey turned on Sheffield. "What the hell is she talking about, Isaac?"

"Nothing, nothing," Sheffield choked out the words. "It's nothing to do with that. I didn't kill him. We did argue that night. That was all.

"I had discovered what he'd done—" His head swiveled toward Phil. "Not what he'd done to my daughter, but what he'd done to the company. I swear he was alive when I left."

The company. "Fauks Copper, Coal and Steel?" asked Phil.

"Yes. I didn't kill him. I would never do that to his family."

"I believe you, Isaac. I think, if Lady Dunbridge will put down her weapon, we might apprise her of the situation."

Now here was a dilemma. Should Phil take chances with her own survival to get information? Mr. You're-on-Your-Own might be out there ready to come to the rescue, but he might just as well be on his way to God knew where.

But the fact that he'd been here at all meant something serious besides murder was going on.

She lowered the pistol, but didn't let go of it. "All right. Tell me what this is all about."

"Please sit down," Godfrey said.

She hesitated.

"So that I can."

She sat. Godfrey pulled up a chair from the corner and sat down. It gave Phil a second to quickly look around. It was more than one room, though they appeared to be in a combination sitting room and kitchen. It was comfortably furnished, though only one lamp sat in the middle of the table to light their conversation. And as far as she could see, there was only one door.

"Go ahead," she prodded Sheffield.

He ran his hand down his face. "As you probably know, the banking crisis was narrowly avoided, thanks to J.P. Morgan."

"Yes," she said a little impatiently. "I understand that he was instrumental in getting banks and others to put up funds to keep things from failing."

"Yes, but not soon enough to save the Knickerbocker bank or many smaller trust companies."

"Fauks?" she asked.

"No. We would have been fine. We were on solid financial ground." He glanced at Godfrey.

"I had just returned from D.C." He blinked several times. "Anyway, while I was out of town . . . in . . . talks." Sheffield continued, "Perry managed to hijack a major portion of the company's ready cash. When I learned about it, I confronted him at Agnes's party. He was in a panic. He—"

"Mr. Sheffield," Phil interjected. "Will you please just tell me what happened, and tell me the truth. Obviously there is something you and Mr. Bennington want to keep from me. I'd like to know what is going on. Gwen is very upset, and that is not good for her health. So the sooner we can put this all behind us, the better for everyone.

"I surmise Perry stole the funds and I'm guessing that you haven't been able to retrieve them?"

Sheffield hung his head. Shook it twice. "He'd heard that the government was about to award a big contract for steel to supply the War Department's new aeroplane program. He wanted to show everyone what a big shot he was.

"He used the company's money to invest in a short-sale scheme. He thought he could buy enough of a competitor's stock to make it big on his own. He used Fauks company money, convinced his friends and associates to invest in a 'sure thing.'

"But the stock tanked before he could sell out and he'd lost everything.

"It's gone, truly gone, and I don't know how many other people he took with him."

He shuddered. "And the worst thing was that while he was looting the company, I was in talks for one of those contracts."

Phil looked at Godfrey.

He returned what for him was a shrug. "Now we have both been burned by that arrogant little . . . Well, never mind."

And Daisy had come to New York to sell her Mexican mines to Perry and invest in his "scheme." She was one of the fortunate ones as it turned out. Daisy and Harry Cleeves.

But how many others had not been so lucky?

"He had to have had insider knowledge of the contract," Godfrey said. "We kept it under wraps to prevent a feeding frenzy of little companies that really couldn't come up to scratch. As it is, with two of the most promising companies headed to bankruptcy, we'll have to start the search over. A major setback, as the department and the Wright brothers are in negotiations for building the planes. We need to have a supplier in place to be able to start production. You can see the ramifications if all this was to become public."

She did. What she couldn't quite imagine was aeroplanes in the hands of the War Department. War with aeroplanes? Phil didn't want to contemplate what they would do to fighting nations.

Phil dragged her mind back to the man sitting across from her. "So you confronted him."

"Yes. He was in a panic. I told him not to show his face at the company until I returned. I left the party and went straight to Pittsburgh to evaluate the situation there. He'd forged my signature on a financial transfer document, though I'm sure he must have had someone working with him, an accomplice, perhaps in the Pittsburgh office. It would be complicated to not raise a red flag with that kind of transaction. I have people on it, but I need more time to try to save the company.

"And I need time to find out who leaked the information to him about the contract.

"The fool," Sheffield cried. "Fauks Copper, Coal and Steel is cleaned out. We'll go under as soon as word gets out and there's a run on the company. It won't be long. Word has already hit the wires. It's just a matter of time."

The wires. The news had already hit. The ticker tape machine in Luther's office. The scrap of ticker tape in Perry's wastepaper basket. The piece that had fallen to the floor when Thomas had put on his overcoat just the night before.

"Unless we can figure out something to squelch the sell-off," Godfrey added.

"I'm afraid it may be too late." Isaac seemed to age in front of them, a totally broken man. He too had lost in Perry's reckless dealings. And where would that leave his poor wife?

Godfrey pushed his chair back from the table. "So now you know what Isaac and I were discussing when we heard your knock at the door."

Her knock? She hadn't made a sound. And then it dawned on her.

That weasel. He'd wanted them to find her.

Over the course of the next few minutes, Godfrey and Sheffield convinced Phil to give them twenty-four hours to staunch the bloodletting, with the promise that Sheffield would then turn himself in to the police. He swore again he hadn't committed the murder.

And having heard his story she might have been sympathetic if he had.

Perry Fauks had betrayed his company's, his family's, and his investors' trusts. Had lost everything for a wild speculation. And if what Phil had learned about Perry's relationship with Sheffield's daughter was true, Sheffield would have every right to feel the need for revenge.

But he also seemed like an honest man who cared about his family and his business. When Godfrey swore he would vouch for him, she acquiesced. There was little else she could do. She

was in the middle of a debilitating fog at the home of a very se-
cretive man and without her allies, who were either up at the
house, back in Manhattan, or who knew where.

"All right. Twenty-four hours. Then we, the three of us, must
tell Detective Sergeant Atkins. He's not a stupid man. He'll understand the more subtle aspects of your situation and he will
be able to use the information you have to catch the real killer."

Phil and Godfrey returned to the house some time later. They
didn't speak; it took all their concentration to find their way back
through the fog.

At last Phil saw lights from the mansion and realized the fog
had gotten thinner.

Inside was ablaze with light, and they hastened toward the
warmth. The front door opened and Tillis hurried them in.

Phil saw immediately that something was wrong.

"What is it, Tillis?" Godfrey asked.

"Mrs. Pratt, sir. Having one of her attacks."

Luther and Daisy were holding a slumping Gwen between
them, walking her toward the back of the house.

Agnes, Harry, Newty, and the others were huddled in the
doorway of the parlor looking worried.

Gwen managed to glance over her shoulder. Looked straight
at Phil. Opened her mouth as if to speak.

Phil hurried toward her.

"Fine," Gwen said.

She was not fine and Phil wondered if the weather or something else had set off her asthma.

"Must fine . . ." Gwen pushed feebly at Luther's arm.

Not "fine." Must find? Find what? "Don't worry," Phil told her.
"You can tell me when you're breathing better."

Phil slipped in beside Daisy. "Has Elva gone to start the
nebulizer?"

"It's missing. They've looked everywhere."

Missing? How could such an important piece of equipment be missing? Was Gwen in danger? Is that what she was trying to say?

"They sent her maid to burn some kind of powders. She's setting it up in the morning room."

They were nearly at the door when a frightening wail went up from inside. At first long and shrill, then ululating like some otherworldly creature.

The door rattled as if someone was trying to get out, then it flung open. The acrid smell of the inhalant filled the air. Elva staggered, grabbed the doorframe, and looked wildly around. With an ear-splitting scream, her arms flew out, her hands curving like claws, and she staggered backward into the room.

"What the hell?" Godfrey pushed around them and hurried through the door.

Phil started to follow, felt a wave of dizziness. "Get her away," she cried. "Everyone get away from . . . door. Now."

She was vaguely aware of Daisy grabbing Gwen around the waist, she and Luther dragging her back down the hall. *Clever Daisy*, Phil thought before the hall began to swim before her.

Godfrey had gone inside. She had to warn him. She buried her nose in the fabric of her sleeve and followed him inside.

And nearly tripped over Elva's body.

The smell was stronger, biting at the fabric that covered her face. Her eyes filled with tears. Godfrey had taken his handkerchief to his nose. He made his way to the smoking vaporizer, turned off the burner, and swept the dish and its contents to the floor.

Motioned her back.

He wavered in front of her, stretched and bent and writhed like some demon. Colors danced wildly inside her head, the plants seemed to waver then explode from their bases, twist and coil in the air. And on the floor at her feet, a figure melted and spread across the tiles.

And Phil's mind said, *Poison.*

Then Godfrey was at her side. They bent as one, grabbed Elva by the arms and dragged her into the hall.

Godfrey kicked the door closed and took over dragging Elva away from the room. Phil swayed on her feet but managed to follow him. He didn't stop until they were in the foyer, then he dropped his burden and threw open the front doors to outside. The fog swirled in and so did fresh air.

Phil grabbed for the door to keep from falling, her mind reeling, her body not her own. The floor looked so far away. She shrank back as a metal monster grew and reached toward her.

This is not real, someone told her. Not Godfrey, but herself. Her real self.

The door to the parlor opened.

"Stay inside," yelled Godfrey. The door slammed. He ordered Tillis to seal off the sitting room and open the windows of all the other rooms, then to send all the servants down to the kitchen.

His voice seemed very strange. Warped, like a phonograph record left in the sun. Phil listened, mesmerized, as she clung to the door and breathed in the fresh cold air.

Her surroundings gradually settled back into Godfrey's foyer.

The set of armor at the base of the stairs no longer tried to tear itself from its base.

"*Aaaare yoou all riiiiight?*" His voice still sounded as if he were down a well.

She nodded. "Yes. You?"

"Fine."

Fine. The world righted itself. *Gwen.* And then she remembered Elva still lying on the marble floor at their feet.

Godfrey knelt down. Felt the woman's wrist for a pulse, tried again at her neck. He lifted her shoulders, shook her, gently at first, then more violently. Called her name. Slapped her face. She did not rouse.

Godfrey looked up at Phil from where he knelt by the body.

The world was crystal clear now and Phil didn't need words to know Elva was dead.

Vincent bounded up the front steps and through the open door. "Good God. What happened?" If a pale man could grow paler, Vincent did.

"Poison," Godfrey said. "Some hallucinogen."

"Is she okay?"

"She's dead."

Vincent seemed to sway on his feet, or maybe it was just the residual poison in Phil's bloodstream. "How could this happen? She didn't take drugs, did she?"

"Not intentionally," Godfrey said and looked at Phil. "Vincent, where have you been?"

"Out to the garage. It seems Mrs. Pratt's nebulizer is missing. I thought it might have been left in the auto by mistake."

"Ah," Godfrey said, and said no more.

And Phil thought they were thinking the same thing. Was this a terrible accident? And if it wasn't, had the intended victim been Gwen, not Elva.

Tillis returned. "The staff is all belowstairs, sir. I've told them to stay where they are."

"Very good, Tillis. I'm afraid that there has been a terrible tragedy."

"I can see that, sir. Shall I cover her?"

Godfrey nodded and the butler strode down the hallway as if producing a shroud were as ordinary as retrieving a guest's coat from the closet. Phil doubted that her own butler would be able to maintain such sangfroid.

"Vincent, please join us in the parlor." Godfrey offered Phil his arm and they went inside.

Gwen was lying on the couch. At a table near her head, a small case was opened showing what looked like glass ampules. Daisy cradled her shoulders as Luther held a syringe with a wicked-looking needle.

Phil grasped at Godfrey's arm.

"Are you sure that's safe?" Godfrey asked.

"I keep it locked in my valise," Luther said. "It's only for the most serious emergencies. It's very powerful." He looked at the syringe, suddenly indecisive.

Gwen scratched at his arm. "Luther, please."

He slid the needle into her vein and pushed the plunger, releasing the medication.

Phil held her breath, watched Gwen's breathing gradually even out. A deep breath, and Gwen said, "Thank you."

Daisy stood and came to stand beside Phil. "I checked the ampule to see if it had been opened or cracked. It seemed safe." She moved Phil a little away from the group and asked in a low voice, "Is the maid dead?"

"Yes."

"Do you think it was an accident?"

Phil shook her head.

"You think they were after Gwen? Who would do such a thing?"

"I don't know," Phil said. "But I intend to find out."

Gwen was breathing easier now, but Luther refused to let her sit up.

She reached out toward Phil and Daisy and they came to her side.

"Elva?"

Phil shook her head. She found it hard to speak.

"Oh." Gwen's mouth crumpled. "She wanted to tell me something. I was short-tempered with her. I was afraid she was going to quit because of the murder. I should have listened. I should have found out what she was afraid of. And now it's too late."

"Don't upset yourself," Luther begged. "Lady Dunbridge will take care of everything." He cast a plaintive look toward Phil.

"Of course I will," she said, but this new murder left her even more confused. And it felt like time was running out.

"Why did this happen?" asked Gwen.

"I don't know." Phil just knew she was angry. Whoever the murderer was must be stopped, unequivocally and without delay. It looked like it was up to her alone to see justice done. And Lady Dunbridge was more than happy to oblige.

22

Godfrey took Phil aside. "How are you feeling?"

"I've recovered enough. What was that? Something substituted for Gwen's usual medicine?"

Godfrey shook his head. "It's the same medicine. Datura stramonium is used in these preparations. It's very effective for asthma, but can be deadly. And in this case was."

"Datura . . . ? What is it?"

"A member of the nightshade family. Jimsonweed."

Phil nodded. "Devil's snare . . . hallucinations . . . and death." She shivered. "A mistake?"

"The doses are carefully premeasured by the pharmacist and sealed in individual packets.

"So someone had to have altered them. And if they did . . . there might be more?"

Godfrey didn't answer.

"But why would someone want to hurt Gwen?" Phil frowned. "Or Elva?"

"Lady Dunbridge. I work for the War Department. I am never called on to deal with individual murder."

Phil stared at him. *Not one at a time, but wholesale killing?* She blinked, recovered herself. "And?"

"I think I have no recourse but to call Detective Sergeant Atkins."

"I agree, but even if you can reach him, will he be allowed to come? This isn't his territory."

"I can reach him and they will allow it, if I say so. I don't often trust the police in matters of delicacy, but I suppose in this case, I must. If you could rejoin the others, I'll make it so."

Phil really wanted to hear those conversations, especially in light of what she'd just heard in the cottage. And now Godfrey had decided to call on someone he'd just dismissed. A man caught between two loyalties? It made her respect him for it. Still, she could never really trust him. She recognized a stronger power than hers when she saw it, and had no doubt he would use that power against her, or Atkins, or anyone whom he felt was a danger to his family or his country. She nodded her acceptance and left him to it.

The others were gathered in the parlor where she'd left them. Gwen was sitting up, Luther on one side and Ruth on the other.

Daisy was at the drinks console mixing cocktails.

"I asked Tillis to bring tea and coffee," she said when Phil joined her. "I for one could use something stronger. What on earth is going on?"

"The maid is dead," Phil said, making herself busy with glasses, mainly to deflect attention.

"Accident?"

"No. Godfrey is sending for the police."

"Good God, what a life you lead." Daisy covered her mouth with her hand. "How heartless that sounds."

It did, but Phil couldn't deny they were all relieved that it wasn't Gwen lying beneath the cloth on the entry hall floor.

"Where are Agnes and that crowd?" Phil asked.

"The girls were close to hysterics, all three of them. I sent them into the card room and told Harry to keep them quiet and calm. He's the only one with half a brain. The brother is useless. The other boy is . . ." She shrugged. "Useless. At least they're being quiet."

Tea came. Ruth poured. Daisy and Phil and Luther opted for gin and tonic water. Godfrey didn't return.

After a while, Phil wandered into the card room. Morris sprawled—it seemed his favorite position—in a chair looking through a magazine. Newty sat in a window alcove flipping a coin and catching it. Harry was building a house of cards on the games table.

The girls were absent.

"Gone to powder their noses," Harry said.

Phil glanced at the back door. "Everyone is supposed to stay put until the police arrive."

He looked up, an ace of spades raised in his hand. "You know how girls are. They'll be back." He carefully placed the card on top of the house of cards he'd built. Looked up. "You don't think they had anything to do with this?"

"That isn't the point. It's important to keep the crime scene— oh, never mind." Phil crossed the floor, opened a door, and found herself in a small octagon-shaped room, comfortable and private, with a window that overlooked a secluded formal garden behind the eastern walkway.

The fog seemed to be lifting a bit and Phil saw Agnes Pratt standing near a stand of yew trees that formed a wall around the garden. And she wasn't alone.

Vincent Wynn-Taylor stood facing her, both his hands on her shoulders. A show of support or something more intimate? Two lovers or two co-conspirators.

Phil was shocked at her own thoughts, but perhaps not as shocked as she should be.

It was an age-old story, a young girl loves someone other than the one her parents had chosen for her. Isn't that just what had happened to Phil?

Only in Agnes's case she'd been set free. Or had she and Vincent helped the situation along by conspiring to kill Agnes's fiancé? Phil couldn't see it. Agnes could have easily said no to Perry. Her parents doted on her, they would never make her marry someone she didn't love. But would they welcome Vincent as Perry's replacement?

That would open a whole new set of motives. And add to Phil's already growing list of possible suspects.

And who knew when Atkins would arrive. They both thought Agnes had held something back when Atkins questioned her. Well, here was something she could do to expedite the investigation.

A quick look around revealed a narrow arched door that led to a set of stairs down to the garden.

Phil didn't hesitate but strode through the geometric plantings to where Agnes and Vincent stood, oblivious to the fact she was fast approaching them.

He was the first to see Phil and dropped his hands in sheer reaction.

"Sorry," he said. He jerked a nod toward Phil and hurried past her and into the house. She let him go. At the moment she just wanted to talk to Agnes.

"I just wanted to get a bit of fresh air," Agnes said.

"Well, we're not supposed to leave the parlor, but since we're already here, I've been wanting to talk to you."

"I-I didn't know that—we should get back."

"And we will," Phil said. "But I'm worried that something troubles you."

Agnes shook her head, but already the tears were welling in her eyes.

Phil tried not to roll hers. Honestly, the idea of this child committing, much less covering up, a murder was a stretch beyond her imagination.

"What is it, Agnes?" Phil carefully modulated her voice to concern rather than inquisition.

"It's . . . nothing."

"Well, it must be something. Let's sit over here and you can tell me. Sometimes it helps to tell someone outside your family or friends when you're worried about something."

"Oh, Lady Dunbridge. I knew you would understand. Mama said you were a modern woman and though you hadn't always made the best choices, you would never back down from a problem."

"Well, I have made some pretty stupid choices in my life," Phil agreed. It was so lowering, that even this young thing knew about them. "Men problems?" she guessed.

Agnes shrugged. "That but something else."

"Something with Perry?"

"You can never tell."

"If it doesn't have anything to do with Perry's—and Elva's—murder, I won't."

"It doesn't." Agnes stopped, looked up. "Elva was murdered?"

"It looks like it."

"Someone wanted to kill my mother? Are we all in danger?"

"We don't know, that's why it's important to stay close and to tell me anything that might be helpful or anything that has upset you." *Gads, this could take all day.* And she needed to find out what was worrying Agnes before Atkins arrived and blundered manlike into the conversation.

"I hated him," Agnes blurted out.

Taken aback, Phil asked, "Perry?"

Agnes nodded. "He was so nice at first, handsome and rich and all the things a girl should want in a husband. Papa and Mama were both pleased that he showed me attentions." She sniffed. "Too much attention."

"He didn't go further than making you feel uncomfortable, did he?"

"He tried. All the time. He touched me in places that were— it was wrong. He said I was unnatural and that all the girls did it. Do they, Lady Dunbridge? Do all the girls let them . . . you know?"

She did indeed. "It is something that you and only you can decide. It shouldn't . . . uh . . ." She was not the person to give this lecture. "Do anything against your will. It should be something you both want."

"Well, I didn't. Not with him."

With whom then? Phil wondered. *Vincent Wynn-Taylor?*

"He tried. He'd stick his fingers in my bodice and rubbed his . . . against me. It was awful. He didn't care about me at all."

Unlike someone else? Phil wondered. Should she ask and risk frightening Agnes? She had to risk it. "Someone like Vincent, who does?"

Agnes blushed. "He's a gentleman and has such lovely manners, and he cares what one thinks, and . . ." Her eyes, red-rimmed but sparkling blue, widened. "Perry was none of those things. He made my skin crawl. But I didn't kill him."

"Do you know who did?"

Agnes stared at her, then shook her head. "No. No. It wasn't one of us. It couldn't be."

"I'm afraid it might be. So you must tell me anything that you know."

"I don't know anything." The girl was trembling. "Except . . ."

Phil squeezed her hand encouragingly. She was afraid to speak.

"I know, at least I think, Maud did it. With Perry. I passed him in the hall one afternoon and he didn't stop to do the things he usually tried with me. So I kept going and Maud was lying on her bed. Her dress was mussed, and she was crying. She tried to hide it, but when I pressed her, she said she loved him.

"I think they'd been—anyway, she said if I didn't want him, she did. And I said she couldn't have him, because it was practically settled and my parents would be so disappointed. I couldn't let them down. And she called me selfish. And oh how I wish I had just said, 'Take him.' But I didn't. Now he's dead. And someone tried to kill Mama. What's happening to us?"

Morris appeared at the door and came striding toward them. It was the fastest Phil had ever seen him move. "Aggie, Mama is worried. We couldn't find you. But I should have known you'd be here." He glanced at Phil. "And now you've upset everyone."

"I'm sorry," Agnes said.

"Well, get along then. No harm done."

Agnes pulled her hands from Phil's and ran to the house.

"You'll have to forgive my sister, Lady Dunbridge. She's as flighty as they come. Pay no attention to what she says. Mama will settle her down."

"What do you think she said?" Phil asked suddenly, looking at Morris in a new light. Maybe he wasn't the lazy, uninterested person he'd been acting like.

"Oh," he said on a sigh. "I have no idea. She gets strange notions. Excuse me." He strode after his sister.

Phil crossed her arms against the chill air and watched him go. Something was amiss here.

So far her inquiries had led her to business dealings. Could it be that she'd missed the signs of that lowest, according to Mr. X, motive for murder, passion?

Well, she wouldn't figure it out standing shivering in the garden. She returned to the house, where she checked on the card room denizens. Harry and Newty were exactly where she'd left them. Morris was back in his chair with his magazine as if he'd never left, and Effie and Maud had returned. She cautioned them all not to leave unless they told her or Godfrey, and she went into the parlor.

Agnes was sitting with her mother, her head on Gwen's shoulder, their hands clasped together.

Everyone was there, except Godfrey. Did he think that being in the War Department meant he didn't have to follow the rules of investigation? Of course he did. And he was probably right. He certainly wielded more power than any of them, including John Atkins and possibly more than her elusive Mr. X.

Phil sat down in a chair near Daisy. She really needed to talk to Lily and Preswick. They might have insight into whether Elva was the intended victim and not just an innocent bystander.

But she didn't dare leave this group to their own devices. Any one of them might be the next victim. Or one of them might be the murderer and try to escape. She would have to trust her servants to proceed with their own investigations—which they no doubt were—and hope to heaven they were taking proper precautions for their own safety.

It was three hours before they heard the sound of an automobile stop in front of the house. The tenuous quiet of the group erupted into a fresh bout of jumpiness, tears, and general anxiety.

Godfrey went to meet the newcomer. Phil heard several voices in the entry hall; one of them was John Atkins. He seemed to be giving orders. So he had brought men with him.

Phil cautioned herself to stay seated. She knew Atkins wouldn't appreciate her presence, and she didn't want to cause any friction between the two men. Atkins was already chafing under Godfrey's thumb. And she, and probably Atkins, knew that Godfrey would have no compunction about throwing Atkins out if he entered areas that Godfrey deigned off-limits. It still wasn't clear what those limits were. Or why.

There were things Atkins should know. She'd had plenty of time to think while she waited for his arrival. Time to try to put the pieces of this puzzle together. Tie what connections she could to Perry's murder and Elva's.

Banking? Stock? Steel? Passion. A mare's nest indeed.

And where were Godfrey and Atkins? It didn't take this long to say hello, there's been a murder, here's the body, and to return to the parlor with Atkins.

Of course. It was because he wasn't coming back to the parlor. He'd taken Atkins straight to the sitting room to view the evidence.

Well, if they thought they could—

The parlor door opened and Tillis stepped inside. "If you could join Mr. Bennington in the sitting room, Lady Dunbridge."

Well, that was more like it. Phil followed him out, careful not to look at the others. She didn't know what they were thinking and she certainly didn't want them to know her thoughts.

Elva's body was still lying just where they had dragged it.

Tillis had covered it with a white linen cloth, perhaps a table-cloth. Phil tried not to look.

The sitting room door was shut but the butler knocked and held it open.

Phil had a sudden vision of him stepping inside and announcing a visit by the Countess of Dunbridge.

"Thank you, Tillis. That will be all."

He bowed and left. Phil went inside and shut the door.

The windows were open. The room was cold. There was the faint residual odor of stramonium and a stronger one of kerosene, which must have spilled when Godfrey knocked the vaporizer over. It was amazing that the whole room hadn't gone up in flames. The vaporizer lay on its side on the table. The glass globe that protected the flame had rolled across the floor. The remains of the inhalant were spread like cigar ash on the table and onto the carpet.

John Atkins knelt, studying the remains.

Godfrey stood observing him from several feet away. "Ah, Lady Dunbridge."

Atkins turned his head, pushed to his feet, nodded. "Lady Dunbridge."

"Detective Sergeant."

"Mr. Bennington tells me you were first on the scene."

Phil frowned. Why so terse? He couldn't be angry at her already.

"Pure coincidence. We were helping Gwen down the hall when we heard this terrifying scream." Phil glanced back at the closed door, picturing the body that lay beyond it.

"Truly terrifying," she repeated, trying to give him a sense of how awful that sound had been. "Elva must have been deeply hallucinating. She staggered out into the doorway, flailing her arms, her face contorted. It was horrible." Phil couldn't prevent a shudder.

"You came in here?"

"Well, of course. Elva collapsed and fell back into the room.

Godfrey ran to turn off the vaporizer. Then we pulled her into the hallway to get her away from the fumes. Unfortunately it was too late.

"Just the little time it took to get her out—" She shuddered.

He didn't say anything, just frowned more deeply. Then he turned to Godfrey. "Did Elva always prepare and administer the stramonium to Mrs. Pratt?"

"Yes, I believe so. But perhaps Luther could best answer that question."

"Most asthmatics use a nebulizer. That is considered the most efficient method."

Godfrey paused. "It seems that the case with the nebulizer in it was inadvertently left in Manhattan. The vaporizer was set up in the sitting room. Fortunately, Luther keeps a syringe and ampules of atropine in his valise that can be used for severe attacks."

"Why not go directly to the syringe if it is so effective?"

"It's my understanding that it is used only in the severest cases. Gwen hates the needles, and Luther hates hurting Gwen. So the vaporizer was the logical choice. And it isn't uncommon for her to use it.

"But Detective Sergeant, these doses are premeasured by the pharmacist. They must be very precise or . . ." Godfrey spread his hands. "A tragedy like this can happen."

"Where is the rest of this incense?"

"I don't know. Probably with the rest of the medicine. Ah, there is the case." Godfrey started to get it.

"Please don't touch it," Atkins said.

"Yes, of course. I beg your pardon. Do you think there are more tainted doses?"

More likely he wants to take fingerprints from it, thought Phil. Atkins might be tight-lipped about his proceedings, but Phil knew he was up to date in his methodology.

"I will need to speak with Mrs. Pratt. If you will provide a comfortable space for her to answer some questions."

The two men eyed each other.

Really, there was a murderer loose and they were fighting a turf war? In the most civil way, to be sure, but still . . .

"I believe I saw a very nice little sitting room on my way to the garden," Phil said.

Both of the men's heads snapped toward her.

Had they forgotten she was there?

"Of course," Godfrey said.

"I suppose you will insist on accompanying her," Atkins said.

"But naturally, she'll need my support. After all, that's why I'm here."

Atkins's expression said he wasn't fooled in the least.

In the end both she and Godfrey were allowed to stay while Atkins interviewed Gwen.

Gwen was surprisingly calm as Atkins asked her about her asthma, the drugs she took, where they were kept when they were not in use. She answered succinctly and calmly, reaffirming what Godfrey had told them in the sitting room.

She really didn't need Phil for support: Gwen Pratt was a remarkably strong woman despite her breathing difficulties.

Several minutes into the interview the door opened and this time, Luther Pratt strode through the door.

"I must insist—"

"Very well," Atkins said with resignation in his voice. "Come in. We're finished here for the moment. I am confiscating the remainder of the Datura powders." He turned to Gwen. "Do not use any medication that hasn't been locked securely. Can you manage or would you prefer to return to the city?"

"I'll be fine, Detective Sergeant," Gwen said. "The young people have so looked forward to the balloon ascension. It's only a day."

Only a day, thought Phil and knew Atkins was thinking the same thing.

"When you return, do not take any medication that was left behind. Order a new supply of everything. I'll confiscate any unused applications when I return to the city."

"You think there's more?" asked Luther.

"It is a possibility."

"But I just gave her a vial of atropine. Good Lord. Gwen?"

"Luther, my dear. I'm fine. It must have been a dreadful mistake. I've used this prescription many times before and it did no harm."

"How many times?" Atkins asked. "The box here has only two doses missing."

"Oh, that is a new batch, I believe, let me see. Oh yes, it came the day after . . . Agnes's party."

And Perry Fauks's murder, Phil thought.

"You're certain of that?"

Gwen's brows knit.

But Phil remembered. "When I visited that day, Vincent Wynn-Taylor had just come in. He said that he'd been to the pharmacy and had picked up your medicine. I saw him hand it to Elva."

"I've used it since and it didn't have this effect."

"They might not all be tainted," Atkins said. "It could have been selective and left to be used anytime. A ticking time bomb, if you will."

"But why?" Gwen asked.

"That way the killer wouldn't have to be present when the fatal dose was taken."

"That's diabolical," Luther said.

"Yes, it is," Atkins said. "Now I want to talk to Vincent Wynn-Taylor."

Wynn-Taylor was not as good a witness as Gwen. He seemed nervous and when Atkins told him about the poison, he cried, "Oh my God, oh my God. I picked it up from the pharmacy. It's my fault."

Atkins sat and listened and looked perturbed when Godfrey finally said, "No, my boy. Not your responsibility. How were you to know?"

After that he calmed down, and Atkins veered into another line of questioning that he hadn't been allowed to conduct after the first murder.

Godfrey didn't stop him. He seemed to have acquiesced to the idea that he needed Atkins to see them clear.

"You were at the ball that night?"

"Yes, I was invited. I'm not a servant, but a man of business."

"And did you have occasion to see Mr. Fauks—outside of the ballroom?"

"I don't remember. It was a crush, we must have passed a number of times during the evening." He thought back, his eyes rolling up in the way people did when they were thinking. It was a habit Phil had broken herself of years before.

Wynn-Taylor shook his head. "Maybe in passing in the hallway. Nothing that stands out. Oh, he was at the other end of the table at supper. No, nothing."

"Did you see any altercations between Perry and anyone?"

He hesitated, just long enough to make Phil wonder.

"I did happen . . . no, it was nothing."

"I'll be the judge of that," Atkins said. "You were saying."

Vincent cast a look at Godfrey.

"Go ahead, Vincent. Anything you say here will be in confidence."

The detective sergeant's eyes flashed but his expression remained even. He was very good at hiding his feelings. But he was clearly displeased with Godfrey's interference.

"I did overhear something, earlier in the evening. I don't know if it's important. I had gone to fetch something for Mrs. Pratt. They were in the study. I wouldn't have stopped but . . ."

"Yes, what did you overhear?"

"An argument. Or at least loud voices. I wouldn't mention it but . . ."

Again the look toward Godfrey. "Mr. Pratt and Mr. Jeffrey."

Pratt and Jeffrey?

"It was about money matters. I-I shouldn't be saying this. I'm sure it has nothing to do with Perry's death, but—"

"Go ahead, Vincent," Godfrey said.

"Well, sir. Mr. Jeffrey was asking for money again. Only this time Mr. Pratt said no. And that he, Mr. Jeffrey, needed to start living within his means, and, well, it isn't the first time. I was about to ease away, when Mr. Jeffrey said that Fauks had ruined him."

"He was speaking of Perry Fauks?"

"I just assumed that, but . . . then he blamed Mr. Pratt for his troubles. Which is a damn lie. Mr. Pratt has been nothing but kind and generous to the man. I wouldn't say anything normally, but it just goes beyond the pale. Mr. Pratt has been more than generous because of Mrs. Jeffery being Mrs. Pratt's sister. And everyone knows it was you who got him his position in the department because of your friendship with the Pratts."

Oh really, thought Phil. She'd half expected an accusation of murder. She relaxed.

"Then he did say something strange."

Phil perked up again. So did Godfrey and Atkins.

"That he was going to confront Mr. Sheffield that very night."

"Sheffield? Not Fauks?"

"Yes. Mr. Pratt told him not to be a damn fool, and he'd throw him out for good if he disrupted Agnes's debut. But that couldn't have anything to do with this."

"Anything else?" Atkins asked.

"No, nothing."

"Then thank you, you may go."

Vincent practically fled the room.

"Well, Lady Dunbridge?" Atkins said.

"What?" Was he actually asking her opinion?

"Sheffield," she said. "Good heavens. We've forgotten all about Sheffield. Godfrey, we have to tell him."

"Tell me what?" Atkins asked.

"He's hiding in the cottage by the lake."

23

Atkins turned on Godfrey. "You knew about this? You've been harboring a possible murderer. Where is he?"

Godfrey's lips tightened. He seemed to deliberate. Then said, "This way, Detective Sergeant." He preceded them into the hallway. "Coats, Tillis," he ordered.

Atkins was still wearing his, but the butler appeared immediately, holding two coats almost as if he'd anticipated them.

When he helped Phil into hers, she expected Atkins to say something, but he seemed to have given up getting rid of her.

Enfin, she thought. Maybe he would finally begin to accept her help.

Godfrey led them through the house and out the side door to the walkway that would take them into the woods and to the cottage. He walked quickly, not waiting to see if they followed, and for a moment Phil wondered if he was trying to get ahead of them to warn Sheffield.

But when they got to the steps where the walk ended and a smaller path led into the woods, he stopped. "The fog is still heavy in places, please follow me closely."

They went single file, Atkins insisting that Phil go ahead of him, which was chivalrous, she hoped, but probably more utilitarian to keep her within reach.

They soon came to the cottage. The lights were out even though it was getting dark. Atkins stepped abreast of Godfrey and held out his arm. Shook his head.

It all looked rather slow motion in the fog.

Godfrey came to stand by Phil, and Atkins motioned them back. He reached into his coat and pulled out a rather large revolver.

Godfrey started forward, but Phil grabbed his arm, shook her head.

Atkins turned the knob and, standing well to the side of the doorframe, pushed the door open, waited for four of Phil's pounding heartbeats, then went inside.

Phil and Godfrey stood rooted to the spot. No gun reports, no sounds of scuffling.

Still they didn't move.

The glow of a lamp filled the doorway.

Dreading what she might see, Phil let Godfrey lead the way. He peered inside then ushered her through the doorway. It was empty. Atkins was just coming out of the back rooms. Shook his head.

Isaac Sheffield was gone. The papers he'd piled on the desk, the briefcase, all gone. The only thing that lingered was the faint aroma of a pipe tobacco she knew all too well.

Atkins ran past them and out the door.

"Detective Atkins, come back, it's easy to get lost in the fog." Godfrey followed Atkins out.

Phil ran to the door, looked to her left, where the men had gone. She couldn't see either of them.

Just like men. She'd probably have to go rescue both of them.

They appeared at her right like two lost phantoms and went back into the cabin, leaving her on the stoop like a servant.

She followed them inside.

"Do you know where he is?" Atkins demanded.

"No. He asked if he could stay here while attempting to recover funds that had been stolen from his company."

Atkins shot a look at Phil. "I suppose you knew about this, too."

"Only because I followed Godfrey." She lifted her chin. She had no intention of letting him scold her like she was some naughty schoolgirl. "Which I might add, it's a good thing I did. Or you might not know about him being here at all."

"Look, Atkins, you can't think that Sheffield killed Perry. He's completely loyal to the company and the family. He's been moving heaven and earth to save it."

"You said that. Save it from what?"

"Perry stole funds to invest in some scheme. Evidently he lost everything. At least, Isaac hasn't been able to find the money. I don't know how many people have lost their investment or if it can be reclaimed. Fauks stock has already plummeted. If the company fails, it will inevitably start another panic. I don't know that the economy can handle another blow this soon. Discretion is imperative."

"My job is not the economy." Atkins's features stood out starkly in the lamplight. "Bringing criminals to trial is. And right now I have the murders of two people on my hands. Hands that have been tied, I might add, from the outset. I've been thwarted at every turn. I don't know whether that was your doing or Mr. Pratt's. But because of that, another murder has occurred."

"Now see here." Godfrey held up his hand. "Isaac Sheffield is not a murderer, but if you need to call out a full-scale search for him, go ahead."

Phil piped in before the men could come to cuffs. "I wouldn't bother, if I were you, Detective Sergeant."

"What do you know about it?"

"Not much, but I have a good idea that Isaac Sheffield did not run."

"Then where the hell is he?"

"I believe he's been kidnapped."

Both men stared at her.

"Lady Dunbridge, really," Godfrey said.

Atkins eyed her speculatively. "What do you mean by kidnapped? Who kidnapped him? And why?"

"I mean kidnapped and I don't know why or by whom."

"Then how on earth do you know?"

Phil had no idea what to tell him. She knew she couldn't tell him what she really suspected. That some other agency was ahead of him. The telltale remnants of Mr. X's tobacco hadn't been a mistake. He would never be so careless. He'd left that clue deliberately.

Guiding her toward something. And he'd left it because he wouldn't be visiting her tonight to tell her in person. He'd taken Sheffield somewhere, probably for questioning. Thwarting Atkins again.

What a mess. Four people, all who wanted to get to the truth, none of them trusting the other, Atkins constrained by his superiors, Godfrey either constrained by his or willing to do whatever he had to do to contain a scandal, Mr. X for whatever reason, and Phil sent here to investigate by some unknown person or agency for some unknown reason.

She couldn't tell them that. Not only would they laugh themselves silly, they would most likely throw her in the lunatic asylum.

And they were getting nowhere. This was such a stupid way to do business.

"Women's intuition," she said finally.

Atkins threw up his hands.

Godfrey smiled. "We can't argue with that, can we, Detective Sergeant?"

Was he humoring her? She didn't like the look behind his eyes. She'd supposed until now he had been on their side. Suddenly she wasn't so sure.

"And as such," she continued, "I think we should return to the house and . . . and continue our investigation over a cocktail."

Atkins's mouth dropped open, Godfrey did a double take.

She didn't blame them. They must think she'd gone stark raving mad. Because in that split second she had come to a disappointing conclusion. She would have to solve this murder without them. And to do that she needed to get back to the house.

"My nose is cold, my feet are wet, and my coat weighs two stone. I'm going back to the house." She didn't wait for them to acquiesce but strode out of the room. If ever there was a day for split skirts it was today and she'd changed out of hers and into her checked foulard for luncheon instead. It was probably ruined from tromping through the woods.

It was a stupid thing to be thinking at such a crucial moment, but it occupied her mind with something besides murder. And she needed to keep her composure intact and her tongue silent to be most effective.

It had occurred to her more than once that she might be no more than a pawn in some game of powerful men. Fine. She was up to the challenge. She'd carry on whether they liked it or not, with or without them.

She started up the path, her eyes and ears alert for any sound that shouldn't be there. Something that would tell her that Sheffield and whoever took him were hiding nearby.

All she could hear were her two companions' footsteps behind her.

Had the others moved out of hearing distance, perhaps even out of the area? They might now be sitting in a comfortable office somewhere grilling their prisoner.

But was Sheffield the murderer? If he had killed Perry why would Godfrey hide him, and given him access to Gwen? Were finances more important than friends and family? To many, they were.

When they reached the house, Godfrey continued inside but Atkins pulled her aside.

"What is going on here?"

"I don't know."

"Godfrey is going ahead to have me called off this case. I don't know why he called me out here in the first place if he was just going to obstruct my progress. And you. I don't know what game you're playing but it's no place for an amateur."

"Amateur?" She clamped her mouth shut to keep her temper in. She had almost said she was no amateur. But her employer "relied on her discretion" and almost a decade in London society had taught her the importance of discretion when it mattered most.

She did, however, see the need for more study in her future.

"I want you and Lily and Preswick out of here immediately."

"It's too late to leave. It's coming on night, too dark to see the roads."

"Lady Dunbridge, I know you're trying to help, but you're out of your depth. Two people are dead. A killer is out there. This is not some game for the amusement of a bored dilettante. And I don't want you to get hurt."

"You arrogant—" She broke off. "You care about my safety?"

"Of course I do." He cleared his throat. "I would for any citizen."

"I'm not a citizen."

"Don't quibble with me. You're going home." He took her by the arm and steered her into the house.

"You can't send me packing—besides you haven't searched Elva's room here, have you?"

"I am about to do just that."

"I'll help you."

"Thank you but not necessary."

"Are you expecting to find clues? Are you conversant with where ladies hide things?"

His eyes narrowed. "Elva was a servant and I'm a policeman— a public servant."

"Touché," she said, trying not to show her chagrin.

They moved down the hallway. Fortunately Elva's body had been removed. By the coroner? Did one live in the area? Or by one of Godfrey's staff?

Phil's patience broke. "You need me—you don't know anything that's been going on here."

He slowed, looked around, then yanked her behind the stairs. She'd been here before and gotten an earful. "This is cozy."

"What do you know?"

"Let's see, where shall I start."

"Don't push me."

She didn't want to push him, she wanted him to cooperate and help her. "I'm perfectly willing to help. Besides discovering Sheffield's whereabouts, dragging Elva out of a noxious room, finding Mrs. Kidmore-Young, shall I go on? The family is frightened; they will never tell you the truth for fear of naming someone they love. You know that as well as I. But I've learned this so far.

"Elva, the latest victim, has been nervous ever since Perry was killed."

"That's only natural."

"Perhaps, but I think there is more to it than that.

"Gwen just today said Elva wanted to talk to her about something that she was worried about. But then Gwen had her attack and they didn't speak. Now Elva's dead.

"I've had Lily and Preswick getting to know the servants and listening for anything that they might have seen or heard and are too frightened to tell.

"I talked to Sheffield. He explained what he'd been doing. I believe him." She held up both hands as if to ward him off. "But I haven't ruled him out."

She stopped to take a breath and to think. She'd gotten carried away. And she still hadn't told him about her theft of Perry's wastepaper basket. She'd been trying to protect Maud, but for all she knew, the Jeffrey twins could be cold-blooded killers and not the silly naïve girls they appeared.

"I . . ." She braced herself. "I found two interesting scraps of paper in Perry's wastepaper basket."

"What?" he exploded.

"Shh. I was trying to protect a young lady's reputation and inadvertently discovered something else, which I would have told you but we all came out here and you were nowhere to be found."

"Uh-huh. And what were these tidbits?"

"One was the corner of what Preswick says is a stock ticker tape. The other was a crumpled newspaper article about the War Department's test of spy balloons."

"And?"

At last, he seemed interested. "The War Department has been testing those balloons all week. Tomorrow's exhibition isn't just a festive day for spectators."

"How do you know this?"

"I saw them when I was at Holly Farm. Bobby said they'd be at it all week."

"And how do you see this as being important in this investigation?"

"Simple, Detective Sergeant. Godfrey, Perry, and lots of money. The War Department needs steel."

"That's a lot of supposition from a newspaper article."

But she'd heard the shift in his voice. He was actually listening.

"And the scrap of stock. I don't know how that fits. Sheffield says Perry embezzled the company funds and they're about to go under. He also said Perry used it to buy stock in another company in competition for a government contract for steel."

Atkins blew out breath.

"And rumor has it that company is worthless, now that J.P. Morgan has bought out some Tennessee company and has secured the monopoly on steel."

"So someone is in possession of a lot of money or a lot of worthless paper."

"Exactly. But who?"

"Amazing."

"What is?"

"You, Lady Dunbridge. I don't know how you do this, but it's further than I've been able to get."

"Because you play by the rules. Actually so do I, but it's a different set of rules."

"I think I prefer mine."

"But you have to admit, in some instances, mine will allow me to get the job done."

"I could get in a whole lot of trouble."

She smiled. "My dear Detective Sergeant, my guess is, it isn't a state totally unknown to you."

He laughed in spite of himself. "You are . . ."

"Anxious to catch a killer. Let us go."

Godfrey was waiting for them when they reentered the hallway. He didn't seem at all surprised to find them coming out from behind the stairs. "I've asked Tillis to hold dinner for a half hour. I thought you would want to get out of those wet clothes before you dined."

He turned to Atkins. "Alas I am unable—"

"I will need to see the maid's room," Atkins said, cutting off the rest of Godfrey's apology.

Phil knew what he was going to say. That he was unable to invite Atkins to dine with them. Ridiculous of course, he could probably seat fifty at table. A slap? Yes. Also a backhanded compliment that he recognized Atkins as someone worthy of being apologized to.

"You've been called back to town."

"Godfrey—" Phil began.

He stopped her with a flick of his hand.

There was a standoff that seemed to go on forever, and Phil couldn't think of a thing that would help the situation.

"You may search the maid's room," Godfrey said. "I'll have someone show you to the servants' wing, and then they will show you out. Nothing personal, Detective Sergeant."

"Good to know." Still Atkins deliberated. Then he reached into his pocket.

"I'll be staying nearby with friends." Atkins handed Phil a card. "The telephone exchange is written there." He glanced at Godfrey. "In case you need me."

"Mr. Bennington." Atkins strode toward the servants' stairs without a backward look. The footman barely got there before him. Phil knew he was fuming, and she didn't blame him.

"Really, Godfrey."

"I hated to do it, Philomena. He's a good man. You can tell, you know."

"Then why?"

"He can be trusted, but some of his superiors can't be. And being an honest man . . ." He shook his head. "He's between a rock and a hard place. I couldn't take the chance."

"What is going on here, Godfrey?"

"On my own honor, I don't know. And I would feel much better with Atkins on the case, but I have my superiors, too." He clicked his fingers and a footman came to relieve them of their coats.

"A half hour then?" He walked off to the back of the house.

Lily was waiting in her room when Phil walked in. She jumped up from the dressing table bench. "What's happening out there? Is Elva really dead? Madam?"

"Yes, I'm afraid so." Phil was suddenly tired. Her body ached, her head ached, her heart ached. For Elva, for John Atkins, for Lily, whose past she didn't even know.

"They say downstairs that someone tried to kill Mrs. P-r-r-att. But I don't think so. Elva was afraid for herself." Lily's mouth worked. Phil didn't know whether to comfort or pretend she didn't see. But Lily turned away, answering the question for her.

"Did she tell you what she was afraid of?"

"No. She didn't say. But I could tell."

Because she too knew fear?

"What will you wear into dinner, madam? The others have gone ahead."

"It hardly matters," Phil said, sinking onto the dressing table bench. "My peach silk taffeta, I suppose. As soon as dinner is over, I'll complain of a headache. You and Preswick will meet me here."

"Are we going to catch the killer-r-r?"

"We're going to try. The detective sergeant is searching Elva's room."

"Why?"

"I suppose, in case she was trying to poison Mrs. Pratt."

"Not Elva. She is dead and not her mistress. And she ador-r-red Mrs. Pratt—madam."

"Fetch me a gown, then hurry back to the servants' quarters and see if the detective sergeant finds anything."

Lily had gone to the door of the dressing room, but she stopped. "You don't think they were after Mrs. Pratt, do you, madam?"

"I don't know, but whoever did this was willing to kill many people in order to reach his goal. Murder is bad enough, but that is diabolical. I'm going to suggest you serve Mrs. Pratt until we get back to the city. I don't think he will try again so soon." Phil stopped. "But not if you're afraid."

"Me? I hope he tr-ries. I will slit his thr-roat."

Phil gritted her teeth as a chill ran up her spine. "I don't think that will be necessary, and please, Lily. Do not put yourself in harm's way."

"I am not afraid."

"But I am. I don't know what I would do without you."

Lily blinked.

"Now get me into this gown. I don't want to be late for dinner. And you don't want to miss anything belowstairs."

24

Dinner was a quiet affair. Luther and Gwen did not come down. Agnes sat, not eating and threatening to dissolve into a flood of tears. Ruth sat between Morris and Newty. Harry spent a few minutes attempting to engage Effie and Maud in conversation and finally gave up. Vincent barely looked up from his plate. Daisy kept Godfrey entertained, for which Phil was thankful.

Phil had plenty to think about and even more to do. She needed to consult with Preswick and Lily, find out if they had learned anything more about Elva and whether Atkins's search of her room had been successful.

Finding the missing letter opener had suddenly taken on more urgency. Something had tied the two murders together. Unless Gwen was the actual target and Elva had been a necessary sacrifice. Why Perry and Gwen? The only thing Phil could see they had in common was Agnes.

She looked across the table at the girl, whose eyes hadn't left her dinner plate. She hadn't liked Perry's advances. Had she complained to Gwen? Had Gwen taken matters into her own hands?

Gwen might have managed to kill Perry and had Elva help her dump his body in the laundry chute. Elva had been with Gwen for many years and, according to Gwen, was very loyal. And according to Lily, very scared. Maybe she'd begun to feel the weight of guilt, had threatened to confess.

Phil's mind balked at the possibility. Which was no excuse for not looking at the facts. Elva toward the end of the party would be upstairs readying her mistress's things for bed. It would be easy enough for them to . . . What? And why in the middle of a party with hundreds of guests?

Unless Perry had actually gone further than Agnes had admitted. Lured her upstairs to her or his room. Gwen had caught them and was furious. Stabbed him with what? The letter opener? She kept it in her upstairs sitting room. The topaz was found on the second floor. There was a good chance that was where Perry was killed, or at least put into the—

"Don't you agree, Lady Dunbridge?"

Phil started. "I beg your pardon?"

Godfrey gave her a tight smile; the meal was evidently wearing on him in spite of his delightful dinner mate. "I was agreeing with your idea that Lady Warwick should do a speaking tour in the States. Perhaps in the spring."

Phil smiled back, thinking how fake they all were acting. "Absolutely. I think people would be interested in her life and her ideas." But mainly in her scandalous behavior, she added to herself.

"Then it's settled."

"Oh Godfrey . . ."

Phil went back to her ruminations. She hadn't gotten much further when dessert was brought in, a light Charlotte russe that was delicious but which everyone ate as if rounding the homestretch at Belmont.

As soon as Godfrey put down his spoon, Daisy stood. "Shall we?" she said, cuing the ladies to withdraw. Ruth gave Daisy a brief scathing look before dutifully standing. Did she actually think she would replace Gwen as hostess?

The ladies withdrew to the parlor. Phil caught up with Daisy. "I have a headache."

Daisy frowned. "Must be the weather."

"No doubt. Please don't sound the alarm if I'm not in my room when you retire."

Daisy's eyebrows rose is supposition.

"I'll tell you all about it later, but try to keep everyone here and things going as long as possible."

"Everyone?"

"Everyone." In a louder voice Phil said, "I must apologize. I have the beginnings of a headache."

"I think I shall retire, also," said Ruth.

Daisy sprang into action. "Oh, Mrs. Jeffrey. Ruth. You can't leave me to fend for myself among all these young people. I depend on you to help me make the best of things." She took Ruth's arm and led her farther into the room, while Phil made her escape.

There were no boisterous voices coming from the dining room. Phil had a feeling the men would not linger overlong over their port.

Making certain no footman was in sight, she lifted her skirts and ran up the stairs to her suite of rooms.

Lily and Preswick were there.

"That detective didn't find anything," Lily said.

Preswick looked down his quite intimidating nose at her.

She made a face and added, "Sorry, my lady."

"Of course. We are all a little overexcited tonight." Phil glanced at her imperturbable butler and thought, *Most of us.*

"So there was nothing in Elva's room that could be any kind of a clue. Did you speak with Detective Sergeant Atkins before he left?"

"No, but I waited for him in the servants' hall downstairs. I knew he'd come down that way. I just knew he would. Mr. Tillis was with him. But as he passed he shook his head just a little at me. Like this." Lily made a deadpan expression and moved her head slowly and minutely to the left. "But he was looking right at me. It was a message."

A message indeed. But did it mean he hadn't found anything or he couldn't talk in front of anyone? And now he was miles away at some friends' house.

"Nonetheless we shall search again. Let us go."

They used the back stairs to the third-floor wing where the servants were housed. They met no one; still, Lily ran ahead to make sure they could enter unnoticed.

Phil and Preswick scurried down the hall to Elva's room and Lily shut the door behind them.

It was a spacious room with a worktable, a wardrobe, and an upholstered sitting chair. The bed was narrow but looked comfortable enough. There was very little indication that anyone had searched through it, evidence of Atkins's neatness as well as thoroughness. And he hadn't found anything.

They searched again, starting with the most obvious—drawers, worktable, mattress, clothes cupboard. They pulled back the oval rag rug; sounded the floorboards; looked behind pictures and emptied the sewing basket.

"Nothing," Lily said.

Phil sighed and sat down on the bed. "I was sure she must know something that made her the target of the murderer. And if she was frightened, and didn't tell anyone, what was she afraid of?

"Tell us again what she said to you, Lily."

"She said there were bad things happening. That she couldn't stop it. And she didn't understand it. And she was afraid."

"She told you all this?"

"Since we came here, to Foggy Acres. I think at first she told me because she didn't think I could understand. Sometimes it just helps to say things out loud."

"Yes, very important," Phil said, hoping Lily knew she could tell her anything without fear of retribution.

"When she started to wind down, I had to pretend to understand and speak a little English."

"Clever," Phil said. "Did she say what she was afraid of? Of getting caught? Of something she saw?"

"I tried to tell her that you would keep her safe but it took too many English words. And I didn't want to give myself away."

"You did right." It had been stupid for Phil to have asked her to speak in Italian. A piece of self-assuredness and arrogance that had surely come back to bite them.

"And there was only one thing that could keep her safe."

"Safe from what? Murder? Because she was afraid of another one happening? You think she saw the murderer?"

"Perhaps, but she didn't say. Maybe she saw what happened and was afraid to tell."

"But why not tell? She had friends here. Employers who cared about her well-being."

"Because, my lady, if I might venture a theory."

"Please do, Preswick."

"Because she was afraid of someone in the household?"

"Possibly," Phil agreed.

"Or because she was afraid someone she cared about was the murderer," Lily added.

"A lover perhaps," Phil said. "Lily, did she mention anyone that she might be smitten with? Someone she might want to protect?"

Lily gave her a look that defied description. "She is a lady's maid. She makes money, lives in comfortable surroundings, and her work is not too hard; she has an amiable mistress. She wouldn't be so stupid."

Phil raised an eyebrow.

"Well, I wouldn't be." She hesitated. "I was thinking of her mistress."

"Mrs. Pratt?"

"Elva was very loyal. She would protect her with her life." Lily frowned. "Which maybe she did in the end."

The three of them grew silent on that thought.

Lily was the first to recover. "But I did see her talking to that secretary once. They were very appassionato."

"Romantic?"

"I don't think so. They were standing close, but I think it was so they wouldn't be heard. And that Morris is always slinking about. He's not very particular, that one."

"But why would Morris want to kill Perry? And then his own mother?" It defied the imagination.

"So what was it? What did she have that could protect her? She must have left a note or something." Phil stood, looked around the room, even to the ceiling. "Or the murder weapon." Phil took a couple of steps away, turned back to Lily and Preswick. "What if she found the murder weapon?"

"And hid it somewhere," Lily posed. "To keep it safe."

"The police searched the servants' quarters at the Pratts' house. So maybe she took extra precautions. Where would she put it?"

She turned to Lily, who glanced down at her own ankle.

Phil frowned back at her. "On her person?"

"She didn't say."

If the murder weapon was actually the missing letter opener, it was, according to Gwen, heavy and clumsy to use. Bending and working all day, it would be a difficult item to carry around.

And if she had, Atkins would have found it when he searched the body, as he surely must have done, and somehow have found a way to tell her so.

"Besides her own person, where would be the next safest place? Somewhere no one else could get to it. But there is no such place."

"What about among the medicines for Mrs. Pratt," Preswick suggested.

"That's good but Atkins already confiscated that and if he'd found anything surely he wouldn't have left us here to fend for ourselves. Where else? What else would a maid have access to—of course, her mistress's dressing room."

"You never go into your dressing room when I'm not there?" Lily asked.

"No. Why would I?"

Lily shrugged, darted a look at Preswick. "Sorry, Mr. Preswick."

Preswick nodded. "That's an idea, my lady. Do you think Mrs. Pratt would be averse to our searching her dressing room?"

"I think we should find out." Phil started toward the door. Stopped. "Damnation. Gwen had dinner sent to her room. Luther joined her there. If he's still there . . . Oh, never mind. Follow me and stay out of sight until I get rid of Luther. I'll come to the door after I've explained to Gwen what we want to do."

They hurried single file down the servants' stairs and back to the second floor. Preswick and Lily tucked themselves into a nearby closet and Phil scratched on Gwen's door.

Gwen was sitting on a small sofa, dressed in a yellow and light green wrapper, looking as fragile as the first bloom of spring. Luther sat beside her but he stood when Phil entered.

"I just came to see how you were feeling."

"She is very upset and can't be excited, Lady Dunbridge."

"Of course."

"Oh, Luther, I'm fine. Run along and have your port with the gentlemen. Philomena and I will have a nice visit."

"Gwen. Are you sure?"

"Yes, my dear. Sometimes a woman just needs for things to be normal and I had an idea about the drapes I wanted to discuss with my dear friend."

Luther looked askance at his wife. Even Phil was momentarily nonplussed.

But when he was gone, Gwen said, "How stupid. But it was the only thing I could think of at the moment. Sit down and tell me everything that has been happening. Luther thinks by not telling me anything, it will be better for me. I thought I might go mad if someone didn't come tell me the latest news."

"We don't have much time," Phil said. "We—Detective Sergeant Atkins and myself, and my two servants, who are quite in the know—we think Elva must have seen or heard something the night of Perry's murder. It's the only scenario that makes sense."

"So the killer wasn't after me?"

"I don't think so, but we will still take every precaution to keep you safe. But I need your permission to search your dressing room."

"My dressing room? What on earth for?"

"We think Elva must have some evidence that she thought would keep her safe or else she would have come to you—or run away."

"But she didn't."

"No," said Phil, slightly distracted as another thought crossed her mind. "To keep herself safe or perhaps indulge in a little blackmail. Surely she hadn't been so naïve to think that would make her safe. Once the killer knew she knew, it was only a matter of time. Oh Elva."

"Blackmail? She wasn't like that."

"Well, we're not sure, but since her room afforded no clues, the only other place she could have safely hidden something was—"

"My dressing room," Gwen said, sounding almost delighted. "I never go in there, nor anyone else."

"May we? Preswick and Lily are waiting outside."

"But of course. I'll help if I can."

As soon as they were all assembled, they went into Gwen's dressing room.

It was rather sparsely furnished since she'd only been outfitted for a weekend visit.

"Are you sure she brought it here and didn't leave it in the city?"

"She must have. Not having it at hand would rather defeat the purpose of having it. She would need to know it wouldn't be found. And outside of a safety-deposit box, which would be difficult for her to get to with her work schedule, I think she would keep it somewhere she could keep an eye on it without worrying about someone finding it."

"What do you think it is?"

"I'll recognize it when we find it." And Phil imagined Gwen would, too, if it turned out to be what she suspicioned.

Preswick searched the furniture and wall coverings, carefully keeping his face averted while the women pulled out gowns, stockings, shoes, and undergarments.

They unfolded and refolded. Shook skirts, felt in pockets. Opened handkerchief boxes and toiletry cases, lifted the rug. Gwen joined in with gusto, though Phil had to sit her down when the carpet set off a dance of dust motes that left her short of breath. From then on she watched from a chair in the doorway.

"You'll be our lookout," Phil told her. She seemed very pleased with the role.

Phil felt along the floor of the cupboard and pulled out a large tapestry bag. "What's this?"

"My needlepoint. Ruth gave it to me last Christmas. I really can't stand needlepoint or knitting or any of those things. But I bring it out for show whenever she's here. It wouldn't do to hurt her feelings, poor thing."

Phil placed it on a chair and opened it up. Inside were skeins and skeins of yarn and a piece of canvas with a patch of small spaces filled in with tiny, uneven stitches. Not Gwen Pratt's forte, to be sure. Phil shoved the frame back into the depths of the bag, felt around until her hand touched something hard. Cold. Metal. She pulled it out, and held it up.

"It's my letter opener!" Gwen exclaimed. "How on earth did it get in there?"

"If I'm not mistaken," Phil said, "it's also our murder weapon."

Gwen gasped. Preswick and Lily hurried over to see.

"Perry was killed with my letter opener?"

"That appears to be the case," Phil said.

"Good heavens. But not by Elva? How could she?"

"It seems unlikely unless she had an accomplice and surely they would have disposed of it in order not to garner any suspicion on themselves. I think she was either blackmailing someone else or using the threat of it to keep her safe."

Preswick took the opener from Phil. "Fingerprints, my lady."

Phil relinquished it without argument.

"Hold it to the light, Mr. Preswick," Lily said excitedly. Then her eyes widened as she realized what she had done; she broke into a spate of frantic Italian that even Phil couldn't understand.

"Yes, do, Preswick," Phil said, hoping to draw attention from Lily's sudden fluency in English.

But Gwen had noticed. "My goodness, Lily. Your English has certainly improved in the last few days." She cut a look toward Phil, more amused than angry, Phil was glad to see.

"A quick learner," she agreed. "Such an asset. Shall we continue?"

They all gathered around the vanity table. Preswick held the letter opener under the light. And Lily and Phil and Gwen, who had left her post at the door, crowded around him to get a closer look.

"Look there," Lily said, pointing to the blade.

Elva hadn't bothered to try to clean it and the blade was still smeared with dried blood. And where the blade met the handle, a ring of crusted blood was embedded in the seam. And at the top of the jewel-encrusted handle a sliver of paper had been wrapped around the handle and tied with a piece of blue yarn.

Phil could see something written on the outside, but letters were partially hidden by the yarn.

Preswick looked at Phil. They should probably wait for the detective sergeant before they removed it. But Phil didn't know where he was, possibly still driving to his friends' house. They could telephone, but what if he hadn't arrived? They would have to leave a message, then he would have to drive back.

It was ridiculous. Phil slipped away and opened the tapestry bag, dumped the contents on the floor; among the yarn was a pair of small sewing scissors. She knew they'd be there. Every girl had had one of these bags at one time or another. Phil was happy to say she, at present, did not, and would not ever again.

She took them back and with one snip the paper fell away to reveal the empty space where the Imperial topaz had been.

Phil started to pick up the paper, but stopped. "Will you do the honors, Mr. Preswick?"

Preswick pulled the cuffs of his gloves tighter, then carefully spread it out on the table. Phil and the others leaned over, beside themselves with anticipation.

Finally, the answer lay before them. The initials VW-T.

25

"No," Gwen said. "No."

"I think, Preswick, you should place that call to Detective Sergeant Atkins. Lily, help me get Mrs. Pratt back to her room."

"No, that isn't necessary. I'm fine. But I just won't believe that Vincent is a murderer. It's true that he wasn't able to continue living in the style of the other boys, but he works hard and without any recriminations."

"Recriminations?" Phil asked. "Why should he have recriminations?"

"Oh, I don't know the half of it. But it was some scheme these men are always getting into. Luther had introduced his father to a brokerage firm that appeared for all intents and purposes very legitimate. Luther certainly thought so. He invested in some funds, as well as Vincent's father, and let's see, Thomas, and Harry's father . . ."

"Godfrey?" Phil asked.

Gwen's lips pursed in concentration. "I don't believe so, though I could be wrong. He prefers to own a thing outright. And plus there's his work for the government. That keeps him in the know."

"So what happened?"

Gwen sat down on the settee. "You'd have to ask Luther for details. I'm not sure. There are always so many deals going on in the life of a banker, most of which are all very hush-hush and most of which they just don't want to bother our little heads with. As I recall, one of them found out about an impending disaster and they all pulled their money out. Except Leonard, Vincent's father, was out of town and couldn't be reached and by the time he was informed of the situation, it was too late.

"Evidently these things happen. It didn't ruin him, but that, with a series of other unfortunate events—his wife died a short while after that—well, he couldn't recoup his losses. Seems he'd been growing increasingly in debt due to her treatments and some bad financial deals.

"It was in no way Luther's fault but he felt he had to do something for Vincent, so he asked him to become his secretary. He thought he might eventually work his way into finding him a position at the bank without him having to go up through the ranks, which would add insult to the humiliation his family endured."

A well-meaning intention, Phil thought, but which only served to increase his humiliation by putting him constantly around the others while he was no longer considered one of them.

Things didn't look good for Vincent. His initials inscribed with the murder weapon would be bad enough. But a lot of things were beginning to make sense.

His pining for Agnes knowing he no longer had the means in which to attain her hand. Why he seemed uncomfortable around the others. Not only because of his position in the household but because of the history of their fathers. Morris's disdain for him.

It was bound to lead to resentment. And a case could be made that he'd just snapped. And taken it out on Perry Fauks. Because of Agnes. It must have been the last straw.

Well, if Preswick had been able to contact John Atkins, they would find out soon enough.

Phil and Gwen sat waiting for Preswick to return, the letter opener wrapped in one of Preswick's blindingly clean handkerchiefs lying on the sofa between them.

"You don't think the detective sergeant will suspect me?" Gwen asked into the silence.

Phil cut her a look. To her discredit, she *had* briefly considered Gwen as a suspect.

"Did you kill him?" she asked.

Gwen blinked several times. "Of course not. Why on earth would you even say such a thing?"

Phil sighed. "I don't know. The murder weapon belongs to you, and we found it in your needlepoint bag. Those are the kind of clues that policemen follow."

Gwen sucked in air.

Phil moved closer. "Do not get upset. I was just getting the possibility out of the way. And I would prefer you not take any more of your asthma medication than absolutely necessary until we get back to town and you have a new supply."

Gwen nodded, took a slow breath, closed her eyes and concentrated on breathing.

Phil concentrated on staying calm, not taking the investigation in hand and begin questioning Vincent herself. But she was not the expert that Atkins was, she was bound to make a hash of it. Still, it was infuriating not knowing.

She fairly jumped from the sofa when Preswick returned. "Did you find him?"

"No, my lady. His friends have not heard from him."

"Where is the man? What good is a telephone exchange if he's not going to be there to answer it?"

"I'm sure I couldn't say, my lady."

"I know." She sat back down. A frisson of unexpected anxiety swept through her as she imagined an automobile accident, a confrontation with the murderer, who managed to overpower him, or an ambush by same as he drove down the road.

Which was absurd, she assured herself. All the possible suspects were here. And most likely sitting downstairs in the parlor, where she'd left Daisy entertaining them.

"I think I should join the others."

"I'll come with you," Gwen said. "I can't stand being out of the know."

Phil totally agreed. Leaving her alone would give her time to worry herself into another attack. Not to mention there was a killer still among them.

With them all gathered in the parlor, Gwen would be safer. They all would be. And while they waited for Atkins to return, she would keep her eye on everyone.

Phil stood, picked up the letter opener. She had no intention of letting it out of her sight again, but there was no place to hide it on her person. The silk of her gown was too thin to be of any use. There was only one choice. She picked up the loathsome tapestry bag, placed the opener on the bottom, then crammed the yarn and scissors back inside.

Giving orders to Lily and Preswick to advise her as soon as they reached Atkins, and holding the bag close, Phil went downstairs with Gwen.

The first thing Phil saw when they entered the parlor was Daisy's tight smile. And the absence of Godfrey Bennington.

"You owe me," Daisy said under her breath when Phil reached her.

"What's been going on?"

Daisy threw her head back and laughed like Phil had just told her an amusing story. "It's like herding goldfish. This is the most peripatetic group of guests I've ever endured. They were not swayed by my discourse on workmen's rights. And Ruth Jeffrey nixed any little tidbit that was of interest. Really, you'd think those girls of hers were still in the nursery."

Phil tittered out a laugh that must have sounded unconvincing, considering the look Daisy shot her.

The doorbell rang, saving them from carrying on with their charade.

Moments later Tillis opened the door. He didn't bother to announce the visitors, for behind him stood John Atkins and Isaac Sheffield.

"Thank you," Atkins said. "I'll take it from here."

The butler stepped aside and Atkins ushered Sheffield into

the parlor. The detective sergeant was holding a pistol trained on the businessman.

Atkins swiftly took in the room. "Where is Mr. Bennington?"

"I'll get him," Daisy volunteered and hurried away.

She returned less than a minute later with their host.

"Good God, Atkins, what is the meaning of this? Where did you find him?" Then he saw the revolver. "Is that necessary?"

Yes, thought Phil. *I'd like to know, too. And where have you been all this time?*

Atkins tilted his head. He was still wearing his hat. He took it off and dropped it on the closest table, but he kept the revolver trained on Sheffield. "You must pardon the unorthodoxy of my visit, but there is only one of me."

Godfrey winced his acknowledgment.

"He's got it all wrong, Godfrey," Sheffield pleaded.

He was shivering so hard that his teeth clacked together, making the words come out in a stutter.

"Get by the fire, man." Godfrey exchanged looks with Atkins.

"Go ahead," Atkins said, and lowered the gun.

Sheffield hurried to the fire and stuck out his hands.

Gwen crossed to the coffee table and felt the pot. Then she poured a cup of coffee and went to hand it to Isaac Sheffield.

Phil started to move to stop her. She had no idea if Sheffield would take the cup or grab Gwen to hold as hostage.

But Atkins had already moved. He took the cup from Gwen and handed it to Sheffield.

Phil came up beside him. "How did you find him? Where was he?"

Atkins looked around the room.

For what? Phil wondered. To make sure everyone was there? Or was he looking for someone specific?

Godfrey strode over to where Sheffield was standing. "Sit down, Isaac, and tell us what is going on here."

Sheffield looked around, sat down in a chair near the fireplace. "I was kidnapped."

Phil sucked in her breath. *Ha.* She'd been correct. She couldn't help but cut a self-satisfied look at Atkins.

He merely looked away.

"Absurd," Godfrey protested. "Why? By whom? Where did they take you? Why did they let you go?"

"I don't know who they were. Or where I was. I think they must have chloroformed me. When I woke up I was in a room somewhere. It was unfurnished except for a table and chairs. And the walls were stone. At first I thought it was a prison. But then I saw the windows were covered over by a thick material."

He took a shuddering breath, either from cold or memory. "There were three of them that I saw. One was stationed by the door. One stood in the corner out of my sight line, and one asked questions."

"Sounds like an interrogation," Phil murmured, which earned her a sharp look from Atkins.

"At first I thought they were thieves or might be holding me for ransom. But they merely wanted to question me about the situation with Fauks Copper, Coal and Steel, and several other trusts. They wanted to know if the company had invested in . . . I can't even remember the name. I said no. They asked about Perry's takeover attempt of this company, and if I had known about it.

"I told them no, but they kept pressing me. Who set Perry up with funds? Who brokered the deal? I kept saying I didn't know. I found out about Perry's theft the day of the party. I don't know if they believed me. I can hardly believe it myself. He had to have accomplices, but until I can do a thorough audit, I can't know.

"I explained this, and cooperated even though I didn't know who they were; I still don't know. But they kept asking me questions, it seemed like for hours, then suddenly I was in the auto again. I don't remember anything until they dumped me in the woods near the cottage.

"So I made my way back there to find Detective Sergeant Atkins waiting for me."

Phil's mouth dropped open in a most unladylike fashion. "You were waiting for him? What happened to your friend? We've been telephoning you for the last hour. No wonder they didn't know where you were."

Atkins shrugged.

She turned a scowl on Godfrey. "I suppose you're responsible for that."

"Yes, I'm afraid a bit of subterfuge on my part. I caught the detective sergeant as he was leaving and asked him to stay at the cottage in case we needed him. I felt things might be coming to a head and that the sooner he and Isaac sat down together the sooner we might reach a resolution."

"That's all fine and good, but while you two were engaging in subterfuge, we found the murder weapon." Phil looked down at the tapestry bag that she now clutched with both hands across her middle. She really didn't want to be the one to do this, but she didn't have a choice.

"The murder weapon?" Atkins asked.

"Yes," Phil said. "And the murderer . . . maybe." She put down the tapestry bag, reached down to the bottom, and pulled out the letter opener.

She could feel the room grow even quieter as everyone leaned in to try to get a look.

She turned to the reading table that held Sheffield's used coffee cup. Pushed it aside, and placed the opener on the table. Gestured for Atkins to unwrap it. But Atkins's eyes were scanning the guests. Alert. Intense. Ready to grab whoever made a move to run?

"Shall I unwrap it?" Phil asked.

He nodded once, slowly. "Carefully."

She didn't comment. She lifted the edges of the handkerchief, unrolled the opener from the folds until the handkerchief lay flat on the table and the paper lay open beside it, the initials plain to see.

Atkins glanced down. Zeroed in on Vincent Wynn-Taylor, who had been sitting with Agnes on the settee when the detective sergeant and Sheffield had entered, but who was now standing by the French doors to the terrace.

Ready to make a run for it?

Phil edged toward him. Atkins made a minute gesture that held her back. He turned to Vincent.

"Mr. Vincent Wynn-Taylor, I am taking you into custody for questioning about the murder of Percival Fauks."

Vincent bolted for the door. Godfrey was on him in the blink of an eye and dragged him back into the room, flicked him into a chair.

Goodness, Phil thought, for a middle-aged government official he was certainly quick on his feet.

Atkins stepped forward, blocking any idea of escape.

"I didn't do it," Vincent mumbled.

"Then perhaps, Mr. Wynn-Taylor, you will tell us who did."

26

Vincent ran both hands through his hair. "I don't know." But his glance flicked toward Agnes. Phil saw it and she was certain Atkins did too.

"Then why are your initials written on this piece of paper?"

There was a communal gasp.

Except from Agnes, who froze as she reached toward Vincent, leaving one hand outstretched, her fingers gracefully curved like an enchanted princess, though perhaps not so enchanted now.

"I don't know, but I didn't kill him."

"Mr. Wynn-Taylor," Atkins prompted, stepping slightly so that he sheltered Vincent from the stares of the others.

Phil understood what he was doing. It was the same maneuver used in ballrooms and soirées across England to give your confidant the illusion of confidentiality. It sometimes worked in society. Here, the spectators merely moved over to get a better view.

"Go on."

"I went upstairs—for something. And there he was, lying there. On the floor in the hallway. The letter opener was still in his back. He was dead." Vincent's voice cracked on a sob.

"And?" Atkins didn't miss a beat. He wasn't about to let the man recover his wits.

"And I shoved him down the laundry chute."

Another collective gasp. A high-pitched cry from Agnes and she threw herself at her mother. Gwen staggered back under the impact and they both ended sitting on the sofa together.

"The letter opener must have fallen out when I did. I was in such a hurry, so afraid someone would come, I wasn't thinking straight, but I didn't kill him."

"If you didn't kill him, why didn't you sound the alarm? Why try to hide the body?"

"Because I panicked."

"Oh come now, Mr. Wynn-Taylor. I don't believe that for a second. If you panicked, it was either because you did kill him, or you saw who did and wanted to protect them. Who would that person be, Mr. Wynn-Taylor?"

"I swear I didn't see anyone."

"But you were afraid someone did it. Who was it? A member of the family?"

Agnes started to protest, but Gwen pulled her back and held her with both arms.

"Someone you cared about and were afraid would be blamed."

"No. No. I did it. Okay? It was me. I did it." Vincent hung his head.

"Now let me get this straight. You didn't kill him. But now you say you did kill him."

"No. Yes. I killed him."

"You know, Mr. Wynn-Taylor, if I didn't know better I would think you were trying to obstruct my investigation of this case, actually two cases. Did you kill Elva Wilson, too?"

It was the first time Phil had heard Elva's last name and it made her death all the more poignant and sad.

"No . . . I mean . . ." Vincent slumped back in the chair.

"But you must have. I think she was blackmailing you for the murder of Fauks. And you, being of a diabolical turn of mind, devised a plan to get rid of her that wouldn't point to you."

"No!" Vincent said as if it was something he couldn't contemplate even now, much less plan in advance. And Phil was inclined to believe that this was the first time he'd even thought this far.

But the detective sergeant plowed on. "You were responsible

for picking up Mrs. Pratt's medicine from the pharmacy. You could easily alter the dose before handing it over to Elva. You were taking an awful chance.

"What if it had killed Mrs. Pratt as well? What if . . ." He swung around to take in the others. His eyes alighted on one person. "Agnes . . . had been in the room."

"No!" cried Vincent at the same time as Agnes yelled, "You're wrong!"

Atkins turned back to Vincent like nothing had happened.

"Is that the way it happened? You killed two people in the house where you were employed and where you had other emotional ties?"

Vincent stood. Atkins pushed him back down.

"If you don't tell me exactly what happened, I'll have to arrest you. Take you to the station and if it turns out that you aren't the killer, that man . . . or woman, will still be free, and these people—that particular person—will still not be safe. Because I will continue to investigate until I get to the bottom of this. So why don't you tell me the truth."

"I killed them. I killed them both," Vincent said in a flat unearthly voice.

"Why?"

"I-I was angry."

Atkins caught Phil's eye. It was barely long enough to register, but she knew where he was going.

"Why were you angry? Why did you suddenly feel the need to murder Mr. Fauks in the middle of a ball where anyone might walk by and see you?"

Vincent just shook his head, refused to even look up.

"Shall I guess?"

"No! Perry had this scheme that he wanted me to invest in. Said it was a sure thing. He wanted to take over some company, he had a contract lined up with a big organization."

"And did you invest?"

Vincent shook his head. "It was tempting. He said I could

more than double my money, I wouldn't have to work for Mr. Pratt anymore. Could be my own man. A real man," he said in lower tones.

"Sounds like a good deal. And yet you weren't interested? Even though it might make you rich. Rich enough, say, to rival him for Miss Pratt's affections?"

Another head shake. "No, my father lost everything we had because of bad investments. I swore that would never happen to me."

"That's enough, Atkins," roared Luther. "Leave the man alone. If he did it, he did it. And I'm sorry for it. Was your life so awful to risk everything to get away from us?"

"No, sir, not at all. I love my job and I—" Vincent's voice cracked.

"Oh, Vincent!"

Agnes broke away from Gwen and threw herself at Vincent's feet. "Tell them you didn't do it. Tell them."

Atkins's eyes rolled heavenward. "Tell us what, Miss Pratt? That *you* killed Perry Fauks?"

Phil would be inclined to laugh if the stakes weren't so high.

Agnes stopped wringing her hands and stared at him. "Me? I didn't kill Perry."

"No, I don't believe you did. But I think Vincent thinks you might have."

Agnes turned back to Vincent? "You thought it was me?"

Vincent didn't answer, but his Adam's apple jerked spasmodically.

"How could you think that?"

"He deserved it, if you did."

"Agnes?" Gwen said.

"I'm sorry, Mama. I hated Perry. He was awful. I had a fight with him that night. But I didn't kill him. I wouldn't kill anybody."

"Why didn't you tell me?"

"I didn't want to disappoint you."

The detective sergeant's jaw tightened. "If we could please contain ourselves for a few moments longer."

Phil forced herself not to look at him. Or Daisy. It was all rather over the top, and she was afraid they might succumb to a fit of laughter, which would be embarrassingly not tonish. And she suddenly realized that this was a family who cared deeply about one another and for whom she did have a certain affection. That was not something to be taken lightly.

"So, Mr. Wynn-Taylor, could you tell us why you thought Miss Pratt had murdered him?"

"He was lying across the hall from her room."

"And so you concluded that she must have killed him."

Vincent was silent.

"What other rooms are in that wing of the corridor?" Atkins looked around for a dry eye. "Mr. Pratt?"

"Well, let's see. There's my room and dressing room at the front of the house. Gwen's room, dressing room, and sitting room. Agnes's room and dressing room. One guest room where Effie and Maud are staying."

Surely, Atkins already knew this. He hardly seemed to listen to Luther's recitation. *He's looking for a reaction,* she realized. An unconscious recognition of guilt. A "dead giveaway," as Bobby Mullins might say. *Fascinating.*

Agnes's room was right across from the laundry chute, so it made sense that Vincent suspected the worst. But the killer could have dragged the body from any of those rooms to the laundry chute in an attempt to mislead. Or had been frightened away before he could get rid of the body.

Atkins turned back to Vincent, leaving Phil no wiser to what he was thinking. "Thank you. Now, if you've pulled yourself together, Mr. Wynn-Taylor, could you please recount the rest of the events of that evening."

Vincent started as if he'd been goosed.

"Why did you go upstairs in the first place?" Phil interjected impatiently.

Her interruption received the frown she admitted it deserved.

But Agnes answered. "Don't try to protect me anymore, Vincent. I'm not guilty and I can take care of myself." She smiled up at him, her eyes adoring.

Phil looked away. Had she ever been that young and naïve? Of course she had—before the Earl of Dunbridge.

On that thought, Phil promised herself to be more sympathetic to young girls in the future.

Vincent straightened in his chair. "I saw him talking to her downstairs. I could tell she was uncomfortable, but he took her elbow and practically forced her up the stairs. She wouldn't have gone, but I think she didn't want to cause a scene."

Agnes nodded, looked from Phil to Atkins. "I told you how he was. I didn't tell you that night he made me go up the stairs with him. I saw Uncle Thomas and Mr. Sheffield coming out of Papa's study and I didn't want to cause a scene in front of them, so I went with him. But when we got there he tried to—tried to, right there in the hall.

"He was acting crazy. Not like usual when he got like that, but crazy, desperate almost. He scared me. I shoved him away and ran to my room and locked the door."

"Oh, my poor child," Gwen cried. "I had no idea. We would never have had something like that happen to you."

"Why not, Mama? You heard the rumors about Mr. Sheffield's daughter. Even I had."

"I had of course. But I thought it was just grief talking. Sometimes when you can't explain bad things it's natural to try to blame someone else. Isaac, I'm sorry. So sorry."

Sheffield, whom Phil had completely forgotten, looked up from where he was sitting. "You're not to blame, Gwen. No one is, but myself for being blind to Perry until it was too late."

"But why didn't you tell us?"

"I did many times, but as you say, everyone thought it was just the ramblings of a grief-stricken, guilty father."

Everyone but Mrs. Ida Kidmore-Young, Phil thought. No wonder Isaac Sheffield chose to spend his time with her rather than with his wife, who would rather blame Isaac than face the truth. They had both been wrong about Perry Fauks.

"If everyone will save your apologies until we've come to the end of this, I would appreciate it. Now tell me what happened next."

Vincent straightened. "I meant to go after them and stop Perry, but Mr. Sheffield stopped to ask where Mr. Pratt was, I told him I thought he was in the ballroom, and he asked me to go find him. I did, and I accompanied him back to Mr. Sheffield. They went back to the study, and I realized that neither Agnes nor Perry had returned downstairs. I was terribly worried, so I ran up to the second floor."

"And?"

"And there he was, Perry, lying on the ground. He was dead and the letter opener was sticking out of his back. It was right across from Agnes's room. I panicked. I didn't know what to do, just that he couldn't be found there. Then I saw the laundry chute and I opened it and shoved him inside."

"Oh Vincent," Agnes said softly and lay her head on his knee.

"Then a door opened across the hall and I ran like hell in the opposite direction."

"What did you do next? Your clothes must have been mussed. Blood perhaps had gotten on your shirt when you moved the body."

"On the cuffs and I didn't have a change of clothes. I was just very careful and went home soon afterward. It was late, around two, I think, and no one thought it odd when I left because I had work the following day."

"And the shirt?"

"Gone into a trash bin on my way to the pharmacy the next morning."

"And the letter opener? How did the letter opener end up in this bag along with your initials?"

"I assumed it had gone down the chute with Perry. It was shoved in to the hilt. It never occurred to me that it had fallen out. I heard the door and I ran. Then next day when I brought Mrs. Pratt's medicine from the pharmacy, Elva said she had found it and she knew what I did.

"I told her I didn't kill him, that I was trying to protect—I was trying to prevent scandal. But she didn't believe me.

"I asked outright, 'Did you see me kill him?'"

"And she said, 'No, but I heard you arguing.'"

"But it wasn't me. I was downstairs, looking for Mr. Pratt. When I finally got upstairs Perry was already dead."

"And how long was it between the time Agnes and Perry went upstairs until the time you followed?"

Vincent pushed his fingers through his hair. "I don't know. Five, ten minutes. The ballroom was crowded and it took a few minutes to find Mr. Pratt."

"And Mr. Sheffield was waiting in the hall for you to return?"

"Yes. He and Mr. Pratt went down to the study and when I went up the stairs Perry was dead."

Atkins looked at Sheffield for confirmation.

"Yes, I stood right there until Vincent returned with Luther."

Back to Vincent. Phil could almost see the detective sergeant's mind working. "She tried to blackmail you."

"Not at first. She was very loyal to the family and to her mistress. She was glad to have Agnes out from Perry's clutches, so she said nothing."

"But that changed?"

"Yes, a couple of days later, she came to me. Demanded money. Said she had to get away and that she would exchange the letter opener for five hundred dollars. I didn't have that kind of cash. I tried to reason with her. And suddenly we were all coming out here and there was no time to find out what had changed."

"She had to get away. Those were her words?"

"Yes. I thought it was odd because she always seemed very happy here. She'd been with Mrs. Pratt a long time, before I came, certainly."

"Yes," interjected Gwen. "She'd been with me since Agnes was little, close to fifteen years. I can't believe she would want to leave."

"I don't think she wanted to," Vincent said. "I think she was afraid, but I was so wrapped up in my own worries, I didn't pay enough attention to her. If I had—"

"You would have been able to save her?" Atkins finished.

Vincent shrugged. "I might have been able to do something."

"If you had told us the truth to begin with you most certainly would have."

Vincent's head snapped back. Agnes burst into a new spate of tears. Even Phil blinked at Atkins's response.

Atkins turned to face the group. "You all heard Mr. Wynn-Taylor's story. Do any of you have anything to add? Or to contradict?"

No one did. Luther and Sheffield corroborated Vincent's time line of events. No one dissented. Even Morris, always at the ready with a dry sarcastic remark, stayed mute. Phil wondered if he had invested in Perry's failed scheme.

"I think we've finished here," Godfrey said. "We have an early morning. Cars will be leaving for the balloon test at nine a.m."

Atkins look nonplussed. They were all going off to a balloon exhibition in the middle of a murder investigation? But he said nothing, so Phil kept mum.

Godfrey went over to Vincent. "Get a good night's sleep, my boy. Things will look brighter tomorrow." He glanced over to Atkins. "Just stay in your room until breakfast."

Everyone took the cue and began their good nights. Gwen pulled Agnes away from Vincent and Luther led them both out of the room.

They'd barely reached the door when it opened and Thomas Jeffrey walked in. "I say. You're all for bed? So early?"

"Oh shut up, Thomas," Ruth said. "I'll explain upstairs. Come along, girls." She practically pushed her husband into the hallway, followed closely by Maud and Effie.

Harry followed them, and with a final sardonic look toward Atkins, Morris sauntered after the others.

Atkins said a few words to Godfrey and Phil sat down with Daisy.

"I don't like that young man," Daisy said, watching Morris close the door behind him. She yawned. "I know Godfrey said for us to go to bed, but I need another glass of champagne. I see that you and the inspector here are going to have a nice long tête-à-tête with Godfrey, and I'll be wigged if I'm going upstairs to drink alone." She lowered her lashes and fluttered them ever so slightly at John Atkins.

He smiled, and Phil wanted to kick him. "By all means, Lady Warwick, I'm sure Lady Dunbridge will join you."

He meant for them to go upstairs. But against the two countesses, John Atkins had no chance. Phil and Daisy sat together on the settee, both sipping champagne and watching him as he stood at the French doors looking out into the night.

He'd refused a drink since he was on duty, at least nominally. He'd also refused to discuss his opinions with them.

And Phil was getting a little impatient. "Do you think one of those two did it?"

"Possibly. Neither has an alibi and both had motives."

"Remind me not to ever do anything that puts me at your mercy. That was a bit ruthless."

He raised an eyebrow at her. "I never said I wasn't good at my job."

"But I think you are wrong."

"Why am I not surprised."

"Do you want to hear what I think?"

He gave her a half smile. "Do I have a choice?"

"Certainly, if you want to go bumbling around waiting for someone to confess." She turned her shoulder on him. "Daisy, pour me more champagne."

"What is it you want to say?"

Phil took her time, waiting for Daisy to fill her glass, took a sip of champagne. "This is your case. But you haven't been around this family as much as I have.

"Think of it. Elva had a good position here. You didn't see her in action, but she cared about Mrs. Pratt, seemed to be content in her job, and she knew she would receive a handsome pension when she retired. Why would she jeopardize that for five hundred dollars?"

"That's a lot of money."

"Perhaps, but it wouldn't last. Elva must have realized that, she wasn't stupid. And you heard Vincent. She didn't demand money at first. I don't think she had any intention of blackmailing him."

"And yet she did," Atkins said.

"I don't believe it was blackmail. Elva said she heard them arguing, but what if it really wasn't Vincent who was arguing with Perry? Elva must have realized she'd been wrong. And that she was in danger. Which as it turns out, she was. She was frightened enough to try a spot of blackmail on Vincent not for greed, but to save herself."

"You don't think Wynn-Taylor is the villain of this piece?"

"I'm not sure. Are you?"

He shook his head. "The evidence so far is pretty damning, but not complete."

"But he said he was in the ballroom when Perry must have been killed."

"If you believe him."

"And you don't?"

"I believe in evidence more than I do in people."

Phil gave him an assessing look. "Why, Detective Sergeant. Is that your experience talking or your philosophy of mankind?"

"Experience," he said drily.

Phil put down her glass and stood. Walked over to the table where the letter opener still sat along with the damning initials.

She didn't touch them but something was bothering her. It seemed to her they didn't even know what the motive really was. Love or greed or desperation.

Why had Elva written Vincent's initials if he wasn't guilty? She leaned closer, perused the writing. Why not, *VW-T killed PF*. No message of any kind.

Just a piece of paper smooth on top and bottom edges and torn on each side of the writing.

Oh for heaven's sake. Where was her detective's mind? She pinched an edge of the paper between her fingernails and turned it over.

"What are you doing?" Atkins reached the table in three strides.

"Looking at the real clue in Elva's note."

He peered at the paper. "What? It's a piece of ticker tape. Pratt has a machine in his office. Every banker, financier, and financial hopeful owns one."

"I realize that now. But look at the date."

"The date."

Atkins turned the tape around with one finger until it faced him. "The day of the murder." Atkins looked more closely. Read. "CCC down to almost nothing."

Phil felt Daisy come up beside her. "CCC, Columbia Copper Company," Daisy said. "That's the trust Perry Fauks wanted me to invest in. I was more concerned with selling my mines than the actual investment, but I'm sure that's the same company."

"That's it," Phil said. "Elva left a message *for* Vincent, not about him. A clue about the murder." She jumped up, started to pace. "She'd figured out who the real killer was. I don't know how she figured it out, but she did. And she was killed for it."

Phil turned back to the others. "Columbia Copper Company. Perry tried to get Harry and Vincent to invest, they both said no. But maybe somebody else said yes and when it went belly-up, they confronted Perry and killed him."

"Huh," Atkins said. "Clever girl, Elva."

"What about me?" Phil asked.

Atkins chuckled. "'Clever' doesn't even begin to cover it."

"Is that a compliment?" she asked.

"I'm not quite sure myself."

"Well, I think she's terribly clever," Daisy said.

The door opened and Godfrey walked in. "Both Sheffield and Vincent are safely tucked away with the advice to stay put. I have servants sitting outside their rooms in case their memories slip."

He went to the drinks table, and poured himself a glass of aged double malt scotch.

"So," he said, after taking a long draft. "You have two suspects, Detective Sergeant. Can we consider the case closed?"

27

The first thing Phil noticed when she awoke the next morning was that it was sunny. At last. No fog plagued the landscape.

She didn't linger over her coffee, but dressed for the day, in a tweed split skirt ensemble suitable for balloon ascensions and chasing criminals, and went in to meet Daisy.

Daisy was up and dressed in a wonderful black and bisque striped day dress, beneath a black velvet vest. For a woman who had eschewed social life, she certainly had some wardrobe.

They went downstairs, where they served themselves from a sideboard set up with the usual country breakfast fare: eggs, ham, bacon, tomatoes, kedgeree. There was also a morning newspaper.

While a maid served the coffee, Phil opened the newspaper. And there were the headlines she'd been expecting ever since she'd called on the Pratts the first day.

"'Tennessee Steel Bought by J.P. Morgan. Fauks Copper, Coal and Steel Price Falls.

"'Steel stocks were holding low but steady this morning at the opening of the New York Stock Exchange. The Columbia Copper Company, after a short rally yesterday, plummeted. It seems unlikely that it will be able to recover and bankruptcy is imminent. The plunge appears to have been brought about by a corner store operation. Business associates, Mr. Charles Morse and Mr. Augustus Heinze, are thought to be responsible for false trading and are being questioned by the authorities, who are also looking for other agents involved in the stock manipulation.

This comes amid demands for stricter oversight of banks and Wall Street.'"

Morse and Heinze. The same names written on her Follies program. Phil sipped her coffee. It looked like Perry hooked up with a couple of dishonest men and lost his company's as well as others' fortunes. *Other agents.*

Did they suspect Sheffield of knowing about this earlier than he said he did? Is that who kidnapped and questioned him? He seemed sincere in his effort to save the company, but maybe it had merely been desperation.

Did that make him a suspect in Perry's murder? He might have quickly gone upstairs, killed Perry, and been back in the foyer appearing to wait for Vincent to find Luther.

Possible, but unlikely.

And where had Thomas Jeffrey gone when he left with Max after Godfrey's dinner? All the way to Washington and back in twenty-four hours, just in time to see Sheffield and Vincent put under suspicion. Why come back at all? Surely not just to watch a balloon exhibition? Perhaps to mollify his wife.

And why hadn't Detective Sergeant Atkins asked him to attest to the other men's movements the night of Perry's murder? Or to his own?

There were still too many unanswered questions.

And where was Atkins? Back at the cottage enjoying breakfast brought down by one of Godfrey's many servants? Or had he taken his two suspects into custody and returned to Manhattan? She certainly hoped not. She wasn't sure either of them was guilty. At least not of murder.

Because she just didn't feel like this was over. Call it her female intuition; she had little else to go on at this point. All clues led to Vincent. And perhaps he had lost his head, lost his money and his girl to Perry Fauks.

It was pretty damning, as John Atkins had said. And yet.

There were still pieces missing. Like motive. Had the murders been perpetrated over love or money? The age-old question, it seemed. The only thing left was revenge. And Isaac Sheffield certainly had every reason for that.

The door opened and Godfrey stepped just inside.

"We're caravanning to watch the balloon ascension, leaving in an hour. I hope you will both be joining us." He seemed in particularly good spirits.

"Wouldn't miss it for the world," Phil said. It might be the last time they had all the players in this tragedy in one place.

Daisy rode to the field with Godfrey, with the others following behind them. Phil insisted on driving the Packard, and Lily and Preswick were sitting in the backseat rather in the servants' carriages.

Phil knew today was the best chance for catching a killer. There would be a celebration after the launch at the field, then they'd return to Godfrey's for dinner. Everyone would be leaving the next morning, including the Jeffreys, who would return to Washington later that afternoon.

The string of carriages and automobiles meandered down a country road and turned into an open field where a number of automobiles were already parked in a cordoned-off area, near a large white tent where the crowd had collected.

Phil pulled the Packard alongside Godfrey's Daimler.

While they relieved themselves of goggles and driving togs, Preswick handed out the field glasses that Phil kept at the ready.

Daisy and Godfrey came to meet them.

"I see you've come prepared," Godfrey said, indicating her field glasses.

"A gift from Bev Reynolds. They're handy at the track." *And for keeping tabs on suspected felons from a distance.*

"It's an excellent day for an ascension," Godfrey said, rubbing his hands together with the enthusiasm of a young boy. "Sunshine, good visibility—no fog—and a good brisk breeze, but no strong gusts." He directed Preswick and Lily to a second-

ary tent where his servants had gathered to enjoy the celebration, then turned to Phil and Daisy. "Shall we go?"

He escorted them toward the larger tent where refreshments
were being served. Small tables were set with linens and silver
service. And a buffet table ran along one side overseen by several chefs.

Phil helped herself to a glass of champagne and looked out
over the field where the ascension would take place. It was a flat
grassy area that stretched for several acres.

Two large domed rectangular structures sat at one end.

"Hangars," Godfrey explained. "Where we store the balloons
and other aeronautical housings."

"It's quite impressive," Phil said. "Where did you find an area
this flat among all these rolling hills?"

Godfrey chuckled. "I happen to own it. Had to do some lev-
eling but it's worth it. I lease it to the government."

Daisy opened her mouth.

"For a dollar a year, so don't scold."

Daisy relaxed.

It was impressive. Several baskets, their balloons not yet in-
flated, sat among the dried grasses. One rose upright, filled and
ready to go, held to earth at this point by sandbags. Another lay
precariously on its side, billowing like a mythological animal
as it was filled from a large pump.

Beyond the balloons, the Long Island Sound glistened blue
and silver in the sunshine.

A couple came up to say hello. Godfrey introduced "Senator
Davies and his wife, Carolyn." A few minutes of small talk, and
they passed on.

"Quite a crowd," Daisy said.

It was. Several military types sporting medals against dark
blue uniforms, the ambassador and his wife, some businessmen
and their wives or consorts, dressed to the hilt. Probably more
than one senator or other government official.

"Ridiculous piece of pomp and circumstance," Godfrey said,

overlooking the crowd. "But we need supporters among politicians and wealthy financiers as well as the government."

"I take it these are not just weather balloons," Phil said.

Godfrey smiled. "We have many uses for them. Still much testing is needed. They're not as accurate as we'd like. Even the best pilot is at the mercy of the wind. But until we perfect better aircraft this is what we have. Ah, it's beginning."

They looked out to where the second balloon began to expand before their eyes.

"Excuse me, I must say a few words." Godfrey left Phil and Daisy to step onto a raised platform. "Good day, colleagues and invited guests. Welcome to today's test of the newest additions to the Army's Balloon Corps." He briefly explained how the balloon was filled—with hydrogen generated by large machines built for the purpose—how the pilot steered—a mechanism housed in the basket—and of the flight on wind currents and balloon manipulation.

"The ascension will begin in just a few minutes if you'd like to find a viewing place."

Phil saw the Pratts and the Jeffreys moving toward the field. Maud and Effie had already gone ahead. Harry, Newty, and Morris lingered over their drinks. Godfrey took Daisy to the front of the crowd accompanied by several dignitaries. Phil didn't see Sheffield or Vincent and had to assume they were on their way to further questioning or still at Foggy Acres.

She did see Atkins standing at the far side of the tent, watching everyone.

Two men passed by her close enough for Phil to catch part of their conversation.

"Isn't that Thomas Jeffrey?" said a man chewing on a cigar. "I'm surprised he'd show his face today. He tried to get me to buy into CCC, the fool."

"Columbia Copper Company? You didn't do it, did you?" said his companion. They walked on and Phil followed.

"Hell no. But Rudy Klemp did. I feel sorry for him. He's

cleaned out. Anybody else who did will be ruined today. Went
belly-up last night. Stock's completely worthless. I heard just before I left town this morning. Rallied a bit yesterday then
tanked.

"Told him I wouldn't deal with those two cheaters he was
working with. They already finished off Knickerbocker Trust."

"Thomas has always been a fool," said the other. "Everybody
but Thomas knows it."

"I heard that Fauks Trust is in trouble, too. And not just
because the son died. They're saying it wasn't an accident."

"The world's gone crazy. That's for sure."

"Damn. The fallout will sound through the financial world;
we might as well get ready for round two."

Phil let them go. She needed to find Atkins. But she didn't
get a chance. A swell of excitement rose as the first balloon
dropped its anchor and ascended over their heads.

Everyone was looking into the sky except Phil, who was trying to find the detective sergeant.

Suddenly a man raced from the parking grounds. He stopped,
looked wildly around, saw Thomas standing between his wife
and daughters, and yelled, "Thomas Jeffrey, you're a scoundrel!"

Thomas glanced over his shoulder, then moved his family a
little farther away.

The man ran full tilt toward Thomas. Grabbed him by the
shoulder, spun him around. "You're a cheat and a scoundrel.
You've bankrupted me."

The men Phil had been following hurried toward the altercation.

"You're drunk," Thomas snapped back. "I don't know what
you're talking about."

The second balloon filled behind them, but not too many
people were paying attention. They were riveted on the argument.

"You told me it was a sure thing. Is that what you told Perry
Fauks?"

Thomas turned on him, grabbed the man by the neck.

Phil stopped dead in her tracks. She'd been thinking that someone had killed Perry in anger. What if Perry had been the angry one, had attacked and was killed?

Sheffield's words came back to Phil. *He must have had an accomplice.*

Perry had lost the company funds, because someone had taken advantage of his näiveté. Promised a sure thing? Not Sheffield. He'd been trying to save the company. Were Perry and Thomas both caught up in the fraudulent stock manipulation?

The newcomer was now screaming at Thomas. His anger had attracted the attention of others and a knot of men surrounded the two men. The excitement of the crowd turned ominous, the balloon launch forgotten by all but the two pilots preparing for the ascension.

Godfrey gestured to several guards, who hurried toward the altercation that was rapidly degenerating into a brawl, as the balloon swelled behind the crowd. The man pushed Thomas, who staggered back.

Suddenly Thomas screamed out, "To hell with you! Leave me alone! I didn't do anything."

His voice was strident, almost hysterical. Phil had heard him scream like that once before—the day he'd been chastising his daughters for spending so much money. Elva had jumped and dropped a glass vase, then behaved strangely afterward. Not because she'd broken something but because she'd recognized the voice. The same voice raised in anger that she'd heard arguing with Perry before he was killed.

It had to be that. Until that moment in the foyer when Thomas had yelled at the girls, she might not have been certain who that voice had belonged to. And after that . . . She knew who had killed Perry. That was why she'd been acting so nervous.

Oh Elva, why hadn't you confided in someone? Because they were family? Because she was afraid they would side with their own over the word of a servant?

She'd tried to get money from Vincent so that she could flee. And when that didn't work she'd left a message for him wrapped around the murder weapon, because he of all of them might understand. But understand what? How could a torn piece of ticker tape point to a murderer?

Elva would never be able to tell them now. Or could she? Phil thought back. She had to be missing something. Finding the letter opener. The ticker tape wrapped around the handle. The ticker tape in Perry's wastepaper basket. The ticker tape with Vincent's initials. The ticker tape falling out of Thomas's sleeve as he hurried to leave with Max.

Columbia Copper Company. CCC. He and Perry must have fought that night, and Thomas had killed him. He'd been in the deal all along.

Of course. Today, with one angry confrontation from a man Thomas had cheated, it all fell into place.

She needed to find John Atkins. Who she found was Daisy, and she remembered the day she'd met her in the Plaza running from the journalists. She was supposed to meet Perry and another man. Not Sheffield, and certainly not Godfrey—she wouldn't have forgotten Godfrey's name.

They hadn't met, but they were supposed to have at the Plaza's tearoom with Perry, the day after Perry was killed. Not Sheffield, but Thomas Jeffrey.

Godfrey was striding toward the group. "Gentlemen!" he commanded.

Thomas saw him and began backing away from the crowd. Past his wife and children, who were staring in disbelief. His head swiveled but there was nowhere to go. The crowd stood between him and the automobiles. The ocean lapped at the far side of the field.

Phil raced to Godfrey. "I think he killed Perry and Elva!"

The second balloon began to rise, but no one was paying attention.

Thomas turned toward the field, and Phil knew in that instant what he was going to do. It was his only chance.

The balloon began its ascent, the basket skimming along inches above the grasses. Thomas ran faster; he was several feet away when the basket lifted off the ground. He threw himself at it and held on as the balloon rose into the air.

The crowd became silent. All eyes watching the spectacle of Thomas hanging onto the side of the basket.

Phil lifted her field glasses, trained them on the balloon.

The pilots were pulling Thomas into the basket.

Godfrey's men had reached the balloon and were attempting to drag it down, to no avail. The two pilots couldn't help. They were standing upright, their hands in the air. Thomas held a pistol. Aimed at them.

As if he felt Phil watching him, he turned, fired. A report rang out and a clump of sod exploded at Phil's feet.

Someone screamed.

"He'll blow them to smithereens!"

The crowd shrank back with a collective gasp. Except for Phil, who started forward.

Her arm was grabbed. "Stay put," Atkins ordered.

"But he killed Perry and Elva. I'm sure of it."

Godfrey hurried up to them.

"Where is it going?" Atkins asked.

"No telling now. It always depended on wind currents but with him giving the orders, there's no telling."

Phil looked up at the sky. The first balloon was a mere dot, traveling north over the Sound, but Thomas's seemed to be veering southwest.

"I have a unit standing by near Foggy Acres," Atkins said.

"Lieutenant Carlton, take the detective sergeant to the radio room. You do have communications?"

Atkins nodded and the two men hurried away.

"This is ridiculous," Phil said. "He's getting away. We'll have to follow it." She ran toward the Packard. She wasn't surprised to see Preswick and Lily waiting there for her.

Preswick started them up and they shot down the road. As she drove away, Phil heard other engines start up behind her.

"How are we going to catch it?" Lily yelled. "It doesn't have to stay on the roads."

"We'll just keep it in sight and leave the rest to Godfrey and his men."

They came to a fork in the road. "Which way?" Phil yelled.

"To your right, my lady." Preswick pointed to the sky.

Phil swung the Packard into the turn. They all toppled to the side until she straightened up again.

When she looked again, the balloon had disappeared.

Phil kept driving; there was little else she could do at this point, except give up, and that she refused to do.

"There it is," cried Lily.

Phil saw the top of the balloon rise above the trees, before it disappeared again.

She turned again. Onto a familiar road. "We need reinforcements." She accelerated and barreled down the highway with Preswick and Lily clinging to the sides of the car and Phil clinging to the steering wheel.

The road curved slightly to the right and Phil recognized the drive to Holly Farm up ahead. She pressed on the brake and made the turn to the farmhouse in a cloud of dust.

She didn't slow down at the house but drove straight to the stable. Several men came out of the paddock.

The balloon was in their sights, seemed to be going right over their heads. She'd hoped it would land on the track as it had the other time that had upset Bobby so much. Indeed, he was coming out of the office at a run.

But the balloon lifted again and floated toward the woods.

Phil slammed on the brakes, and the Packard screeched to a stop. "Bobby, the balloon! A killer is escaping."

Bobby's mouth opened as he looked up at the sky and scratched his head, then looked back at Phil. "He's in that contraption?"

"Yes."

"Want me to shoot it down?"

"No! It will explode and there are two pilots with him."

"Huh." Bobby raised his arm. "Well, fellas, what're you waiting for. Get those work nags out and go after 'em. Not the thoroughbreds. Mrs. Reynolds'll have my head if they get hurt. Jaime, take the truck."

"Come on, your lady, I'll show you how to drive over rough ground." Bobby jumped into the back of the Packard. "Follow that track around to the back. Ground's hard there."

Seconds later four jockeys were galloping toward the woods.

Phil and her passengers bounced along a rutted farm track that led into the woods.

"Steady," Bobby yelled. "Straight, straight, it's gonna curve to the right."

Phil gripped the steering wheel, willing the Packard not to veer from the narrow passage. Silently apologized to Bev each time a branch scraped along the sides. At last they drove out of the trees into a small field where two of the jockeys had stopped and were looking at the sky.

Phil slowed the Packard.

Another jockey returned to the field. "Lost it, Bobby. Sorry."

They were all searching the sky but there was no balloon in sight.

"Where'd it go?" Bobby asked.

"Musta crashed somewhere. You want us to spread out and look for it?"

"I think it went down over there." One of the jockeys pointed to the left.

"No, I saw it go in that direction," said another, and broke into a string of Spanish.

"What do you want us to do?"

"Heck, it could be anywhere," Bobby said. "And I can't use the other horses, they wouldn't know what to do if they ain't on a track."

"Of course not," said Phil.

"They could go on foot, but—"

A sound of an engine overhead stopped his speech. They all looked up.

"Holy cow," Bobby said. "What the heck is that?"

One of the jockeys made the sign of the cross.

"It's an aeroplane," Phil said. "Lily, get my field glasses." She realized they were still around her neck. She lifted them to get a closer look.

"Where did it come from?" Bobby twisted around to follow its motion.

The aeroplane dove and lifted then tilted and turned to come back the way it had come, but instead of passing overhead, it turned again, until it was flying in a circle one, two, three times.

"What is it up to?"

"He's showing us to the balloon," Phil shouted.

"Don't know if the auto will make it," Bobby said. "You know how to ride?"

"Bobby, I'm a countess."

"Rico, give the lady countess here your horse."

Rico slid from the saddle. "It's not side, lady."

"Not a problem," Phil said. "Give me a leg up, Bobby."

Bobby laced his fingers and braced himself. "Turn your heads, boys." And he hoisted Phil into the saddle.

"Follow that aeroplane." *Thank heavens for split skirts*, Phil thought as they galloped away.

They found the balloon crashed at the edge of a hillock dangling in the trees. The two pilots were standing next to the balloon trying to untangle the moorings from the basket.

"We confiscated his weapon," one of them called. "He's over there by that tree." He went back to assessing the damage.

Thomas lay on the ground, holding his shoulder and trying ineffectually to get up and away.

The jockeys slid off the horses and grabbed the desperate man. Phil stayed put. She wasn't sure her legs would hold her.

Overhead the aeroplane came back for a final pass.

Phil lifted her field glasses as the plane dipped and Godfrey Bennington saluted her before lifting the nose and flying off into the sky.

28

"Now what do we do?" Phil wondered aloud to Bobby as they watched the jockeys tie Thomas's wrists and ankles and carry him back to the field where they'd left the Packard. Once there they decided that Bobby would drive the Packard back to the farm, and they tossed Thomas in the backseat, where he fell over to his side like a trussed turkey.

"I'll just ride back to the farm," Phil told Bobby. She wasn't sure she wouldn't fall off the horse trying to dismount and end up on her derriere in the dirt. This riding astride would take some getting used to.

But back at the farm she managed a respectable dismount and didn't feel too bad in the scheme of things. She and Bobby stood in the yard looking over their captive.

"He didn't actually confess to murder; so far he's just guilty of stealing a government balloon."

"I could give him some motivation to talk," Bobby said, flexing his chubby fingers.

"Thank you, but I don't think the detective sergeant would agree."

"Naw, he wouldn't, and where is he by the by? Shouldn't he be doing some arresting?"

"I imagine he's on his way. Shouldn't be long now."

And indeed only another few minutes passed before a cavalcade of vehicles drove up the Holly Farm drive.

Godfrey's Daimler led the way. And Phil wondered at the alacrity at which he'd flown back to the balloon field, and then driven to Holly Farm. Flying was definitely the way to travel, except for the terrible accident that Orville Wright had suffered a few years before.

That aside, she wouldn't mind trying out the controls of an aeroplane someday.

Godfrey stopped at the paddock, and John Atkins brought the Panhard et Levassor to stop beside the Daimler.

Daisy, Harry, and Morris all piled out of Godfrey's car and hurried toward Bobby and Phil.

"Lord, what a day," Daisy said. "I haven't had this much excitement in years. And I must say your inspector certainly has a dashing car."

"It belongs to the department," Phil said. She watched as Atkins left his car, not even slowing down for a thank-you as he made his way directly to the Packard and Thomas Jeffrey. He leaned over the prisoner and seemed to be talking to him, though Phil couldn't hear what was said.

Obviously she needed to be closer.

"Excuse me, Daisy." Phil strode over to where Atkins was hopefully wringing a confession from Jeffery. But he'd stood and was talking to one of the jockeys.

Phil came up beside him. "What did he say?"

Atkins glanced at her. "That he wanted his lawyer."

"Did he confess to murder?"

"I didn't ask him."

"Why?"

"Lack of evidence so far."

"You're hoping for a confession? We have evidence. He brokered the deal with Columbia Copper. He and Perry must have fought—"

"'Must have' isn't 'did,'" Atkins returned, only half listening. What was he thinking about? Making a plan? What? He could be so infuriating.

"Thumbscrews?" she quipped.

"Hmm," he said and returned to the prisoner.

She hurried after him. "We do have evidence of sorts. Maybe not evidence exactly but clues."

She was distracted by the sound of more vehicles, then doors slamming. Luther and Gwen climbed out of one, Ruth and Effie and Maud got out of the second vehicle. A third was a gray, imposing-looking van. Godfrey motioned it forward and it stopped, blocking the drive back to the road.

Preventing a car chase? Phil wondered wryly.

Godfrey turned to Atkins. "The van will extricate the equipment from the basket. Then they will transport the prisoner to Foggy Acres for questioning. I'll be able to accommodate your prisoner there until you can arrange to have him transported to jail.

"Don't worry, Detective Sergeant, once the government debriefs him over this situation—he's all yours. I suggest we all make our way back to Foggy Acres for supper. You too, Detective Sergeant. You'll join us while you wait for a detail to arrive. I think we've all had quite enough of the outdoors for one day."

Phil thought Atkins might argue, but he just clamped his teeth together and watched as two men in military uniforms untied Thomas's ankles and escorted him to the van.

Gwen had been supporting her sister as they watched, but Ruth broke away when she saw Thomas being led to the van. She ran toward her husband.

"What's going on?"

"Sorry, ma'am," one of the guards said and gently set her aside.

Luther wrapped an arm around her waist. "Enough, Ruth. Come away."

Gwen came up to support her sister's other side. "Do as he says, Ruth. We'd all like to hear what Thomas has to say. I'm sure the detective sergeant would not deny us that opportunity."

They all looked at Atkins; he had gone a shade whiter but he kept his feelings to himself.

Thomas was put in the van. The Pratts returned to the automobile. Godfrey accompanied the guards to the van.

"Could you give a girl a lift?" Daisy asked Atkins in her best dance hall girl imitation.

He tried not to smile, but Daisy wasn't the most beautiful woman in England for nothing. And though she was probably a good ten years his senior, he couldn't resist. "It would be my pleasure," he said, smiling at Daisy. The look he shot Phil dared her not to comment.

They all met back at Foggy Acres. Gwen immediately sent the girls upstairs to rest and dress for dinner. They didn't want to go. Maud and Effie were worried about their father and Agnes was worried about Vincent. Gwen held firm and waited at the bottom of the stairs until they disappeared down the hall.

The rest of them stopped in the parlor to indulge in a preprandial cocktail before changing for dinner. Besides, no one wanted to miss the moment when Godfrey returned with the miscreant in tow. Even Atkins, who had accepted a whiskey after cajoling from Daisy, stood at the window, looking over the others.

"What do they think he did?" Ruth wailed at regular intervals, until Phil wanted to tell her, but she held her tongue.

Phil was certain now that Thomas had been the broker of the deal that bankrupted Fauks Copper, Coal and Steel, and probably others, too. She was fairly certain he'd also killed Perry Fauks. And if he'd put his own money in the deal, there were more distasteful surprises to come.

"Why don't I take you upstairs," Gwen said. "Luther has something he wants to tell you." She glanced toward her husband, who was standing in the doorway.

Phil and Daisy exchanged glances. What next?

"No. I'm going to stay here until someone tells me what this is all about."

"I really think you should go with Luther."

Ruth lifted her chin.

"You're broke," Luther said, ruthlessly. "There, now you know. Gwen wanted to spare you the humiliation of learning this in front of our friends, but you have never listened to reason. I don't know why Gwen, good soul that she is, thought you would now."

"That can't be true," Ruth said.

"Well, it is. Your husband has lost his—and your—last dime. He stole a government balloon and now he'll most likely go to jail if Godfrey can't hush it up. Either way, you haven't a penny to fly with."

Ruth subsided, too stunned to remonstrate or even rush from the room. Phil was afraid she had more unwelcome news ahead of her.

Phil looked up to find Atkins watching her. She crossed over to him. "What do you think? Is he the murderer?"

"Perhaps."

"What more do you need?"

"You don't have to announce your question to the whole room."

"Sorry." Phil moved closer, and they looked out the window, not quite the same as huddled together in the fog, but a close second.

"I wager that Godfrey will get some kind of a confession out of him."

"That's what I'm afraid of," Atkins said, looking into his glass. "But this is a matter for the New York Police, not the feds."

"Does it matter who gets him?"

"Yes."

She smiled. "Well, let's see what we can do. We know he sold that poor man at the ascension, CCC stock. And that Perry was also selling it. Perhaps they didn't connive together but found Messrs. Morse and Heinze separately, though I doubt it."

"So do I. But it doesn't prove he murdered Perry or Elva."

"It doesn't prove he didn't. And where was he while the deed was being done? Where was he while Vincent was looking for Mr. Pratt? And before Vincent returned and found the body?"

"Killing Perry Fauks, I imagine."

Phil bobbled her glass. "But how can you prove it? The nearest thing to a witness is dead. I could testify in court."

The look he gave her defied description.

"Perhaps you can get him to confess."

"I plan to."

The sound of vehicles ended that somewhat unsettling statement. Moments later, Godfrey strode in, followed by Thomas between two guards.

They deposited the man in a straight-backed chair in full view of all the guests.

Atkins was first to see them.

But Ruth beat him to her husband. "What have you done, Thomas?" she demanded.

"It wasn't my fault."

The look his wife gave him made even Phil quail. "Oh, Thomas. It never is."

Luther tried to pull Ruth away, but she wouldn't budge.

"They say you cheated all those people. Tell them it isn't true."

Thomas's eyes flitted around the group as if looking for an escape. There wasn't one. He hung his head. "It's not my fault."

Gwen eased Ruth out of the way and stepped menacingly toward her brother-in-law. "How could you? After all Luther and Godfrey have done for you?"

"How, sister-in-law? You would never understand how hard it is just to survive in Washington. You sit here in all your luxury, never giving it a second thought. Never worrying about what tomorrow might bring. You have everything."

"Thomas Jeffrey," Gwen said. "How dare you talk in that manner. Don't presume to know how we feel. You've been given every opportunity to succeed, thanks to Luther and Godfrey, I might add. If Luther hadn't talked him into getting you a position at the War Department, you'd be groveling as a clerk in some little office in New Haven."

Phil was impressed. Luther was right about his wife—she might look frail, but she was amazingly tough.

Thomas coughed out a derisive laugh. "Some help. It's a constant struggle. Travel and parties and meetings and the girls' expenses. I can never get ahead." He turned to Ruth. "Didn't you ever wonder how I was paying for all of this?"

"I-I—" Ruth looked blindly around the room, but no one had an answer for her.

Phil did. "Your husband and Perry Fauks devised a scheme to get rich by embezzling funds from Fauks Copper, Coal and Steel and cheating people who trusted them."

Ruth looked stunned. "No, tell them it isn't so. Tell them."

Luther stepped toward his brother-in-law. "Who came up with this scheme? Not Perry, he wasn't that bright. It was you. Oh, good Lord. You used your position in the acquisitions office, the job Godfrey got you as a favor to me, to get inside information on the government contracts. God, man. How could you?"

"How could I not?"

A twisted cry erupted from Ruth. "You cheated people? Broke the law? Talked that poor boy into stealing his family's money? What more must I endure?" She stopped to suck in a terrible breath. In a much lower voice she asked, "Did you kill Perry, too? Did you? Did you?"

Thomas hung his head.

"Did you?"

Phil glanced toward Atkins. He cut his eyes toward her, but he didn't intervene. He was letting Ruth push Thomas to the breaking point. And it was working beautifully.

"Did you?" She screamed the words at the slumping man.

"You don't understand. I'd lost everything. I just wanted to talk to him, explain, but I saw him taking liberties with Agnes and I knew he had to be stopped. I followed them upstairs. But when I got there no one was in the hallway.

"I was afraid he'd forced Agnes into her room, but I heard voices coming from Gwen's sitting room and a cry and I knew he must have taken her in there. So I opened the door. He had forced her to the settee and was holding her down as she struggled."

"It wasn't me," Agnes cried from the doorway.

Gwen started toward her, but Phil held her back.

Agnes stepped just inside the door, not looking at anyone but Thomas. "I went to my room and locked the door."

"Well, Thomas?" Ruth's eyes never left his face. "Which one of you is lying? Do I even need to ask?"

Everyone waited for the answer.

"It wasn't Agnes," he said, his voice barely above a whisper. "It was Maud."

Ruth gasped, swayed. Luther took her arm but Ruth shoved him away.

"Maud?"

"Yes. I rushed in and pulled him away. Ordered Maud back to her room. But she pled with me not to hurt him. She said she loved him.

"He just shrugged, said, 'Are you surprised your daughter is a little'—I can't even say the word. He was insolent. Said I had bankrupted him and his company and it was only right that he got some compensation. He said that of Maud. *My* daughter. Like she was just another commodity. He just stood there leering at me, daring me to do something.

"So I did."

"You killed him?"

"The letter opener was lying there on the writing desk. I grabbed it and lunged at him as he walked away. I didn't think. I was as surprised as he was when it plunged into his back."

"You could have called for help," Luther said.

"I didn't know what to do, I couldn't leave him in the sitting room. I dragged him into the hall. I thought I could get him to the servants' stairs so it would look like he'd caught one of them stealing or something. I don't know what I meant. But then I heard someone coming so I just left him and took the servants' stairs back to the main floor.

"The next day, I heard he'd been found in the laundry room. I don't know how he got there. Maybe he wasn't dead and fell in. I don't know. Columbia Copper was failing and I was too busy trying to do something to worry about it."

"And Mrs. Pratt? Did you not mean to kill her, too?" Atkins asked from where he stood. His voice cutting through the charged atmosphere.

All eyes turned to Thomas.

Ruth's voice cut through the silence. "You tried to kill my sister?"

"You tried to kill Gwen?" Luther lunged for him.

Atkins grabbed him and wrestled him back.

"No. Not Gwen. I'd never hurt Gwen, but Elva had figured it out. She didn't say anything, but the way she watched me. Ran from me whenever I walked by. I knew she knew, and I knew I had to do something about it."

"So you stole the nebulizer from the luggage so she would have to use the incense," Atkins began.

Thomas shrugged. Actually shrugged.

Phil felt like lunging for him herself. But she just clenched her fists while her anger threatened to explode. At Perry and his abuse of money and young women, at Thomas and his cheating, at Maud for her stupidity.

But mostly at herself for hearing Maud tell Effie that she was afraid Thomas had killed Perry and brushing it off as normal schoolgirl exaggeration.

And because of her, Elva had lost her life.

She caught Atkins watching her, lowered her eyes. She didn't feel so self-satisfied now.

"I had to. We would be ruined. I didn't mean to hurt Gwen. I knew Elva always set up the incense before Gwen's treatments. And see? I was right."

"Right?" screeched Ruth. "You think you were right?" She was across the floor before anyone realized what she was doing, hauled off, and swung. Her slap resounded through the room, Thomas's head snapped back; the rest of his body followed.

But Ruth wasn't finished, and Atkins was uncharacteristically slow to stop her.

Ruth lunged at him, grabbed his lapels. "You have ruined us. The girls and I will take what life brings, but not with you. Not anymore."

She released him and Thomas fell back against the back of the chair, raised his arm to protect himself. But Ruth merely reached over it, grabbed a handful of hair, and yanked so hard that strands came out in her hand. Thomas yowled and Atkins finally put an end to the assault.

"I'm getting a divorce," Ruth said, straightening up and patting her own hair as if nothing had happened. She took a last look at her husband, who cowered in the chair. "Gwen has been trying to talk me into leaving you for years. But I was a faithful, stupid wife. Now I hope you rot in hell."

"To be sure, he'll at least rot in gaol," Daisy observed.

"If the electric chair doesn't get him," Phil said.

"But the girls," Thomas cried.

"The girls will survive. They'll have to learn how to work, they have no choice now. Oh, what a fool I've been."

She turned and threw herself at Gwen's feet. "Can you ever forgive me?"

Gwen looked startled. Then she reached down to pull her sister to her feet and settled with her on the sofa.

"Well, they needn't worry about Mrs. Jeffrey surviving," Daisy said under her breath. "She can always make her living on the stage."

The doors opened, Tillis stepped inside, and looking at a point above all their heads said, "Dinner is served."

Atkins declined to stay for dinner. He was anxious to get his prisoner back to the city. He stopped Phil on her way to the dining room. "Just so you know, Elva wasn't your fault."

"I heard Maud talking to Effie. I could tell she was afraid her father had killed Perry. I should have pressed Maud on why, but I thought it was schoolgirl histrionics. If I had, Elva might still be alive."

"If Elva hadn't tried on a bit of blackmail on Vincent, instead of telling her employers or the police what she suspected, we might have found the killer sooner and she'd still be alive."

"She was frightened."

"As well she should have been."

"What happens now?"

"Thomas Jeffrey will be charged with murder and possibly fraud. If he'd confessed right after he killed Fauks, he might have gotten away with manslaughter, defense of his daughter. But I've seen it more times than I care to think about."

"What's that?"

"The committing of one crime leading to more heinous acts in an effort to cover up the first."

That had certainly been true in Thomas's case. He'd killed two people, destroyed his family with his greed.

Phil hadn't done very well. Maybe she wasn't cut out for this job after all. If she found herself locked out of her apartment on her return to the city she would know that her superiors were of the same persuasion.

Atkins coughed out a mirthless laugh. "Stop it. You can't prevent every evil deal in the world." He didn't sound sympathetic, for which she was grateful. "God knows, we all have our regrets." He tipped his hat to her and strode out the door.

Spoken like a man who knew his worth and accepted his limitations. Phil didn't think she would ever reach that point. But surely all those years navigating the scandals of London society wouldn't go for naught. She'd just have to try harder.

She took a breath and went in to face the family.

29

"I don't know how to thank you," Gwen Pratt said the next morning, as Phil and Daisy, dressed in their driving togs, waited outside for the last of the luggage to be loaded onto the Packard.

Phil smiled, but she just wanted to get home.

Daisy and Godfrey, who were deep in conversation, didn't seem to be quite so eager to part.

Luther trotted down the steps. "Lady Dunbridge. How can we ever thank you. You are just as clever as everyone is saying. It's a terrible business, but you got to the bottom of things with the least scandal."

"I must warn you, Luther. There will likely be speculation."

"Ah, speculation. The bane of bankers everywhere."

"I meant—"

"I know exactly what you meant and there is nothing to worry about. We are ready to help Ruth and the girls weather the future. They'll be all right."

"Yes," said Gwen. "Thank you from the bottom of my heart. I hope we'll still be friends, now that the worst is over."

"I'd be delighted."

"I hope I'm included in that," Godfrey said, bringing Daisy over.

"But of course," Phil said.

"And thank Detective Sergeant Atkins when you see him. I will be sure the commissioner is made aware of his excellent work."

Phil smiled at that. She wasn't sure that Atkins wouldn't

prefer to stay out of the spotlight. Not everyone in the force approved of his adherence to the former commissioner's sweeping reforms. It wouldn't do to ruffle too many of those feathers.

"Isn't she the cleverest?" Daisy said, taking Phil's arm. "Dear Godfrey, thank you for your hospitality. And for your sage advice."

He kissed her hand, lingering a little too long, Phil thought. Then kissed Phil's.

They said their goodbyes, Preswick cranked up the Packard, and they were soon jostling down the drive toward home.

Two hours later, Phil pulled up to the Webster Hotel. "Well," Daisy said, as they waited for the concierge to take her luggage inside. "It was quite an exhilarating weekend. You certainly know how to pick your friends."

"I might say the same for you."

"He's a darling, isn't he. When he came soaring overhead in that aeroplane, it was beyond thrilling. Air travel. Amazing. Godfrey says it's the wave of the future."

"And what is in your future?" Phil asked.

"Godfrey has arranged for me to talk with an impresario about a speaking tour this spring. I'll be returning to England tomorrow or the next day. There's much to organize. But I hope to see you on my return."

"But of course, you must."

"And Phil. I don't know quite what you're up to, but keep up the good work."

Phil, Lily, and Preswick dropped the Packard off at the hotel entrance to be sent back to the garage. Everything looked quite normal, just as if they hadn't witnessed a murder, participated in a balloon chase, and caught a killer over the weekend. Taxis queued up at the curb. The shoeshine boys, none of whom looked anything but the young boys they were, were plying their trade in their usual places along the sidewalk. Across the street Just a Friend, wearing a new coat heavy enough for the severest weather, hawked his papers. He dipped his chin at Phil; she could imagine him winking though she couldn't see from where she stood.

"Well done, Preswick. He looks quite toasty."

"Quite, my lady."

While Preswick directed the luggage to the cargo elevator, Lily and Phil took the elevator upstairs.

"Nice weekend, madam?" Egbert asked as he rode them to the fifth floor.

"Delightful, thank you."

Lily turned her head to roll her eyes.

The elevator stopped and Egbert opened the gate.

"Welcome home, Lady Dunbridge."

"Thank you, Egbert. It is good to be home."

Phil let them into the apartment.

The first thing she saw was the gardenia on the entrance table and the note and folded newspaper beneath.

The gardenia was fresh. She pushed it aside, tore open the envelope, and pulled out the single sheet. *Nice work, Countess. Page 1, column 3. Not bad for a weekend in the country.*

She dropped the letter and opened that morning's edition of the *Times*.

Third column. "Fauks Heir Killer Caught. Stock Manipulating Ring Brought In for Questions. Another Panic Averted."

Stock manipulating ring. So that was what Mr. X had been after all this time. He didn't care about the murder. He was after the fraudulent stock manipulations.

"How does he do it?" Phil wondered out loud. How could he already know the outcome of the investigation, much less get here before she had?

"I think maybe he's a sorcerer," Lily said.

"I think he may be," Phil agreed. "A bath, Lily, and then a

martini," Phil said, dropping her purse, shrugging out of her coat, and leaving hairpins behind her as she strode down the hall.

An hour later Phil was sitting in her parlor stretched out on the Louis Quinze chaise sipping her second dry martini, when the doorbell rang.

"Preswick, are we expecting someone?"

Preswick appeared in the doorway. "No, my lady. Shall I answer it?"

"Yes please, but no sneaky newspapermen, unless . . . Never mind, yes please."

She heard the door open, a bustle of activity, and low conversation.

Then a woman burst through the door. She was dressed in the latest Paris fashion, a confection of a hat tilted rakishly above her blond curls.

"Did you miss me?"

"Bev, what are you doing here? I thought you were staying in Paris through the spring."

"I was, but I was bored. And I couldn't—just couldn't—miss the New York season." Bev Reynolds tossed her hat onto the nearest table and sat down, leaning back and throwing one leg over the other. "I heard Daisy Greville was here. Did you see her? Have I missed anything? Tell me, has anything the least bit interesting happened while I've been gone?"

Phil laughed. "Not a thing in the world."

"Then mix me a martini and let's cause some trouble."

"An excellent idea." And Lady Dunbridge was happy to oblige.

Turn the page for a sneak peek at
the next Lady Dunbridge mystery

Available October 2020

1

Philomena Amesbury, Phil to her friends, the Countess of Dunbridge to everyone else, handed her armful of packages to the footman of the Plaza Hotel and stepped out of the red Darracq taxicab.

"Lovely day, isn't it, Mr. Fitzroy?"

The doorman, dressed in the full fawn-and-gold braided livery of the Plaza, smiled and looked dubiously at the gray clouds that overcast the sky.

"Indeed, Lady Dunbridge. Did you enjoy your morning of shopping?"

"I did. Everyone is so festive." Of course there had been that unsightly shoving match between two ladies over who went first up the escalator at Bloomingdale's and the disappointing moment when the proprietor at the little bookstore across the street had informed her that he'd sold his last copy of the latest Arthur Conan Doyle novel, which she had been hoping to buy as a present for her butler, Preswick.

A misstep on her part. She shouldn't have waited until ten days before Christmas to reserve a copy. But after six months in Manhattan and three at the Plaza, she was still learning her way in a place where countesses did things for themselves.

"There are more packages in the taxi and even more being delivered, if you'd please have them stored until I call for them."

"Yes, Lady Dunbridge." Mr. Fitzroy nodded to the bellman,

who reached into the taxi and took the remaining packages into the hotel.

The taxi drove away, and Phil took the opportunity to look across the street to where a small boy hawked his newspapers at the entrance to Central Park. He had designated himself as her small but vigilant lookout, and who went by the soubriquet of Just a Friend.

Phil waved, though he wasn't looking her way. He was wearing a new scarf and mittens to add to the winter coat Preswick had bought him a few weeks before. Her butler might be a tad old-fashioned in his ways and a bit long in the tooth, but he had a heart warmer than the bag of chestnuts nestled inside her purse.

Oh the freedom of leaving England, with its peerage and restrictions, for America where she could come and go as she wished at any time of the day and be whatever she wanted. If it hadn't been for the earl dying and leaving her a dowager at twenty-six, and her last rather public indiscretions with a certain Frenchman, she would never have known the excitement of life in Manhattan.

Well, to be honest, there had also been that little incident of a murder that she'd inadvertently solved and that had made all the major newspapers—much to her father's chagrin. Her father might look the other way at *affaires de coeur* and other minor eccentricities by his daughter, but he wouldn't stomach her hobnobbing with the metropolitan police. He'd intended to pack her off to Great-Aunt Sephronia in the wilds of Yorkshire, hence Phil's quickly organized trip to the New World.

And as it had turned out, that one little involvement with the London police had done much to insure her success in New York. For there was no one people admired more than someone with a title who could solve their most dastardly crimes while keeping their family secrets locked in her breast—and a few others locked in the safe in her apartment upstairs.

Phil headed toward the bank of bronze elevators where

Egbert, her favorite operator, nodded and gestured her inside the cage.

"Lovely day, Lady Dunbridge," he said in a melodious voice that always sounded like a song.

"Indeed, Egbert. Do you think we'll have snow for Christmas?"

"Perhaps."

Phil opened her handbag and pulled out a brown paper cone of chestnuts. "I thought you might enjoy these."

"Ah, roasted chestnuts. Thank you." Egbert quickly slipped off one white glove and took them from her.

"Make sure you enjoy them while they're still hot," Phil said.

He slipped them into his pocket and slid his hand back into his glove just as they reached the fifth floor.

He opened the gate and waited for her to reach her door and let herself inside.

All was quiet. She'd given her maid, Lily, and Preswick the day off to do their own shopping and to enjoy the festivities of the city. This would be their first Christmas as a household and they were all looking forward to it.

Preswick, after a rough start, had taken to life in Manhattan, and Lily was thriving.

At least Phil thought she was. Phil actually knew very little about Lily before the day Phil had first encountered her as she fought off several sturdy British customs officials who had discovered her attempting to stow away on the ship to America. Recognizing a kindred spirit, Phil had paid her passage and hired her as a lady's maid, her own maid having refused to board the ship at the last minute. When she refused to give her name, Phil called her Lily because of her porcelain complexion. Preswick had done the rest.

They'd become quite a team, the three of them.

Phil unpinned her hat and tossed it and her handbag onto the occasional chair set next to the hall table. A white envelope lay on the floor by the door.

Strange. Usually when there was a message, the concierge, a kind but inquisitive creature, made sure to stop her on her way upstairs.

She picked up the envelope and read one handwritten word. *Countess.*

There was only one man who called her that, a deliberate misuse of proper address. She was certain he knew better. Perhaps he was letting her know his opinion of titles. A form of challenge? Or, dare she hope, a term of affection? Whichever, it sent a thrill of excitement through her.

She ripped open the envelope, let it fall to the ground as she perused the single sheet of paper. *Theatre Unique. 1:15 Last Row.*

It was written in the bold classic script that she knew well. She glanced at the Ormolu clock on the mantel. Twelve forty-three. She'd never make it. She didn't stop to equivocate, but grabbed her purse and hat from the chair and hurried back down the hall to the elevator.

It was infuriating, Phil thought, looking out the passenger window of the taxicab inching its way down Fifth Avenue. The streets were congested with holiday traffic. Pedestrians clogged the sidewalks, jostling each other as they hurried from one shop to another.

The subway would have been much faster, though there wasn't a station near the hotel and she'd as yet never taken one of the underground railways, something she should probably remedy as soon as the weather was better.

She checked her lapel watch. Almost one o'clock. He could have given her more notice, or left the note with the concierge and saved her several lost minutes of going upstairs. But that was not Mr. X's way. *Mr. X.* She still didn't know his name or what he looked like, since he always appeared in disguise, when he bothered to appear at all.

But though she might not know what he looked like, she

knew how he felt, every luscious contour of him—until he'd disappeared, always before the light of dawn.

She leaned forward and tapped on the glass window that separated her from the driver.

"It's most urgent that we hurry," she explained.

"You shoulda left earlier. It's Christmastime."

It wasn't like she'd had a choice. Though she enjoyed the excitement of notes slipped under the door or left on pillows, and chance meetings at balls or in dark alleys, it just wasn't efficient. They needed a better system of communication.

She could imagine him sitting in the theater, dressed as who knew what, waiting for how long? He was taking an awfully big chance if it was something urgent.

And things always were with him.

"I'd be ever so grateful, if you could see your way through this traffic."

The driver turned around long enough to scowl at her.

She lifted her eyebrows and clasped her handbag suggestively. "Very grateful."

Almost immediately the taxi swerved out of line and swung around the truck in front of it, nearly coming to blows with another taxi attempting the same thing in the opposite direction.

The taxi lurched and swerved back to its side of the street. Phil adjusted her hat, which she hadn't secured properly in her haste to get into the taxi. A block later he turned in front of a trolley and headed toward Park Avenue, which was not quite as heavily trafficked. It took them straight down past Union Square to Fourteenth Street, where he turned and stopped at the curb.

Phil tipped him generously and the taxi squeezed back into traffic. Across the street the Academy of Music, now no longer the center of the arts, stood shoulder to shoulder with Tammany Hall, headquarters of the most powerful politicians in Manhattan.

The Theatre Unique was located on the south side of the street, sandwiched between a row of small storefront businesses, several theatrical agencies, an oyster bar, and a cigar shop. THEATRE UNIQUE was picked out in the new electric lights across a curved arch that led to a rather byzantine-looking ticket kiosk. Above the arch, nude gods held up garlands of flowers, while above them, cherubs played a fanfare on plaster trumpets.

There was no end to excess in America, even in their theaters, Phil thought as she headed to the kiosk.

She handed over fifteen cents, snatched her ticket, and fairly ran to the entrance.

Only as she stepped into darkness did she realize that she was entering a nickelodeon.

She couldn't begin to guess why Mr. X wanted to meet her here. But he must have had his reasons. He always did and she never questioned him. At least not out loud.

She stood just inside the door, silhouettes of seated people coming in and out of focus as the moving images cast them in flickering exchanges of light and dark.

Still, she didn't venture farther, but swept a look around the perimeter of the room, peered into the dark corners, along the back wall to the square of light through which the images were projected. She perused the rows of seats, picking out as many details as possible, as Dr. Gross in his handbook *Criminal Investigation* had recommended.

Everyone seemed mesmerized by the screen, which was showing speeding race cars that normally would have interested her. But not today.

She was intrigued by her summons, and just a little wary. Anticipation tickled the hairs on the back of her neck as the cars silently raced across the screen and an unseen pianist plunked away at a tinny rendition of Scott Joplin's popular "The Entertainer."

Really, life had been much easier when gentlemen callers

appeared at the door with a card and a bouquet of your favorite flowers. But so much less interesting.

A single gentleman sat alone at the near end of the back row. He appeared to be asleep. There were no other people sitting in the last several rows.

Taking a final quick look around the flickering room, Phil pulled her skirts back, eased into the row, and sat down.

He didn't greet her. Didn't even appear to wake up. Purposely ignoring her? She felt a little niggle of irritation.

Though perhaps they were being watched. She leaned back, gave her outward attention to the screen.

"I'm here," she whispered, keeping her eyes focused on the racing cars.

No response.

She risked a sideways glance. He'd gone all out today. And, she had to admit, she was impressed.

He seemed shorter, more heavyset than usual, almost paunchy. Dressed in corduroy trousers and nondescript jacket. No hat that she could see, just thinning hair that was slicked back except where several strands fell over his forehead. He looked the epitome of a middle-aged working man.

And still he ignored her. He was obviously perturbed that she was late.

Well, really, was she expected to sit quietly at home waiting for instructions?

"You've made your point," she whispered. "It's the holidays. I was out shopping. I came immediately upon returning home, but traffic is particularly heavy this time of the year."

Nothing from her companion.

"Don't you think you're taking this a bit far? I apologize. It won't happen again, though I don't know why you just couldn't have skulked around the hotel dressed as a shoeshine boy and told me what I needed to hear. Why are we here?"

Nothing. They were definitely being watched or he would have acknowledged her by now.

She turned her head slightly, pretending to look in her bag. She was certain no one had been behind her when she sat down.

And she was filled with an unnamed dread.

She touched his shoulder. He slumped forward. She leaned closer but couldn't see his face or smell the faint aroma of the exotic pipe tobacco he favored. But she did smell something sickly metallic, and her stomach heaved.

With a herculean effort, she pulled him upright; his head rolled, then snapped back over the seat back.

The race continued inexorably on the screen.

The gash where his throat had been slit, and the black stain, soaking his collar and spreading down his woolen jumper, appeared and disappeared in the flicking light and dark, light and dark, of the moving picture.

Her mind—and yes, her heart—reeled, as logic fought for purchase.

She had learned much about the science of psychology since beginning her detectival career. The mind could play tricks on you, or show you the way out of a maze. At times it was hard to distinguish which was which.

This was not Mr. X. This man was shorter, stockier, his neck thicker. Even with his talent for absurd disguises, Mr. X couldn't possibly change so much.

Besides, Mr. X would never succumb to the indignity of having his throat slit in an afternoon nickelodeon.

But whoever he was, he was definitely dead. No one could survive that much blood loss. Whoever had killed him had been efficient and ruthless—and might still be in the theater.

She instinctively reached out and touched the man's hand. Still warm. Her stomach revolted, but she felt down the rough wool of his coat and slipped her hand in his pocket. A stub of a pencil, a notebook, what felt like a smashed packet of cigarettes, and a small rectangular box. Matches?

She didn't think twice but pulled the items out and shoved

them in her handbag, knowing full well that she was interfering with a crime scene, one that might somehow involve her.

She reached out again, slid her hand beneath the lapel of his jacket . . . and was nearly swept away on a tide of relief.

This definitely wasn't Mr. X. Her eyes might deceive her, but her touch never would.

But who was he? And why was she sent here to meet him?

She quickly felt inside his jacket, reached over and tried the other pocket, and found nothing more.

A scream pierced through the music that accompanied the racing cars—through the erratic lights and the pictures that flashed and jumped and seemed to suddenly grow very bright—bright enough to see a young woman standing at the end of the aisle.

"No!" the girl cried. "No!" She turned and ran.

There was a sudden stir around the theater, murmurs as heads began to turn, looking for the source of the scream.

Phil, suddenly galvanized into action, ducked her head and sidestepped to the end of the aisle.

Someone yelled, "What's happening?"

A man stood and turned from his seat. "Back there, in the last row! Call the cops!"

The girl had disappeared. Phil turned back to the suddenly silent theater. The music had stopped. The race cars continued to whizz across the silent screen.

Someone slipped up beside her, took her by both elbows. She immediately tried to strike out.

"Don't turn around," he whispered. "I'm the theater manager. You need to get out of here. This way, please."

He gave her a push, then grabbed her by one arm and propelled her down the aisle toward a back door, past two other men attempting to restore order as the patrons fought their way to the entrance in the opposite direction.

"Hurry," he hissed. And just as the house lights came on,

he pushed her through a door camouflaged by a mural across the back wall.

Things were happening too fast. But she knew he was right. She couldn't be found here.

The door closed behind them and they sped down a narrow dark corridor. Phil couldn't see where they were going. She stumbled; he dragged her up and didn't let go of her until they'd reached the end. He unlocked a door, opened it a crack, and peered out.

"Turn right and go to the street. Be careful not to be seen." He shoved her out the door.

She whirled around just as the door shut in her face. She rattled the handle but it was locked. Pounded on the door to no avail.

"What's going on? Let me in!"

But there was no answer.

Phil turned around, senses alert. She was in an alley surrounded by trash cans and cast-off furniture. She covered her nose, lifted her skirt, and ran toward the street. She just managed to throw herself against the brick building at the sound of police sticks clacking against the wall, summoning help. Two constables ran across the end of the alley toward Fourteenth Street.

When their sticks could no longer be heard over the pounding of her heart, Phil peeked around the edge of the building. Finding the street empty, she stepped out onto the sidewalk.

Why had the manager been so anxious for her to be out of the theater? Why pick her out of the rest of the audience? Did he know who she was? She hadn't even gotten a good look at his face. Had that been on purpose? He'd stayed mostly behind her, guiding her by the arm. She couldn't have turned to look at him if she'd tried. Which she hadn't.

When she reached Fourteenth Street, instinct told her to walk in the opposite direction toward Union Square, to take a taxi home and wait to be contacted.

But curiosity propelled her back toward the front of the theater.

She kept close to the storefronts, pretending to look at the notices at the booking agencies, the menu of the oyster bar, as she slowly made her way down the sidewalk.

A black motorcar screeched to a stop in front of the theater, and two men got out. Phil ducked her head to peruse the boxes of Tiparillos and Cubans in the cigar-shop window. One of the men she recognized immediately. Sergeant Charles Becker, the scourge of the Tenderloin, known as the most corrupt policeman on the force. She had no reason to doubt that it was true.

He'd tried to railroad Phil's friend Bev into admitting she'd killed her husband, which she hadn't. He was tall, broad, and muscular, with a mean expression even when smiling. He preferred the round crown of a bowler hat, which had inspired Bev to dub him the Fireplug.

A shiver ran up Phil's spine.

What on earth was he doing here, outside his district? And how had he arrived so quickly? The Tenderloin was on the far side of town.

The mere fact that Becker had been summoned could only mean someone was trying to cover up something. And his quick arrival must mean Phil wasn't the first to discover the body.

And with Becker on the case, did that mean Detective Sergeant John Atkins would soon be following?

If she'd only been on time—which she would have been if she'd known about it earlier—she might have been able to prevent the murder.

Becker and his companion went inside, and Phil decided it would make better sense to leave them to it. She had no intention of crossing paths or swords with Becker if she could help it. Once had been enough.

Her knees were suddenly weak. Denial and fear had kept

her going. But now, the relief she felt when she realized that whoever the victim was, it wasn't Mr. X, threatened to overcome her. That and the stab of guilt for her own relief, when some poor family would not be seeing their husband, son, or father ever again.

Phil's steps faltered as much from the thought as from the pile of horse manure she had to sidestep in the street. Last year she would never have even considered the possibility that someone might murder a person in a theater. But since coming to America, her eyes had been opened. The Americans were such an ingenuous—somewhat ruthless—lot.

She reached the far side of the street just as a black morgue van drove past and stopped behind the police car. Two men jumped out, opened the back, and pulled out a stretcher before rushing into the theater.

Phil watched in dismay. Neither Becker nor the morgue van could possibly have arrived so quickly.

Not unless they had already been waiting nearby.